DISTORTED LEGACY

Henry M'ule Musenge

Printed in the United States of America.

Library of Congress Control Number: 2024930788

ISBN   Paperback   979-8-33278-468-2

Boundless Script Ventures
99 Wall Street #210
New York, NY, 10005

www.boundlessscript.com

DEDICATION

"Hello gorgeous!" I whispered in the young lady's ear, as a way of greeting.

"Hi!" she responded coyly.

"You certainly look like the Victoria Falls!" I complimented her.

"What do you mean 'like the Victoria Falls'?" she asked quizzically.

"In the words of Dr David Livingstone a face with 'such breathtaking beauty should have been gazed upon by angels in their flight'," I clarified.

She chuckled and gently smiled before asking, "Are you a poet?"

"No-o!" I replied candidly.

That was my very first exchange with Rosemary Chileshe Chaongopa as we were practising dancing routines in preparation for her elder sister's wedding. Even though we met twice after this, we went our separate ways to pursue our quest for further studies.

However nine years later, we met again after our post-graduate studies and became inseparable. The rest is history. We courted for a year and tied the knot on 27th March, 1982; the happiest day in my life. Three months later, I declined a better paying job offer from an international organization to be based in Lagos, Nigeria, while Rosemary was unable to take up a government assignment in Foreign Service; thus we were firmly grounded in Mother Zambia. The Lord blessed us with three lovely children: Kasali, Chikumbi and Tekela.

In government, Rosemary rose steadily and eventually became Permanent Secretary at Cabinet Office and served six Republican

Presidents. Despite her promotions and enhanced status at work, Rosemary remained a committed spouse and a loving dotting mother to our children. She played many roles in my life. Not only was she a loving spouse, she was my everything. Being broughtup by my grandparents, I learnt a lot from her about family and forgiveness in marriage. Losing Rosemary to cancer on 15th July 2019 was undoubtedly the most painful loss in my life.

In recognition of her hard-work, dedication to duty, long service and contributions to government services, Rosemary was posthumously awarded by the Republican President on 24th October 2019, the highest recognition for a civil servant: The Order of Distinguished Service – First Division.

I thank God for her life and her sharing more than half of it with me.

Her love remains permanently inscribed on my heart.

I dedicate this book to my late wife, the love of my life, my best friend and confidante, Rosemary Chileshe Chaongopa Musenge.

MHSRIEP.

ACKNOWLEDGMENTS

Firstly, I am eternally grateful to God, my Creator, for giving me such a fulfilling life and enabling me to put pen to paper.

Secondly, I wish to acknowledge the unwavering support and encouragement from my children: Mukonde, Kasali, Chikumbi and Tekela. I love you guys.

For reviewing the manuscript in its early stages and sharing thoughts and ideas to make it the finished product you hold in your hands, I owe my deepest gratitude to: Mzee Chapa Yotam Chikamba, Dr. Peter Machungwa, Late Hon Ng'andu Peter Magande, MHSRIEP, Mr Alex Chiteba, Mrs Roleen G. Liboma, and the late Joseph Kunda, MHSRIEP.

My appreciation goes to my editor Dr. Mbono Dube, for her commitment and numerous suggestions.

Special thanks to Ms Namuumbwa Mantina and Mr Field Kasoma for researching on some special topics, patiently transcribing, and typing the manuscript. I owe you both.

Finally but not the least; I appreciate the authors and acknowledge the sources of some quotations in this book.

Table of Contents

CHAPTER 1

Becoming Zambica

Like much of Southern Africa, Zambica had a pleasant climate and was endowed with vast natural resources. Zambica, located in southern central Africa, is surrounded by other countries rich in minerals, expansive virgin lands and thousands of wildlife. European colonialists developed a ravenous appetite for more and more once they sampled Zambica. Their yearning was urgent and without limit. They did not care if the Africans were ultimately left with nothing. They insatiably enacted laws that discriminated against Africans. They introduced colour-bar in order to enhance their predilection to make Africans as second-class citizens in their own country. Consequently political consciousness among Zambicans was induced because of greed and selfishness by the Europeans' insatiable appetite for power and wealth. Worse still was that the British South Africa Company (BSA Co) acquired the territory in the 1890's largely for the purposes of prospecting for minerals.

Quite a number of Zambican kings and chiefs even to this day own vast tracts of traditional land. They are custodians of these lands for their people. Just like in present Zambica, these traditional rulers had the right to apportion land to whomever they deemed fit. Using this convenient loophole, the BSA Co dubiously obtained land rights to the territory by a series of treaties with the traditional rulers. A number of these treaties were vague and lacked legal backing. In many cases, the land was neither demarcated nor on title. In fact, it is said that one Lomba King proudly showed off huge tracts of land that he claimed to be his to Mr MacPherson, a BSA Co official. Mr MacPherson, from Dundee, Scotland, had the nerve to ask the king to show him the extent of his land knowing pretty well the king had no map or knowledge of how big it was. In the company of his Kateka (Prime Minister), the king majestically walked towards the nearest anthill with the white man trailing behind him.

"I have a huge tract of land in my kingdom." Said the Lomba King.

"How big is it?" asked Mr MacPherson.

"Very big. Too big to measure," replied the king.

"Very big," repeated the official. "Do you have any drawings? Do you have any title to the land?" the excited officer said with much interest.

"No! The land is too big!" exclaimed the king. "It can't be drawn on a piece of paper." He reasoned retrospectively.

They strolled up the anthill as the chief panted for breath. He looked northwards while pointing into the horizon, "Very far, very far," he said in the local Lomba language when in actual fact part of the land he was pointing at belonged to other chiefs.

"Very good!" Exclaimed Mr MacPherson even though he too had no idea about the actual extent of the land.

The king was aware the white man was not just paying him a courtesy visit. He definitely had a lot tucked under his sleeve. He knew that many of his colleagues had already fallen prey to the antics and sweet but sour language of the colonisers. He had to be extra careful. Wasn't he one of the wisest kings in the country? He was not called a Lomba King for nothing, he mused. This MacPherson must be taught a lesson.

"Eh Mr. MacPherson. You're aware that your people have come to our region mainly for our precious mineral, copper. We have ears to the ground, you know. We hear there is an increasing world demand for this our ancestral given mineral and, of course, other minerals. Also, copper mining has grown rapidly in this country and the value of exports has been increasing in the last few years," the king said, giving MacPherson a sideway glance, calculating the effects of his knowledge.

"I wouldn't say it that way, Your Majesty." Mr MacPherson was fast becoming uncomfortable with the king's knowledge. He had expected a naïve and ignorant African ruler; far from it.

"Whom would you blame for the rise of the African desire for political inclusion in this country? You people are excluding us, exploiting and oppressing us," said the king as MacPherson was thinking of how to reply.

"Despite the expansion of mining activities in this country," the king continued, "there are still marked differences between the quality of life for Europeans and Africans. Government policies, such as taxation of Africans, forced labour, unfair land and agricultural policies, all have contributed to the deterioration in the quality of life of people in the rural agricultural communities," the king put it to him.

MacPherson nodded silently.

"African farmers are restricted by law in the crops they can grow. This is a deliberate ploy on the part of the government to limit the farmers' alternatives to extra income thus making working in the copper mines more attractive," he reasoned.

The king paused to allow his visitor to make a contribution. He sure was a wise and clever king.

"You're right, Your Majesty," MacPherson eventually responded. "But the BSA Company has invested well in a railway across this country and indeed other activities. We definitely won't carry all these back to our motherland, the United Kingdom," said the Scotsman with some elevated pride.

With the right hand raised, "Hold it there!" said the king in a deliberate emphatic manner. "What about the rural areas? Have they been covered? No! Look at this!" he spread his hands in frustration. "Aren't these your so-called developments; the ones leading to migration of Africans to the mining areas? Is that fair? Hmh, just don't go there Mr MacPherson," he warned.

"Your Royal Highness, the King of the industrious Lomba people, you are very right. It is not fair. That is why some of us are pulling out of the system and trying to stand alone," MacPherson tried to explain. "We are seeing the atrocities inflicted on the locals. If you give me…"

"Lies! All lies!" the king exclaimed cutting in. "You people are all the same. What do you say? Ah, 'birds of the same feathers, flock together.' You all think we are all a pack of toothless wild dogs. Right?" he questioned.

The king suddenly stopped walking and looked MacPherson straight in the eye. Mr MacPherson was suddenly intimidated. He had played roughly with a lioness' tail without knowing it had teeth or not. He had to quickly find an appeasement. He dared not wait for the vicious animal in the tough king to open its mouth and snarl.

"Your Royal Highness, the king, it is true what you say. This country was planned as a settler's colony, reserved for European skilled workers. Unfortunately, those who came ahead of us restricted Africans, the rightful owners of the land, to unskilled labour and they are being governed by different wage scales based on race. A lot of the kings and chiefs unknowingly endorsed this barbaric practice. So, in the eyes of the whole world, there is mutual understanding."

"'Mutual understanding,' you say? To perpetuate this unfair practice! Is that the reason why there is very little investment in African education to perpetually keep the African at the bottom of the ladder?" queried the king.

MacPherson was becoming hot under the collar. He remained silent.

"Coincidentally, the colonial government has left most of African education in the hands of the Christian missionaries whose main concern are tithes and offerings! This makes me sick!," he spat in disgust. "I guess it is best we get back to the house," he said pointedly.

The bodyguards got the signal and led the king, his visitor and the Kateka back to the palace. Meanwhile, Mr MacPherson was convinced something was surely and truly amiss.

They walked back in silence.

After what seemed like forever, MacPherson said, "Your Royal Highness, I thank you for opening my eyes today," he said, trying to weave his way into the king's good books. "I now understand why all these insecurities, anger and distrust of the foreigners which have led to the protests. This is indeed a rare occasion," he continued. "There is still one more thing," he paused to get the king's attention. Making himself comfortable by stretching his legs and leaning backwards on the wooden chair, a sure sign that he was not ready to leave yet, MacPherson asked, "Why did congress change its name?"

This pleased the king. His visitor from a foreign land fore, fore(very far, very far), was feeling at home in his palace.

"Oh, that! In 1953, the name was changed to African National Congress (ANC). Through ANC, a push for independence is growing while the party's popularity is also increasing. ANC was formally formed in 1950 and was led by Nalumino Mukelabai Lisulo, a Lomba from the royal family as its first president. After the 1954 ANC general conference, Lisulo was succeeded by John Mweene Mwendalubi, a powerful speaker and charismatic leader from Southern Province. He was originally perceived to have the drive and stamina to push the liberation struggle forward. However, by 1960, the ANC leader had become flatfooted," the king said disappointedly.

By the time the king put a full stop to his narrative, it was time for lunch. Because Mr MacPherson had a mission, he joined the king. He needed to be friends with him if he wanted land, especially that the king was proving to be a hard nut to crack. His colleagues had warned him though that penetrating the Lomba Kingdom was not that easy.

"Mr MacPherson, I tell you what, these young people will emerge victorious one of these days. I say days; not months, not years. The logs, the grass and the match are ready. We just need one young person to strike the matchstick. Then 'boom'!" His Majesty professed. "How

I pray for my ancestors to allow me to witness that day," the king wore a cheeky and mischievous smile that unsettled the white man.

Interestingly, as predicted by the Lomba king, the people of Zambica did not lose hope. They knew that what they were fighting for would benefit generations to come. In 1960, the radicals in ANC became frustrated with the pace of the liberation struggle under their leader, Mwendalubi, fondly called Old John and his secretary general Jerome Jumbe, who was sometimes called JJ. Under Mwendalubi's lukewarm leadership, ANC was seen as going in circles, probably destined for nowhere. Furthermore, other radical leaders were concerned with Mwendalubi; he seemed to be increasingly influenced by white liberals and was seen as willing to compromise on the fundamental issue of majority rule. Consequently Simon Mulenga Wampanga, a childhood friend of Jerome Jumbe, led a rebellion within ANC and formed a new political party. After his training in India, Wampanga with his colleague Ngenda Mwanawina returned home changed and ambitious youngmen, largely influenced by the effective political organisation they had observed in India led by J Nehru, a disciple of Mahatma Gandhi. A similar metamorphosis had happened to Muyunda Lubasi when he returned from attachment in Ghana, where he had observed a fired-up Kwame Nkrumah in active political action. Rejuvenated and impatient, the three realists and a few others in the ANC, met secretly at Wampanga's home. They resolved that their party ANC, was almost moribund and going nowhere. They cited poor and uninspiring leadership as the main reason for their sudden move. They yearned for serious agitation in order to liberate their motherland.

Lubasi and Mwanawina wanted Wampanga to be interim leader of their new party. However, before holding elections to select interim leaders and registering the new party, Wampanga articulated and prevailed on his fellow belligerents. Wampanga's towering features made him stand out and influential. With great height, a heavily bearded face, often with an open neck dressing in chitenge (bishop collar) shirt and slippers, which he adopted as a result of his experience in India, he cut quite an imposing figure.

"Let's take Jerome with us," he suggested in a commanding voice. "He's a good organiser and our party will benefit from his vast experience in organising party politics in rural areas."

"Why should we tell him now?" asked Mwanawina. "He's too slow and too obedient to the president; the same president who has failed to move the liberation of our country forward."

Wampanga nodded without saying a word.

"While I understand the views of my good friend Mwanawina," Lubasi said, "I think it will be an advantage for us to bring Jumbe on board with us," he stated. Then, he explained his reasoning, "The fact is that it will spell the end of the ANC; without us and JJ," he argued.

"That will remove any competition and will be good for our party," Mwanawina conceded. "I really like that."

Wampanga was satisfied with winning over his colleagues concerning Jumbe with little effort. He nodded silently again as he took off his glasses and gazed into the distance, like a seer, contemplating the future of a free country. He polished his glasses as he listened to the conversation.

Jumbe's education, his roots in Lembaland were often questioned, and he and his family were locally regarded as foreigners.

In fact, Jerome Jumbe had believed during his childhood that he would one day return to Masaland where his parents originally came from. After losing his father at an early age, Jumbe's insecurity increased and could only be overcome by local friendships through Wampanga, Chanda Mumbi, and Mwamba Mulewuka. When they moved to the Copper Province, Wampanga and Mumbi had relatives there from Northern and Luapita provinces, while Jumbe had none. It was again these friends, who provided Jumbe with security and testimonials for him being a 'Kwitonta boy', while he lived and prevailed in their shadows.

Earlier in Northern Province, Jumbe's political organization only survived with Wampanga's support, and equally on the Copper Province, it was Wampanga who had to introduce Jumbe. With the political organization growing, it was the shadow of Wampanga that kept Jumbe from being ousted as a foreigner. However, other tribes later saw sense and salvation in keeping Jumbe in leadership; he served as a buffer to the unknown because kicking Jumbe out meant Wampanga taking over leadership as some of them feared his perceived extremism and following.

When Wampanga returned from India, the British suspected that he had been under Nehru's political influence, which they detested, as encouraging socialism. This was also influenced by the early uneasy postcolonial encounters they were having with Ghana's Kwame Nkrumah. Thus, together with their American supporters, the British government could not allow Wampanga, a communist suspect, to assume power. Therefore, for them, Jumbe was convenient; a vouched teetotaler, which suited the Maccathy era. Subsequently, Jumbe's activities from this time onwards were centred at image building for himself, with the help of his new white friends.

"Mulenga, why did you call me to come quickly and to come alone?" he asked.

"I shall go straight to the point," Wampanga said. "We need you to join us," he said. "No, I need you to join us," he corrected himself. "I have convinced the others."

"Wait a minute Mulenga. Join you, where?" Jumbe asked anxiously. "Where are you going, back to India?" he teased. "And who are the others?" he asked eagerly.

"Mwanawina, Lubasi and a few others. We have left ANC," he revealed. "We are wasting our valuable time sticking with the slow and scared Old John," he said.

"But why?" Jumbe asked. "When the ANC collapses, we shall all be seen as failures."

"Yes, to some extent," he quickly agreed. "But still, the buck stops at the leader's door."

Wampanga pointed to some of the weaknesses in ANC.

"You know what?" Wampanga asked. "Our party has fundamental challenges."

"Like which ones for instance?" Jumbe asked.

"As a party, we have failed to establish an effective working relationship with the African trade union movements," Wampanga said. "And yet it is only the unions which can paralyze industries through strikes if we work closely with them," he continued while Jumbe nodded.

"The party also failed lamentably to prevent the formation of the Federation of our country with Masaland and Southern Rhodesia due to our leader's laissez faire approach," he concluded.

JJ nodded again.

Wampanga pointed out some other weaknesses in the party; lack of a steady income due to the absence of effective financial arrangements, which in effect encouraged misappropriation of funds by officials at all levels.

"Yes, these weaknesses are known by some of us," Jerome agreed. "But all of us should share the blame under collective responsibility," he reasoned. "If only there was intra-party democracy and objective debates were not stifled," Wampanga countered.

Wampanga continued, "Unfortunately, my friend, this is not the case at the moment." Adding, "Ever since we came from India, the National Executive Committee meetings are poorly conducted with very little debate. Minutes and matters arising are hardly debated upon. The Federation is siphoning our country's resources from copper to develop Southern Rhodesia and Masaland."

"You can't say that!" Jumbe protested. "We need to liberate our country together, you know that. We made a commitment, remember?" he reminded him.

"That's exactly the point; liberate our country," concurred Wampanga. "However, with the current leadership, it will take another 15 to 20 years to liberate this country from this colonial yoke," He moaned. "Our people will soon be disillusioned."

Wampanga provided more worrying details to show that their president had been compromised; he was secretly dealing with some white man from the intelligence office which was privately monitoring the party.

"For gratification, the president was handsomely rewarded and distracted."

He mentioned a white's only hotel in which the party president would be smuggled to eat special white men's foods, drink his favourite whisky, smoke his preferred Cuban cigars, have fun and so on.

"He unwittingly leaked valuable information on the struggle, which is why he had been targeted."

Jumbe's jaw dropped.

"Are you sure, Mulenga?" asked a shocked Jumbe.

"Absolutely," Wampanga responded. "Because of our friendship and the mutual trust we have for each other for years, I can't afford to leave you behind in a sinking ship. It is up to you." Wampanga shot a serious eye at his friend, forcing Jumbe to nod in agreement and understandingly.

"Are you sure the ANC has no chance?" Jumbe asked.

"It will soon sink like the Titanic," Wampanga predicted.

They talked further. Wampanga reminded Jumbe that it was public knowledge that Mwendalubi was lax in handling party affairs; how he was fond of arriving late at important public meetings and sometimes failing to make any appearance. Worse still, the party president often declined to delegate authority even when he knew he would be away. Wampanga further told Jumbe that the British would never hand over independence on a silver platter. They would have to fight for it to get it back. Jumbe promised to make a decision the following day after consulting his wife.

The following day, Jumbe called Wampanga to meet up with him. While his mind was already made up, he wanted to clear one burning issue.

He put it to him, "You know we have discussed this issue a number of times in the past," he lamented. "Some of our colleagues have great doubts about my nationality."

Wampanga nodded.

"If it were not for you and Mwendalubi trusting me," JJ continued, "I would not have been accepted as Secretary General of the party."

"I am fully aware, Jerome," Wampanga replied calmly. "I've already discussed it with the others. There will be no problem from now on."

"Are you sure, Mulenga?" Jerome Jumbe asked anxiously.

"As you are aware, nobody in politics today knows you as much as I do. I shall convince them in Lusiku and the trade unionists on the Copper Province." He promised.

"With that out of the way, I'm game!" Jumbe announced excitedly.

"Good!" Wampanga responded happily. "Welcome on board." He said as they shook hands. "What we expect is to form a more serious and assertive political party unlike the African National Congress."

That afternoon, Jumbe resigned from his position as Secretary General of the African National Congress Party to join Wampanga and his colleagues. His sudden move greatly disappointed Mwendalubi; Jerome Jumbe was one of his most loyal senior members of the party.

While the rebelling group agreed on their burning desire to accelerate the struggle for independence, they faced a number of challenges. The immediate ones were to choose a name for the party; two: elect a leader who would be accepted nationally; three: develop an impeccable fundraising strategy and four: develop a clear political plan of action, in order to scare the British government. They had to make a big impact compared to Mwendalubi's timid approach.

The initial interim leaders were Jumbe, President; Lubasi, Secretary General and Wampanga, Treasurer with Ngenda Mwanawina as Vice Treasurer while Sakwiba Mwangolwa was elected Publicity Secretary. The other positions were to be filled later. However, Ngenda Mwanawina and Muyunda Lubasi were not comfortable with the initial leadership of their party. They wanted Wampanga, a fellow realist and leader of the rebellion against the ANC, to lead the new party.

Wampanga's colleagues were also apprehensive that Jumbe might in actual fact turn out to be just as moderate and indecisive as Mwendalubi, the man they had just run away from. But Wampanga pointed out that his friend, Jumbe had been senior in the ANC to all of them and therefore deserved the presidency. Unknown to his fellow realists, Wampanga had a vision; use a moderate person like Jumbe who was tolerated by the British, in order to fool the colonial government with the so-called non-violent approach to the liberation process when, in actual fact, serious and effective programmes were going to be directed by him and his fellow radicals.

To choose a party name, they needed the country's name, but Wampanga and his fellow realists were totally opposed to the country's name at that time, named after a British explorer and entrepreneur.

Wampanga said to his colleagues, "There is no way our beautiful and rich country could be named after a foreign exploiter."

The others nodded in agreement. "We must choose a befitting local name," said Ngenda Mwanawina. They considered a couple of local names, but could not agree on any.

Wampanga had a huge library at home and used to read extensively. He also kept a diary, which he worked on a daily basis. In his readings, he had come across what the Portuguese used to call Zambesia, referring to parts of central africa. Focusing on the two major rivers in the country, he suggested to the others about a possible combination of the names of the two great rivers.

"What's the name then?" asked Mwanawina impatiently. They toyed with the name Zambesia, but could still not agree on it.

"How about Zambica?" Wampanga recommended.

"Sounds great!" Muyunda Lubasi concurred.

So, Wampanga was the first to pronounce the name Zambica, and the country would later be known as Zambica. After that, it was easy to name their new political party. That is why many people credit the country's name, Zambica, to the realists and Wampanga in particular. Hence Zambica African National Congress (ZANC) was officially born in September, 1960.

The first general conference of ZANC was held in Dented Hill in November, 1960, at which sixty hastily summoned delegates confirmed

Jumbe as President, Lubasi as secretary general and Wampanga as treasurer. The remaining positions were filled by others.

Leaders of the Zambica African National Congress had an easy and upfront start. They quickly took the provincial leadership and some structures from the party they had ditched, the ANC.

In Luapita province, the ANC provincial leader, Mubanga Nkole, abandoned ANC and walked away with structures, top leadership and most members and delivered them to ZANC.

Using their secret plan, they moved across the country, and explained why they had left the non – performing ANC. Then, the new party's plan of action was swiftly put in place and implemented, with instant effects; burning of bridges, cutting of trees and barricading tree trunks across main roads, breaking windows of government offices and schools, especially in Copper, Northern and Luapita provinces and part of Central Province.

As arranged with the trade union movement, the violent activities were instantly joined by wildcat strikes on Copper Province and Dented Hill, including the boycotts of European shops selling merchandise to Africans through small windows, a rather humiliating racial practice. The trade union was supportive of the approach of the new militant party, which openly supported workers' rights. This was the very opposite to John Mweene Mwendalubi's cowardly approach; preferring to stay away from trouble and direct confrontation with the British government.

In the process, some innocent people were injured, after being caught in the crossfire. To put it mildly, the country was suddenly shaken by the new wave of violent activities, never experienced before. Besides the worrying wave of violent actions, ZANC's secret plan of action had been leaked to the government by a paid informer pretending to be sympathetic to the new political party. From the leaked document, the government knew that more and worse violent actions were to follow, including serious harm to Europeans at the hands of their maids and houseboys.

Jumbe and his radical partners were taken by complete surprise one night. The British governor of the territory, Sir Andrew Dickson, made a sudden radio statement, announcing that the Zambica African National Congress was banned with immediate effect due to its violent and terrorist activities. He gave some details of their violent activities, resulting in extensive damage to government property and other planned illegal and destructive actions.

Besides outlawing ZANC, all prominent leaders were restricted in various remote parts of the country. The ZANC leaders were arrested and ferried to various localities, the night before the governor's announcement. Each District Commissioner had received arresting instructions two days before the arrests were made nationwide. The country's Police was beefed – up with Federal troops and police from Southern Rhodesia and Masaland. The military action taken by the British government was a complete surprise to ZANC leaders. There were posters in major towns titled 'ZANC BANNED' but the ZANC youths rewrote the posters in black ink – ZANC NOT BANNED.

To neutralise the party further, detained ZANC leaders were confined far away from areas where they came from. This was also aimed at crippling the movement by taking away their leaders considered as rubble rousers. Thus, detained ZANC leaders were scattered to different remote parts of the country, leaving their followers like orphans.

When ZANC leaders were in restriction from public life, freedom fighters met in Julien Chikafika's house and discussed the formation of a new party. Chikafika; 'a no nonsense fiery woman organiser of the party ' also mobilised a large number of women in the country to take part in cutting down trees and used them to barricade roads. The women also prepared meals for freedom fighters. In addition, Chikafika was at the forefront of calling women to politically oriented meetings, organised demonstrations and composed tunes for freedom songs and slogans.

Thinking that he had decapitated the African serpent by detaining all the troublesome politicians, the British governor got a shock of his life when another political party, named 'African Freedom Party',

(AFP) was formed, led by Patrick Kalikeka and later changed its name to United Liberation Party(ULP), led by Miyoba Chuma, a lawyer. It was a plan the forceful elements had already put in place. While the new party had different leaders, their manifesto and overall objectives were almost similar to those of the banned ZANC.

A few months after its formation, ULP looked much more of an amorphous collection of splinter groups, which were soon joined by a number of ZANC officials returning from restriction. United Liberation Party's early activities were largely centred in Dented Hill, Lusiku, the Copper Province, Luapita and Northern provinces. Surprisingly, when the detained ZANC leaders were released from prison, the ULP leaders led by Miyoba Chuma willingly and jointly surrendered their positions to the former leaders of ZANC, as if they were merely warming the chairs for imprisoned leaders; another strategy of the banned leaders of the party.

In the arrangement, Jerome Jumbe became the President of the ULP. Thus, the main objective for detaining former ZANC leaders was nullified. While they were expected to tone down after imprisonment, the behaviour of the new ULP leaders was the opposite; they were more critical of the government, describing themselves as 'prison graduates'. Later, it became important and more fashionable to be a prison graduate; it enabled one to boast of being a tested political leader.

To avoid what had happened to ZANC, the realists led the formation of secret parallel structures, which could continue in case the party was banned and 'official' leaders were arrested, another concept learnt from Ghana. This concept streamlined fundraising activities, largely through the Indian community and African businessmen and women. They mostly used influential and educated women, who couldn't be easily suspected by the police. Through these structures, funds raised were used to support party operations and the livelihoods of families of political prisoners.

In 1962, a ULP 5 point master plan was born under the leadership of Lewis Chanda, popularly known as LC. The 5 point master plan, code-named 'ShaShaSha' was known only by a few trusted leaders in the party. It was a revival of ZANC's military approach copied from Kenya's Maumau. Apparently, the campaign for civil disobedience, political awareness, arson and strikes was named after a popular dance in the 60's, called 'ShaShaSha' and symbolized that it was time for the British to face the music of Zambican independence. The master plan had 5 stages.

The ULP cadres involved in executing the plan were immersed in secrecy and took oaths of allegiance to the motherland.

All the stages were commenced in earnest in 1962 but implementation was staggered.

Stage 1 was commenced on the same day in Copper, Luapita, Northern, Central and Eastern Provinces. Fitupas or ID certificates were burnt at once. In addition, for Luapita province, speed boats were demobilised on lakes Bangweulu and Mweru and tyres for police vehicles in Kabombe, Kaole and Lubwe, were punctured, therefore demobilizing the police. Traditional chiefs and their kapasos were threatened and could not arrest anybody.

At the height of the implementation of ShaShaSha, an innocent British woman, Mrs Linda Smith, was killed in Kafulafula. She was in her car with her two daughters when she was stopped at a roadblock mounted by militant ULP youths who demanded that she vacated her vehicle. When she resisted, probably fearing for her life, the youths removed the children from the car, smashed the car windows, splashed petrol over her and one overzealous youth torched the motor vehicle and unfortunately, the woman was burnt alive in the vehicle. This criminal act annoyed the British government, and it retaliated by immediately banning ULP activities on the Copper Province and threatened to abandon the idea of granting independence to the territory.

Immediately, the police mounted an intensive manhunt for the suspected murderers; four were caught, tried, convicted and sentenced to death while two youths connected to the killing were never caught. They were ferried out of the country secretly and it is believed that ULP structures assisted in hiding the suspects, who were eventually sent abroad for training. The two, who happened to be brothers, returned to Zambica after independence, one as a medical doctor and the other as an accountant.

Subsequently, ULP became a formidable political party which seriously mobilised for membership and effectively agitated for independence. In a relatively short time, ULP became a progressive and respected political party with Jumbe and some of his colleagues frequently going on hunger strikes to attract local and international attention. Like the banned ZANC leaders, the ULP President and his friends organised protests and destruction of selected government property and infrastructure. As punishment, Jumbe and his friends were detained like before, in different parts of the country.

In any case, party mobilization continued because the underground fundraising set up by Wampanga's team continued to send money to the party headquarters. The women provincial treasurers, who were not part of the official ULP structures, worked hard in mobilising the needed funds. The safety net of the secret arrangement was that the families of detained leaders were looked after by those who were not 'official' party leaders and therefore not caught up in the government dragnet. This was a strategy developed way back by Wampanga and his colleagues in the treasury. Wampanga had emphasized, "Money or finances are critical in party mobilization. We cannot run the party effectively without adequate funding."

The British government now took notice as stage 1; civil disobedience was being implemented. They couldn't believe Africans could be so highly organised. The organisation, co-ordination, and magnitude of destruction of property immediately brought shivers to the British government which had never been shaken by ANC in the past.

Caught totally napping, the governor requested for urgent support and Federal mobile units were sent in from Salisbury and Blantyre to manage the urgent situation. To decongest prisons, the government decided to release some of the non-political prisoners, as instructed by the governor, but more people volunteered to be jailed.

"We can't take in any more political prisoners," said the prisons commandant to the governor.

"Why not?" the governor asked. "They must be taught a lesson or else more trouble will brew in the country."

"Sir, we have no capacity. We have no food. We have no beddings," the commandant moaned.

"Can't you release more of the non-political chaps to create more room?" the governor asked.

"We can do that if you offer them a special pardon. But this action will not decongest the prisons much." He said regretfully. "More are volunteering to be jailed." He told the governor. The governor promised to look into the issue as soon as possible. Meanwhile, he immediately reported the worrisome incidents to the colonial secretary.

As the political agitation turned into more violence, resulting in the deaths of some of the agitators and innocent citizens, the British government gave in and opted to negotiate for a peaceful handover of power. The British government quickly called a constitutional conference for the country. While Mwendalubi's ANC was readily available to attend the meeting, the ULP refused to attend due to the influence of their militants.

In March, 1962 James Duncan, the British colonial secretary was dispatched to Zambica and Julien Chikafika and a few other assertive party women went to the airport to meet him. Chikafika was not only an organiser, but was always in the forefront in demonstrations. The brave and determined Mama Chikafika along with her female friends demanded immediate independence and self-rule and showed their displeasure by baring their breasts.

When Duncan was surrounded by the half-naked weeping women, he began to cry too. She was later quoted in the press saying that it was the most amusing incident in her life, to see a white man cry. Her high spirits and optimism were a great encouragement to everyone during the pre-independence days. The heroism of Mama Chikafika is legendary in the history of Zambican politics.

The government also presented details on the spate of destruction carried out by ULP in the country to the colonial secretary.

Subsequently, ULP convened a conference in Southern Province at Nagoye in 1964 at which they agreed to participate in Ian Duncan's 15/15/15 elections. Mubanga Nkole led articulation of the position of his delegation from Luapita Province on political strategy ULP needed to adopt, in order to end colonial rule. "As we approach independence, let's enhance democracy in the party." said Nkole. "yes! yes!" shouted several delegates, especially, the budding democrats.

"Keep quiet! No noise," said the chairperson intimidatingly. "Let comrade Nkole complete his contribution."

"Thank you, Mr chairman for your protection," Nkole appreciated. "My delegation from Luapita Province is strongly advocating for real democracy in our party. We want all our structures to be strengthened."

"How do you suggest we do that?" interjected the chairman.

"It is straightforward, Mr Chairman," he said. "As we do in our province, we want ordinary party members to elect all party leaders. This will enhance accountability of leaders to the party structures." He ended to resounding applause from most delegates.

Unfortunately, the ULP leadership rejected Nkole's proposals, even though they were popular among most ordinary members. Instead, the conference adopted a strategy of democratic centralism, which allowed leaders to appoint leaders; creating more powers for the party president.

The resolutions at the party conference gave Jerome Jumbe powers to appoint members of the National executive council and to select candidates for the 15/15/15 constitution elections. They also abolished a powerful party position of Divisional President. Surprisingly, the passing of the three undemocratic resolutions at Nagoye was seen as a triumph by the budding dictators.

Wampanga, Sakwiba Mwangolwa, Lubasi and other senior party members were quickly sent to raise funds for the elections. They went to Egypt, Ghana, Tanzania, Nigeria, Liberia, Algeria and a few socialist countries. Leaders of some of the countries they visited were generous and gave motor vehicles, equipment, and cash for the elections. Discipline, dedication and commitment characterized the spirit of party members sent to fundraise, as they focused on the final objective of attaining independence.

Local support was available too especially through the indian community and African businessmen. In particular, most Indians had yearned for a change of government after experiencing discrimination from whites and the colonial government. In any case, while the majority of Indians were flowing with the wind and supporting JJ's ULP, most Indians from the southern province supported Mwendalubi's ANC, even though cautiously.

While Indian support to the liberation struggle varied, it was described by one Hindu informant as 'moral' or silent and was largely clandestine and in kind, but it was nevertheless vital to the struggle. For instance, the Hindu community allowed African nationalists to hold meetings and rallies in the Hindu Hall in Lusiku. At the time, several private Indian spaces were also used by the nationalist agitators. Through this process, offices of one prominent Indian businessman were used and out of his generosity he subsequently donated his big property in Lusiku to the first governing party of independent Zambica, the ULP. The building block on Independence Road became ULP's Headquarters.

Then came the country's controversial and highly divisive elections of 1964. After the votes were counted, ANC obtained 7 seats, ULP 14 seats while United Federal Party (UFP) had 16 seats, the highest number. The Liberal Party and Lombaland Party got no seats. With no party obtaining an outright majority, Mwendalubi's ANC was the most beautiful bride to form a coalition government with in the most racially divisive and non-representative election the country had ever witnessed.

Before the coalition government was formed, ardent discussions and speculations abound in most clubs and bars especially in the capital city. The white only' gymkhana club was full to capacity the night before partners of the coalition government were announced.

Most patrons in the club were almost certain Jumbe and his ULP were headed for political humiliation and a funeral. Banking heavily on Old John Mweene Mwendalubi to keep his promise to partner with the whites only party was almost a certainty for them. Most of them were drunk, happy and continued celebrating in advance.

"I will drink to that," shouted one fat drunk patron. "After all, Old Mwendalubi would be a fool to walk away from the UFP, which has guaranteed him leadership of the coalition government."

"I agree entirely with that," chipped in another but slim patron. "There's no way Mwendalubi would partner with the ULP whose leaders always virilised him, calling him a fool, unpatriotic and a drunk!"

That mood and high expectations were mirrored in almost all drinking places patronised by whites in the country, including the well-known Lusiku golf club.

The Indians who had played an important role in the liberation struggle were equally anxious. Thus, the views of the Indian community could not be left out. Most Indians proclaimed, "When the country becomes free we shall all be free inside and outside." Despite some young community members often calling Indians 'Mwenye', a local term for Indian, many Indians actually felt at home and mostly never mentioned their Indian citizenship.

That night, most Indians were praying for a breakthrough between JJ's ULP and Mwendalubi's ANC for the sake of the country. Inevitably, Indian views and wishes were well represented at the Lusiku Indian's Sports Club, whose name later changed to Lotus Club. At that time, Indians could not trust whites who had generally discriminated against them and had earlier attempted to restrict Indian entry into the country. They therefore prayed for the unlikely coalition government between ULP and ANC. They quietly sent emissaries to Mwendalubi to that effect through Livingstone-based Hindus, who were more aligned to Mwendalubi than JJ.

For Africans, the situation was very different. While they didn't suspect any manipulation of the election results by the all white officials, they were sad about something else, the outcome from the tricky constitution. Subsequently, the mood was sombre in most African watering holes, as bars were often called by Africans in the country. In the popular Chinika beerhall, located in the western side of the capital city, most patrons condemned John Mweene Mwendalubi as a fool, unpatriotic, and a traitor for siding with the whites against his fellow blacks. He should change his colour and name, they insisted.

The opportunity, however, had finally come, for Mwendalubi, to teach a big political lesson to those vehemently opposed to him in the ULP, especially Jerome Jumbe and a few others. Mwendalubi had signed a pre-election pact with UFP and seemed inclined to form a coalition government with the white dominated party. As the whole world watched the latest drama unfolding in Zambian politics, Old John surprised many people by reneging on the loose pact made with the white party. Instead, Mwendalubi opted to form a coalition government with the ULP, paving the way for the first ever popularly elected African government in the country.

It is reported that despite being offered to lead the coalition government by the white party, Old John made a firm decision. He went to his party's secretariat, where his party's National Assembly group were in a closed door meeting. Most of them were willing to teach the ULP politicians a big lesson for having betrayed ANC and showing Mwendalubi disrespect. Their leader, however, stormed their meeting in the company of JJ and asked only three questions in rapid succession; "How many of you favour an African government? How many want an African government now? How many are behind me?"

Most hands in the crowded hall went up in answer to the questions.

"So be it!" the ANC leader declared and quickly walked out.

Immediately, Mwendalubi and Jumbe, the ULP leader, drove to Government House to inform the British governor that they had agreed to form a coalition government; the first black government. What a relief to the whole nation!

Initially, Jumbe and a few other ULP leaders were nervous about negotiating with Mwendalubi, whom they had often criticized and insulted. The man they had often described as a drunkard thus taught them a political lesson, by driving a hard bargain, resulting in the six ministerial positions available being shared equally between the ANC and ULP. During the struggle for independence, the ANC and ULP had fought some fierce political battles. Mwendalubi was subsequently praised for his maturity and patriotism by casting aside old differences and agreeing to form a coalition government with the bitter rival ULP in national interest. However, it is Simon Mulenga Wampanga who is credited with success in persuading his friend Mwendalubi in accepting the coalition with ULP.

By the end of the coalition government, negotiations were concluded for a constitution for one man one vote elections. Surprisingly, Jerome Jumbe's name was inscribed in the constitution to be the first Republican President; which was strange. It is rumoured that after closely watching the leadership of ZANC and its successor, ULP, the British were quite scared of the hawkish and straight-talking Wampanga, who was also perceived to be inclined to socialism. They did not trust him to lead the first black government.

The campaigns were highly charged and bitter exchanges and name calling was common, until the highly contested elections were held, with ULP and ANC being the chief competitors. The rivalry between the two parties was intense and acrimonious, as if they were not partners in the just ended coalition government.

After winning the one man one vote elections, Jerome Jumbe became first Republican President of Zambica in September, 1966.

Jumbe and the ULP inherited a relatively strong economy. Initially, Jumbe was praised as a good and fair leader; he tried hard to balance his cabinets along tribal lines, except for the omission of Luapita Province from his first cabinet. Many observers were surprised, especially in view of the tremendous contributions to the freedom struggle made by the people from that province led by a fearless politician, Mubanga Nkole. Was the President implying that the province was not important, or was it punishment for delegates from the province having voted against resolutions empowering him to have absolute powers against the party constitution?

President Jumbe also worked hard to improve education in the country by providing free education and setting up the University of Zambica, after inheriting only a few graduates at independence. Jumbe's government also tried to develop infrastructure in the country in general and for research and development, in particular, which was a good sign as most of the pre-independence leaders had low education.

In a relatively short time, the President's dictatorial tendencies started to manifest, starting with intolerance to divergent views and the isolation of those perceived to be potential rivals. As he pushed his socialist agenda, the President seemed less prepared to listen to alternative views, even constructive criticism and anyone in his way was dealt with firmly. Punishment meted out often included demotions and or expulsion from the party. While such high-handed actions silenced most of his critics for a while, an undercurrent of resistance and dissent was slowly building-up in the country. Nevertheless, the silencing of political enemies gave Jumbe some breathing space to do whatever he wanted.

The President also embarked on socialist programmes, such as the nationalisation of major companies, thereby scaring away potential direct foreign investment; implementing consumption rather than production oriented programmes such as generalised food subsidies which benefited top civil servants, miners and indians instead of vulnerable citizens and the introduction of an ambiguous philosophy called 'Humanism.' He also implemented politically correct but economically suicidal programmes, like providing massive support to liberation movements in Southern Africa, whose cost was way beyond the country's financial capacity, also implying that the President's constituency was far and way beyond Zambia and exporting heavy minerals by air and by road making the exports non-viable.

Support for liberation movements in the region was important but on President Jumbe's scale and solo approach, it was too hefty for Zambica to shoulder alone. Consequently, the country, besides spending colossal amounts of unbudgeted funds on these liberation wars for neighbouring countries, also invited trouble as Zambica was often invaded by white led armies from the south, east and west, all of them much superior to the ill-equipped Zambican army. In the process, some of the country's valuable infrastructure was bombed and destroyed while some Zambicans also paid with their precious lives after being caught in the crossfire. The President and his colleagues should have known the dire consequences of provoking better armed armies; it was suicidal.

Subsequently, the President's policies directly led to a serious downturn of the country's economy, as the negative impact filtered right down to the citizens; some started wearing patched clothes, which had nothing to do with the fashion of the day. Also, poverty levels increased, while the proportion of households failing to have three square meals per day escalated. With increasing poverty, even ordinary citizens started resenting the government for diverting huge resources meant for national development to purchasing military equipment for the sub-region, at the expense of the needs of the citizens. Was this a regional government? some of them wondered. Economically, the country has never recovered since.

Nevertheless, after losing support in the traditional stronghold areas, including Northern and Luapita provinces, President Jumbe knew the end was near. Before exiting, he thought of a quick survival plan. He devised a self – preservation scheme. He and his colleagues decided on what they had to do for survival. In 1969, President Jumbe said that one-party state would come through the ballot box; implying that eventually, opposition parties would lose popularity and win no seats in parliament. However, this is not what actually happened, probably due to increased discontentment among the people. In fact, from 1971 when he used Wampanga and Sakwiba Mwangolwa to pass the referendum to end all referenda, the President began to plan to dismantle and throw out all opposition.

After deep soul-searching, JJ tactfully targeted the most difficult province to capture in the country then; Southern Province which had remained solidly loyal to Old John and his ANC. He also remembered that he had been personally condemned by southerners for betraying Old John, when Wampanga's group ditched ANC to form ZANC. He had no choice, under the circumstances, but to deal directly with Old John himself; his former boss in the ANC. At a meeting instigated by the President in Macha, they reconciled, with the ANC being given positions in the ULP Central Committee. The pact is generally referred to as the 'Macha Declaration.' In this pact, former ANC leaders were made to believe that they were in ULP unconditionally.

In February 1974, the President announced that there had been a constant demand for the establishment of a one-party state in Zambica. He said the demands were coming from all corners of the country, in different ways, including meetings, conferences, and by similar calls from traditional leaders. He added that the ULP National Council meeting the previous year also charged the Central Committee to work towards what he called one-party participatory democracy. The President added that the numerous demands were made in order to preserve unity, strengthen peace and accelerate development in freedom and justice. He made a bold pronouncement that his government had decided that Zambica would become a one-party participatory democracy and that practical steps would be taken to implement the important decision.

The practical steps included the appointment of a National Commission, consisting of many members with Miyoba Chuma as chairman. The major mandate of the commission was to recommend changes to the ULP constitution in order to bring about one-party state. It was clear from the President's announcement that the terms of reference of the commission would not include asking the people whether they wanted a one-party state or not; it was already decided by the President and his government; a fate acompli!

After receiving the commission's report, the President went through the legal minds' blueprint with a keen eagle's eye. He then took off on a working holiday to Kasaba Bay, a beautiful resort on the shores of Lake Tanganyika. His main intention was to rest, review, and look at any possible lacunas in the document. The President had to be very certain on which recommendations to accept, which ones to reject and probably which ones to sneak in. Upon his return from the highly publicised working holiday, the President held a highly hyped press conference, dubbed 'the master of all press conferences'. He gave a long and winding introduction, lasting almost thirty minutes, pausing, and drinking vodka-like water in between.

Eventually, the government published its white paper indicating which recommendations it had accepted from the report. The government then formally proclaimed Zambica a Presidential one-party system with the United Liberation Party as the supreme institution of the state. This brought about the end to the existence of Zambica's First Republic.

So, the independence constitution which had permitted a multiparty system, was now replaced with the new constitution that was formally adopted by the ULP dominated National Assembly in 1975, thus heralding Zambica's second republic. To show the seriousness of his declaration, journalists from international and locally accredited media were refused to ask any questions. This signalled the commencement of a new repressive era and was a major departure from the President's previous press conferences.

Jumbe's landmark pronouncements would silence all and sundry in the country and would be passed as law in Parliament. From that day on, no one would ever speak ill of the President or his autocratic party. The President beamed with delight; he would legislate to silence everyone. From that moment onwards, President Jumbe would rule with an iron fist, insulting any critics, threatening innocent Zambicans and detaining without trial, anyone with divergent views. After all he was protected by legislation through the hushed constitution.

In the new one-party participatory state, the party became superior to the government while the party and its government became one. Subsequently, government revenue became party revenue. While compromised lawyers on ULP's payroll had belaboured and considered all possible eventualities, they had nonetheless forgotten one little item. They never legislated against the labour movement, led by one gifted little orator, James Francis Chaluma, fondly referred to as JFC by his followers.

Using the labour movement platform, JFC made loud noises, protested and at times alone, and literally painted black, the undemocratic agendas and poor economic actions undertaken by President Jumbe and his ULP. In return, Jumbe used all tactics at his disposal to frustrate the labour leader. He intimidated the little man by all means; he called him inept, said he was only a 4 feet man while he was a giant at over 6 feet.

He went on to say that Chaluma was a cheat, who had been expelled from school but ended-up with a 'stolen' Form Two certificate. He made several unsubstantiated allegations against the man in order to finish his future political prospects for good. Hence, the father of the nation set an example that political competition was equivalent to total war, just as he had done in the ULP tantamount to discrediting of any political opponent.

Old President Jumbe was still full of plans and intrigues. He wasn't done yet with the little trouble maker, the chairman general of the Zambica Congress of Trade Unions. He thought of one of the oldest socialist tricks in the book he had used so well in the past against his perceived enemies.

When JJ realised he was headed for embarrassment if he continued on the same trajectory, he changed his tactics and appeared to have gotten over the 'spat' from the 4 feet midget. He invited Chaluma for lunch at state house with the First Lady in attendance. When Chaluma checked the food on the table, he noticed that there was no Zambican dish on the menu. Chaluma loved nshima with okra (lady's fingers), ifinkubala, ichochela, fisashi and many such traditional dishes. Without wasting time, Chaluma undiplomatically expressed his disappointment.

"Your Excellency, I can only see European dishes here before us. I am afraid I don't indulge in such exotic and expensive meals more especially that I represent the poor and suffering workers of Zambica," he said.

President Jumbe was obviously taken aback and could not hide his shock at Chaluma's observations. He thought he was pleasing the 4 feet midget by preparing food which was beyond many Zambican families. With his jaw drooping, JJ told his wife: "Bana Mpundu (Mother of twins), make sure to give Chaluma what he likes to eat when next time he visits us as our guest." His wife nodded obediently.

After lunch, they went into a private one on one meeting. As they sat at close range, Jumbe looked observantly at the man again; extremely small, short in multi-coloured clothes, contrasting red socks and brown elevated shoes, probably to compensate for his short height. His eyes were also small and deeply set into his skull.

"I could easily deal with this small man," Jumbe thought. "After all, I have effectively dealt with bigger men before", he stared at him once more, almost forgetting the real objective of their private meeting.

Nevertheless, he made him feel at home. "Can I offer you a drink?" he asked him generously.

"No, thank you, Your Excellency," Chaluma replied nervously. A close friend had advised him; "If he offers you a drink, don't drink it unless you are both drinking from the same glass!"

Despite his internal animosity to the small man seated close to him, Jumbe pretended and praised Chaluma for his leadership of the Labour Movement. "This," said the old man, "has made the Central Committee of the United Liberation Party recognise your immense achievements." The guest nodded gently and relaxed, somewhat.

"This is the main reason for calling you to State House today." He quickly inhaled and exhaled slowly. "To communicate the message in person, on behalf of the Party and its Government."

"Thank you, Your Excellency," Chaluma responded. "The pleasure is all mine," he said with some deep American accent.

"The Central Committee under my leadership has therefore decided to honour you in this way," the Head of State said, handing over a big envelope to his almost nervous guest.

"Thank you, Your Excellency," Chaluma replied. "I never expected such praise and honour from your party, and you, the founding father of this great nation." He praised him in return.

"You can go ahead and open the envelope," the President enticed.

James Francis Chaluma fidgeted a bit in opening the large white envelope. He quickly perused through the letter: In the letter, Chaluma was offered the position of Member of the Central Committee of ULP, the ruling and only political party in the country. It was unbelievable.

Instinctively, Chaluma was extremely excited. All the perks would wipe away his financial blues in a relatively short time, and to be addressed as MCC was the highest title in the country. Many people perceived the title as higher than that of a PhD holder or even Professor. Was he dreaming?

Chaluma smiled broadly and was inclined to accept the appointment there and then. However, something else bothered him, as his sixth sense quickly dictated; wait and consult. He therefore quickly thanked the Republican President.

"Thank you, Your Excellency for the great honour," he said. "I never expected it, to be honest with you." He confessed.

"You are most welcome Mr chairman general," the Republican President responded, expecting a positive response there and then.

"I am sure we can now forget the differences of the past and work closely like brothers." He sounded genuine. "We are brothers, as national leaders, aren't we?" he asked.

"Yes, Your Excellency, we're brothers although I consider you the father of the nation." He responded. "Let me assure you, Your Excellency," Chaluma sighed, inducing more suspense from JJ. "I shall respond in the shortest possible time after consulting my family," he promised.

"Twit!" Jerome Jumbe breathed. "What family?" he wondered. "Does he mean the entire Labour Movement?" He suspected.

As he had promised, Chaluma consulted widely, well beyond his nucleus family and the labour movement. In particular, he was surprised that the praise showered upon him was exactly the very opposite of what the President had always said publicly about him at several rallies and private meetings.

He concluded that while the offer was extremely attractive, it was most likely a trap. He therefore, quickly sent a polite letter to the Republican President, full of praise and gratitude but in conclusion, he regretfully declined the offer, for personal reasons.

"Twit!" muttered the President after reading the letter. "He is a clever little fellow! But I am not done with him yet. I will fix the midget one day." The President vowed.

What Chaluma didn't know was that his latest rebellious act was perceived as an affront and an open declaration of war against the President. It was apparent that JFC was astute. In addition, he knew for a fact that President Jumbe had become extremely unpopular in the country. The short leader was therefore apprehensive, least he tarnished his own image.

It is often whispered that James Francis Chaluma declined Jumbe's attractive job offers twice, like Shakespeare's Julius Caesar.

CHAPTER 2

Riding a Tide of Fortune

There is a tide in the affairs of men which when taken at the flood, leads on to fortune…. On such a full sea are we now afloat. And we must take the current when it serves or lose our ventures.

"~William Shakespeare~"

There was barely a day passing without people talking about James Francis Chaluma or JFC. News spread fast and wide that the 4 footer gentleman had dared the number one guy in the whole of Zambica. He knew people were also talking about him. JJ too knew that he had contributed to JFC's popularity. Now JJ's uncalculated moves were fast putting him in trouble. Wampanga, his childhood friend and once upon a storytime trusted most trusted friend was also elusive these days. He should have sought counsel from him before offering JFC the most prestigious position in the country; MCC and the midget had the nerve to turn him down! Now, every Jim and Jack was talking JFC at breakfast; JFC at lunch; JFC at supper. "I bet my bottom kwacha, many are dreaming of JFC in their sleep. Some even dream of that piece of an excuse of a man. Makes me sick to the core!" JJ concluded by carrying his hands on his head. He was troubled. Who was this short JFC to challenge his authority?

Meanwhile, as JJ was spending sleepless nights over JFC, the whole country was abuzz with mixed feelings about what was happening politically as well as socially. Debates about JFC's nationality were the entertainment of the day.

"My friend, I heard that just like JJ, JFC is not Zambican. I wonder what is true nowadays." A woman drawing water from a stream confided in her friend.

"Awe, Bana Bwalya, (No, Mother of Bwalya). My father went to the same school with his father. He was born the same year and month just like my father. They are age mates. He was born in April, 1945 in Chitwe Nsofu on the Copper Province. His parents hailed from Mwansanga village, in Luapita Province. His late mother and father were Diana Kombe and John Francis Chaluma, respectively. While his father's birthplace is questioned by some people, it has been simply blown out of proportion. His relatives and early childhood friends have confirmed that his father's birth on the Democratic Republic of Congo side of the Luapita river was purely by circumstances prevailing at the time." She paused as she was placing her 20 litter water-bucket on her head.

"The nearest medical facilities from their village at that time were at Jonathan Falls Hospital in the south and Miles Mission Hospital in the north-east. These, however, were both very far to take a heavily pregnant woman to. Thus, the pregnant mother of John Francis Chaluma was taken to the nearest hospital by canoe across the Luapita river at Chibombe Hospital in Congo DR. It is stated that the hospital in Congo DR could be seen from the Zambican side and that most people above 80 years now were either born across the Luapita River by this practice, or at home using traditional birth attendants. Imagine people calling me a Congolese just because my grandfather was born on the other side of the river!"

"No way, my friend. Impossible! We still cross the river to go and get medical treatment at Chibombe Hospital, come to think of it."

"Imagine that my friend. My father says young Chaluma went to Jonathan Falls Primary School which belonged to Christian Missions in Many Lands (CMML) in Luapita Province and completed primary education in 1958 after which he was admitted to Junior secondary school studies at Kabombe Secondary School."

"No wonder Chaluma's speaking prowess! Most of those who went to those schools are gifted in oratory."

Yes, JFC emerged and was noticed early in public speaking. A schoolmate at his primary school testified that when he was in Form 3 at the same school, Chaluma was the centre of school debates at the time. He said that most students would not miss a debate when they knew that Chaluma would be speaking for or against the motion. He added that once the classroom was full, spectators perched on window sills, with all their focus on the articulate, star debater from standard iV. He said, due to his charisma and eloquence in speech, Chaluma's team won their motions most of the time.

While at Kabombe Secondary School, Chaluma belonged to the ULP youth wing through which he and other young freedom fighters organised, agitated and protested against a myriad of injustices of white colonial rule. The youngsters regretted Africans being stripped of their dignity and doors closed to basic human liberties and opportunities for socio-economic development. At the material time, students were striking over poor food. They were fed-up with constantly eating beans and nshima, a thick porridge made from maize or cassava meal, which though a staple food for the people is of very little protein. The two women were so intrigued that they laughed out loud clasping each other's hands. They couldn't imagine people could fight for food.

"Awe bana Bwalya!" (No Mother of Bwalya!).

"True, my friend. My father says that the students were also unhappy with the slow pace of works by a white owned company, Costain Contractors, engaged to renovate and build new dormitories. These grievances sparked riots and a strike by the students, including Chaluma. Unfortunately, the white Provincial Education Officer (PEO) sent by the authorities from Kaole to investigate the student unrest did not help matters either. Unable to understand the local language used by the students, he relied entirely on a messenger, who had a very poor understanding of English for help in interpretation." The woman paused.

"Eeee, you seem to know a lot about JFC, my friend. Let me not disturb the flow of information. This is very interesting. What then happened next?"

"Oh yeah. I heard people concluded that the report on the incident was not backed by what prevailed on the ground. The PEO never consulted the headmaster before calling on a fellow white Provincial Commissioner and the Special Branch to summon the Federal Mobile Unit to break-up the school strike and riot.

"After investigations identified the ringleaders of the strike, the PEO directed the school management to act quickly and six students including Chaluma, were immediately expelled. However, the expulsions were deemed unusual and led to a split between the school headmaster's team on the one hand and the PEO on the other. The latter demanded instant dismissal of the so called ringleaders while the former recommended punishment and final warnings. However, due to his seniority and the political nature of the offence, the PEO's wish carried the day. Most people believed that the expulsion of the six students, including Chaluma, was politically motivated. It was sanctioned by the then Minister of African Education-Musambila. My friend, this JFC has story after story. No wonder he is the talk of the nation." The narrator paused for effect. She felt great that on this day she was the giver and volunteer of information. Tables had turned. This made her feel significant for once. All along, her friend would always be the deliverer of the hottest news in the village. She added that Musambila himself was a discredited black minister who behaved whiter than whites themselves.

"I know," her friend chipped in. "Isn't that the reason why everyone calls him 'makobo'?" she asked, waiting for her friend to respond.

"Yes, he spies on fellow blacks, reports negative and exaggerated aspects to whites. That is why he was awarded the position of Minister for African Education so that he could spy on African students as well.

No wonder he backed the expulsion of the six black students without hesitation. That's what he was being paid for."

As the two women separated, they knew they would continue hearing a lot more about this JFC.

It was common knowledge that the then school captain, Yotamu Bwalya, mostly called YB, was also unhappy with the expulsions. He argued that the identification of the ringleaders was biased, and that the interpretation from the local language to English was wrong. In any case, YB felt responsible for failing to control the student body, and volunteered to be expelled, instead of the six students, a proposal which was rejected by the school administration. On the advice of Kabombe School headmaster, Bwalya changed his mind and stayed. Bwalya was a popular local student football star and was admired and respected by the school administration, the local community, including the King of the Lunde people, Mwata Mukulu. For instance, YB starred and scored spectacular goals in his team's victories against visiting teams including one from Katanga Province in neighbouring Congo DR and a visiting team from Mwamona Blackpool from Copper Province.

Chaluma initially worked in different capacities, including manual jobs when he was a teenager. He is also reported to have worked on a Tanzanian Sisal Plantation. However, his first formal employment was with Southern African Road Services (SARS) in the Copper Province as a bus conductor on a long-distance route. He was an unconventional bus conductor though he ensured that passengers on board the bus had bought tickets for the route. But as the bus was moving, he would often go to his favourite seat at the front of the bus and take out one of his reading materials or assignments from a red bag and focus on his Form Two studies.

Chaluma's behaviour was a clear indication from the onset that he missed school and was determined to advance his academic qualifications no matter what. The route inspectors often scolded young Chaluma for what they termed antisocial behaviour on the bus, for his apparent lack of interest in the passengers. One particular inspector, Mr John Lubinda scolded him one day. "You are not fit to be a bus conductor because you are always reading at the front of the bus instead of moving about checking and talking to your passengers."

Chaluma apologised and told Lubinda how he really wanted to study at Kabombe Secondary School but had wrongly been identified as one of the ringleaders, which led to his expulsion from school. After that, a sympathetic Lubinda encouraged the young man to continue studying on the bus as he was impressed with the young man's determination to study.

The main reason for Chaluma leaving his employment at SARS was to search for a place where he could work and study at the same time. But he made sure that within one year he completed his Form Two before leaving employment at SARS; yet many people including President JJ thought he had not completed his Form 2.

In 1968, he got employed as an accounts assistant clerk with Atlantic Company (Z) Limited. In 1969, he was promoted to the post of cost shipping clerk, after doing well in the previous position. In 1971, he was promoted yet again to the position of credit manager. He should have been doing something right to deserve the quick successive promotions.

Chaluma and his first wife had two children. His first marriage ended in a disaster. It is rumoured that he was betrayed by his best friend. In 1970, Chaluma married his second wife, Veronica Phiri Chaluma with whom he had many children.

To fulfil his burning ambition for higher education, Chaluma continued his private studies with the Rapid Results Correspondence College. He subsequently completed the University of London GCE 'O' Level Certificate and an additional 'O' Level Certificate in Economics, English Language, Principles of Accounts and Bible Knowledge. From these achievements it is explicit that Chaluma was a fast and disciplined learner who passed his examinations with minimum supervision and also worked hard to earn his rapid promotions.

Chaluma also did training related to his position as Credit Manager through private studies organised in New York. He obtained a certificate in Advanced Credit Analysis as well as in collection and credit. In 1979, he attended a course in Industrial Relations at the Henley Staff College in Reading, England. He also completed the London University 'A' Level Studies in Government and Political studies.

Later while in office as Republican President, James Francis Chaluma studied by distance and obtained a Masters of Arts degree whose dissertation was published into a book titled 'The Challenge of Change'.

While at Atlantic Company (Z) Limited, Chaluma was a busy and active participant in the trade Union affairs of the country; he was elected shop steward for the engineering and ordinary Workers Union at his place of work. This was followed by his election as District chairman of his trade union two years later. Then, he was elected as District chairman of the mother of trade unions in the country, the Zambica Congress of Trade Unions (ZCTU). In another vertical upward move, Chaluma was soon elected chairman of the National Union of Building Engineering and Ordinary Workers. It is apparent that Chaluma had greatly impressed the membership of the trade unions. This is evidenced by his rapid rise and promotions.

Chaluma's dapper as well as his short stature, was noticed by both his supporters and opponents, especially President Jumbe. The first Republican President famously referred to him as the 'four-foot dwarf' during his rise in opposition politics.

By taunting and humiliating Chaluma, President Jumbe actually made a big political blunder as the victimised Chaluma became a household name in the trade union circles and the nation. In addition, Chaluma's leadership skills, tenacity, and courage did not go unnoticed in the labour movement; leading to his rapid rise through the ranks of the union. It was not surprising therefore, that at their Annual General Meeting in 1976, James Francis Chaluma was elected unopposed and became Chairman General of the Zambica Congress of Trade Unions (ZCTU), the co-ordinating body of all the country's major trade unions. This was largely due to his dedication to the defence of workers' rights and his almost solo opposition to ULP and its leaders. What a jump!

From a junior position of Credit Manager at an engineering firm to becoming head of the national body of all trade unions in the country.

Chaluma heaved a sigh of relief! He couldn't believe it himself! While he had ambitions, as many people did, he never, ever thought, let alone dream of becoming boss of the much respected and sometimes feared labour movement. He reflected on his unexpected achievement. In retrospect, he thanked President Jumbe for unintentionally making it easy for him to quickly climb the otherwise difficult and long ladder to a lofty position in the trade union movement in the country. All the negative names he had been called by the President were worth the lofty prize. His name would now be known all over the world, he reckoned. Was he destined for something bigger? Was he riding a tide of fortune? He asked himself.

Ironically, Zambica Congress of Trade Unions (ZCTU) was established by the ruling ULP as a means to communicate with the labour force. Therefore, ZCTU had historically supported ULP. In the mid-1970s, Chaluma had urged the government not to regard ZCTU as a pressure group and reiterated the union's support for the government. However, through the 1980s, the relationship soured as ZCTU resisted the government's attempts of incorporating the union organ into the ruling party. From that time on, Chaluma's attitude changed.

Nevertheless, the ZCTU still maintained that it had no intention of becoming a political party. But 1983 marked the first major conflict between the government and the union movement when Chaluma and sixteen other leading unionists were expelled from ULP and detained following their refusal to cooperate with the government's Local Administration Act of 1980. With the state of the economy deteriorating and the price of maize meal, a staple food of the Zambican diet doubled, the trade union called for strikes, leading to a major uprising in most urban centres in 1988.

As a strong and vocal representative of the workers in the country, it was not surprising that Chaluma was unpopular in government circles but was greatly appreciated by the workers and the general population;

after all he remained almost the only discernible voice against President Jumbe's one-party dictatorship when all credible opposition had been threatened and silenced. As Chaluma and his colleagues continued to press for workers' rights and improvement of their conditions of service, including higher wages, the government acted swiftly by confiscating their passports hence putting a stop to their foreign travels.

JFC as a credit manager was responsible for credit management of the company. It was a senior position by the standards prevailing then and taking into account his level of education. JJ, in his quest to silence him, intimidated the Engineering and General Contractors' Union to exclude JFC by virtue of him being in a managerial position. Fearing dire consequences, the Union leadership succumbed to the pressure and expelled JFC from their membership for no good reason. This pleased President JJ.

It has to be said that when destiny makes an appointment with you, no one can stand in your way. Whilst Atlantic Company (Z) Limited was a 100 percent private company, the entity that came to Chaluma's rescue was surprisingly dominated by government controlled parastatal companies – the Zambica Union of Financial Institutions of the Zambica State Insurance (ZSI) group which was a 100 percent government owned and had monopoly of insurance business after nationalisation in 1970.

The financial union group adopted Chaluma as its patron and therefore through an extraordinary stroke of luck, he continued to be at the helm of ZCTU. Thus, while JJ thought by eliminating Chaluma from his original union he wouldn't be eligible to stand for the chairmanship of the ZTCU, Chaluma's destiny thwarted the President's highly calculated and punitive move. Unfortunately, by the President's own actions, even those who hadn't heard of or really known Chaluma now took an interest in him; who was this little fellow, who was giving old and mighty President Jumbe sleepless nights? In those days only, JFC and sometimes the students' union, Zambica National Union of Students spoke on behalf of the people, after the introduction of the bullying and dreaded one-party state.

The President and his colleagues tried other means to delink the labour leader from the union. For instance, in 1989, Chaluma successfully withstood a government 'sponsored challenge' to his leadership of the National Union of Builders and Ordinary Workers. He won; probably continuing to ride a tide of fortune. However, had he lost, that would have put his ZCTU position in jeopardy.

President Jumbe went to the extent of publicly declaring that Chaluma was harbouring political ambitions and was after his office.

JFC cunningly responded, "Your Excellency the President, yes as a human being I have ambitions because I am not a vegetable. But to say that I am after your office is a lie! However, when my time comes to challenge you, you will hear it from me and not from some obscure sources. For now, my interest is to protect and fight for the welfare of the suffering working Zambicans. Meanwhile, let us work together for the betterment of the country."

Nevertheless, Chaluma and his colleagues were undeterred and continued to agitate for workers' rights. As further punishment, Chaluma and his colleagues were in 1983, detained at a remand prison by the President for calling a wildcat strike that paralyzed the Zambican economy, aimed at disrupting industrial peace and to eventually overthrow the 'democratically' elected government. But Chaluma and his union knew that the President was now more desperate. The union simply reacted, "Our mandate is to correct bad actions and stop repression of workers' rights by the state, but not replace it." Later, all union leaders were released after a judge ruled that their detention was unconstitutional.

While in prison, Chaluma is said to have read the Bible extensively. It is not surprising that later, most of his political speeches contained biblical references; he seemed to have come out of prison a much more ardent Christian than before. One wonders, was the detention a blessing in disguise for Chaluma? At least, it made him a prison graduate even though he was no politician then. The small man was also exposed to a wide range of international affairs; in September and December, 1975,

Chaluma, as a Zambican delegate attended the United Nations general assembly in New York.

It is interesting to note that JFC had some amazing qualities which stood him apart from the crowd. Where others would have easily sold out, he stood firm and did the unthinkable. At one occasion, Jumbe had made overtures to JFC by offering him a cabinet portfolio.

JFC was first offered the position of Foreign affairs Minister. He told JJ that he needed to sleep over it and also consult his family. When JFC, then chairman general of the ZCTU, told his wife, Veronica, she was ecstatic at hearing the news of her husband's appointment to the prestigious office of Foreign affairs Minister. However, after reflecting on his mandate as the chief defender of the workers' rights including the down-trodden or so-called common man, his conscience could not allow him to betray the people of Zambica. He called JJ and politely told him that he was unable to accept the offer to serve in his cabinet. He intimated that he was happy where he was looking after the interests of the Zambican workers. His wife who was already spreading news to her family and friends was devastated when JFC told her that he had declined the offer.

President Jumbe was not a man to be challenged and take it lightly. But he swallowed his pride and later extended an olive branch to JFC. Notwithstanding, JJ was a man who didn't like to be slighted even a tiny little bit. However, the only common thread between JJ and JFC was that both were April babies – stubborn to the core.

JJ amended the act regulating public enterprises by including on the Board of Zambica industrial and Mining company the chairman general and Secretary General of ZCTU. That was how JJ temporarily brought JFC into his sphere and JFC knew it, too.

Chaluma was elected Workers' chairman of the international Labour organization (ILO) technical committee dealing with the provision of collective Bargaining. Later, he was elected Workers' chairman of ILO's technical committee dealing with social aspects of industrialisation. In view of his commitment to labour issues internationally, Chaluma was also later elected as chairman of various influential technical committees of the ILO.

As political repression and the detentions of innocent 'citizens' increased, coupled with the biting economic challenges, and the continuation of rampant shortages of essential commodities, a few brave patriots started talking openly. They resolved to do something, despite the fact that they had no right of assembly under the existing one-party constitution. After meeting privately, a sensitization group tasked itself to contact other potential supporters of the idea, to form a democratic movement. This group included Isaac Mwangolwa, a former minister in President Jumbe's first cabinet and two academicians, Mbepa Fitala and Mukelabai Lisulo.

The nucleus group contacted a few others, including former ministers under President Jumbe's government and a few trade union leaders, including Chaluma. The group decided to form a working committee to organise strategies and programmes for further expansion and recruitment of citizens advocating for the reintroduction of multiparty politics in the country. The committee was tasked with organising a conference at Victoria Falls in Livingstone and when they failed to raise the needed funds, they went for Plan B; holding the meeting in the more centrally located Lusiku, at Forest House Hotel.

The meeting was successfully held, and Isaac Mwangolwa was chosen interim leader of the group. The major challenges facing the group were: how to operate as a political grouping under the one-party constitution. For this reason, the meeting agreed that the grouping be called a movement, advocating multipartism. The other challenges were how to raise funds for operations and mobilisation, when any donations would be deemed unlawful. Last but not least, finding a credible leader, when several people had been intimidated by President Jumbe's autocratic rule. These were daunting challenges.

For a potential leader, they made a short list of three possible candidates, with Chaluma, as number 3.

Number 1 was contacted, a former minister in President Jumbe's first cabinet. He had all the necessary credentials and was reported to be one of the richest Zambicans then. He was excited first and promised to reply in a week's time. It was the end of the second week, but he was still dilly dallying. They concluded that the guy had chickened out. He was probably scared of facing his tricky former boss, who kept secret red files, containing compromising details of his opponents which he could spill to the public.

They sent an emissary to number 2, who didn't help them either. First, he gave one excuse after another, and then finally declined without giving any good reason.

While it had been easy to approach number 1 and number 2, it was more difficult to contact Chaluma since no one among the organisers knew him personally.

After consultations, they sent Yotamu Bwalya, often called YB, a successful businessman who had known Chaluma since their school days at Kabombe Secondary School to break the news. Bwalya was the school captain at the school when Chaluma and five others were expelled. Chaluma had sometimes lamented fighting President Jumbe alone; it was dangerous daring the strongman, who was backed by the whole state security machinery. Thus, the idea of working with other citizens would somehow minimize the risks on his life.

JFC had only one serious concern, though, and he put it to YB. "Please thank the members of the organising committee for me, for considering me worthy of their trust." He paused; Yotamu Bwalya looked at him expectantly. "However, I cannot accept the invitation because I am a poor man," Chaluma continued, YB coughed unintentionally, but uttered no word.

"I have no money to fight President Jumbe," Chaluma explained. "Being on the opposite side, the President's men have ensured that I remain a pauper perpetually," he moaned.

"No sir, Mr Chairman General," YB interrupted, "We have already put in place a fundraising committee."

Chaluma nodded.

"The needed funds for this very important project will be raised by us," he assured. "Some monies from well-wishers have already been deposited in a suspense account."

"Are you sure, YB?" inquired Chaluma.

"Yes. I can assure you of that," YB responded. "We didn't know until now that President Jumbe has annoyed so many citizens by his tricks, and some are ready to fund this important project well." He revealed.

"In that case, I accept to be considered," he told him. Bwalya smiled broadly. His mission had been accomplished. In a way he was personally interested in the project, having been imprisoned by President Jumbe for suspected but unproven foreign exchange related dealings.

"As you know, I am a firm believer in democracy," he said. "I would therefore like us to conduct elections democratically," Chaluma suggested.

"That's already part of the agenda," YB responded.

"Very good," Chaluma intoned. "We should not behave like President Jumbe and his ULP, who do not even respect their own constitution," he said.

Changing the subject, they talked about their former school in Kabombe, where they had been schoolmates. YB promised to raise funds for books and computers for the school. As YB left, he was almost certain that Chaluma would be the best candidate to face President Jumbe in any possible election; all the others, including number 1 and number 2 had already been compromised. In addition, Chaluma was now almost a household name, due to his continued opposition to President Jumbe and his ULP, he reasoned.

What YB didn't disclose to the members of the organising committee was that since Chaluma had been financially crippled by the state machinery, he was the one who had secretly sustained him.

One of his gifts to the cash strapped labour leader was a two-storey house in Southrise in Kafulafula.

When the movement held elections for interim leaders, Isaac Mwangolwa was elected chairperson while Chaluma was made Director for Mobilisation, a position which enabled him to tour the country extensively. Seven others were appointed to different interim positions. Subsequently, members of the interim committee were sent to various parts of the country, to introduce and promote the new movement. By early 1992, Chaluma became more involved in the activities of the movement. In order to manage, he obtained unpaid leave from his company to devote full time to the growth of the organisation.

In December 1992, while on one of the mobilisation trips in Macha, Chaluma and nine other members were arrested. The charges made against them were: participating in an unlawful assembly and belonging to an illegal movement, as the movement was not yet registered. Some of the nine arrested members paid fines for the offences, while others, including Chaluma were later acquitted, on grounds of conflicting evidence.

<hr>

The sun bathed in a golden path, emanating a bright and illuminating glare; in appreciation, birds sang sweet melodies and flew gently while flapping their feathery wings, before heading to their next perch. That same windy Saturday morning, Chishala headed for the Lusiku club, the oldest recreation club in the country. The club also housed the Lusiku tennis club, at the corner of Angels Boulevard and Lowly Sellassie roads, in a modest short Hectors suburb of Lusiku. He parked his grey SE 500 Mercedes Benz and carried his new tennis kit with pride. He was always proud of his Benz; it was a status symbol at the time; only owned by a few well to do Zambicans, like him.

Chishala liked his tennis too. He loved the sport as if his whole future depended on it. Somehow, he had a sneaky feeling that tennis, which he believed was a sport for the affluent, would clearly distinguish him from most of his colleagues, whose preoccupations were womanising and boozing, like his old friend Kaluba. Sometimes, Chishala considered non-sporting colleagues lazy and boring. No wonder some of them looked much older than their age and carried their protruding tummies, often referred to as patriotic fronts, as if they were more than five months pregnant! He placed Kaluba in that category, even though he was now learning how to play tennis.

On the contrary, Chishala was slim, athletic, and physically fit. In fact, many people thought that he was actually ten years younger than his real age. Nevertheless, he was somehow surprised that some of his friends, especially Kaluba, described him as 'Mr John come lately,' where the sport of tennis was concerned. Seriously, Chishala did not mind that description, which was for a man who learnt the sport in his early thirties, but immersed himself in it both heart and soul. While exaggeration could not be ruled out, he often responded that there was no harm in developing a passion late, rather than never. For him, what mattered most was that he was able to play tennis well and sometimes competed with the so-called early starters.

Chishala had another good reason for his belated but elated drive for the sport of tennis. He had a new racket given to him as a birthday present at the office by Theresa, whom he secretly adored though he didn't reveal his admiration for the young woman. He regarded her as the most intelligent and beautiful woman at his place of work. He was therefore, pleasantly surprised that she bought him such a valuable present; an indication that she might consider his proposal favourably, should he decide to make one. Somehow, he considered her lucky; otherwise he would have already made a fast move on her.

For his calculated campaigning and related manoeuvres, Chishala was recently elected to the prominent and enviable post in the tennis circles, that of president of the Zambica tennis association. His victory was much sweeter because Kaluba was one of the candidates he defeated in the first round of the elections; he considered him a thorn in the flesh at times.

In any case, as an added incentive, the new tennis president basked in the publicity and glory that went with the position at the time, especially that he was the first Zambican to fill the luminous post which previously had been held only by whites and Indians. As expected, Chishala did not hesitate to take advantage of the opportunities, especially those involving young female tennis players or fans alike.

At the Lusiku tennis club, Chishala was participating in the men's singles tennis tournament that weekend. Nonetheless, for those who knew Bwana Chishala's limited tennis prowess, it would be a miracle for him to go beyond the quarter finals and even progress through to the semi-finals. Little did he suspect that there was actually a plot behind his back, a conspiracy in his favour; to let him win the prestigious tournament largely for two reasons: giving him a great sense of victory and to motivate him to raise funds for the association. Being well connected politically and in the business circles, the conspirators were convinced that Chishala was a perfect vehicle they could use to propel the almost bankrupt association back to its previous prominence and sporting glory.

However, the secretly concocted scheme hit an unexpected snag at the last hurdle. Chishala's opponent in the final was a no nonsense and ambitious young tennis player, who took no prisoners on the tennis court. The younger finalist knew that he could beat the president in straight sets, if he so wished; because he knew that his opponent in the final talked more tennis than he could play it!

Nevertheless, the younger finalist didn't want to embarrass the president, who he greatly respected as a politician and businessman. Besides, he also believed, like many others in the association, that Chishala had the capacity and zeal to revive the financial position of the association. Despite reasoning like that, he was in a dilemma as he was aware with certainty that losing to old Chishala in the finals would jeopardise his own tennis ratings in the country and the region.

As a compromise, young Pick-up Zulu deceptively played along with the scheme by letting Chishala take the first set by a decisive 6 – 4 score line. That gave Chishala an early lead and elated ego about the prospects of winning the tournament. Nevertheless, the young man made no mistake in the second set, which he took, by a 6–3, score line.

The third and decisive set was somewhat intriguing. Zulu tactfully let old Chishala lead by three games to nil. Then, he rolled over his older opponent and as his name suggested, picked-up five consecutive points to lead by 5–3. Just then, something more dramatic suddenly happened. The tennis president abruptly stopped playing. He raised his right hand to the chair umpire, limped a bit, and quickly slumped in agony onto the hard ground, facing the floor near the service line. When two male attendants approached, Chishala shouted, "No men needed, they are too rough! Girls will do a better job," he suggested, causing laughter among the large crowd of spectators.

In compliance, two slim young ladies rushed in to massage the president's stiff limbs from suspected cramps. Thus, the much talked about final match dubbed as a contest of ages, between the promising young player against a determined old player, was suddenly abandoned due to the president's injury and according to the tennis guidelines, victory was awarded to young Pick-up Zulu, who won by default and like his name suggested, picked up the trophy, and a winner's cash prize. The losing finalist, Chishala, was presented with cash equivalent to half of the winner's amount, which he immediately donated to the tennis association.

The dramatic and unexpected end of the final created abundant speculation among players and some well-informed spectators. Those who knew the tennis president well, had no illusions whatsoever; they openly professed that the tennis chief merely feigned injury, in order to escape the embarrassment of direct defeat at the hands of a much younger opponent. Zulu, too, harboured the same opinion but wisely kept it to himself.

"Sorry about the injury, sir," said a feminine voice. "But congratulations are in order! You played very well," she complimented him, as she smiled gently. He stared at the young woman, scrutinizing her closely. She was slim and he thought she was extremely pretty.

"Except for the injury, sir, you deserved to win the tournament," she continued.

"Hello young lady," Chishala greeted. "Do I know you?" he asked while she kept quiet. "Have we met somewhere?" he continued, still mesmerized by her beauty. She beamed him a gentle smile again and he encouragingly smiled back at her.

"I don't think so," she responded belatedly. "But who doesn't know the most famous president of tennis the country has ever had?" she asked back intelligently.

"Is that so?" Chishala asked, smiling cynically. "You should have been doing some homework." Chishala critically examined the beautiful and well-dressed young lady. She had pale rounded legs; the type he most fancied. He swallowed hard, moved closer to her, and said almost in a whisper, "Can I give you a ride home?" She hesitated, without uttering a word.

He noticed her trepidation and added, "No strings attached of course," he assured her. She subsequently nodded in the affirmative.

He asked if it was all right to pass by his office to pick up a document before dropping her off wherever she was going. They quickly headed for his office located on the first floor of the imposing electricity house on Egypt Road. When she quietly observed him at close range, she realized he was older than he had looked on the tennis court. Nevertheless, she let him dominate the small talk as they walked up the stairs.

He bubbled on and on about his profitable business in the importation and distribution of second-hand clothes, popularly known as salaula or Sally's Boutique. He volunteered that he was the first Zambican to make it in a business largely dominated by an Indian business cartel in the country. Chishala also boasted about his large and well-furnished office before offering her a drink from his small, but well stocked office bar. She however declined saying, "Maybe next time, sir." She knew there and then that he had an interest in her.

"Are you in a hurry?" Chishala asked.

"Yes," she replied. "I've some urgent homework to do and the deadline is approaching," she said. She didn't want him to think that she was a pushover.

After chatting for a while, they headed for the hostels at the National Institute for Public Administration (NIPA), where she studied and resided. He further learnt that she was Nsenga from Eastern Province, and a final year student for the Diploma in Public Administration at the college. Instantly, Chishala felt a great sense of victory as he lustfully gazed at her firm youthful behind, until she disappeared into the hostels.

He was elated, as if he had just won a state lottery jackpot. He assured himself that he had already conquered the beautiful but naive-looking young student from Eastern Province. Little did he know that in spite of her pretence and feigned initial resistance, she too, fancied him. While Chishala was suddenly happy over the prospects, Mboniwe on the other hand projected that finally, she had hooked a prospective sugar daddy. He would instantly improve her wardrobe and enrich her social life, during her final college days in the capital city.

She imagined that he could be such a contrast with her current poor and immature college boyfriend, who had literally nothing to offer and could be described as 'a boy of straw', using the college girls' terminology. In addition, the young man was well known as a troublemaker at the college and she at times regretted dating him.

"Where do you think you are going?" shouted a tall young man, as Mboniwe was about to step into Chishala's Mercedes Benz one Friday evening. She hesitated for a while, feeling embarrassed as some students were getting curious and showing interest in the confrontation. This was the third time that Chishala was picking her up from the hostels.

"Why are you asking?" she asked in a low voice.

"You know why," he replied loudly for everyone to hear.

"I shall come back soon," she promised.

"Over my dead body," he yelled. "You're going nowhere."

"This is my uncle from Petauke," she replied meekly. "We are just going to visit our relatives in Chilenje." She said, as Chishala tightened up in surprise.

"Shut up you whore," the tall muscular young man replied.

Mboniwe suddenly froze.

"I know all about your little affair," he inhaled and then quickly exhaled emotionally.

She hesitated, and was overwhelmingly embarrassed by the presence of other students around, who were now paying undivided attention to them and laughing excitedly.

"Do you think I'm that stupid?" he asked her. "I've been trailing your secret movements with this randy old man; he is old enough to be your grandfather!" He was shouting again at the top of his voice. Mboniwe kept quiet while Chishala listened silently in the car.

"I can beat him up and no one can stop me," he threatened. She tried to persuade him to leave but to no avail. Some of the students around laughed loudly and pointed fingers at them and the old man seated in the car, as they speculated and gossiped among themselves.

Having had enough and uttering no word, Chishala drove away at a fast speed to avoid further embarrassment. His plan for a romantic outing with his new catch ruined, he went to Lusiku tennis club, to drown his sorrows and for a quiet reflection and certainly to lick his wounded ego.

Like in a dream, he remembered how his previous relationship with a beautiful young woman almost had a fatal ending:

The young woman used a friend to lace rat poison in Mwansa's tea at the office. Even though the girl's cousin had no reason to wish any harm to Mwansa who was her senior as secretary to the Land Commissioner, she had been persuaded and paid handsomely to put a brown powdered concoction in her colleague's tea. This she implemented perfectly one cold morning in June.

Mwansa had thirstily gulped her tea offered by her trusted officemate as she had done on numerous previous occasions. However, two hours later, she experienced excruciating abdominal pains and was rushed to the nearby hospital after she foamed at the mouth and started vomiting profusely.

At the hospital, she was put on a drip to dilute the poison in her blood. Her temperature was gradually lowered and that's how her life was saved.

Laboratory tests later confirmed that Mwansa had ingested poison about mid-morning the day she fell ill. While his wife was still recuperating in hospital, Chishala had only one main suspect, his then girlfriend, who had earlier threatened to harm his wife; a threat he had considered as a joke.

He rushed to her flat near NIPA and confronted his secret lover.

Although she initially denied it, she eventually confessed, saying confidently, "If I used initiative to put a little poison in her tea, so what?" to Chishala's disbelief.

"Are you crazy?" he asked in utter surprise.

"Yes, I'm crazy about you and I don't want to share you with anyone else," she replied, in a firm voice.

"How can you do a stupid thing like that?" he asked.

She hesitated for a moment before responding, "Don't you know that your wife is the obstacle here?" she asked him bluntly.

"Obstacle to what?" he asked in bewilderment, shaking his head.

"Have you forgotten, darling?" she asked. "Preventing us from getting married, of course," she said, sounding delusional.

"You are mad," he charged. "You have gone totally potty. You should be in Chaputuka Mental Hospital," he fumed. "I shall have nothing to do with a deranged woman like you anymore," he swore.

She thought he was joking, until he slowly started to walk away. "Chishala," she called, "you can't do this to me. No! You can't do this to us," she pleaded. "I love you!" she shouted.

"No way," he responded. "Damn you! Our fling was a mistake from the start. It is all over," he stormed from her flat, banging the front door.

He never saw that 'crazy' woman again.

Subsequently, as he came out of his reminiscing daze, he concluded that it was unfair for him to start dating another girl, soon after the near fatal incident, involving his wife, he lamented.

Saturday was equally frustrating. Chishala was supposed to travel to the Eastern Province for another mobilisation trip. As the advance team leader, he had to prepare the ground before the arrival of his party President. He later found out that the delay was caused by the slow processing of travel funds. Therefore, he could not leave immediately for his latest political assignment.

With time on his hands, Chishala had to deal with a frequent domestic challenge. His wife had tried to buy some essential commodities but, as was often the case, she failed to find them.

He decided to go on the hunt himself, just like many disappointed Lusiku husbands often did. He was encouraged when he found a long queue to a supermarket on Egypt Road, even though he didn't know what it was people were queuing for. He was in the queue for a good twenty-five minutes but the movement was rather slow. Later, he was told that the long line was for one of the rarest items in the country then, cooking oil. Regardless, several people in the queue became agitated with the lack of movement and shouted obscenities at the supermarket staff.

In due course, word went round that the supermarket was closing for the day because cooking oil had just run out. It wasn't long before a van offloaded several police officers, who chased the disappointed customers away, including Chishala. He remembered that chasing potential customers by police officers or ULP vigilantes when commodities had run out was now a common practice in the country.

He was naturally disgusted with the development, especially after having spent almost one and half hours in the long queue. Left with no option, he drove to the black market on Katanda street, and found some salt and cooking oil, which he bought at almost four times the market price. Despite the inconvenience and the escalated cost of essential commodities, Chishala hoped that this would be one of the key-determining factors against the ruling party on election day. He smiled wistfully that his party would probably benefit from a very sad economic situation.

He drove home and was welcomed by a very happy wife, who smiled broadly at him, as a resourceful husband. Still smiling gently and singing her favourite song, she dutifully packed his suitcase in the evening in preparation for his long trip the following day.

Mwansa was delighted that her ingenious and caring husband managed to find rare commodities, which she had failed to find herself. She recalled how her neighbour, Mrs Lubinda, often came to ask for salt or cooking oil from her since her husband had no car and found it difficult to source the rare but essential commodities. No wonder many Zambicans were now complaining about inconveniences caused by the frequent shortages of essential commodities in the country.

She was convinced that her imaginative husband was not too worried about the frequent shortages of the needed items in the country. On the contrary, he knew that the shortages would provide fodder to his party's campaign, as one of their promises to the voters would be to end the constant, and annoying shortages within a short time after assuming power.

The second trip to Eastern Province was tiring, what with bad roads, filled with potholes in some places. Chishala led a small team to reassess the situation in a few districts. It was clear that right from Lengwe Bridge to the provincial capital, the road had not been maintained for a long time. Since they had not yet established structures on the ground, they wasted a lot of time searching for who could become interim district officials. But it was evident from the hostile responses and negative reactions of the local people, that ULP was still very strong and popular in the area.

As if Chishala's team needed any permission from them to belong to another political party, the majority of the people spoken to stressed that they were very happy with ULP and that there was no need for another political party in the area. Of particular concern to Chishala and his team was the high popularity of the ULP leader. The people there seemed to adore President Jumbe almost to the point of worshipping him. He had sacrificed so much to liberate the country; anyone trying to wrestle power from him was regarded as a traitor! While the majority of the voters in the area were not well educated, they nevertheless felt strongly about continuity and the liberation heroes.

The summary of the report on Eastern Province was again negative, concluding that it would take a miracle for a new political party to dislodge the ULP, from its stronghold.

CHAPTER 3

The Beginning of the End

"Comrades, Jumbe has betrayed us! How can he keep quiet when everything is going haywire like this? This is annoying. We seem to be where we started." A visibly disgusted Mubanga Nkole addressed his friends as he pulled out a chair to sit. Of a small stature and physically unassuming, Nkole's commanding voice was however, unsettling. They were still at the ULP conference and discussing the passing of those three unpopular resolutions.

"Nkole, you seem to forget who Jumbe is. Why do you waste time talking about opportunists, bootlickers and banana backbone people surrounding JJ? Heh?" Ngenda Mwanawina cut him short and threw his hands in the air.

"We all know what JJ really wants while bootlickers support him without thinking."

"Yes, comrades. We have been used and dumped by Jumbe and a few yes men" Nkole advocated. "Suddenly, our contributions have been discarded just when we can all smell independence."

Everyone looked up and all their foreheads registered frowns that spelt out concerns of what was at stake.

A year after independence and back in Luapita Province, they were still talking about that Nagoye Conference.

"Everything we had worked for was gone."

Nkole held his head with both hands and brought them slowly to his chest. He later let the hands rest tightly around his stomach. His friends' eyes followed his movements quietly.

"Do you all remember the 1964 Nagoye Party Conference?"

They all nodded vigorously in agreement.

"That is when early polarisation of ULP factions started. All of a sudden, a powerful party position of Divisional President was abolished and we were all shocked that the party granted Jumbe sweeping powers to appoint members of the central committee as well as to select party members to contest the elections under 15/15/15 constitution. This was contrary to the party constitution."

"You're very right, Mr Nkole."

"Iyee!" Another man butted in. "That conference was deadly. Nkole and all delegates from Luapita Province were almost expelled from the party for opposing those undemocratic resolutions. It became crystal clear that what was happening certainly suited Jumbe. Instead of defending democracy, Jumbe had kept quiet. Some people find it very easy to be chameleons. That's Jumbe! I've never trusted him since." He stood up and moved around aimlessly; a sure sign of frustration taking its toll.

"But iwe (you), How could Jumbe not do that?" Ngenda Mwanawina who had been quietly following the conversation joined in. "He knew very well who Nkole was and is."

Everyone including Nkole burst out in laughter. "He knew very well that even foreigners upheld him very high. For example, the British governor then described Nkole as the most effective political organiser in the ANC and later ULP. That clearly made Jumbe uncomfortable."

"But was that my fault?" Nkole asked as a matter of fact.

"Yes, it was your fault, comrade," Ngenda Mwanawina pointed a shaking finger at Nkole.

Mwanawina was visiting Luapita Province on a party mission as head of delegation a year after independence. "If you are not careful with your moves and your words you will leave that beautiful white wife of yours to vultures I tell you. However, Jumbe knew very well that our friend Nkole here, was a committed and intelligent political organiser in Luapita Province. Unfortunately, he paid the price for speaking out and I can assure you that is why he will never be given a senior position in government. I know Jumbe very well. He is quite vindictive."

"Whew! You're right my friend. I paid heavily. In the same vein, Luapita became a black sheep province and was not allocated even a single cabinet position at independence despite having made tangible contributions to the liberation struggle. Imagine! This was an early indication that the President was vengeful and did not forgive perceived offenders." Nkole spoke with a heavy heart and a voice that spelt that enough was enough.

However, observers pointed out that by endorsing the three controversial resolutions, the conference actually promoted dictatorship and one-man rule right from the outset. The party's decisions at Nagoye disappointed many who had worked very hard at provincial level; it was like getting rid of genuine contributors when independence was just around the corner.

A stern acid test for Prime Minister Jumbe and his ULP was a conflict at the dawn of independence, described by JJ's government as a rebellion, but termed as a massacre by independent observers.

"Remember Alice Mulenga Lubusha and the then English Missionary Society Church in Kwitonta District?" Nkole reminded his friends. They were still discussing their President, Comrade Jumbe.

"Don't even go there. Oh, that was the worst Jumbe and his cronies could ever do." Mwanawina recalled. Mwanawina was speaking freely, over 600 kilometres from Lusiku, crowded with JJ's spies and cronies.

"Massacre of the very innocent. Smearing one's hands with the blood of God's ordained!" Mwanawina contributed irritably.

Nkole and others nodded in agreement. They all remembered it all sadly and vividly, as if it had happened the previous day.

Before her death, Alice Mulenga Lubusha belonged to the English Missionary Society church in Kwitonta district. In 1955, Alice woke up during her funeral and rumour circulated that she had met 'Jesus' in her death, who commanded her to go back to earth and work. After her 'resurrection' as Regina or Lenshina, she started to preach and had some healing powers. However, as a woman, she was not allowed to preach to the male congregants and the Lubwa-based church permitted her to preach only to the female congregants. But men also started flocking to her services to listen to her captivating sermons. Not amused and perceiving her to be a threat to church unity, the missionaries cancelled her services all together as punishment.

This led Lenshina to start her own healing and preaching ministry in her village, which grew rapidly, attracting followers from other provinces and even from outside the country. In Kwitonta district, Lenshina followers' praying times conflicted with ULP's campaign schedules and the latter started implementing punitive measures. To avoid further victimisation, Lenshina's followers set up their own villages, mostly near rivers, and they were quite enterprising and established small scale businesses. The success of their businesses seemed to annoy many ULP leaders.

It is reported that to punish Lenshina's followers further, ULP members began burning Lenshina villages within Kwitonta district. In turn, the brave victims started to retaliate by burning government buildings. Traditional chiefs stayed aloof in the matter, preferring integration of their subjects instead of them living in separate villages. At that time, the ANC and ULP campaigns for the 15/15/15 constitutional arrangement exacerbated the situation as Lenshina followers were inclined to support ANC which was not harassing them. This further offended ULP leaders.

In 1966, the coalition government between ULP and ANC ended and Jumbe as Prime Minister became the sole ruler. Scared of further victimisation, Lenshina followers refused to be reintegrated in their former villages. Jumbe saw this as a rebellion against his government. He decided to send over 2000 hastily recruited and ill-trained soldiers and police officers. While troops were under the control of the British military, the communication between British officers and the troops was very poor. This contributed to misunderstandings which in turn led to huge numbers of fatalities, especially among Lenshina followers. Government sources reported that over 1000 people died following the attack and Lenshina's retaliation. But independent observers said that the figures were highly suppressed. Also, the number of casualties did not include those who died after the security operations or those that starved to death while hiding in the bush or during the long march to 'safety' into war-torn Katanga province of DRC.

The government blundered in the handling of the Lumpa Church incident that lead to the massacre of either unarmed citizens or those armed with inferior weapons, such as pangas, spears, or home-made guns. They killed church members, some were shot while running away and some were women with babies strapped on their backs. Surprisingly, as Lenshina's followers were being killed, and others running away, some ULP members were heard thanking Jumbe or simply urging troops on and shouting, "Kill them! Kill them! We are now in charge."

There is a high possibility that Prime Minister Jumbe could have been tricked by the governor whose government had always resented the activities of Lumpa church members. The church activities were suspected to be an expression of African resentment to colonial rule. While ready to pull the trigger, the governor knew too well that the massacres would be blamed on the new and inexperienced African leader.

Despotic rule and indecision by Jumbe were obviously largely responsible for future resentment against him and his party; leading to future disintegration of the ULP. While the President could be held responsible for this, he didn't initially set off as an autocratic leader; for most intents and purposes, he was made despotic by some of those he led. For instance, Dombwa Shimunda, ANC Member of Parliament for Maala Constituency said in Parliament, just after independence,

"President Jumbe, at a rally in Chipata, allegedly deplored the police for favouring ANC." That became a serious boiling point.

"What? Dombwa Shimunda, those are false and unsubstantiated allegations. Mr Speaker, I move that MP Dombwa Shimunda be suspended from Parliament with immediate effect," the ULP youthful chief-whip in Parliament, Sakwiba Mwangolwa, roared. He felt what Dombwa Shimunda had said concerning the conduct of His Excellency the President was far-fetched.

"Hear! Hear! Hear! Hear!" the ruling party members of parliament all screamed in unison.

"It is going to be positive proof that not only are we on this side of the House, but that ULP is not going to brook any nonsense in the running of this country," Mwangolwa continued after receiving thumbs up from his supporters. "But that once and for all the idea must be drummed home; and I mean, drummed home Mr. speaker, that I mean the name of His excellency the President of the Republic of Zambica must never be taken in vain." The ULP Members of Parliament applauded.

Surprisingly, Mwangolwa was not alone in pursuit of justice; the then Minister for Eastern Province and Simon Mulenga Wampanga rose to contribute. In support of the motion, Wampanga said, "When you make a mistake with your father, he whips you, if you make another mistake to your mother, she will whip you, or you may not have food. This is our philosophy. This is our own foundation and we are going to continue because it is right!" Wampanga went on to portray the picture that the President always made correct decisions.

While the motion was meant to intimidate the opposition member of parliament for Maala, it certainly placed President Jumbe beyond reproach. Little did the ULP Ministers realize then that they were creating a personality cult around President Jumbe, making his name synonymous with – His excellency the President. In any case, some ULP leaders, including Wampanga himself, were later on the receiving end, after President Jumbe's autocracy became fully entrenched. While all Members of Parliament enjoyed parliamentary immunity for anything said in the House, it was dictatorship and abuse of ULP parliamentary majority that led to the censure and finally suspension of the ANC Member of Parliament for a harmless statement made in the House.

More cracks and crevices in the ULP continued emerging much earlier than expected. However, ethnic tensions became evident. Nevertheless, the development of deep divisions in the party were not adequately addressed. While President Jumbe's strategy for unity was tribal balancing, elite party members repeatedly mocked this noble venture as promoting inefficiency in the party and the government. Unfortunately, President Jumbe's supporters were unmoved and felt that the practice was a sure way of promoting unity.

With the forthcoming general conference and party elections in 1969, Wampanga was told by the President not to stand for the position of party Vice President because if he won, he would automatically become Republican Vice President, according to the ULP constitution. The President argued that since both of them hailed from Kwitonta, it would be totally unfair to the rest of the country if both the Republican President and his Vice came from the same district.

But President Jumbe was in trouble even before the party elections were held. While he did his best to back Speedwell Nkutukunve to retain his Vice Presidency, he could not openly back him up because by doing so, he would be seen to be anti-Wampanga, his 'kingmaker'. In addition, Nkutukunve had been accused of misconduct at the office by his colleagues, for which President Jumbe was accused of covering up. Consequently, President Jumbe publically seemed to play a neutral role.

Wampanga listened more to his group of ardent followers, urging him to go for it, in view of his presumed popularity. He put his name forward as a candidate for the position of Party Vice President, in effect, rebelling against his President's advice. Many senior party officials had told him bluntly that he had no chance against a candidate quietly endorsed by the Republican President. The radical element in him ignored them all and he went for it after forging an alliance with a few senior party members from Southern Province.

With his craftsmanship and effluent oratory, Wampanga defeated his opponent hands down and many people noticed him as a fearless political organiser. To add insult to injury, Wampanga's alliance scooped 5 out of the 7 contested central committee positions. No doubt, Wampanga's stunning victory at the 1969 party polls was the first major embarrassing moment for the President. President Jumbe, as he did to Nkole in 1964, never forgave his childhood friend. His camp regarded Wampanga's act as 'rebellious' against the sitting President, as the victorious camp celebrated openly. To them, their man's victory was testimony that he was the more visionary in the party. After all, was he not the one who instigated the rebellion in ANC which led to the formation of ZANC, the forerunner to ULP?

The ULP faction that lost the 1969 elections seemed prepared to use any means at its disposal to acquire political power in future and to make the work of Wampanga as ULP deputy leader and Zambican Vice President difficult. This was tantamount to rejecting the results of free and fair elections. They falsely accused Wampanga and his supporters of promoting regional chauvinism. In earnest, they seemed to have developed political anxiety and fear of not being in control of the party. That fear was evidenced and associated with a profound distrust of political opponents, leading to political competition in ULP being considered as total war.

Without a doubt, Wampanga's election success had other serious ramifications. His supporters monopolized senior positions in the new party central committee. This upset members from other provinces, especially Eastern Province, where the defeated candidate came from, while those from Western Province were equally upset that they had lost senior founding members of ULP, who lost in the party elections, as they had been discredited by the President and were not aligned to Wampanga's pre-election alliance.

The President did not help matters either. Probably feeling rebuked by Wampanga's supporters, he added the Ministry of Finance to Wampanga's Vice Presidential portfolio, which was unusual. This act was resented by some non-Lemba speaking members of the party, alleging that power had now shifted into Lemba hands. However, instead of celebrating, Wampanga's critical elements saw the President's generosity differently. They saw it as a ploy meant to overburden him so that he fails. This was at a time when miners were revolting against the government's introduction of taxes for miners. In reality, the government was probably looking for a tough guy to handle the miners or someone to fail and take the blame!

ULP central committee lost its tribally balanced composition as tribal interests took root. The tribal feuding came to a head in an orchestrated anti-Lemba fashion during a ULP National Council Meeting in 1970. Having set it up, Jumbe sought a proof of loyalty, as far as Wampanga was concerned. But some members pointed fingers at him, as the one who had failed to control the situation in order to benefit from it. A few others were more blunt at the meeting, shouting and implying that Wampanga, the owner of the party throne was going to retrieve it. Annoyed, President Jumbe quickly stood up and walked out of the all-important meeting. He declared that he was not prepared to preside over a federation of tribes and tendered in his verbal resignation there and then.

That night is commonly referred to as 'a night without a Leader'. Jerome Jumbe withdrew his resignation the following morning, after he received several delegations, pleading with him to rescind his decision. It is rumoured that Wampanga locked the door to the conference hall, saying "No one will leave, until we resolve this." While Wampanga's bold action was a mark of leadership, analysts, however, suggest that President Jumbe was a major beneficiary, as this was a show of homage to him, that he was the only person capable of leading the party. In reality, President Jumbe actually never resigned. After consulting Chief Justice Jonathan Smith on how he could resign, Jumbe never sent his letter of resignation to the CJ. So, he was merely testing his colleagues' loyalty.

Another consequence of the 1971 ULP party elections and the ejection of two former political heavyweights from Lombaland was the loss of power in the province. The irony was that they lost to nonentities, from a newly formed political party that was predominantly Lomba. The new party clearly benefited from the confusion in ULP, winning all but one of the parliamentary seats.

Besides losing power in Lombaland, ULP also lost control of Northern and Luapita provinces once it became clear that Lembaspeaking members of the party were being resented, while others were being discriminated against. As the breaking up of the ULP continued JJ and his closest allies sensed danger. One of the actions taken to forestall the situation was the renaming of Lombaland as Western Province, a move that was resented by most Lombas.

In 1971, another divisive and racial issue occurred involving the white Chief Justice, Jonathan Smith who had supported the ULP during the struggle for independence. After a judgement by white judges, seen publicly as favouring two whites, who had strayed into the country, President Jumbe stepped in and publicly asked the Chief Justice, "Are the judges defending the interests of the people or foreign interests?" When the Chief Justice responded publicly, emphasizing the independence of the judiciary, all hell broke loose, and party protests were organised, accusing him of racism, and demanding that he be deported from the country forthwith.

Some of the incensed protesters carried placards hostile and critical of the Chief Justice and were actually racist. Two of them read: 'A White Man Will Never Be a Zambican' and 'The Only Good White Man is a Dead One'. Some disgruntled party members including a close ally of the President blamed Wampanga's supporters for orchestrating racially toned protests against the chief Justice, and surprisingly absolved the President who had started the nasty saga, in the first place.

Contrary to suggestions that Wampanga was a racist, it has been established that he had many white friends and admirers who liked him for being honest and talking openly on racism, and the need for emancipation of Africans. One of his daughters confirmed that Chief Justice Smith and their father were very close friends. A day before leaving the country, the former Chief Justice visited the Wampanga residence to say goodbye.

He said to him, "Simon, my friend, you are a good and honest man. I'm leaving because I cannot continue working under double standards; one standard to please the public and a different one expressed privately."

They embraced and parted as good friends. They continued writing to each other, thereafter.

All in all, Wampanga's tenure as Vice President was a short and unhappy one. Some people in the party accused him of alienating too many people. Others said that he was a victim of weak leadership, unwilling to accept the realities of democracy. However, in high places, Wampanga was a feared and marked man; he threatened many who didn't want to face him on a ballot paper in free and fair elections. Otherwise, he possessed political talent; he had teamed up with so-called nonentities from Southern Province and had convincingly beaten a sitting Republican Vice President who had been endorsed and supported by the President.

His team of supporters, therefore, said that everybody ganged up against him and concocted unsubstantiated charges against him. Some feared that his next move was to contest the Presidency and he had a realistic chance of winning! The question remained the same: what was the President's role in the unfolding divisions in the ULP? Certainly, the ugly developments had serious ramifications on the governance of the state and unity in the party and the country.

In 1971, Simon Mulenga Wampanga resigned from ULP and therefore as Republican Vice President. He declared that some of his colleagues never recognized his position as Vice President. He stated that some Lemba-speaking people were persecuted because of his position. But his resignation provoked another bitter intra-party war and inter-ethnic rivalry which forced the President to dissolve the 1969 central committee. This further illuminated Wampanga's political aptitude.

As a sequel, President Jumbe resigned as party President and became secretary general of the party. He dissolved the central committee and appointed an interim central committee of 11 members, including Wampanga, who had agreed to withdraw his resignation. Ignoring his usual practice of tribal balancing, President Jumbe appointed four Lembas in the new central committee and three from the Eastern Province. The composition of the new central committee favouring Lembas was seen as a triumph for Wampanga against the President. It was, however, observed that the President's behaviour became more erratic, as the political tensions in the party now spread to the whole country, bringing to the fore other hidden grievances.

The intense political crisis within ULP since 1969 contributed to the loss of popularity and deep divisions in the ruling party and was largely caused by lack of internal party democracy, leading to deep polarization. This was mostly linked to the ULP leader himself and his non-Lemba loyalists, who lacked appreciation for rules on which operations of a democratic government depended. Some people concluded that the first Republic under ULP failed due to ethnic divisions. President Jumbe and ULP loyalists' actions fueled ethnic hostility. The regional chauvinism of Wampanga and his Lemba supporters was deliberately exaggerated for purely political reasons. President Jumbe seemed to encourage political instability by balancing political factions, even at the expense of good governance.

When that delicate balance was rudely disturbed in 1969, it was observed that President Jumbe became increasingly authoritarian. When the nationalist coalitions in ULP finally disintegrated with the defection of the dominant Lemba faction and the formation of Wampanga's United Popular Party (UPP) in 1972, President Jumbe decided to maintain his grip on power culminating in legislating against opposition political parties by forming the one-party state. This was against the wishes and interests of the people of Zambica.

Wampanga stood on his new party's ticket in the Mwamona byelection on the Copper Province and won overwhelmingly. It was a victory many pundits predicted he would not achieve due to the

President's dictatorship. He had been barred from campaigning and yet most ULP political heavy weights had camped in the constituency, campaigning seriously for weeks for fear of being embarrassed by the man who had the ferocity to win but they often described him as 'pretender to the throne.'

ULP spent a lot of government and party resources insulting Wampanga and assassinating him politically, in order to finish him for good while the President was conspicuously silent. The country and the whole world could not believe what continued to unfold in Zambica. Hailed as a beacon of peace in the region and considered relatively democratic, the increased patronage to President Jumbe under the circustances was frightening and simply unmatched in the region as timid liberation heroes preferred to be safe by remaining mute.

In any case, the oppressive nature of the ULP regime made it difficult for anyone in the UPP to openly campaign for him. Anyone found openly supporting Wampanga and UPP would probably find himself or herself unemployed or severely beaten and or risked being petrol bombed. There was so much fear and tension in the nation. However, the ZCTU was unhappy with the brand of dictatorship being exhibited by the President. Risking prohibition, the labour movement quietly campaigned for the man, who they knew had done so much for the liberation of the country, though the ULP government had banned him from entering the constituency during the campaign. What type of democracy was this?

A strategy was, therefore, mooted whereby most miners agreed to openly campaign for UPP and Wampanga within their communities. On the other hand, it was agreed that campaigns be centred in the mines' premises and most importantly underground. The messages from the mine working areas were further disseminated to each miner's respective family in their homesteads and drinking places.

However, against the odds, through the tactic of conducting campaigns on the mines, homesteads and drinking places, Wampanga won in Mwamona with a resounding landslide majority. It was an indictment that the people were fed up with the misrule by ULP.

Asked by reporters on how he managed to win without campaigning and without entering the constituency, a calm Simon Mulenga Wampanga said, "By the grace of God and the will of the people." He added, "But the President' who is still my brother, knows too well that the repression and dictatorship he has adopted is not what we fought for. Many people lost their lives for the freedom of this country, that is now being taken away."

Wampanga had just attended parliament, as the new Member of Parliament, for Mwamona Constituency, on his party ticket. Despite President Jumbe's manoeuvres to disparage the growing popularity of his new party, the mood in the house was totally different. There was unseen jubilation in parliament when Wampanga was brought in and introduced in the chamber, as the new Member of Parliament for Mwamona Constituency. All members of the opposition clapped while a sizeable number of ULP members of Parliament had no choice but to clap too.

Someone from the opposition bench shouted, "The future President!" Echoed by others, the embarrassed Mr speaker had a problem controlling the proceedings to enable the new member to make his maiden speech. The spectacle in the House had never been experienced before, and must have upset ULP big wigs, who had thought that Wampanga was dead and buried, politically. But the man was still alive and politically popular. Wampanga had offended and embarrassed the President once again by standing in the Mwamona by-election against the President's wishes. This sounded more like a fulfilment of the statement he had made earlier, during the launch of his UPP, that just as he was instrumental in destroying ANC and helped form ZANC, and that now, he would destroy the ULP, using a totally new strategy.

After parliament that day, Wampanga was driven to Kamwala to inspect offices for his new party headquarters, apparently donated by an Asian businessman and sympathiser. As he walked towards the building, he was stopped suddenly, insulted and attacked by ULP youths, led by a known ULP youth leader who was later promoted.

Simon Mulenga Wampanga was held to the ground by ULP vigilantes, while a known ULP youth leader beat him up. The mob thought he had died, when he passed out. A good Samaritan disturbed the attackers, picked him and took him to the hospital. It is rumoured that a close friend of both the President and Wampanga, also a member of the central committee of ULP, was terribly upset with the sad incident. He visited the former Veep at his home in treelands; he found a bloodied, heavily bandaged Wampanga with a swollen face, cracked lips, and ribs.

Meanwhile, the President never issued any statement condemning the unfortunate beating of Wampanga. In February, 1974, he banned the UPP on flimsy grounds after realising that the growth of the new party and Wampanga's popularity would be unstoppable. Wampanga and top UPP leaders were imprisoned. Many citizens suspected that the ULP scheme was to remove Wampanga from Parliament for good, as any Member of Parliament missing sessions for six months automatically lost the seat.

Seeing that his party support was waning and his personal popularity had nose–dived in the northern traditional areas, President Jumbe was apprehensive of his one-party rule holding the country together much longer. Besides Southern Province, he desperately wanted his former strongholds, especially Northern and Luapita Provinces, as well as Copper Province, which had remained aloof, due to inter party squabbles; they also leaned more towards Wampanga's destiny. He had to find a way of bringing back his childhood friend, who had gone back home to Kwitonta, after his release from prison, the previous year. He sent an emissary to Kwitonta, inviting Wampanga to state house.

Upon arrival, he was warmly received by the President as if there was no rift between them. Their meeting was over lunch, which for obvious reasons, Wampanga almost declined. In the prayer before the meeting, the President made a passionate call for forgiveness and reconciliation with his brother! He confessed that he was only human and had made a lot of mistakes politically, and requested for forgiveness from god and from his brother. He finally asked for a fresh start, and the guest and his team were highly touched by the moving prayer, from the President.

During lunch, President Jumbe, observant as usual, noticed something unusual. He asked Mulenga, as he still fondly called him, if he too had become vegetarian. Replying, Wampanga said with humour that he instinctively turned vegetarian, a decision largely directed by ancestral spirits of Kwitonta. Everyone at the table laughed, but rather uneasily. On a serious note, Wampanga was not at ease having lunch with his childhood friend; so much acrimony had taken place, putting a serious wedge between them. For self-preservation, he only picked foods from the plates where the President had picked his.

After lunch, the President and Wampanga held a one on one meeting in the President's study, at Wampanga's request. The guest said, "thank you Mr President for inviting me to state house. But I want you to know that it hurt me extremely to be humiliated and tortured by young people in prison." He said bravely and bluntly to him as they always did way back in Kwitonta.

"I am very sorry about what could have happened in prison. I heard and some of those overzealous officers have since been fired."

"To be honest, I worked so hard and made sacrifices for us to form this government." Wampanga said. Jumbe nodded, knowing that what his guest had said was true.

"And I also protected you while in Kwitonta, on the copper province and then at national level, and promoted you to become our first President." He put it bluntly to him.

"I know Mulenga. I know." The President said. "I can assure you it won't happen again." He promised.

Standing a bit taller than the President, the only difference between them was that unlike the President, Wampanga never publicly bragged about his imposing height.

Deep down, President Jumbe knew that Wampanga was his kingmaker; no doubt about it. He therefore regretted his friend's mistreatment in prison. However, concerning the implementation of their 'childish' secret agreement while swearing on the Bible, he was not sure. He now knew just how sweet power was and also feared something else.

The rest of the meeting went as to plan; Wampanga was thanked for coming over such a long distance and for his unforgettable contributions to the struggle and the government. He was finally invited to re-join his old party, which had missed him so much. They discussed anxiously for a while, until he was assured that he would be re-joining ULP without any conditions, as a full member and with all rights and privileges. In addition, Wampanga was offered a position on the ULP central committee, which he declined.

He said, "Mr President, you know me better than anyone else. I don't believe in leaders handing out party positions like business cards." He said to his host. "I believe in electoral competition, to allow the people to choose their best leaders." He, however, thanked the President for the offer.

In national interest, Wampanga finally agreed after a short but serious reflection. The President was now at ease; he had conquered his stubborn friend, his most serious rival for the party leadership; a man who often gave him sleepless nights. But he also knew that his friend was a smart crowd puller. He recalled a time when he was Foreign affairs Minister, and they used to travel together to the Copper Province. Coming out first from the aircraft as President, the crowd would loudly shout, "JJ! JJ!" However, when Wampanga came out after him, the intensity of the chants would increase to "Shimpundu! Shimpundu!" (Father of twins! Father of twins!), to almost a deafening tempo. It was clear then that the Foreign Affairs Minister was more popular than he was on the Copper Province. Later he tactfully decided to travel without him on such trips.

Nevertheless, he now imagined the popularity of the ULP bouncing back to its heydays, what with his tact of persuading the crowd-puller to re-join ULP. He would deliver huge votes especially from the northern parts of the country and the copper province. What the President didn't think about, however, was that many people in the country were watching the new developments with keen eyes, to see whether the reconciliation was genuine or not. He therefore, had his own obligations, to stick to the letter and spirit of the rushed agreement. He would also bank on support from Southern Province, after he had earlier convinced Mwendalubi and his team to join ULP, at the advent of the one-party state.

Meanwhile, Wampanga travelled back home and broke the news to his family about his decision to re-join politics and the ULP in particular. After a stunned moment of silence, he was asked by one of his daughters, Chola, "Dad, why go back into politics? You contributed so much to the liberation of this country. Look at what you got in return; imprisonment, torture and betrayal by people you trusted most; even those you propelled into the highest office in the land. Is it worth it, Dad?" she asked in a highly emotional voice.

He smiled gently before responding. "Ba mayo (my daughter), I did whatever I did for my country and not for an individual." He added, "I believe in the Lemba saying that goes 'Umwaume tatine mfwa. Afwaya amala yakwe yashala kuchishiki!' (A brave warrior is not scared of death. For the right cause, he would rather his intestines are found hanging on a tree stump)."

His wife sat by watching in silence but listening to the exchanges, with tears rolling down her cheeks. She knew better than anyone else did just how far they had come and the immense sacrifices her husband had made; she was greatly hurt by the betrayal.

In 1980, as the ULP general conference was just around the corner, many people were anxiously waiting to see any new faces in the ULP Central Committee after the scheduled elections at the Chibwe Conference. The meeting would also provide a stern acid test to the reality and genuineness of both the Macha Declaration and the President's agreement with Wampanga.

Meanwhile, unknown to most people, Wampanga and Mwendalubi had been meeting secretly to strategize on a common stand to challenge Jumbe for the ULP presidency. Their secret plan was for one of them to stand, to avoid splitting the votes. However, their strategy looked like the 1969 North to south pact, which worked so well, but divided the ULP for good. Surprisingly, the two politicians announced their candidature on the same day, sending shock waves to President Jumbe and other senior ULP members. A Lusiku businessman, Robert Chalwe also announced his intentions to challenge Jumbe for the party presidency as an independent. Despite the unexpected set back, President Jumbe swiftly planned a counter strategy against his 'new' political enemies.

To plan and avoid undue publicity, Wampanga was at a secret location in Lusiku-West, about 26 kilometres from the capital city. He often used the farm, belonging to a sympathizer for political retreats, to get away from the President's informers. Despite always being under the microscope of the President's intelligence, he had found an effective way of evading them. Nevertheless, at about 01.30hrs one Tuesday morning, and four days before the ULP convention, Wampanga heard a gentle knock on the southern window of his room. Apprehensive but alert, he did not respond, but crawled to the master bedroom and gently knocked on the door. His host, Chapwa Chileya came out carrying a shotgun and called out, "Who is it?"

"It's me, Mwelwa," a voice familiar to Wampanga responded from outside.

"It's okay. He is innocent." Wampanga said with relief sounding in his voice. Mwelwa was apparently driven to the farm by a senior MCC of ULP, who was among the MCCs, who had secretly pledged to vote for Wampanga at the party conference.

Mwelwa, a trusted office orderly at the ULP Party Headquarters, presented an alarming document to them. The ULP Constitution had been changed: "For one to contest the party presidency, one should have been a member for five years continuously with no criminal record. Such an aspirant also needed two hundred supporters from each province, amongst the delegates at the congress."

That knocked out the breath in Wampanga and his jaw dropped; the anticipated showdown with President Jumbe on the ballot paper would not happen! If anything, Wampanga's only wish had always been to face President Jumbe in a free and fair contest which he believed he would win.

The second amendment was on a technicality, targeting Mwendalubi, who had just joined ULP following the dissolution of the ANC.

That day, frantic efforts were made; Mwendalubi came to Wampanga's hiding place with two experienced and trusted lawyers who were joined by Wampanga's constitutional lawyer, a state counsel. The team looked at a number of options, including obtaining a court injunction, to prevent the holding of the conference while the case went to court. They left the legal option alive.

While greatly disappointed with the lack of democracy in the ULP, both Mwendalubi and Wampanga decided on plan B to attend the conference. There, they had planned to make political noises, meant to embarrass the President for hiding behind rushed, unconstitutional amendments of the party's constitution. In any case, the President's move confirmed what some party members had suspected all along; President Jumbe was a dictator and coward. He did not believe in fair competition through the ballot box.

In Chibwe, Wampanga and Mwendalubi stayed at two separate houses in case they were tracked down by the President's secret police. Anything could happen; one of them had to live to tell the story. More importantly, in order to continue the struggle against a man both had trusted so much in the past but had betrayed them.

On the first day of the conference, their drivers were stopped and ordered to turn around by heavily armed police, as both men were barred from entering the conference premises. The main reason for keeping them out of the venue was to quickly allow party delegates to approve the amended constitution by acclamation instead of secret ballot provided for in the constitution. However, by barring the two old politicians from the conference, the proposed amendments to the party constitution were implemented even before approval by the delegates!

One of the invited dignitaries to the conference, a visiting President from a neighbouring country, and President Jumbe's old friend, regretted the undemocratic episode. He said, "it is dictatorial to prevent people who fought for independence from standing for a position of their choice in the party. This will unfortunately erode the needed competition in young African democracies."

Meanwhile, Robert Chalwe was sorted out differently. They made sure he was clobbered and could not manage to raise the required number of supporters. Furthermore, he was declared bankrupt; after his bank accounts were frozen. According to the law, he could not stand for the presidency or any other public office. He sure paid a heavy price for attempting to exercise his democratic right.

The Lusiku High Court criticized the amendment of the constitution by acclamation; it however turned down Wampanga's and Mwendalubi's appeals against their disqualification. This paved the way for President Jumbe to be unopposed as the sole Presidential candidate.

While the ULP cadres and leaders were dancing for their great leader, the country was being choked by rampant shortages of essential commodities, especially mealie meal, bread, cooking oil and salt. This led to constant increases in food prices and the mushrooming of the black market, offering goods and services at almost four-fold the normal price. Besides shortages and high prices, citizens had to constantly endure standing in long queues, where they were sometimes harassed by ULP vigilantes.

Simon Mulenga Wampanga died of suspected poisoning by a known police officer, who later became Police Chief for Eastern Province. According to publicly available information, while visiting his daughter in Filamba mining town of Copper Province, Wampanga suffered a stroke and died two days later. After suffering a stroke and while he was still conscious, Wampanga asked for a pen to write something but the stroke had paralysed his right side and he couldn't write with his left hand. It is reported that due to frustration, Wampanga tossed the pen away and whatever he had wanted to tell the nation and the world before he died, went with him to the grave.

Many of Wampanga's followers wept uncontrollably over his death; they had held him in religious affection. He's the one who first proposed a more viable approach to the freedom struggle; he's the one who led the rebellion from the ANC to form ZANC; he's the one who first pronounced the word Zambica......! Some of his ardent supporters described him as the best President Zambica never had. His speeches and writings reveal him to have been a great thinker, patriot and Pan Africanist who had a great moral sense of right and wrong. Politically, the man was feared and exercised influence even when he had no political office; his death shook the whole nation. His enemies however, sighed with relief as they had considered him a radical, a racist but much more, their greatest political threat.

Later two friends, Somone and Musonte, admirers of the late politician, went to Filamba Mine Hospital in the hope of viewing the body of Wampanga before its departure for Kwitonta. Upon arrival at the hospital, the two were shown to the mortuary and were ushered into a fairly roomy place where several people had gathered. In the centre of the room on a table was a gleaming casket containing Wampanga's body, cordoned off by fierce looking men. The late politician's supporters were the people that were allowed to view the body and the two men took advantage and also viewed the body. Somone said to his friend Musonte, "This is a proper mortuary, unlike mortuaries in government hospitals, here the room is clean, there is no foul smell, and everything is orderly."

After viewing the body, the two men left for North Downs Airport – where a government buffalo military aircraft was waiting to fly the body to Kwitonta.

About 15:00 hrs the cortege arrived at the airport. Immediately in front of the hearse was James Francis Chaluma, bearing late Wampanga's famous walking stick. The hearse was flanked by two traffic police motorcycles with flashing lights moving at walking pace, followed by a crowd of walking mourners fronted by the same fierce looking men earlier seen at the mortuary.

Upon arrival at the airport, the casket was loaded onto the plane and those travelling boarded, including Chaluma. The government had designated Ngenda Mwanawina, then a government minister to accompany Wampanga's body to Kwitonta. Mwanawina was regarded as a political ally to Wampanga since both had been detained by President Jumbe for differing with him and forming political parties.

The atmosphere at the airport was sombre and full of grief, people were crying openly at the untimely departure of a political icon many thought would succeed President Jumbe. The feeling of a political vacuum was written on people's faces as they mourned.

Suddenly someone shouted from the steps of the plane, "Somebody should say something before the departure of our great leader's body. Mr. Mwanawina representing the government should say something."

Mr. Mwanawina responded that he had not been mandated to speak on the occasion.

The man then said, "In that case, let Chaluma speak."

Unfortunately, Chaluma was so overcome with grief that he was sobbing and failed to say anything. The doors to the aircraft were shut and the plane took off. It is significant to note that while holding late Wampanga's walking stick, some people from the crowd were murmuring and pointing at Chaluma, "Nomba niwe!" (Now it is you to take over the fight for this country).

Somone and Musonte looked at each other with tears welling in their eyes as the plane carrying Wampanga's body finally took off.

The socialist President was reluctant to stop subsidies of food commodities, which had added to the total distortion of the country's economy for a long time. Appearing on national television one night, he, while responding to a related question, bragged that he would not stop food subsidies, which had cushioned the livelihoods of poor families. He further said that Zambica would never experience food riots as was happening in some neighbouring countries. He sounded confident that he would always remain on top of things and would manage the threatening hunger situation.

While he continued procrastinating on the subsidies, the situation suddenly got worse. Under immense pressure from the World Bank, that they would withdraw the agreed support package, the President ate humble pie and finally capitulated. He suddenly announced the withdrawal of food subsidies, which led to a sudden increase of mealie meal prices, subsequently increasing the price of the family food basket.

In a short time, the majority of affected families cried foul and blamed their President and his government for lying to them and failing to keep the promises concerning food subsidies. In a matter of days, food riots started from Copper Province, spreading rapidly through Dented Hill to Lusiku Province, turning ugly and escalating to the destruction of government property by angry and hungry rioters. The President and the government were embarrassed; it was only a matter of three weeks since the head of state had assured the nation that food riots would never take place in the country. President Jumbe and his ULP colleagues were certainly losing control of the developments in the country.

President Jumbe was embarrassed further at the Lusiku Patriots Stadium where he had gone to watch an international football match as a mob suddenly came forward despite heavy security. The people were complaining of starvation at their homes and pelted the President with over ripe tomatoes; something that had never happened before. The writing was certainly on the wall for the head of state. It is reported that the President was terribly upset that while the crowd disparaged him at the stadium, the same crowd cheered and showed respect to Chaluma who was not even a government official. He is reported to have brooded over the incidence for a couple of days.

There was also a coup attempt by one captain Lwatula, who stormed Zambica National Broadcasting Services (ZNBS) station in the capital city and announced that he had taken over government. The attempted coup was the climax of the economic undercurrent that reduced the once rising and affluent young nation to a beggar state. On the material day, President Jumbe was away from the capital city to officiate at the annual Zambica international trade exhibition on the Copper Province. However, the head of state mysteriously disappeared briefly from public view, during the duration of the announced coup.

Some sections of the public spontaneously took to the streets to celebrate the downfall of President JJ and the ULP government. President Jumbe seemingly lost the backing of the citizenry. Apparently, some people were tired of the degenerating economic conditions and living under one-party rule. An impulsive commentary by an apparently excited ZNBS radio announcer on duty voiced what was apparently on the minds of many citizens. He said in one of the vernacular languages.

"Kale sana, Lesa atupele Mankangala Jerome Jumbe ukutulubula kubusha bwaba mwisa, nokutungulula ichalo chesu pamyaka amakumi-yatatu. Lelo Lesa wesu naumfwa amasali yesu nokutupela umushilika, Captain Lwatula, ukutufumya mubusha bwa makwebo ubwaletele ba Jumbe. Nifwe bani ukususha umulubushi mupya uyo Lesa wesu atuletela?"

('Long time ago, God gave us Jerome Jumbe our liberator from the yoke of colonialism, who presided over the affairs of our great nation for almost thirty years. Behold, our unfailing Almighty today has listened to our plight and has given us the economic liberator, Captain Lwatula, to take Zambica's economic destiny to a better level. Who are we to question the will of God?').

The attempted coup brought to the fore that President Jumbe was no longer liked by the majority of Zambicans. The Copper Province in general and Kafulafula in particular, woke up to the news of the coup and many people trooped out of their homes in their thousands to celebrate and congratulate the gallant men in uniform.

Fate had it that in no time, the courageous radio announcer would be among several civil servants to be axed from their jobs in the aftermath of the botched coup. It is reported that a commando unit of the Zambica Army loyal to their deposed Commander-inChief swung into action in the background. Leaving the Copper Province, they headed for the capital city by air.

Two helicopters secretly flew towards the capital, while a dispatch of four smokescreen-armoured troop carriers travelled by road, a distance of about 300 kilometres. Two of the vehicles were actually decoys, packed with sugarcane, pineapples, bananas and mealie meal. However, beneath the camouflage merchandise was sophisticated communication equipment, capable of both eavesdropping and jamming the enemy communication system at the press of a button. The driver was a commando trained in communication with instructions to drive away from the target and confuse the enemy in case of trouble.

The loyal forces were in high spirits. They arrived in the capital incident free and assembled at a military facility, camouflaged as a farm on the outskirts of Lusiku for a briefing. Their commander was a young and athletic Major Nshimbi, an artillery and close combat connoisseur trained in the Soviet Union and Cuba. Major Ngulube, a veteran map reading and town combat expert, provided the necessary last minute instructions about the layout of the ZNBS buildings and general terrain. The two Majors led the march by the loyal forces onto the radio station, and the commando dispatch swiftly surrounded the coup plotters, and first captured those guarding the outer perimeter of the premises without firing a single gunshot.

The enemy troops guarding the entrance to the inner building, however, put up a brief but desperate fight, but they were quickly disarmed and captured. The 'triumphant' Captain Lwatula meanwhile was unaware that the tide had swiftly turned against his coup plot and ironically continued to urge the tv station announcer to make intermittent blood-chilling announcements about the takeover as he played reggae music and other sombre music in studio 2.

General Silutongwe, the Zambica Air Force Commander flew by helicopter to Mandeni to meet the respected ULP Secretary General, Comrade White Phiri. As the chopper landed at Phiri's farm, the aging Secretary General, still in his pyjamas, rushed out of his house and ran towards the banana plantation nearby, fearing that the chopper was carrying soldiers who had come to kill him.

A calm and collected General Silutongwe disembarked from the helicopter and saluted the party Secretary General as he emerged from hiding. He informed him that he had come to fetch him so he could be taken to ZNBS studios to make an important announcement to the nation. Comrade Phiri however refused to go with him and stated in his native Ngwani, "mufuna kunipaya," meaning "You want to kill me". He insisted that the announcement should be made by the President himself.

General Silutongwe explained, nonetheless, that the President was not available and he, as second in command, was expected to step in as a matter of urgency. Comrade Phiri still refused and heaped all the blame on JJ, his boss. "I told him many times that we should retire and leave politics for the young people, but he wouldn't listen," he moaned. "He is a very stubborn man!"

After much persuasion and patience, the general finally convinced the Party Secretary General to go with him to ZNBS.

Within two hours after ZNBS was recaptured by the loyal forces, an unshaved and visibly terrified ageing Phiri appeared on national television and made a counter-announcement in a trembling voice that the coup by a few disgruntled soldiers had been crushed. Later, it was alleged that the loyal forces effortlessly foiled the short-lived coup and captured Captain Lwatula, the coup mastermind because most of his troops were already celebrating and apparently dead drunk. They lamentably failed to coordinate their planned military manoeuvres.

It was later reported that the coup backfired largely because the anticipated rebel reinforcements expected to capture key positions in the capital city grew cold feet; they did not turn up to support their brave but drunken colleagues.

However, this was a real wake-up call for President Jumbe. His first action when he ambled out of his hideout was a major cabinet reshuffle.

With political uncertainty in the air, the general mood in the country kept on mounting to a crescendo, with increased agitation, protests, and involvement of the church mother bodies. President Jumbe finally succumbed. He announced the holding of a referendum to decide whether to return to multiparty politics or not. Due to increased pressure, President Jumbe changed his mind and abandoned the referendum campaign after two weeks. He dissolved Parliament during ULP's convention and revoked an appropriate article of the Constitution and set the last day of October, 1993 as Election Day. In doing so, plural politics were ushered into the country.

Many observers had said that President Jumbe was never the same man he used to be, since the foiled coup attempt. While pretending to be strong, that single event was probably the final nail that punctured his otherwise tough skin. The Movement for Multiparty Restoration (MMR) was immediately formally registered as a political party in 1993. Subsequently, the interim executive committee of the MMR organised a National council meeting at a posh conference centre, in Lusiku, where delegates from all the provinces met to elect the executive committee of the new party.

In February, 1993, the MMR held its national convention at which the national party executive was elected. At that first convention, the pintsized and outspoken President of the labour movement, James Francis Chaluma was elected as its first leader, in addition to ten other executive members. These included the Vice President, the National Chairman, and the National Secretary.

Thus, the convention elected the small man, Chaluma, who soundly beat former interim leader Isaac Mwangolwa. Unlike his opponent's long and rather academic manifesto, Chaluma had a very short manifesto, two pages long, entitled 'Why I Must Win'. For some, it was unexpected that JFC would beat the former interim leader, who was more educated, with a Master's degree and had vast political experience. It was observed after the elections that Chaluma's main advantages over his opponent were his unmatched oratory skills, which endeared him to the party membership; he was also regarded as new and independent, as he had never served in any of the President's cabinets.

However, as agreed, the Presidential election was held first, in order to give a chance to the losers in that position to contest at a lower position. But the actual implementation of this loose arrangement proved to be difficult. Originally, three candidates officially lodged in their nominations for the position of national chairman, but two of them quickly withdrew, including Mukelabai Lisulo the leading contender, in order to give way to the losing Presidential candidate, Isaac Mwangolwa. While they expected the third and only remaining candidate, Elias Chipango, to also step down, Chipango stood his ground and stated that being the only candidate remaining for the position, he should be declared unopposed instead.

They tried to promise him this and that, for the sake of party unity, but he was adamant and stuck to his guns until he was declared unopposed and became chairman of the MMR, rather by default. While the attempted undemocratic manoeuvres to persuade Chipango to step down for the sake of party unity caused laughter among the majority of the delegates at the convention, student observers from the University of Zambica were, however, not pleased.

Their short spokesperson addressed the press and disclosed his group's utter disappointment, saying, "The formation of the MMR gave hope and fresh air to the student movement, thinking that a new political dispensation had come to our beloved country," he said with disappointment sounding in his voice. "Alas, we were terribly mistaken." He continued.

"Hear! Hear!" shouted other student observers who were joined by a few disgruntled losers.

"The attempt to abrogate their constitution in favour of a losing candidate is a shame and should be condemned in the strongest terms possible. By this serious undemocratic attempt, we, the students' body have no option but to conclude that democratically, there is not much difference between the old undemocratic ULP and the new so-called democratic MMR." Many delegates laughed. This statement from the students was certainly sweet music to the ears of ULP leaders, who were looking for any faults and cracks in the new party they knew would be their main opponent in the anticipated elections.

The development however, meant that Isaac Mwangolwa, who had spearheaded the formation of the new party and also led it as interim chairman was left empty-handed, without any position in the party's top hierarchy. Some delegates blamed Chaluma for his greed and ambitions; why couldn't he allow the former interim chairman to lead the party now since he was much older than him?

However, budding democrats who constituted the majority of the delegates scoffed at the allegations and proposal. They sang songs in support of their popular new party President, whom they described as, their Moses and 'aka Red' meaning the chosen one. Some of them said Chaluma knew he was very popular, and went for it and surely obtained the crown he rightly deserved at the convention. Others among them laughed at the loser, for failing to accept the fundamental rules of democracy, which had been a perpetual problem in the ULP, where he had been a senior Minister in President Jumbe's cabinet.

"He should have seen it coming during the campaign." Was a sentiment that was often heard expressed by many delegates.

It had been observed during the campaign that quite often, once Chaluma had spoken, the majority of the party members left the rally, indicating that most of them came largely to listen to the little man, with a magic tongue of an orator. This was obviously embarrassing for the interim leader, scheduled to speak last. In the end the interim committee swapped the speaking schedule for the top two; making the interim leader speak before Chaluma, which was also demeaning to say the least.

James Francis Chaluma was considered by many as an articulate orator, while only a few people knew that he had invested a lot of his family time in improving and perfecting the art of speaking. He would rehearse a speech several times. He had a tape recorder which he used to record himself, pacing up and down in his small room at home. He usually did that when preparing for Labour Day celebrations which were always graced by President Jumbe. He repeated this feat for all labour functions at which he was requested to speak.

He would rewind the tape, listen to what he had presented before an imaginary audience, edit it and start all over again until he was happy with the outcome. Only then and only then would he venture out for an occasional bottle of castle beer!

Surprisingly, JFC was a down to earth person. On a weekend, he would visit some local pub selling 'chibuku' beer where he would mingle with the lowest of his membership of the labour movement to get the feel of their plight. He would drink the chibuku beer – sold in bulk, in 2.5 litre and 5.0 litre containers which everyone in the group took turns in drinking the brew from.

Some people thought he was a genius, but genius or not, it came with a lot of hard work. His signature pose when he wanted to stress a point was to hold his hands akimbo, his glasses drawn further down the nose bridge so that instead of looking at the audience through lenses, he looked at them over the ream of his spectacles.

CHAPTER 4

Contrasting Tactics and Fortunes

"MMR!" Chishala shouted at the top of his voice.

"Movement for Multiparty Restoration!" the ecstatic multitude rumbled, whistled and ululated. This was good. This was promising. He decided to dare them once more:

"M!" Chishala shouted.

"Movement!" the crowd responded. The Kwitonta, Northern Province party cadres had done a good job.

"M!" Chishala's voice borrowed a few more decibels.

"Mul-ti-par-ty!" The crowd competed and beat him at his own game. This was interesting.

"Raaaaaaaaaaaaaaaaaaaa!" Chishala pulled the last abbreviation turning round and round to the chagrin of those who were on the platform with him, including candidate Mumbi. Politics!

"Resto-ra-tioniiiiiiiiiiiiiiiiiiiiiiii!" the crowd followed suit. The noise made was deafening. The party colours in the form of cloths, t-shirts, placards, and others went up in the air. Chishala's security guards could not stop the cadres from lifting him up. He felt good and honoured by this constituency.

No wonder MMR fancied itself to win the forthcoming elections even though it was the clear underdog! However, many thought it was folly for the new party to contest the elections against the old and well-oiled ULP. The latter had solid structures on the ground, resources and a network of rich admirers and supporters overseas and within the country, they argued. The incumbent President himself had repeatedly booed and demeaned the MMR saying: "What can they do? They are just a bunch of frightened little boys and girls(Ba Kasuli)."

The MMR on the contrary, had nothing on the ground, no structures, no motor vehicles, and no cash. But it was fast proving to be with the people. What Chishala and his entourage had just witnessed was beyond comprehension. It reminded him of what had happened in one of the neighbouring countries where people voted for an 18 year old young man to be a member of parliament. The incumbent president of that country was heard saying just to oust him, people could have even voted for a hyena! The way people were responding to the campaign slogans in Northern Province was a thriller and reminded Chishala that people did not measure the new party by material possessions.

In his campaign and monitoring trip to the Northern Province as his party's delegation leader, Chishala had many days of reckoning. He grew up politically. He learnt that the kicks of a dying horse are the most dangerous. Most MMR candidates he had visited so far in the province had expressed concern over the lies and negative tactics that were being used by most ULP candidates.

"Sir, we may lose the elections, not because the voters don't like us," she paused, "but because of lies and negative propaganda being used by the ULP candidates!" The candidate in Kwitonta constituency exclaimed.

"What lies? What tactics?" he probed.

"For instance," she replied, "at his rallies, my ULP opponent keeps repeating that I, Mumbi, am not Zambican but South African, born in Soweto."

"Where were you born then?" he asked her bluntly.

"I was born right here in this constituency of Zambican parents", she said firmly. She further revealed, "My umbilical cord is buried in Chashi village about 15 kilometres from here".

"Why then would he tell such blatant lies?" he asked her.

"To discredit me and win the seat obviously," she reasoned.

"I see", Chishala said, reflecting for a moment.

"My husband is South African", she continued speaking, "and the ULP has taken advantage of that to confuse the people."

"Those are serious allegations" he stated, "which we have to refute as quickly as possible." He suggested.

"On our part, we shall do our level best to do so, sir", she assured him. "But they are also intimidating the voters by telling them that anyone found voting for the opposition will be killed."

"Leave that to me." he told her, "our President will be addressing a press conference in two days' time. He will challenge the Police command and assure our voters not to have any fears."

"Thank you, sir. Your assurances are greatly appreciated and will be conveyed to our officials and the voters as we continue campaigning." Mumbi spoke with a voice full of appreciation and confidence.

"Otherwise," he stated, "how do you generally assess the mood of the voters in this district where old Jerome Jumbe comes from?"

"The majority of the people we have spoken to are very supportive," she responded. "We might obtain good results from here, sir." she assured him.

"That's good news," he said. "Nevertheless, I wish to caution you and all our other candidates to be on the lookout, be alert." He urged. "ULP are getting desperate now."

"I see," she replied.

"Just be on the alert," he told her. "They will bring cash and rare essential commodities to bribe villagers," he predicted.

"Thank you, sir, for your timely warning," she replied.

"Let me ask you a personal question, Mumbi. From what I have read in the party briefs on you as a candidate," he paused. She nodded as he continued speaking, "and from what the President had personally briefed me about you." He reflected on those briefs from the party President for a moment.

"You are a very rich woman even beyond Zambian standards." He continued, "Why are you in the MMR and more specifically in this race, where you will most likely be maligned and insulted by desperate thugs in ULP?" he asked her with total puzzlement showing on his face.

"Thank you, sir, for your compliment", she responded and continued with wonder in her voice and on her face, "I didn't know that our party President even has interest and information on me."

What he didn't disclose to her, however, was the party President's reference to her as a 'Powerhouse'.

"She is short like me," he told him, "but unshakeable," as Chishala nodded. JFC had added, "No wonder they say terrific gifts come from small packages!" he had said, probably referring to himself as well.

"I see Mr President," Chishala had concurred.

"As a party, MMR is lucky to have her on its ticket because she's strong, funding her own campaign and has also given generous donations of cash and materials to the party. She is our torch bearer, not just for Kwitonta, but for the whole nation!"

Chishala smiled as he belatedly responded to her, "It's not just you, but all the 150 MMR candidates. As you know governments are formed with a majority in Parliament, and it's a wise leader who knows about the strengths and weaknesses of the people he will have with him to form government."

She nodded.

"Hence the need to have an interest and information about all candidates," he continued.

He explained further that, that was the reason the MMR President had travelled to all the provincial centres, to chair interviews for all shortlisted applicants for all constituencies, before winning candidates were adopted.

Mumbi nodded again with understanding and explained, "We have made some good money in different business ventures, especially in the export of beef, fruits and vegetables within the region and also to West Africa."

"So, meaning that by our standards, you are a very rich woman?" He probed once more.

"No doubt about that, sir," she responded confidently. "I joined politics largely because President Jumbe has overstayed in power. He has personalised the presidency and government and has also destroyed the environment for doing business in this country," she stated, seriousness inscribed all over her small face.

"So besides national issues, you also have a personal calling for wanting to win in this constituency?" he asked further.

"Certainly, sir", she affirmed. "I cannot stand on the fence while all that I've worked for most of my life is being wiped out through one man's poor economic policies," she sighed deeply. "Things must change," she said emphatically.

"Very well. So you have no need for extra motivation, have you?" Chishala asked.

"None whatsoever," she said confidently. "If I beat Lezu in this election, who has been the MP for ten years in this constituency, then I will certainly be on top of the world," she declared.

As he left, Chishala recalled what the party President had told him about Mumbi. That she was a strong and intelligent woman and had a personal reason for wanting to beat Lezu in their so-called backyard constituency of Kwitonta.

Chishala also realised that he had left her strongly energized. While she needed no motivation from him for the campaign; she had her own personal and strong reasons. His party delegation moved on to a neighbouring constituency.

As he made himself comfortable inside his personal vehicle which he had recently branded with party colours, his self-styled chauffeur cum cousin shot him a lasting smile. Chishala was a bit confused. He wondered what he had done to deserve such a long and pleasant heart-warming smile from his elderly cousin.

"Bakalamba (my elder), nga chinshi (what is it)?" Chishala could not help but smile back.

"Hmm, Mune! (my friend). You are good. I don't regret offering to be your chauffeur. When did you learn all this game? Mumbi was literally eating from your hands! If I hadn't been with you 24/7, I would have said you went to get charms before meeting that strong woman. My man!" He nudged Chishala with his elbow.

"Ah, what are you saying now? What have I done?" Chishala was trying to remain calm so he could find out what his cousin was intimating.

"Haa! Relax, mune. Relax! Did you know that that woman you had been talking to is feared by both men and women; not only in this constituency but in the province as well. She is a tigress, they say. But you handled her very well. I'm proud of you. Our fathers, may their souls rest in peace, would be walking tall because of you, I tell you."

"Ah, bakalamba, the president also referred to her as a powerhouse for the party. He respects her a lot," Chishala quickly recalled.

"Most of the people I had a chat with, refer to her as 'Madam Boss'. She is rich, authoritative, innovative, and creative and you name it. I gather she is a guest of honour at almost every event. She sponsors needy children to school but makes them work for it after school. Do you know where they work?"

"That's obvious. Where else but on her farm?" Chishala answered, no longer showing much interest. He had guessed his cousin was suspecting that he was flirting with Mumbi. On the contrary he was just confirming the greatness of the small woman.

"No! Mune! Then she would not be this popular. She requires them to work either on the chiefs' farms or palaces or elderly people's homesteads and small pieces of land. I'm told she even goes to supervise them. She ain't called a powerhouse or torch bearer for nothing! She is more than Lake Kariba. If only this country could have five or six Mumbis, we would never go hungry because there would be very few lazy people."

"You're right. She has surely made a name for herself. This constituency is on fire because of one woman who decided to strike the match. Can you imagine Kwitonta has electricity partly because of her? How I wish all of us could be as independent as Mumbi. Did you know she has sponsored 100% our whole Northern Province single handed? That is why we have to win."

They continued talking about 'Madam Boss' until they arrived at Bwanga's place. Bwanga was the MMR candidate in the neighbouring constituency. Just like Mumbi, Bwanga had other fears. He didn't want to go to prison after the elections.

"Are the stories going round the constituency true?" he asked Chishala anxiously.

"What have you heard? What stories?" Chishala asked puzzled.

"We have been told that President Jumbe has pardoned 1,000 prisoners this week from different prisons around the country." Bwanga told him.

"That's news to me!" exclaimed Chishala in total surprise. "Why would he release such a huge number of prisoners at once?" he muttered in total puzzlement. "Most of them are hardened criminals who would go back to committing serious crimes once again." He stated.

"It's to empty and create space in the prisons for all the parliamentary candidates on the MMR ticket and their supporters!" Bwanga answered fearfully.

Chishala thought for a moment before he asked the visibly shaken Bwanga, "So what do you want me to do about this threat?"

"I'm not sure. That's why I want confirmation from you, sir." He said. Chishala smiled encouragingly for him to continue.

"To be honest with you, I'm scared, sir," he revealed. "I have a young family. I can't afford to go to jail. Maybe we're fighting a losing battle." He speculated pessimistically.

"It's a lie!" Chishala told him. "It's meant to scare our candidates and voters. ULP's constant fear is losing; they now know they can only win by hook or crook" he assured him.

"You think so sir?" Bwanga asked. "But they are also saying that when they win the elections, they will kill all the MMR candidates," he said, still sounding scared.

Chishala took time to reassure Bwanga by explaining to him that it was all a plot by ULP to scare the MMR candidates so that they quit the race before election day.

After a long chat with the scared candidate, Chishala felt that Bwanga was a weak and timid candidate. What a contrast with the strong and brave Mumbi, the Kwitonta constituency candidate, who had guts and showed willingness and determination to take on the ULP crooks.

That evening, he filed an urgent brief to the party President via his hotline with the President's special assistant for press; it had to be included in the President's press conference brief the following day.

But clearly his party leader's instructions were still ringing in his oracular organs.

"Your duty is not to pontificate or theorise, but to follow my instructions," he directed. "Many people have told me that we cannot win these elections because we are not ready", he paused.

"What about you, Mr President, what is your take on this?" he asked him.

James Francis Chaluma smiled gently before he responded. "Being ready is beside the point," he paused. "What I know is that Jerome Jumbe and his socialist colleagues have done most of the work for us."

"Really? What do you mean, Mr President?" Kaluba asked puzzled.

"Kaluba," JFC intoned, "Jumbe and his ULP have destroyed this country big time! They have suppressed our people for a long time. There are shortages of essential commodities every day."

Kaluba nodded.

"What more can the people of this country take?" he concluded with a question.

The party President sent Kaluba to assist Chipulu mobilise the party and commence the campaign in Lake constituency; one of the most difficult constituencies to access due to the blocked channels from overgrown vegetation in the swamps of big lake Bangweulu, because the channels had not been maintained since 1964.

The constituency was itself composed of dotted small islands totalling 19,000 people at the last census with 11,000 of them being registered voters. They parked Chipulu's car, a Ford Cortina, on the mainland at Bwangwa, some 45km from Lubwe.

They hired an ordinary banana boat, a coxswain and 2 paddlers after negotiating fees. Unfortunately, that's all Chipulu could afford.

Kaluba also knew that like other MMR candidates, Chipulu had no funding from the party for all the campaign expenses. This was in stark contrast to the well-funded ULP candidates, including Katobwe, Chipulu's opponent who was also ULP's MP before Parliament was dissolved by President Jumbe.

As the muscular paddlers struggled to move the slow boat through plant choked channels, a 12 – horse power propelled engine motor boat zoomed close and bypassed them, surging forward and leaving the passengers on the slow banana boat wet, and splashed with dirty brownish water.

"Oh! Who is that?" asked the surprised candidate.

"That's Katobwe and his team" the coxswain informed them in response.

"He is the ULP candidate for Lake Constituency."

Chipulu recoiled with a shudder, apprehension covering his face. Wasn't he foolish in risking the little money he could raise by spending it on a campaign that he might not even win? He thought to himself. Had he known that his party had no money to fund its candidates, he would not have resigned from his job at Tubombe Council as a Director of research. In any case, it was now too late anyway.

Chipulu also knew Katobwe personally; a talkative and boastful fat chap. He projected the possibility of a dirty campaign; Katobwe would most certainly try to malign him and cut him to threads during the campaign. At that point, Kaluba could read the trepidation on Chipulu's face. He quickly decided to reach out to him to reassure him before he could throw in the towel.

"All is well," he said. "The party is raising funds for the campaign to support all its candidates. In addition, don't forget that most of the people in the country are on our side." He emphasized, remembering what his party President had whispered to him.

To calm Chipulu down, he spoke softly into his ear about the US$ 8.0 million promised by sympathisers from a certain kingdom for the MMR campaign.

Exhausted and hungry, they finally reached the first islands at 22:30 hours, exactly seven hours since leaving the mainland. The first main challenge was accommodation; there were no hotels or lodges on the islands. Where on earth were they going to sleep? The village headman who received them took them to a dilapidated primary school and showed them an old and dirty staffroom.

"While you are here, this will be home," he said to them and quickly left them. It was clear he was not ready to entertain any more pleasantries with these total strangers.

Kaluba noticed that Chipulu was rather uncomfortable and embarrassed with poor sleeping arrangements, compounded by the fact that he had not carried appropriate camping beddings. He asked him as he was curious. "When did you last visit this place?"

"Oh, I was born here," Chipulu answered hesitantly. "My parents left the islands when I was 8 years old," he stated avoiding Kaluba's direct question.

"Have you been here to visit any relatives since then?" Kaluba asked further.

"No, I haven't," he responded, "I have grown up on Copper Province."

"Oh boy!" sighed Kaluba mentally, "We have a lot of work to do!" He thought to himself. This was a clear indication of negligence. They had to strategize intelligibly. The question of acceptability of a prodigal son lingered long on his already disturbed and tired brain.

African mentality! For a second, he was also persuaded otherwise. "I've relatives though," Chipulu said belatedly upon realising the worried look on Kaluba's face. "They can take us around and introduce me to the people here."

"Good idea," Kaluba replied but rather unbelievingly.

They slept for a few hours but were awake most of the night due to the numerous and noisy fat island mosquitos that disturbed them.

Chipulu feared they would all catch malaria from mosquito bites. Was this venture worth the trouble? Time will tell.

In the morning, as dictated by local practice, the candidate and his team paid a courtesy call on the senior chief for the islands at his palace. Chipulu introduced his team and they discussed the mission of their trip generally. The chief welcomed them as if all of them were his subjects. Just before they left him he called Chipulu aside.

"Let me show you something," the senior chief said, leading him into his inner chamber without his guard. Chipulu followed blindly and obediently. He was not sure on how to behave. He had never met a chief at close range before.

"Sit down, Chipulu." he commanded.

"Thank you, Your Royal Highness," Chipulu said as he sat down involuntarily.

"You are welcome," said the senior chief.

"Thank you very much, Your Royal Highness." Chipulu said.

"Can I trust you?" asked the chief once they were both settled.

"Yes, you can trust me, Your Royal Highness," Chipulu answered while barely concealing his pride that the chief would ask that of him and wondered what it was that he was about to tell him.

"Good." the chief intoned. He continued, "I want to tell you that my people and I here don't trust President Jumbe and his party. For all the years of his rule, Jumbe has never visited the islands even once."

Chipulu nodded.

"ULP has destroyed our country for a long time. In addition, all the chiefs on these islands know that this constituency is the most neglected of all 150 constituencies in the country and our people are not educated and are extremely poor," he moaned.

"I know, Your Royal Highness. This is why we want to remove them from power in order to repair the grave damage done to our country," Chipulu said.

"Great!" exclaimed the senior chief. "Now your strategy. No," he corrected himself, "our tactic will be that I and the other chiefs will pretend to be neutral in these elections," he revealed.

"Yes, Your Royal Highness," Chipulu concurred.

"We shall even attack you and your party sometimes, and praise the Republican President and his candidate. Don't be scared because we are on your side."

"How about your subjects, Your Royal Highness," Chipulu asked with apprehension showing all over his face, "Won't they vote according to your public pronouncements?"

"No they won't. This is just a political ploy to protect you and your party." Chipulu nodded in agreement.

"That is good news for our party, Your Royal Highness." Chipulu appreciated.

"The ruling party shouldn't know, though, that most chiefs and their people in Lake constituency are on your side" he advised.

"Thank you so much, Your Royal Highness," Chipulu said in appreciation.

"You're welcome, my son," the chief answered. "We know for a fact that President Jumbe has pumped in millions of Kwacha in this campaign so that they can cling to power."

Chipulu nodded.

"That money could have been used wisely to develop rural areas like ours!" said the chief, without bothering to hide his disappointment and anger at Jumbe's lack of regard for the people in the rural areas. Chipulu nodded again. The chief also warned him about his main opponent from ULP.

"Be very careful with him. Have your people watch all his moves at all times," he cautioned.

"How dangerous is he?" asked Chipulu.

"Very good question," said the senior chief. "He is vicious and could be malicious. He's already spreading rumours and falsehoods about you and your origin" he revealed.

"What is he saying, Your Royal Highness?" Chipulu asked curiously. "While I am prepared for a good political fight, I am not interested in underhand methods and lies," he said firmly.

"It is good to be honest, my son, but take him on and be ahead of him through your tactics," he advised. "For instance, he has told the voters that you are a foreigner," he continued.

"But Your Royal Highness," Chipulu stated in protest, "I was born right here in Chinso Village before my father and mother moved to the Copper Province," he moaned.

"Not to worry, my son. My people have already done research on you and you are a local man." He breathed in deeply, "I also know your father very well; we went to the same primary school", he revealed, letting air out.

"Really?" he said excitedly, "Dad didn't say anything about that to me," Chipulu said. "God is good!" he exclaimed.

"And one more thing," said the senior chief, "He has also lied about your education. He has told the people here that your PhD is fake; that you bought it from the notorious Matero University."

"Oh, my God!" Chipulu exclaimed again, "But I spent four years at Wisconsin State University in the US studying for my PhD! How could I come back home and buy a cheap certificate from Lusiku?" he asked.

They talked a little longer before Chipulu was given a traditional blessing by the senior chief and permission to leave.

Chipulu came out of that secret meeting totally motivated. He was more confident and determined to face the mischievous Katobwe, come Election Day.

The candidate, with Kaluba's help now combed the islands, introducing the MMR and stating why the ULP should be voted out of power. They formed some structures and appointed party officials. They also invented strong slogans for the area, generally antagonistic to the ULP candidate and his party.

Kaluba was impressed. He praised the mostly uneducated islanders. The slogans would be effective due to their linkage to the peoples' livelihood, being dependent on water, fishing nets and fish.

The following day, Kaluba filed a confidential report to the secretary general of the Party, informing him that the senior chief of the islands was quietly but solidly behind the MMR. The attraction was that the senior chief's islands were the largest, having more than 5,000 registered voters in the constituency.

They moved slowly to the next islands and arrived there after paddling upstream for two and half hours. Then they walked about 1km to the nearest village.

The first port of call, like at the first islands, was to visit the local chief and introduce themselves and explain their mission. Those islands' chief, however, seemed indifferent and asked Chipulu some difficult questions. He also despised the MMR Presidential candidate as inexperienced and a cheat. Chipulu later learnt that the chief was related to Katobwe through marriage.

A trained expert in human behaviour, Chipulu was not heartbroken by the apparent hurdle. He just concluded, "All is not lost. After all, you win some and you lose some."

Later, they went to three more groups of islands; those with reasonable numbers of registered voters.

After their post-mortem meeting, Kaluba and the candidate concluded that most of the people visited on the islands were generally sympathetic to MMR and in rebellion against ULP.

However, the biggest challenge they faced was lack of financial support. They were facing a very well-funded candidate, who had also been the sitting Member of Parliament for the constituency. In addition, the panicking ULP government had suddenly released K1.5 million for the clearing of blocked channels in the swamps; something they should have done years back.

The MMR candidate used the sudden release of a large amount of money to his party's advantage; it was his party forcing ULP and its government to do something positive and beneficial to the people of the islands at last, he frequently pointed out at his campaign rallies.

Kaluba's report to the secretary general the following day gave necessary details and emphasized the need to provide financial support to all the MMR candidates in the race.

He also donated some money to the candidate after seeing him struggle to pay bills on the trip. He had just received a good payment for consultancy work he had conducted for the British government through DFID.

They returned to Lusiku the following day.

Somewhere in Eastern Province, battle lines were clearly drawn between uncle and nephew, in an intriguing political contest described by some journalists as the battle of one family. The uncle, Reverend Benson Zulu, commonly called Uncle Ben, was standing on the United Liberation Party ticket, while the nephew, Alfred Tembo, popularly known as AT, was the candidate for the new political party the Movement for Multiparty Restoration.

In the province, it was almost contemptuous for anyone to challenge Old Jerome Jumbe's authority, as he was regarded as some kind of a semi-god. That's why the province was now the most loyal to the ULP after being a stronghold to the ANC in the past. Though politics was the topic on everyone's lips, young or old in the whole country, in the Eastern Province, especially Linda constituency, the topic was everyone's breakfast, lunch and dinner. People greeted each other with the interesting and sensitive turn of events in their once upon a storytime village. How could an uncle and a nephew oppose each other? It is unheard of.

"Wonders shall never cease, Make Thandi (Mother of Thandi). Abomination!" a marketer addressed her friend as if in a whisper.

"What wonders, Make Mabvuto (Mother of Mabvuto)? What abomination? Weo (you), you love hot news! What's cooking? What's boiling these days? spill the beans!" Make Thandi shifted in her plastic chair so that she directly faced her friend. They certainly did not want other marketers at Linda Market to hear them talk about the unthinkable.

"My friend, as if you do not know. Is it not the Tembo fiasco? I hear there is pandemonium in the whole clan." Make Mabvuto stood up, rested her hands on her hips and then sat down.

"Why wouldn't there be?" Make Thandi showed quite some degree of irritability. "Who does not know that in this area, it is an abomination, a taboo of the highest order in fact, for a nephew to dare an uncle in any contest? Furthermore, the uncle is well known in this constituency, while his nephew, a successful businessman from Lusiku, has bought a big farm which has created employment for many people. Aren't these vegetables we are selling here from that AT farm? Isn't his grocery shop the best and most well stocked in the whole district? Isn't he driving the best car in the whole province? What has he not done to improve the livelihoods of one and many in this community? It makes me sick you know."

"It beats me to imagine why a handsome and popular guy like that would soil his name like this. He is so determined to wrestle political power from the uncle. For what? For a party that may not even win? In any case, who dares Jerome Jumbe and lives? If I were him, I would concentrate on my farm and family. You heard what happened at their family gathering on Saturday?" Make Mabvuto asked her friend.

"What happened? I did not hear anything. How could I with that flock of mine and that good for nothing husband I married? When I get home, it is one chore after another. He demands too much from me."

"Those who were there say there was a heated debate that ended up violently. The highly esteemed Reverend Benson Zulu pointed a shaky finger at his nephew and called him 'a boy still suckling at his mother's tired breasts'."

"Ah! Ah! Ah! That was an insult indeed. Was the mother there? How could the Reverend utter such words? Had he forgotten he is a man of the Bible, a man of God? Yoooooooo! For sure wonders shall never cease!" Make Thandi clasped her hands together as if to wring them.

"Listen to the juicy part of the fiasco. In anger, the nephew pulled a small gun from his side pocket and shot three times in the air before pointing it at his old uncle. Family members scampered in all directions. Reverend Benson Zulu fell on his bulging tummy and raised his hands in surrender. AT then jumped into his car and drove off at high speed."

It was clear that Make Mabvuto was happy that she was the deliverer of the hottest news in Linda. They clapped each other's hands and attended to their customers who had just arrived and were watching them.

However, despite his determination, he was told by a few of his close friends that victory was assured for the President and the Reverend; what was not certain was the magnitude of their triumph.

Alfred Tembo was vying to stand on the MMR ticket and had to pass hotly contested interviews which were chaired by the party President himself, in Chipata, the provincial capital.

Despite stiff competition, he fancied his chances as very good; because he knew JFC personally, having interacted with him in Kafulafula, where they had both worked.

Before he was adopted, he belatedly developed a phobia about standing against his own uncle. His mother had secretly warned him not to stand against her brother.

"He will bewitch you, should you try to challenge him." She moaned and then continued. "As his sister, I know that he uses strong charms from Mawali against his enemies."

Alfred Tembo nodded before responding, "But mum, witchcraft is not real," he countered. "It only affects those who believe in it." He said.

"No!" she screamed. "It works and there is evidence to that effect," she said.

"Are you sure, mum?" He asked.

"I don't want to lose you," she said with a voice filled with emotion and fear and avoiding his direct question.

Alfred remained silent.

"You are the only educated son I have," she cried. "You are my only pillar. Your brothers are all drunkards and do not support me, as you well know," she ended with a sob.

They discussed further, but came to no conclusion. Despite his mother's fears and misgivings, once his adoption was made official, he quickly accepted thus, ignoring her strong advice.

Alfred Tembo's support mostly from the younger generation did not, however, prevent the strain and polarization of the Tembo and Zulu families which were now divided into two camps; one stacked against the other and failing to see eye to eye. As a result, during and after the elections, his mother's camp declined to attend family functions, such as weddings and funerals if Uncle Ben was in attendance.

At the peak of the campaign, it was apparent that Alfred's team was facing a mountain of challenges. The older generation in the area often scoffed at his contemptuous contest against his uncle, after they had tried but failed to convince his mother to instruct her 'unruly son' to withdraw from the race.

In the end, a number of spanners were thrown into his campaign run in order to destabilize and frustrate him. Sometimes, hostile groups organized by his uncle or with his permission, publicly insulted or mocked him. They would compare him to a mad man, who never listened to wise advice from the elders.

While Reverend Ben Zulu was firmly supported by the people in the area, he also had other advantages such as use of government vehicles, a large campaign team supported by government resources and the use of government structures.

On the contrary, Alfred Tembo and his small team depended entirely on his personal resources, and had no access to any government facilities.

With just one week left before the general and Local government elections, all the reports emanating from the office of the President, the service chiefs from the army, air force and the inspector general of the Police were very positive and projected a large voter turnout and a huge majority for the President and his ruling party. President Jumbe was obviously over the moon and very happy with the positive reports. He whispered his joy to his second in command, Comrade White Phiri, the Secretary General of the party.

The following day the President received a delegation of women members of the Central Committee he had sent to the North – Western Province, led by MCC Martha Mulonga.

"Welcome from our beautiful province, comrades", he greeted them warmly in a socialist tone.

"Thank you, Your Excellency, our great leader," Mulonga responded on behalf of the delegation. As always, she smiled at him broadly. "We bring special greetings and commendations of the highest order from our party leaders and traditional leaders in North – Western Province." She said as a matter of prelude.

'Thank you very much MCC Mulonga and members of your delegation," President Jerome Jumbe replied. "How was your journey, comrades?" he asked, smiling broadly.

"We travelled well, Your Excellency." Mulonga replied, "but all is not well in the province," she mumbled.

"Why do you think so?" the head of state asked anxiously.

"Initially, we observed that children we found on the roadsides in the province instead of responding to our party symbol or our party slogan, as they have done in the past, were instead responding with the MMR slogan, 'the hour has come' or the symbol of the clock at 13:00 hrs!' she complained as she continued, "an overwhelming majority of them, Your Excellency."

"But surely those are only children who don't vote," Jerome Jumbe answered in astonishment. "What are the actual findings on the ground?" he insisted, dismissing Mulonga's opinion.

MCC Mulonga replied, "The situation is the same. We have to take drastic measures to reverse the negative development. The elections are just around the corner, Your Excellency," she ended.

The President cleared his throat and then spoke with other members of the delegation, to see if they had a different view from the delegation leader, but their analysis was just the same; negative. The President was visibly annoyed. He consoled himself by thinking that these were mostly uneducated women. Therefore, their analysis could not be more accurate than the more positive ones from the educated and experienced service chiefs and the most trusted Director General of the Intelligence Division.

He tried to persuade them to change their report to a more positive one but the senior women were adamant; the province had turned against the liberation party. In the end, he dismissed the women abruptly.

The party women left the President's office completely bewildered. "Had the head of state and party President just expressed indifference in order to force them to change their assessment of the situation, from what they had found on the ground? Of what use would that be?" They wondered to themselves.

Despite dismissing the report from the senior party women as baseless, President Jumbe reflected further. "What if their verbal report and sentiments were accurate?" He asked himself. It could spell doom for him and the party. What if that short fellow came to power through the elections he had generously granted him by shortening his own rule?

He wondered with trepidation, "No! there is no way those inexperienced chaps from the MMR could be trusted by the people of Zambica. Not after the sacrifices he and his colleagues made to liberate the country!"

It was the final day of the campaign and some people in the ULP camp in Kwitonta Constituency sensed trouble. Their candidate, Lezu who had done everything he could in order to retain the seat had been drawing smaller crowds compared to the MMR candidate. This was despite pro – ULP media reports insinuating that she was no match to the popular ULP candidate; all total fabrications.

In fact, due to misinformation by the biased media, she had received her first born son the previous night, who had been sent by his father.

He said to her, "Mum, pack your things. Dad said I should take you back home!" He commanded.

"Oh, hell no!" said Mumbi. "I will do no such thing! The elections are taking place after tomorrow."

"What's the point of staying here when you have already stopped campaigning?" he asked.

"That's a lie, young man. Turn round and go back to Lusiku. I'm on the final campaign day and I've no time to waste," she affirmed.

Her son immediately produced copies of negative newspaper articles purporting that she was scared for her life because of hostility from voters who didn't want her and she had subsequently gone into hiding.

Mumbi scoffed at the false reports and explained that those were tactics from the desperate ULP after realising that they were not wanted by the majority of voters in the constituency. Her son nodded but was not convinced.

Mumbi scrutinized the reports further. They were all pro-ULP and funded by President Jumbe's party. She explained to him how ULP influenced public media editors, whom they told what to write or suffer the consequences. In some cases, they even wrote editorials and gave obedient editors in chief to publish them unchanged, she explained.

She said to her son, "I thought we have clean politics in our country. No! I was totally mistaken," she breathed in. "There is so much cheating and mudslinging. I've learnt a lot on this campaign trail." She told him gently, breathing out. He nodded.

"If we've to correct the situation, certainly, this isn't the best time to quit." Then she asked her son, "If I were in hiding, would you have found me so easily at night?"

"No, Mum", he replied. "I now understand. I'll tell Dad everything!" He concluded. He rested for a while before returning to Lusiku, to allay his father's fears.

With renewed vigour, the MMR candidate proceeded to Mwandu village which had a voter's population of about 900, a big number by rural standards. The crowd there immediately confronted her.

"What do you have to offer?" one of them asked sarcastically.

"Unlike you, Lezu is very generous!" stated another.

"If he is generous, what exactly has he done for your village?" Mumbi asked them.

"Oh, many things!" replied the ringleader. "Things like bags of mealie meal, packets of salt, sugar, and bottles of cooking oil and many other nice things, you know. While you are stingy and have given us nothing," he complained.

"What about you, have you brought anything for us?" they interrogated her further.

Mumbi thought for a while. She had already done her homework; she knew that Mwandu's village was Lezu's stronghold. She had to tread very carefully.

"I'm sure that my opponent has done all the good things for you people for a good reason," she said.

"He is a good man, just like his father," said a big, dark middle aged man.

Mumbi explained to them about the dangers of bribes and corruption, and how both of them were illegal before asking them another question.

"During the one-party state, that Lezu has represented you in Parliament, has he ever brought such large quantities of rare commodities here?" she asked cleverly.

"No!" they responded loudly.

"Very good." Mumbi said. "It means that the ULP, represented here by Lezu and the whole ULP government, are therefore responsible for the terrible shortages that this country has been having for a long time."

"Yeah! Yeah!" the crowd resoundingly responded, with some chanting "Sense! Emano ayo!" ("that's wisdom").

"Because we have important elections, he has brought you these rare goods in order to buy your votes." she explained.

"He is clever. He is just mocking us," another voice came from the crowd.

"Be smarter," Mumbi advised. "Receive his goods, and even ask for more. But after tomorrow, vote for me as Member of Parliament and President James Francis Chaluma as the Republican President. Be wise. Vote on the clock," she advised. "the Hour has come!" she shouted.

"The hour!" they responded, "has come."

Many people clapped, with some chanting "Yes, Mumbi! Yes, Mumbi!"

Others quickly caught on and began to chant the MMR slogan, "The Hour! The Hour!", while others responded, "Has come!"

"However, those who do not experience suffering brought about by the ULP government, such as shortages and high prices of essential commodities, difficulties in sourcing and buying fertilizer, and lack of public transport etc. those people can vote for Lezu," she teased.

"No!" came a loud shout from the crowd. "These people have been cheating us!"

"Kanshi pakusala," she advised in the local dialect of Lemba, "come out in large numbers and vote for Mumbi as Member of Parliament and James Francis Chaluma as President. Vote on the clock, the symbol for MMR," she ended to a thunderous applause.

She then led the villagers in shouting the slogan for the MMR, "The Hour!

"Has come!" and the crowd responded in a thunderous shout.

"That hour?!"

"Is now!" the villagers responded in unison.

Mumbi smiled broadly; confident that she had managed to convince Lezu's supporters to vote for her on the final day. In doing this, she achieved one of the strategies that had been taught to them by a US NGO, "the last campaign days are the most critical. That's when you can undo what your political opponent has done, especially in their stronghold."

It was getting dark and Mumbi and her team were heading out of Mwandu village. To their surprise, Lezu was driving a truck alone. The truck was branded with his party symbol and had his picture and that of the President and was loaded with bags of merchandise.

"What are those things on Lezu's truck?" Mumbi asked curiously.

"I have seen bags of mealie meal and sugar," answered one of her officers.

"And cartons of cooking oil," said another.

"It's getting late," Mumbi observed. "Where the hell is he going?"

"Where else, Madam?" another officer chipped in, "Mwandu village. These are the commodities he has been giving to voters so that they can vote for him and today is the last campaign day, you know," he emphasized.

"What desperation!" Mumbi observed. "The candidate is corrupt and desperate."

Meanwhile, on the islands of Lake Bangweulu, Chipulu was facing a last minute crisis, just a day before the elections. A negative document attributed to him was circulating. The letter insulted the island chiefs and their subjects. It read in part:

"I am very educated while most of you are illiterates. I shall not come back to this mosquito-infested and backward place. I made a mistake to choose to contest in this God-forsaken constituency where travel is so difficult, sanitation is poor and the whole area is poverty stricken.

Therefore, if you don't vote for me, you will continue to suffer, but I will be okay in town!" The letter was signed by Dr Alexander Chipulu.

The MMR candidate was obviously worried and almost panicked. He had very little time left to exonerate himself. He therefore made an urgent strategy to vindicate himself.

He sent three agents to three island groups while he himself went to the senior chief's palace for support.

In hurried meetings, they refuted the letter as a forgery and not coming from the MMR candidate; they showed his genuine signature against the forged one in the letter. They argued that the only beneficiary to the forged letter was Katobwe, the ULP candidate.

They also charged that the ULP candidate was the only one in the habit of lying about and maligning his political opponents. Further, they proved that Katobwe had lied about his main opponent, in the previous by-election, two days before the elections, which made him win those elections.

Fortunately for the MMR candidate, the senior chief also dispatched his kapasos to tell the people through the village headmen not to believe a word of the malicious letter.

The final day of the campaign in Linda constituency was even more frustrating for Alfred Tembo's camp. After assessing the impact of their campaign strategy and their chances at the polls, AT and his small team mapped out a final day strategy; to address four rallies in four different locations; a mammoth task.

As they proceeded on the only road leading to the first location, they found huge logs across the road. They turned round and headed on the road going to the second location. They also found similar obstacles and the same was the case on the road leading to the third location. Alfred Tembo was immediately reminded of exactly what used to happen during ShaShaSha, in the freedom struggle. Freedom fighters would block roads with huge tree trunks in order to prevent the police and soldiers from pursuing them after they had destroyed government property.

Fortunately, for AT and his small team, the logs rolled on the main road leading to the fourth location were smaller. After being helped by sympathetic onlookers, they managed to partially remove them, leaving enough space for the two vehicles in their convoy to pass.

As they proceeded, a group of thugs armed with machetes and wooden sticks suddenly emerged out of hiding shouting obscenities at AT's team, and probably trying to ambush his small group. In a panic, and fearing for his life and the lives of his team members, AT pulled a revolver from his pocket and shot twice in the air! To the relief of the candidate's team, the attackers scampered away shouting, "Chili na futi! Chili na futi!" (He has a gun! He has a gun!).

On that disappointing final campaign day, AT only managed to address one rally out of the scheduled four. They later learnt that the obstacles found on the roads and the thugs that waylaid them were all part of Uncle Ben's strategy; to teach his raw and politically inept nephew a political lesson he would remember for the rest of his life. Apparently, Uncle Ben used to be a youth leader for ULP during the struggle for independence; he certainly remembered some of the old political tactics. With hindsight, AT reasoned that Uncle Ben had a mole planted in his camp! Otherwise, how did they know exactly where they had planned to hold their last campaign rallies?

Political campaigns were concluded on the eve of the elections in accordance with the Republican constitution. Some ULP zealots projected Jumbe to win by a landslide. The pundits gave almost no chance to his shorter and smaller opponent.

Among the patronizing media; some emanated from established and well respected international newspapers; such as News Month and the New Castle Times. They sounded genuine. President Jumbe was therefore, bubbling with exaggerated energy and confidence.

The President's latest trademark was a pair of jeans. At most rallies, spotting in a pair of tight blue jeans, Jumbe would swagger on the double, to the podium like a youngster in order to dispel the assertions in some quarters that he was an old and spent political bulldog.

Then, a cadre would often scream, 'Moneni, Kanshi achilimo, Mudala!' (Look, the old man, still has what it takes!). A chorus of blind supporters would take up the prompt and cry out with increasing emotion, 'Uh huh, Achilimo! Achilimo Mudala!' to which super JJ, as his followers fondly called him, would waive his green bandana with renewed vigour.

The final rally for the United Liberation Party was held in Lusiku, and the Republican President was the main speaker. Billed as the 'Mother of all rallies', it attracted huge numbers of people from far and wide.

By importing attendees from many provinces, an impression was created that the party had the largest following in the country. This was a strategy used by all big parties and an indication that they would win the impending elections, thereby attracting undecided voters to their side.

But some among their huge crowd were actually lured by a last minute rumour that at the final rally, President Jumbe would finally put a steel nail in little Chaluma's coffin by revealing the short man's top secrets; why he had been expelled from school in Form 2; the identity of his biological father whom he had rejected publicly; how his first marriage had ended in disaster; how he had married his current wife and stuff like that thus, the crowd's expectations were at pitch high.

However, diplomatic etiquette seemed to have overwhelmed the old politician. Instead, old President Jumbe emphasised the need for peace and national unity through his old unifying slogan, 'One Zambica, One Country', which had glued the country's several ethnic groups together, for almost three decades.

The ageing Zambican ruler argued that the inexperienced, short, and immature leader of the opposition party would plunge the country into a political crisis. Responding to JFC's constant attacks about the ailing economy, Jerome Jumbe finally explained that the economic challenges the country was facing were largely due to the unavoidable international economic crisis, at the centre of which was the plummeting copper prices, the country's chief export, and foreign exchange earner.

The President ended with a stern warning, for JFC and his colleagues, when he said, "I have never been insulted so much in my whole life, like I have been in the last ten months from this group of young boys and girls."

As his excited supporters shouted: "JJ! JJ!" at the top of their voices, he got a thumbs up to go on.

He continued, "While I've forgiven them during the campaign, there will be no forgiveness in a few days' time after I've formed my new ULP government," he ended to a thunderous applause.

Held on the last Wednesday, before voting in the south of the capital city, the rally for the Movement for Multiparty Restoration had JFC as the chief speaker, and was slated as the 'Father of all rallies.' The main roads leading to and from the venue were deliberately blocked by the police, in order to frustrate the attendees. But undeterred, they parked their cars and in large numbers walked a long distance to the venue.

The MMR final campaign rally was attended by a huge and anxious crowd, from many places in the country. The rumours circulating in the MMR circles at that time were that because President Jumbe had insulted and belittled him for so long, JFC was going to have the last laugh.

It was rumoured that he would do that by exposing Jerome Jumbe's well-guarded secrets, including why he started fasting when he was growing up in the village; his purported links to the Dul Hindu cult; why he had been nick-named Hitler; the real reason why he was scared of political competition, and other sensitive things.

Instead, JFC told the Zambican people at the final rally that they had had enough suffering under the ULP one-party dictatorship. He emphasised the need for a peaceful change of government through the ballot box, in order to repair the country's shattered economy, create employment and end the rampant and choking shortages of essential commodities.

JFC also teased the President when he stated that for the first time President Jumbe would experience his Waterloo by facing a real man, standing against him; as opposed to standing against a drawing of hyenas or frogs which was the case under the one-party rule. He warned the Zambican people not to trust the ULP which had destroyed democracy, ruined the country's economy, and distorted their destiny through socialist activities. The final message from the opposition leader seemed to resonate well with most of the people at the rally, going by the chanting and ululations. JFC's speech at the rally was judged by many analysts as hilarious and factual, which brought traffic to a standstill in many parts of the capital city.

While neither political leader revealed any dirty secrets about the other, some political analysts concluded that the two political opponents had behaved maturely. They probably reached an amicable political truce; not to reveal each other's old secrets, irrelevant to the current political arguments and to let bygones be bygones, in national interest.

Cleverly, ULP tried to avoid any debate on Zambica's dismal economic performance. Rather, the ruling party tried to project an image of a steady and experienced party, which had steered the country clear of the civil wars and ethnic unrest that had plagued other African countries.

President Jumbe repeatedly emphasised that Zambica was one of the few nations on the African continent that had maintained peace and did not have refugees streaming across its borders to other countries. He claimed that a vote for the inexperienced MMR on the other hand, might plunge Zambica into chaos.

On the other hand, MMR electoral strategy aimed to tie all of Zambica's economic ills to ULP; only ULP's gross mismanagement of the country's resources had led to the nation's penury.

MMR also claimed that ULP was rife with corruption and inefficiency that always accompanied one-party states. A vote for ULP would merely continue a pattern of confused policies that benefited only the party hierarchy, leaving the rest of the people without adequate schools, hospitals, homes or jobs. MMR slogan, 'The hour has come,' embodied the party's attempt to ignite the intense desire of Zambicans for change.

CHAPTER 5

The Fall of the Ulp Citadel

"What would you say about the elections Your Excellency?" JJ was asked by one of the inquisitive reporters following him.

He smiled broadly for effect before a television crew. "Everything is going well." President Jumbe was naturally bubbling with exaggerated energy and confidence as he replied. He was actually playing golf trying to send a message to one and all that he had absolutely nothing to worry about. "What about the results? Are you really confident of winning Mr President?"

"I am very confident young man," he replied waving his famous green handkerchief, "because I know that we are winning comfortably." "Are you sure Your Excellency?" another reporter chipped in.

"Yes, very sure" he said, "with a landslide," he boasted, adding that he was in a hurry to announce his new cabinet in two days' time, to the annoyance of some people who voted against him and his party.

Before the election results were announced, some United Liberation Party zealots projected President Jumbe to win by a landslide, as the pundits gave almost no chance to his short political opponent.

They sounded genuine. Therefore, to emphasize that he was walking over his inexperienced rival whom he thought was probably politically inept, President Jumbe went to play golf, his favourite sport, at Lusiku golf club. He had cast his vote in the morning. He was accompanied by some senior Ministers and a few members of his central committee.

"Your Excellency, these newbies in politics are interesting characters. How can a household name, father Zambica, the founder and the person who gave birth to the anthem "one Zambica one country", be trampled on his head by newcomers in politics?" One senior minister strangely attempted a conversation with the President.

"Comrade, wait and see how they will all come crawling to state house next week. Haven't you heard they have gone into hiding? I tried to make friendship with their small leader, my main competitor by inviting him to come and play golf with me. My messengers could not trace his whereabouts." They both laughed and the other senior ministers joined in. The journalists, for some reasons best known to them were not tickled by this weird humour by the President and other honourables.

"Maybe they have already crossed the Congo border as we speak. Cowards!" another minister joined in the conversation as he was handing the President a bottle of mineral water. "Didn't we hear that the chap's father is a Congolese from next door? He could probably be in hiding there as we speak."

"That four feet person is daring. It is true what they say: short people are argumentative and stubborn. They are also resilient, disrespectful and bad mannered. Now, their day of reckoning is just by the corner. We will all here have the last laugh Mr President." Another minister, a pure spelling of a bootlicker, competed with his colleagues in trying to please Father Zambica. It was very clear that they were hitting the nail right on its head. What hypocrites!

Not even one of them dared update the incumbent President of the likelihood of the fall of the Jericho walls. They were convinced that the years of their founding father will not just go down the drain. They were very sure he will only abdicate the presidential seat by retirement or through death.

In the truest sense, the whereabouts of the MMR Presidential candidate was not known; journalists trying to get a comment from him had failed to track him. As his party secretary general made some feeble comments on behalf of the party, speculation was rife that JFC was in hiding because he had lost the elections.

That evening after voting, Chishala and his wife went to visit General Silutongwe and his wife at their posh house near state house on Liberation Avenue. As expected, they were warmly received by Mrs. and General Silutongwe, the Zambica Air Force Commander. He was with his close colleague, General Ikolo, the Commander of the Zambica Army.

Chishala, a former housemate to General Silutongwe at a secondary school near Kasama in Northern Province noticed that the two generals were in an ecstatic mood; he wondered what it was all about. He was invited to join the party.

"Thank you so much," Chishala replied. "What are you two generals and also powerful members of the ULP central committee celebrating?" He asked them bluntly.

"Oh, you mean you don't know?" General Ikolo retorted. "Election results of course." He gulped two more tots of double malt whisky at once. Chishala's jaw dropped.

"But the results haven't been declared yet." He said, picking up courage. "In any case, counting of ballot papers has just started in many polling stations. So generals, how do you know the results already?" He interrogated.

"Not a problem," General Silutongwe answered. "We have our privileged sources," he boasted.

"In that case, what exactly are your projections?" Chishala cross examined.

"The old man is winning by a huge margin," General Ikolo joined in. "No less than 75 per cent of the vote." He affirmed.

"By that much?" Chishala asked with anxiety ringing in his voice.

"Believe it or not," General Silutogwe said, "Our sources are impeccable and our projections are accurate," he paused, "and they have been confirmed by our M16 friends," he said, confidently. "We have even told the President and commander in chief to relax and take it easy. Didn't you see JJ playing golf this afternoon?" Chishala and his wife kept quiet.

Silence pervaded the room. To break the obvious silence, Mrs Silutongwe coughed uneasily and then said, "I think your figures are really exaggerated," she cautioned.

"Why do you think so, woman?" General Silutongwe asked his wife. "Did you vote for the short chap?" General Ikolo laughed carelessly in appreciation.

Not intimidated, the general's wife cleared her throat, "you know very well that I couldn't vote for him. Not with the support that President Jumbe has given us and the rapport that you and the family have with him," she explained.

"That's that then," General Ikolo concluded. "United Liberation Party is destined for a landslide victory tomorrow," he emphasised "and no one can change it. ULP will rule for yet another twenty nine years." He bragged.

"Actually, my apprehension has a good basis," Mrs. silutongwe clarified. "At Forest B school where we voted and from the long queues I have seen on TV, the overwhelming majority of voters were men this time," she ended, taking in air, and slowly letting it out.

"And what is wrong with that woman?" General Silutongwe asked his wife in a harsh voice. "Aren't we men telling you that we are winning?"

"I know, and that's why I am married to you darling," she said, beaming him a rather shifty smile. The general smiled back and then relaxed. "However," Mrs Silutongwe continued, "more male voters is bad news for Jumbe and ULP, and good for MMR and their pintsize Presidential candidate," she said. The two generals looked at each other, while Chishala and his wife nodded simultaneously.

"Why is that?" General Ikolo asked, "I don't understand."

"Because most male voters hate Jumbe, largely for overstaying in power; 29 years is a long time you know." she hinted. "Then add the erosion of the country's economy, the high unemployment rate, passenger transport blues and the shortages of essential commodities", she suspired.

Silence pervaded the room. Then, she continued. "You may not know it because we are privileged and insulated from the harsh realities in this country; we don't experience the hard times that many families do, due to your substantial benefits," she suggested.

"I agree with my sister's accurate analysis," Mwansa cut in. "In addition, we women always think with our hearts, while men often think with their heads," she said.

"I think she has done a better job than most analysts quoted in the local and international print media," Chishala added. The two generals looked at each other in total bafflement without saying a word.

They continued chatting, largely based on their individual expectations and projections on the expected outcome from the elections.

When Chishala and his wife left the general's house, the arguments were still ringing loudly in their oracular organs. But one thing was certain in their minds – the discussion was inconclusive.

Nonetheless, Chishala's mind drifted way beyond the debate; he now suspected that the two generals could have been involved in a secret operation of rigging votes for President Jumbe and his ULP; otherwise, why were they so sure about the 75 per cent margin? He was also upset about something else. The possibility of his party the MMR losing the election to President Jumbe was not far-fetched. He was apprehensive though that should President Jumbe win the elections, the old man would become even more repressive than before.

"My wife," Chishala cleared his throat, "do you honestly think that the two generals made any serious points worth losing my sleep over tonight?" He put it to her.

"I think the two generals were very subjective and naive," she replied. "In any case, I can't see any reason for President Jumbe getting a landslide in these elections. However, JJ is very smart; he has bought the loyalty of many influential people in the country, including the two generals," she reasoned. Chishala nodded in agreement.

"As you know, the two generals are in the President party's central committee. They are enjoying themselves while the people out there are suffering and wallowing in abject poverty," she explained.

"Their appointment into the inner circle of the ruling party was just a crooked scheme to look after key members of the armed forces and gag them against any possible military reprisal. In the process, the privileged positions insulated them from economic hardships."

"I agree with you entirely my wife," he said. "As a party, we knew that the majority of our people can't vote for a man who has maliciously ruined the country's economy through socialist tendencies." He concurred. "This is what we have tried to put across to the voters at our campaign rallies," he told her. She nodded in agreement.

"As our party president has said many times, JJ will lose these elections whether he likes it or not," he continued.

"That would be the most logical outcome of these elections." she said. "How about Mrs. Silutongwe?" He asked. "I thought she had valid points. Don't you think?" He asked.

"I found her very objective," Mwansa concurred, "especially for a woman whose family has received so many favours from the President's regime. However, I do not share her view that all women would have voted for President Jumbe."

"Why?" he asked, "and who did you vote for, mother of my children?" He asked teasingly and Mwansa smiled mischievously.

"Don't be ridiculous," she answered. "You know exactly who I voted for and why," she challenged him, looking him squarely in the face.

"As for your other question, many women are actually annoyed with President Jumbe because they are often transported to the airports to be paraded and dance for the President instead of selling their wares in the markets," she said. "They don't like being turned into JJ's dancing queens," she said. "I know," he replied. "I was merely pulling both your legs," he teased.

"Were you?" she asked. "Don't forget that my legs are fragile." she joked back.

"Yes. On a serious note," he said, I was encouraged by what I observed during voting," he said.

"What did you see, my husband?" she asked.

"While most voters were quiet," he replied, "occasionally some men paced up and down and asked about the time, even though they all had watches on them." Mwansa smiled knowingly.

"I observed that too," she concurred. "And since the clock is the political symbol of MMR," she reasoned, "any reference to time was an indication of who they would be voting for."

"That was quite smart," he said, "it was as good as covertly campaigning for the MMR without apparently breaking the law, which forbids campaigning 24 hours before polling day."

"I agree with you," she said. "I had the same impression," she added. They locked their eyes and smiled at each other meaningfully.

Encouraged, Chishala downed a few more glasses of Mosi beer; now more optimistic that despite the subjective predictions by the two generals in President Jumbe's pocket, his party, considered by many as the David in the elections, was most likely destined for the unexpected victory at the polls at the expense of the well-resourced and giant Goliath.

—————◇•✳•◇—————

In Kwitonta constituency, in the Northern part of the country, Mumbi vividly reflected on what they had been taught by a US NGO, educating opposition candidates in the province on the electoral process in order to be alert and vigilant, to prevent loss of votes by any tactics that could be used by the ruling party.

As one of her precautions, she assigned each of her five personal motor vehicles in the constituency to each election committee of Zambica (ECZ) truck carrying ballot boxes from different voting centres to the central counting centre. All her vehicles were branded with the MMR symbol and slogans, including her picture and that of her Presidential candidate.

On one route, the ECZ truck carrying cast ballots stopped three times and at all the three places, the vehicle Mumbi had assigned to it also stopped right behind it. At the fourth point, the officer from ECZ that was on the truck was upset. He got out and shouted at the driver and his passengers.

"What's wrong with you chaps? Just proceed and stop trailing us! Don't you have anything else to do?"

"No sir!" The driver shouted back, "we only take instructions from our boss and no one else."

"Who is your boss?" the officer asked in a firm voice as he stood close to the MMR trailing vehicle.

"Madam Boss. The MMR candidate in the constituency is our boss, and our instruction is to trail your vehicle everywhere you go until you deliver the ballot boxes intact to the counting centre," he stressed.

"That short woman is there anything she couldn't think about!" He exclaimed with frustration. "She seems to have taken all the necessary precautions!" He complained as he walked back to start the engine of the truck.

At the counting centre, Mumbi, was witnessing the counting of votes for the first time. She could not comprehend exactly what was happening in the big hall. She however, noticed a trend; the basket with her counted votes was filling much faster than that of her opponent.

"What does this mean?" she asked one of her party officials.

"Just wait and see." He said excitedly.

"Wait and see what?" She asked in bafflement.

"The initial signs are that you are winning. We should take this constituency by a landslide," he projected.

"Are you sure?" Mumbi asked, "don't get me excited for nothing," she cautioned.

"Calm down" he advised. This constituency is of great significance and has national ramifications for these elections." He advised her.

"I don't understand. What ramifications?" she asked in a hushed tone. "Because the Republican President comes from here, and his son is former Member of Parliament here and running against you," he paused and sighed. "Your win in this constituency will imply that ULP and President Jumbe have been totally rejected by the people." He reasoned.

"But this is just one constituency out of 150 in the whole country," she told him, "I can't see the connection."

"That I know," he replied. "But if they are rejected in their own village, it would be worse in the rest of the country." He explained. "I see. I would be very happy to be part of the historic group meting out a crushing defeat to the President and his son" she responded. Just then, the lights in the counting centre suddenly went off.

"What!" screamed supporters of the opposition parties, "What's going on?" They all asked in unison.

"Turn on the lamps and torches," shouted the MMR candidate. 'Madam Boss' continued giving commands as silence dawned on the big room. "Watch all the ballot boxes closely. Don't allow them to steal any votes from us." Mumbi instructed.

"This woman is smart!" Shouted one ULP supporter, "she knows exactly how to safeguard her votes."

Mumbi had earlier on instructed her son to park one car in front of the open entrance to the hall and that he should sit in the car and never doze, not even for a second. When the lights suddenly went off in the counting hall, her son immediately switched on the car lights at full beam, as directed by his mother. Others in Mumbi's camp also switched on their torches and lighters immediately making the hall fully lit.

Mumbi smiled, she knew that of the already counted votes, she was ahead of the ULP candidate by far and that there would be attempts to steal her votes in order to avoid their looming defeat.

After one hour, the lights came back on and the counting of ballots continued unabated. Mumbi was happy that she and her alert team had just prevented a possible attempt by the ULP to steal her votes. As his opponent's votes continued to pile up faster, the ULP candidate became agitated. "No! it can't be!" He said. "She must be using black magic," he alleged shouting at the top of his voice.

When the votes from Mwandu village polling station were finally announced, he only managed 14% of the votes while the rest were given to Mumbi. He shouted on top of his voice again. "No!" He repeated, "the majority of voters in Mwandu village promised to vote for me. I can't believe this." He said in shock, while sweat was dripping from his beard. At this point, the ULP candidate became more agitated. He was shouting at the top of his voice, bullyingly. A police officer threatened to eject him from the hall and that's when he behaved and calmed down.

In Luapita Province, Lake constituency was one of the three constituencies in Lubwe district. For counting, ballot boxes were transported to Lubwe Boma by road from two other constituencies and by a banana boat using a 25 horse-powered outboard engine from the islands.

The counting of votes started in earnest for the two mainland constituencies while counting for the Lake constituency started 8 hours later, due to communication challenges.

As the counting of the votes from the mainland constituencies progressed, the atmosphere in the counting chamber was tense, and it was evident from the full ballot boxes that voter turnout was very high. Early indications were in favour of the MMR candidates to the annoyance of ULP supporters. Chipulu relaxed after noticing that the heaps of his votes were much bigger than those of his opponent's. But he decided to remain calm, knowing that counting of votes would take time. On the other hand, his opponent, Katobwe, decided to stay at a motel nearby and sent two agents to represent him at the counting centre.

At the motel, the fat ULP candidate was busy dishing out alcoholic and soft drinks to anyone in sight. Apparently because of his character assassination letter attributed to the MMR candidate in the last two days of the campaign, he was certain that he would retain the seat on behalf of ULP. After all, a similar last minute tactic had worked well for him in the by-election.

But Katobwe's other reason for celebrating prematurely was that he believed he had insurance, in the unlikely event that he lost the election. According to the constitution, anyone working for the government or allied institutions had to resign their position before nomination day. The ULP candidate had confidential information that his opponent, Chipulu, had actually not resigned from his post at his company in Chibwe.

As they celebrated while the votes were still being counted, Katobwe told his supporters to be calm and enjoy their drinks.

"We will win either through the ballot box or by petition through the courts of law." He boasted. Thus for him, the counting of votes from his Lake constituency was just a futile academic exercise. "We shall beat Chipulu either way." He bragged.

Alfred Tembo (AT), the MMR candidate in Linda constituency was scared of the threats from villagers who had Uncle Ben's backing.

However, the day of vote counting at the district center was different. While he had fancied springing a surprise on his uncle, the atmosphere in the counting hall was rather intimidating. It was noisy and hostility inundated the air circulating in the big room. Nevertheless, the ECZ staff completed the counting of two other constituencies in the district which all went to the ULP candidates, who won by large margins. The ULP winners were announced and declared by the returning officer, sending a freezing chill down AT's already nervous spinal cord.

Then, the counting of ballots for Linda constituency begun. As if rehearsed, a few supporters from Uncle Ben's camp shouted in unison "Muchione ichisilu ntawe yolila yafika(Look at the mad man; his hour of reckoning has come)." Alfred Tembo really tried hard to conceal his reaction to the noise and nuisance caused by some people from Uncle Ben's camp, he could not help it, he shuddered, feeling highly intimidated.

At the same time, the filling of counted votes into his opponent's basket was much faster compared to his. This caused excitement among some of Uncle Ben's supporters, who sensed sweet victory and started making irritating noise and celebrating, while his small crowd remained mute and somewhat subdued.

Alfred Tembo finally realised that his uncle and now political opponent had a commanding and unassailable lead. Suddenly, he felt embarrassed to be losing to his old uncle, whose chances he had totally underestimated. He looked at the unruly chaps in his opponent's camp again; loud noise and hostility was still emanating from there, and yet the biased returning officer was unable to control their disturbing behaviour, which was not allowed by electoral guidelines. Was it because the ULP was the governing party? He wondered.

Disturbed and incensed by the noise and commotion coming from his opponent's supporters, he instinctively made a decision. He whispered to his senior most assistant on his right. "Let's get out of here! This is getting out of control," he commanded.

"Are you sure sir?" the assistant whispered back. "Won't we stay up to the final count?"

"No ways!" He replied standing up. "I have lost this election and there is no point waiting here, probably to be lynched by these thugs!"

His assistant raised his hands towards members of the team and they all swiftly left the counting chamber, to the delight of Reverend Benson Zulu's supporters. Some of them were shouting, "cowards!" "losers!", in their local language, while their confident candidate punched his fist in the air and smiled broadly, realising that he had finally taught his rude nephew a big lesson, in the 'battle of one family'.

The day following the 1993 elections was an interesting one; it was full of surprises and intense anticipation was across the broad spectrum of voters and even those who never cast their votes for various reasons.

Everyone was anxious to know the outcome of the much-publicized elections. In any case, only a few toyed with the idea of the remote possibility; a change of government.

At 15.30 hours, initial results started trickling in and the announcement was beamed live on national television and announced on radio.

As the announcement of election results continued from around the country, a trend emerged: JFC and the MMR were headed for a landslide victory. Counting centre after counting centre reported the opposition outpolling ULP by wide margins. The people of Zambica, speaking through the ballot box had made their choice loud and clear.

As results continued coming in, it became increasingly clear that the Movement for Multiparty Restoration had swept the country. Subsequently, the United Liberation Party was left as a minority, regional party, winning in all 20 seats in the Eastern Province. The United Liberation Party won 5 other seats, to bring its total in the country to 25.

According to official final results, JFC received 76 % of the electorate votes, almost what the two generals had predicted for JJ. He collected at least 70% of the vote in each of the 8 provinces that he carried. In the Copper Province, he outpolled Jerome Jumbe by 91% to 9%, while in Luapita Province he outpolled him by 90% to 10%. Only in Eastern Province did Jerome Jumbe win a majority; his 75% to 25% victory win there demonstrating ULP's entrenched support in the province.

The MMR's parliamentary candidates fared equally well against their ULP rivals: The MMR won 125 of the 150 seats in the National assembly, that is, 83.3%. By these results, the electorate ousted top ULP leaders, including members of the ULP central committee and cabinet ministers.

Thus, the most unlikely had happened. President Jumbe sent a modestly worded congratulatory message to the President – elect, who he praised for his oratory skills, guts, and determination. His message ended, "Mr President-elect, let me take this opportunity to offer my services unconditionally to your government, whenever they are needed." It was clear from the tone and content of President Jumbe's statement that he sought reconciliation with the small man. This marked the end of his 29 years of uninterrupted rule.

However, the MMR top leaders received President Jumbe's reconciliatory message with caution; they knew the man, and anything could still happen before inauguration. They withheld the location of the winning candidate, while their party secretary general appealed for calm and that the President – elect would issue a statement at an appropriate time.

But some citizens were still anxious despite the new development. During the campaign, they were often told that the sun would not rise if ULP lost to MMR, but they were surprised to see the sunrise, after a humiliating loss by the ULP. Thus, the myth was broken, while the MMR dream became real!

For former ULP leaders, the loss was far beyond politics. The loss ignited a looming economic catastrophe. Their own policy dabbed the leadership code barred political leaders, holders of senior government positions and parastatal chiefs from owning businesses and property. This included residential houses and personal transport. It dealt a severe blow to almost all of them, with the exception of a few, who had been allowed to build their own houses, own farms and businesses. Like in the book 'Animal Farm', some top ULP leaders were therefore, more equal than all others were. In any case, election results against them would change all that.

The pathetic situation of the ULP leaders was worsened by the new MMR government's decision to abrogate a law that was passed at the end of the ULP government; to provide a pension scheme to all former leaders. That was the last stroke that broke the camel's back. Suddenly, the ULP leaders who always basked in opulence and power were overnight reduced to downright paupers and the ULP's government machinery crushed like the biblical castle built on firmless sand.

Comments from some international observers were that the electoral environment had favoured the ruling party, but they were surprised that the MMR won, with such a landslide, against all odds. A President from a neighbouring country stated, 'We had never seen a ruling party in Africa humiliated at the polls to such an extent.'

The international community attributed the MMR victory to the depth of the economic crisis in the country, the broad composition of the MMR, the increasing assertiveness of the judiciary and the elections committee, the professionalism and determined work of the monitoring teams, and the commitment of political leaders to the democratic process.

Honestly, while everyone is entitled to their own opinion, political analysts, and pundits including the two generals got it all wrong! A critical independent analysis would have projected a win for Chaluma and his new MMR, but probably not with the magnitude that they did. Why? President Jumbe and his ULP had alienated most of the country for a long time.

Thus, the 1993 elections presented a rare opportunity for the majority of voters in the country to vent their frustration and anger at someone on the ballot. Who else would be at the receiving end, between President Jumbe and Chaluma? For those projecting a landslide victory for President Jumbe, where else could the projected votes be coming from? In reality, the 1993 elections presented a rare payback opportunity for an overwhelming majority of voters; and the results showed. By hindsight, even Chaluma had gotten it right, when he told Kaluba not to worry about lack of resources for the MMR; after all President Jumbe, and his ULP had already done most of the work for them.

Nevertheless, some die-hard ULP followers still hero-worshiped the President's political craftsmanship. How else would they describe a man who managed to hoodwink and unite the vast country under his famed, 'One Zambica, One Country' slogan? They admitted that he was, otherwise, a shrewd negotiator who spearheaded the attainment of the country's independence from the British while presenting himself as a democratic moderate. Compared to many neighbouring countries, independence in Zambica was achieved with minimum bloodshed because the militant wing of ULP organised innovatively before the British woke up.

President Jumbe was a political engineer of some sort, who managed to instil fear in other political leaders in order to keep them in check. But he also used party leaders and members' fears of tribalism to his own advantage. Of humble education, it was believed that President Jumbe's personal will power and self-discipline earned him respect and international recognition. Those who knew him better, however, said that while he portrayed gentleness from outside, he was deep down, a dictator and those at the receiving end included Chaluma, the President-elect.

President Jumbe had also deftly worked to ensure that all people of influence were brought under his control, including chiefs, company chief executive officers, senior NGO officials, and many others. He unflinchingly fired leaders from the party or government positions if they failed to follow his line or if he felt they were also vying for his topmost posts in either the party or government.

But many Zambicans and the international community praised the President for his act of great statesmanship, by humbly accepting defeat, at the hands of Chaluma and the MMR. This allayed earlier fears that in the event of an MMR victory, President Jumbe would be unwilling to relinquish power. Many people were also wondering about the moods of the President, and that of the President-elect.

A close friend of the President found him in quite a state. He was devastated and couldn't believe Zambicans would humiliate him like that, after all his sacrifices during the long and sometimes violent independence struggle.

Inevitably, on a Saturday, just two days after the elections and indeed before all the counting centres had reported final results, tens of thousands of Zambicans and hundreds of foreign dignitaries gathered outside the High court to witness James Francis Chaluma take the oath of office as first President of the third Republic. There was dancing, singing and jubilation, coupled with the constant chants of "the hour –the hour has come."

A born-again christian, the new President opened the ceremony with a prayer. The President-elect delivered a stirring and motivating speech. He admitted that "the Zambica he had inherited was destitute" and then using his oratory skills, exhorted the people of Zambica to go back to work. "The hour has come," he said, "to put Zambica first ……. Let's do whatever we can, every day, to slowly pull ourselves, through our sweat and toil, out of the mud and build a new Zambica."

Evidently, the inauguration and the new President's fiery speech signalled the death of the second Republic and the birth of the third Republic, at the same time. Strangely, the coronation of James Francis Chaluma realised late Simon Mulenga Wampanga's prophetic words to him when he told him at a secret meeting in Kafulafula. He said, "you are the only one courageous enough to wrestle power from President Jerome Jumbe since most leaders are cowards." This also resonated well with what Wampanga's supporters said to Chaluma during their dead leader's funeral, "Now it's you to take over from our late great leader to liberate this country from dictatorship."

The election contest between President Jumbe and James Francis Chaluma in 1993 can be truly likened to the contest between David and Goliath of the old testament. David, a young but brave Israelite shepherd, killed Goliath, a well-trained and well equipped undefeated Philistine champion, who boasted that he would kill anyone who stepped forward to fight with him from the Israelite camp. In the uneven contest, little David slung a little stone that struck Goliath on the forehead and Goliath, the feared giant dropped dead.

Clearly, the towering President Jerome Jumbe, having ruled Zambica undisputed for 29 years and enjoying the incumbency and state support was over confident that he would easily win the elections. However, the diminutive, fluent, and charismatic Chaluma enjoyed a lot of support throughout the country which gave him the unexpected land slide victory.

"I need to send you to your grandmother's son." A mother said as a matter of fact to her son. She could not see that her son was on edge. The noise, excitement and hooting all around was inviting. How could mother talk about sending Mabvuto on an errand when he should be with the MMR cadres on the streets of Lusiku?

"But bamayoooo! Can I do that later? My friends are calling me. Please mum! Just this once." Mabvuto was now kneeling on one knee and rubbing together his hands. He knew very well that both his parents were not amused at all by the MMR victory. They were staunch ULP do or die supporters. But their children were over excited because they had won. They were over excited ever since the announcement. Mabvuto's father went straight to his bedroom and announced that no one should dare switch on the radio or TV. He was in mourning. To make matters worse, his own children were making the loudest noise for him. How were they going to survive?

Mabvuto, the youngest but notorious MMR cadre, had come back home to pick up whatever he wanted to pick up. His father, upon seeing him, felt his intestines twist. His head was pounding with unbearable throbbing pain on his temples. That was why he decided to lock himself in the comfort of his bedroom. His son's voice was annoying and irritating. No one had taken the MMR seriously, including himself. He wondered how JJ was fairing. Since he had locked himself in the room, it meant going on a forced and unplanned fast.

"Are you going to obey your mother or your friends, son?" Mabvuto's mother was very good at manipulating both her kids and husband. But on this day Mabvuto could not budge. Before she could utter another word Mabvuto was gone like a wind. MMR had come and MMR had divided families. The ULP camp was mostly populated by old people and the MMR was infested with young blood. It was sure a new era.

"My friend," Mabvuto's father shouted, "let that foolish boy go! Ah! We are trying to lick our wounds and he comes to rub in salt and pepper. Let him go before I do something I would later regret.

Politics!" He crossed his legs and threw his hands in the air. The 29 years of ULP monopoly was now history. He lamented.

"Up! Up! JFC! Welcome JFC! Plot Number one here we come! MMR rocks woyeeee!" The chants went on and on. Mabvuto and the many other cadres meant business.

It was clear and obvious that the MMR victory was greeted and continued being greeted with much jubilation and great expectations. This was surprising for a party that had been formed only the previous year. A large number of motorists drove towards city centers; some honking their car horns or waving to the crowds along major roads. Others simply mingled aimlessly at shopping centers, where numbers of people were assembling. Some among them were extending their right thumbs, together with their index fingers, making the MMR victory symbol. Chaluma had won. MMR had won. Zambica had won.

Initially, small crowds began to assemble cautiously, due to the fear instilled in the citizens under the one-party dictatorship, but eventually huge crowds materialized, they sung and ululated in support of the victorious MMR and their hero and new liberator James Francis Chaluma. Never had such widespread euphoria been witnessed since the country attained political independence. This was indeed the dawn that ushered in the third Republic.

CHAPTER 6

President Focuses on the Economy

While the President's office was a short walking distance away from the residence, power and its entrapment surrounded his daily activities. President Chaluma sometimes wondered whether he really needed all that expensive security. Who could wish to kill him in any case? He considered cutting down on the unnecessary cost of Presidential pomp and ceremony; he would decide later after consulting the Minister of Defence and his service chiefs.

That same cool windy morning, the President reckoned that the performance of his regime would largely be judged by how well he handled the country's ailing economy and democratization. Whereas enhanced democracy largely needed government's political will, it was more daunting to repair the economy. For consolation, every informed person at home and abroad knew that he had inherited a fragile economy. But this should not remain an excuse for too long.

He reflected upon how the issue of the economy took centre stage during the previous one-year election campaign. He also vividly recalled how he had criticized the ruling party then, concluding that they had ruined the economy, largely due to their socialist programmes and huge appetite to borrow for consumption rather than production. That had led the country, he had argued then, to become highly indebted. Eventually, the national debt escalated to over US Dollar 7.0

billion. On further reflection, he concluded that his party's argument on the poor economy made it easier to defeat JJ and his party.

Now that he was Republican President, it was imperative to tread carefully lest he too would be condemned as a failure, like his predecessor. He also recalled vividly how he had constantly criticised Jumbe on the size of his cabinet. How strange that he had also failed to trim his cabinet, in order to satisfy various constituencies that had played key roles in the campaign, leading to his memorable victory. By hindsight, he now felt that he should have found another way of rewarding some of the people, now sitting in his bloated cabinet and contributing to the escalation of government expenditure. Had he done that, no one could have blamed him for failing to keep that particular promise. While it was now too late to change the size of his cabinet, he felt he would do something else one day, aimed at controlling government expenditure.

Having been Jumbe's chief critic on the economy, it would be shameful if he fell in the same trap. President Chaluma was alive to the fact that the economy by 1993 was in a mess. He reflected further:

Earlier around 1989, President Jumbe had divorced the IMF, accusing the top world financial institution of imposing harsh and unrealistic conditions on the country.

He then declared that the country would only pay its debt obligations when it was ready. He directed that the government would abandon reliance on foreign handouts, arguing that instead of borrowing from international institutions, local resources would be used. Subsequently, President Jumbe introduced a policy of 'growth from own resources.'

But the country's debt crisis escalated largely due to the choking of the accumulated interests. It, however, didn't take long before JJ's government finally capitulated and went crawling back to the IMF two years later. Under the circumstances, Jumbe and his government surprisingly ate their humble pie, and accepted harsher conditions than those they had rejected. That single act by JJ and his government made many people in the country conclude that, the ULP government had run out of ideas and was probably governing the country by trial and error.

Apparently, Chaluma's message on the economy was convincing during the protracted election campaigns that crowds loved it, and often went wild and applauded whenever he expounded on how JJ had ruined the economy through careless and unworkable policies. He reflected further, he gave credit to the party's think tank, which included his own Minister of Defence. Chishala and five other colleagues had worked extremely hard to understand the state of the country's economy at the time. Their recommendations had proved instrumental in attacking President Jumbe's poor performance on the economy.

Now the President appointed a small think tank to look at the challenges in the economy in relation to the recommended changes for liberalising the economy. They had read extensively and analysed pertinent issues and compared the state of the economy to its strength at the time of independence in 1966. They looked at inflation; the depreciation of the local currency and causative factors; the country's foreign indebtedness, and the impact of the costly support to the liberation struggle in Southern Africa, which the country could ill afford. The previous government's reluctance to implement effective structural adjustment programmes with the IMF was also studied and analysed; there was a lot at stake.

The report of the think tank outlined in detail measures that could reverse the country's economic malaise, under a liberalised open market environment. The President also tasked his economic advisor to write talking notes on the economy for him, which with his photographic memory and as a brilliant orator, he would internalise and use effectively to put the message across to the people.

The President and his economic team had just returned from Washington where they held difficult but encouraging talks with the IMF and the World Bank about the state of the country's economy. All considered, a final decision had to be made on the way forward. There was no value in procrastination on the issue any more.

Later in January 1994, the Minister of Finance pronounced policy measures which brought in the fiscal discipline in terms of government public expenditure which were absent in Jumbe's one-party socialist reign and the economic policies that were targeted at transforming the economy. They included a cash economy – where government committed itself to spend on public programmes and projects, only to the extent of the revenue generated through tax and non-tax revenue from government wings, departments and agencies. This measure was aimed at having predictable expenditure and control on debt.

The elegantly dressed President Chaluma often had spent sleepless nights over the country's economy and the high poverty levels in the country; a contradiction in a country endowed with rich minerals and other resources. In any case, not knowing the cause of her husband's insomnia exacerbated the first lady's worries. She reflected a lot about her husband's unpredictable new sleeping habits. She now suspected that he was sick, probably due to the pressures of the Presidency or maybe he was infected with one of the new devastating diseases at the time, like AIDS. The President didn't help her curiosity either. He didn't allay her fears concerning his lack of sleep. The President's main concern was what his government had to do to reverse the crumbling economy; his number one challenge in office. He revisited the party manifesto; there was a clear plan on economic liberalisation.

But his biggest fear was that after being elected as a very popular President, he would easily lose popularity should the measures to put the economy back on track be too harsh to bear for most people. They had already suffered so much under Jumbe's half-hearted liberalisation measures, which paid no dividends. He had to be careful in handling the pernicious economy he had inherited from Jumbe.

Bold decisions had to be made to transform the economy using privatisation as the main tool. Government identified state run companies and trenched them lining them in stages for privatisation. Then, a law was passed on privatisation. The Zambica Privatisation Act was passed and the Zambica Privatisation Agency (ZPA) was created to execute the important task. A technical committee was also created to value all public companies and assets lined up for privatisation.

Following the evaluation and assessment of the companies, the technical committee also recommended the various modes of privatisation, either by open bidding, management buyout or asset(s) sale or liquidation, when company liabilities could not make it into a viable running entity.

After reading the economic report, the President's economic advisor prepared a simplified but detailed executive summary, for the head of state. For a second opinion, he summoned Chishala after he had understood the gist of the root causes and main recommendations. Being a weekend, Chishala went to meet the President at his official residence in the company of two of his youngest sons. In an informal setting, the minister clarified what the head of state thought were contentious issues, especially concerning the essence of the major recommendations for the way forward.

After understanding the challenges and the recommended actions, the President believed that for development to take place, political and economic liberalization should be undertaken simultaneously. He therefore approved the implementation of a series of market – oriented reforms, such as the removal of subsides on maize meal and petroleum imports, and the liberalization of foreign exchange. He is quoted in Forbes as saying "we are determined to move away from a life of subsidies and consumption to a life of sacrifice and production. We need commitment to transform Zambica's economy from one dominated by large inefficient state companies and parastatals (companies managed fully or in part – by a national government) to a market driven, private sector led economy."

The President reminded his cabinet of the party's vision to change the country's political and economic landscape, clearly articulated in the manifesto with priorities for policy change. This he emphasized, "we promised the Zambican people. The 1993 transition and policies being adopted by my government were influenced by Zambica's recent history and my predecessor's uneasy relationship with the international donor community."

Among the nations of sub-Saharan Africa, Zambica had suffered one of the greatest and most rapid economic declines starting in the early 1970's. According to one estimate, GDP declined by 30 percent between 1977 and 1992. Zambica's relationship with the multilateral financial institutions started in 1975. The stability measures, and later structural adjustment programmes, introduced between 1975 and 1992 by JJ all failed to address the underlying structural problems of the Zambican economy. These were; a large and wasteful state sector, inefficient agricultural production and an unsustainable policy of food subsides. The World Bank and IMF's reforms proposals focused, among other things, on reduction of food subsidies to the urban population and an increase in agricultural production by promoting small – scale farming and better price incentives for farmers.

Before implementing economic reforms, President Chaluma was aware that the political costs of the proposed reform measures were, however, high in a society where workers were protected by strong and vocal labour unions. He remembered that faced with 'food riots' in the urban areas each time comprehensive reforms were attempted, his predecessor, abandoned the economic reform programmes due to an escalating debt burden and increasing donor co-ordination. Zambica was therefore unable to draw on financial assistance from the multilateral finance institutions and, hence, from commercial sources. The unbaiting decline of the Zambican economy had now become the main issue, which he himself had capitalized on during the previous election campaign.

A long cabinet meeting, going into late evening approved policy measures for economic liberalisation to lead to a free open liberal market economy, to remove subsidies and for all Zambicans to bear the costs and challenges of the change together.

Immediately, the leadership code, which had prohibited leaders from doing business or owning property under the ULP administration, was revoked and the exchange control regulations were abolished. The

Lusiku stock exchange was established – giving business a feeling of optimism. Many people now felt that the time was ripe for embarking upon new business ventures. Eventually, people's attitudes were being liberated, and made to accept that being rich or making money were no longer considered as antisocial activities, as was the case under Jumbe's regime. Now, many people woke up to freely trying this or that business venture, without any restraint.

Foreign exchange regime and interest rates were liberalised, leaving them to the open market of supply and demand, while excess liquidity was mopped up, through open market operations. These policies were envisaged to make a major impact on the stabilization of the macro-economic situation in the country. Also, other supportive policy actions were taken to make the business environment conducive for private investment and profitable operations.

Liberalisation of trade imports and exports was expected to trigger the economy that had been riddled with chronic shortages of essential commodities. Now, both small and big trading companies took advantage of the policy to import various needed commodities. Through this policy, shortages of essential commodities were expected to end. However many citizens were sceptical. Could the short little President truly achieve the impossible, where big old Jumbe had completely failed?

The deregulation of prices on goods and services was also implemented. With the open market liberalised economy, the Prices and Incomes Commission became redundant. Nevertheless, the key structural reforms changing the economy from state-owned public companies to a private sector-led economy were done through the privatisation process.

The privatisation process had commenced with small companies first and proceeded onwards. The process took time before the most treasured public asset; the Zambica Consolidated Copper Mines (ZCCM) was privatised. It was evident that some western governments tried hard to influence government on how it could be done and who finally got it. President Chaluma refused to be intimidated and in the process crossed paths with some very powerful western governments for not heeding their wishes on how this particular asset was privatised; he later paid a heavy price for his intransigence!

Partly due to increasing criticism, Chaluma and his ministers had realised the great need to involve people who had expertise and vast experience in the sectors up for privatisation, even if they had worked closely with Jumbe in the past. For instance, they appointed John Chanda to head negotiations for the privatisation of mining companies. Chanda was without a doubt, one Zambican who clearly understood the country's mining sector. The professional he was, John Chanda accepted the challenging assignment with humility.

Public transport was a nightmare during Jumbe's one-party era. Due to lack of foreign exchange and other resources, fleets of buses could not be properly maintained and new vehicles could not be procured. With a critical shortage of buses, there were long delays and queues on almost all public routes. To resolve the problem, government made a policy to remove duty on all public transport. All Zambicans, all investors who wanted to do business in the public transport sector were allowed to import buses duty free for a period of two years.

With this development Chaluma was happy that, former President Jumbe's command economy was no more. The President was well advised by the blue print of the think tank report on the immediate actions to take in order to get the economy back on track and on the move again. He also addressed the debt crisis inherited from the former regime, on which interest repayment had been frozen, leading to the country almost being declared insolvent.

After rather difficult and tense negotiations with the Bretton Woods institutions, the new administration under Chaluma was allowed to borrow some US$ 600 million to service the accumulated loan repayments. The rolling of the debt created a new economic lease and some breathing space for the country. This created marginal financial stability and enabled Chaluma and his economic team to start negotiations for a fresh structural adjustment programme. Unlike in Jumbe's case, President Chaluma's regime was now able to do business with financial institutions, from which the country had been divorced due to Jumbe's intransigence. It was evident early in Chaluma's administration that the very serious and committed decisions would turn around the country's economy for the better.

After perusing the relevant documents and having consulted extensively he was now ready to address the country, on the state of the nation, with the economy taking centre stage.

The President convincingly reasserted his incumbency at his third press conference since he was voted into the highest office of the land. Unlike at the two previous ones, when he stood up for more than thirty minutes, he took his chair and sat down immediately like his predecessor used to do. President Chaluma made brief references to the state of the nation generally. He then skilfully treaded on the familiar economic ground most Zambians wanted to hear about. He gave a lengthy rendition of how the previous regime had mismanaged the national economy. "Jumbe and his ULP political sycophants were drunk with power," he intoned. 'They abused earnings from copper. Their ill-conceived programme of indiscriminate nationalization of major companies discouraged foreign direct investment and eroded donor confidence."

He stated how his MMR had taken over a socialist inclined communist economy, where all economic decisions were made to satisfy socialist politicians. He announced that 80 percent of the country's economy fell under state-run public enterprises, while only 20 percent was in the private sector. Thus, economic decisions of state enterprises always followed socialist directions. He also revealed that he was shocked to find that the per capita government debt he found was among the highest in the world, while all of the copper earnings for the following year were already mortgaged, to pay for the past government expenditure. How could a government be run like that? He wondered.

He concluded, "it is evident that Jumbe's socialist-humanistic state enterprises model of development had failed over a long period, from the mid-1970's to the late 1980's. Without a doubt, the country needed change from the one-party state controlled economy to a multiparty liberalised open market economic system." He went on, ignoring the applause from the highly charged crowd. "This would create a conducive environment for economic investment, economic growth, and tax accumulation, to stimulate economic growth and subsequent economic development."

The President paused, sipped a glass of water, took off his reading glasses, and polished them for dramatic effect. The crowd went wild. They clapped while some whistled in appreciation. The President exchanged glances first with the First Lady on his left and then with his Minister of Defence next to her. Then, he looked at his Vice President seated immediately on his right. They were both exhilarated and joined the chanting crowd. James Francis Chaluma deliberately slanted his eyes, jabbed the right forefinger in the air and the crowd was silent as soon as he opened his mouth to speak again.

"My government through a think tank of eminent experts has carefully analysed the negative impact of JJ's socialist policies and has decided to take some bold steps to redress the situation." The crowd liked the President's gallant declaration and broke into an encouraging uproar and once more fell silent when he opened his tiny mouth to speak. "The immense damage to the national economy perpetrated by the ULP regime on our people was tantamount to criminal acts! It was utter misuse of workers. How could a soldier be appointed a Minister of Health? They made an economist serve as Minister of science and technology. The ULP government lacked professionalism. One man pretended to know everything and appointed our qualified men and women to wrong positions. The ULP government baked bread in shops they erroneously called Zambica Consumer and Buying Cooperation (ZCBC) mubwipi (in short)."

The journalists at the press conference almost forgot about their cameras and pens as they laughed derisively when the President inadvertently referred to ZCBC as in short. This was in reference to the small stature of the President. The President too, joined in the laughter when he realised the jibe in his choice of words. He nevertheless, continued, "they sold the bread, and appointed relatives to manage

ZCBC and many other parastatal companies. Fellow citizens, my government will not run the economy. That is clearly not the duty of government. We shall endeavour to provide an enabling environment, so that the economic gurus can have the propensity to do what they know best," he said.

"Furthermore," he continued, "we are committed to let qualified professionals in the social and economic sectors take up their appropriate positions. That is proper governance. The damage inflicted on all spheres of our national life by the twenty-nine years of ULP's dictatorship was immense and it will take some time and sacrifice to reverse the negative effects." He sighed.

"Fellow compatriots, there is need for major actions to arrest the existing economic malaise and to put the economy back on track. In this respect, mother Zambica must undergo labour pains and finally achieve political emancipation. The hour to say enough is enough has come! Zambica will no longer be a laughing stock. Zambica must join the economically progressive nations of the world. That is our paramount duty in government: to deliver our people from the dehumanising poverty, ravaging almost all parts of our country. Our men and women voted me President so that I deliver and we shall deliver. The MMR will never betray the Zambican people, the way ULP did. Compatriots, let us all rally behind the MMR leadership, and take our country to another level; a higher level." He said.

"To rescue the economy and to attract assistance from foreign governments and international institutions, the new government needs to implement radical economic reforms, including lifting price controls on maize meal." He said.

"Zambica, endowed with countless natural resources must arise from the ashes like the phoenix, and be counted among the economically successful nations of the African continent. Behold, the hour for change has come. However, I want to emphasise that the twenty-nine years of political and economic mismanagement by JJ and his ULP cannot be resolved overnight." He paused before continuing, "are you ready to suffer now so that Zambica is economically free and prosperous tomorrow for our children and their children's children?"

"Yes!" the crowd echoed in unison.

"I repeat compatriots, are you ready to sacrifice for a better Mother Zambica?"

"Yes! Yeess! Yeeesss!" The crowd, like sheep, ecstatically bleated in agreement. The President was happy; he got the mandate he was looking for there and then. Therefore, no one could call him a dictator.

This was President Chaluma, bodily a pint size but a legendary giant and undisputable master of oratory at his pinnacle. Everyone was silent. Those following the proceedings of the press conference by television or radio in markets, bars, hair salons, or homes felt overpowered by the strong and convincing words pouring from the mouth of the President. Minibus drivers parked their vehicles, lest the crew and passengers miss a word. Babies strapped on their mothers' backs too seemed to discern the pervading extraordinary silence and stopped their irritable yelling. The press conference assumed the central heartbeat of the nation. It was as though everything and everyone across the nation hung on to Chaluma's piercing voice at the press conference.

"My government henceforth declares the implementation of the Structural Adjustment Programme (SAP) with support from the International Monetary Fund," declared the President.

Chaluma said that the MMR approach showed transparency as ZPA would account for the privatisation process and proceeds in detail. This transparent approach was unlike the manner in which Jumbe conducted the nationalisation programme, using a favoured few, accountable only to himself.

He added that up to the end of his rule, only Jumbe and the favoured few knew exactly what took place during the nationalisation process. He elaborated that while there would be no sacred cows in the privatisation process, the programme would however, be phased after evaluation, to take into account the security nature of the companies involved.

There was a sudden deafening applause from a section occupied mostly by MMR party officials and cadres. The President paused as planned. "Thank you Zambicans," he exchanged looks with the inner circle of his cabinet and beamed, "thank you Zambicans," amidst persistent ear shattering applause.

The economic reforms of the new third republican government had an unquestionable semblance of a people driven mandate. That was a great reprieve. The foundation for Chaluma's and MMR economic agenda for Zambica was set. The surge to liberalise the economy seemed unstoppable, as JFC the political engineer, had set Zambica's economic liberalisation in motion like a speeding electric locomotive during the rush hour. The whole thing was on course and at top speed, ready to erase the socialist appendages of the previous regime. The hour was in full swing; it would proceed unopposed as planned. The President looked at a smiling Minister of Defence. He recalled that the political and economic ingenuity was one of Chishala's ideas during their private meetings at state house.

The President nonchalantly glanced at his official speech, handed it to his aide decamp and raised the symbol of the clock at 13:00 hours and chanted, "the hour!" the incensed crowd retorted, "Has come!" the President repeated, "the hour!"

The crowd once more screamed louder than before, "Has come!"

"The implementation of SAP will not be easy," the President now spoke with ease, without notes. "Implementing the structural adjustment programme is like taking a bitter pill in order for the patient to subsequently get better."

At the end of his address, JFC's press aide invited journalists from accredited press institutions to make comments or ask questions on the President's landmark economic speech.

"My name is James Phiri, from the Zambica Daily Mail," said one reporter. "Mr President, at your two previous press conferences, you stood up for a long time, probably to show that yours is a working government." The President nodded in affirmation. "However, today you sat down, throughout the press conference," he continued as some people burst out laughing. "Is this a sign that you are already tired like your predecessor?"

The President cleared his throat and said, "that is a good question." He stood up with both his hands holding his waist as further laughter erupted. "You see." said the President, "I can still stand up, as long as it takes. This answers your question," he paused. The President added, "Until I came to state house, I never knew just how sweet this chair can be." More laughter followed.

"My name is Nyambe Mundia from The Past Newspaper," another reporter introduced himself. "Mr President, your SAP is quite comprehensive and should swing the country's economy to the extreme right. I hope it works," he said cynically. The President nodded. "You also gave the impression that yours is the first SAP in this country. Is that correct?" He asked and quickly sat down. "Thank you for your good questions," the President said. "One, yes, SAP in Zambica will work, as long as all the people are prepared to make the needed sacrifice," he paused. "Two, yes. A very mild version of SAP had been reluctantly tried by my predecessor JJ, before and then suspended. No wonder such reforms couldn't work." He said. "Reforms are just like a doctor's prescription. You must take the recommended strength or dosage for the prescribed period for your health to be restored. Nothing like I shall only take half the dosage of the drug for half the duration. No!" He concluded. Laughter ensued.

"My name is Goodson Mwamba from The Inquirer, the paper that digs the most," he introduced himself as most people in the audience laughed. "Mr President, you said at several of your campaign rallies that your predecessor made wrong appointments in placing Ministers in ministries where they had no qualifications or experience," he paused for effect. "But here is your own Minister of Defence, a qualified economist apparently in a wrong ministry. What is your take on this, Mr President?" He sat down as some people in the audience clapped.

The President realised that Mwamba's searching question was not anticipated by his experts, and therefore not in his brief; containing possible questions and answers. To create time and think quickly, he went through his common routine of taking his glasses off, cleaning them and perching them at the tip of his nose, as he was thinking of a possible response. "Thank you so much Mr Mwamba", he said, "your question is truly from a paper that digs most." Some people in the audience laughed; as his senior aide quickly placed a little handwritten paper in front of him, containing possible answers. "Yes, it is correct that I condemned wrong appointments," he paused, glancing at the handwritten paper. "But remember what I said about the criteria for appointments in the Defence and security wing?" He asked, looking at the possible answer again, and then looked at Mwamba directly in the face. "I am afraid it also applies to the Minister of Defence, from whom I expect and demand 120 percent loyalty." He ended as the audience burst out laughing.

'Mr President. We all know that JJ's economic reforms never worked. Why should Zambicans believe in your SAP this time around?' Another reporter asked.

"Thank you for your tough question," he hesitated. "It is not for me, but for the Zambican people to judge. They have already suffered so much, endured persistent shortages of essential commodities, lost their hardearned savings through sharp devaluations of the local currency. The hardworking people of Zambica have failed to have three square meals per day, and yet, this was promised by the ULP government. The list is endless. But please don't compare this SAP to half-baked socialist programmes, which have never worked anywhere, including cuba." Many people clapped. Some gave him a standing ovation. He paused to allow the noise die down.

"I want to assure you that this SAP will work in Zambica," he continued. To stress the point, he held his hands akimbo, his glasses drawn further down his nose bridge and he looked at the audience over the ream of his spectacles, instead of looking at them through the lenses. "Because I feel certain about this," he said, "I can kiss SAP in the morning; I can kiss SAP at mid-day and I can have SAP at dinner time." He concluded, with a resounding applause from the audience.

"Any more questions?" asked the president's press aide. "The President can take two more questions," he invited.

"I am Dickson Makwaza from The Times of Zambica," another reporter introduced himself. "Mr President, you had a distinguished service in the labour movement, rising to the highest post of chairman general," he reminded him, as some people in the audience laughed. "Now, you have just announced an interesting but capitalist – inclined economic reform programme," he paused. "Shall we take it that you have now gone full circle, from the extreme left to the extreme right?" he asked. "What is your comment Mr President?" he added.

President Chaluma smiled before answering. "They say that there is a time for everything," the President replied. The audience didn't know what he was driving at. "So, the same goes for socialism. For Zambica and Africa in general, socialism was appealing during the liberation of our continent. At that time, communists gave unconditional support to Africa, which was not the case for capitalists, most of whom sided with colonialists." He explained. The reporter nodded, even though he was not very sure of the essence of the President's long response. The audience too kept quiet. "But as Republican President," he continued, "it is my sworn duty to protect and defend all Zambicans. Therefore, it would be unwise of me to just support a dogma which is on the left but does not put food on the table for my people; but has led to poverty and food insecurity in our country." Most in the audience laughed.

A few more questions were asked and the President answered some of them, while tactfully evading a few. The press briefing was concluded by the singing of the national anthem.

Chishala smiled broadly. The President had performed extremely well and his personal advice to the head of state had been followed to the letter.

President Chaluma in the following days, weeks and months would take centre stage to drive the strong message of the inevitable economic liberalisation to Zambicans across all locations and lifestyles. They listened to his oratory, punctuated with vernacular words and phrases. President Chaluma was set to turn round Zambica's ailing economy for the better.

⊃•✳•⊂

It was now almost one and half years since President Chaluma's ascension to the helm of Zambican politics and surprisingly, the country's economy steadily started to pick up. The macro-economic indicators were stabilizing and showing a positive course. Most important for the common man was the availability of essential commodities in the supermarkets, shops and markets. This had a stabilizing effect on the prices of most commodities. Long queues, characteristic of the previous regime were relegated to the past for the interest of concerned historians. The only limiting factor now was an individual's capacity to pay.

The MMR government inherited a choking debt of over US $ 7.0 billion from the previous government. At that time the international community was looking at actions of helping poor countries reduce their indebtedness, especially countries reforming their economies. Zambica was included in this group of highly indebted poor countries (HIPC) initiative. This added another impetus to the Zambican reform programme; the privatisation of Zambica Consolidated Copper Mines (ZCCM) in particular was being monitored globally.

With the subsequent privatisation of the mines, Zambica almost reached HIPC completion point, but stuttered due to over expenditure, largely attributed to the elections in 2003. The adjustments were however, corrected, as more revenue came into government's coffers, from increased copper revenue prices. Thus, both the World Bank and the IMF acknowledged Zambica's HIPIC completion point in april, 2007. While another MMR leader President Luka Mwambwa and his then Minister of finance Joseph P. Habenzu received accolades for the debts cancellation, many people didn't know that it was the policies and the actions started by President Chaluma, when he was in office that made this achievement feasible.

Thus, privatisation worked for the country's economy, enhancing investors' perception of the economy; in both local and foreign investment. The improved economic environment continued to bring in fresh capital in funds, machinery, equipment and technology needed in productive sectors of the economy. Through liberalisation, the economy was empowered to shift resources to productive areas to create employment, and make new economic opportunities feasible, as seen by more mines opening up, production going up, and new manufacturing companies coming up with a variety of new products, and shopping malls springing up all over the country.

CHAPTER 7

Magnificent Cape Point

It was a Thursday and Chishala had told his wife that he would be on an official trip to South Africa the following day, but withheld the rest of the travel details. He was driven to the Lusiku international airport. As the car inched towards the airport departure terminal under the careful control of his experienced chauffeur, he and his wife said very little to each other. At the airport, she escorted him to the VIP departure lounge and in public view, he embraced her tight for a long, long moment and then let go.

As Minister, a protocol officer did all the immigration and checkin formalities and presented a boarding card to him. When he got in the business class cabin, there was Mboniwe looking elegantly dressed. She greeted him with a toothy smile. He broadly smiled back at her.

While the two had travelled and stayed at secret rendezvous in Zambica before, this would be their first flight abroad together. Champagne was served, as soon as the aircraft was airborne.

"Is this a restaurant?" she asked after observing the refined preparation of the flap tables.

"This is the business class cabin sweetheart, but in any case," he paused, "the service is first class." She nodded in agreement, although not fully convinced with his explanation.

"Can I order anything I like honey?" Mboniwe asked, smiling at him auspiciously.

"Why not?" Chishala responded. "You are welcome my love. Anything at all," he encouraged.

"On second thoughts, I don't want to make you broke," she said as an afterthought. "Especially that you have many expenses to incur while in South Africa."

"Far from it," he responded. "One, because I am loaded right now," he countered, "and two, because all the food and drinks you are going to have on the flight are already paid for in advance," he explained.

"How come?" she asked. "How could they know the value of what I shall eat and drink in advance?" she wondered innocently.

"Food and beverages are included in the price of the ticket," he explained. "Calculated on average." He added.

"I see. I didn't know that," she admitted. "I still think that this foreign trip we are taking is very expensive." She maintained.

"Don't worry my darling," he assured. "I shall take you to many more new nice places in the world," he promised. "Then, you'll know everything you need to know; you'll be more informed than the ordinary Zambican woman." He predicted.

"Really?" she mumbled excitedly.

"Yes," he replied. You'll know a lot more than all the women in Chandevu, Matapedia, and Kuku compounds put together," he boasted further.

"Thanks a lot my angel," she appreciated, "you were sent to me from heaven." she smiled gently, and felt a great sense of accomplishment. The future with Chishala looked bright. She looked to the future, with great anticipation.

"And you were a special little gift for me," he countered, "delivered to me on the Lusiku tennis court, when I deliberately feigned injury." He revealed.

"Really? Why then did you feign injury that day?" she asked. "I never suspected anything. I thought you were genuinely hurt."

"I didn't want the foolish looking young chap to defeat me and humiliate me publicly." He confessed. Mboniwe laughed. She laughed with such mockery which brought tears to her large eyes.

"Why are you laughing?" He asked. "This is a serious matter you know."

"I shall never forget that moment," she paused, "your act on the tennis court that day actually brought us together." She affirmed causing him to reflect for a while.

"I think you are right. I did a smart thing you know." He paused. "Otherwise you and I could have not met." Mboniwe nodded, smiling broadly. He then explained to her that now all members of parliament had just received their hefty tax-free mid-term gratuity payments. He promised to buy her many good things from his parliamentary benefits if she continued being a good girl.

"But I have always been very good to you," she reminded and smiled at him gently.

"Are you sure?" he asked teasingly.

"Absolutely," she affirmed.

"Except for one evening," he said.

"Which one?" She asked innocently.

"At the college," he reminded her. "After we first met." She looked at him timidly, expecting the worst.

"When your naughty boyfriend insulted me in front of so many other students." He paused. "And you lied that I was your uncle from Petauke. When I drove off, I thought I would never see you again," he revealed.

"Oh, that silly boy," she said. "He was just a naughty boy with nothing to offer."

"Go on," he encouraged her. She hesitated.

"First, his behaviour was always unpredictable," she said. "Nevertheless, I dropped him for good when you came on the scene," she said. Chishala smiled; he recalled just how she later went on her knees to make the apology; from her body language, he knew that her apology was genuine.

"Minister, you also have a blemish you know," she reminded him, to break the obvious silence, and to prevent him from referring to her lie again.

"Me? What blemish?" he chuckled. "It's not possible." He defended his honour.

"Yes mister Minister. You!" she teased him. "Your blemish almost turned fatal." she hinted.

"What happened and when?" He asked inquisitively.

She reminded him about his former girl friend who shouted at her at the college, and threatened to kill her in the presence of other students. She told him it was the most embarrassing moment in her life.

"Oh! that. I was so upset. I could have killed someone when I heard the news," he told her.

"Were you really?" she asked, and then laughed.

"Why are you laughing again?" He asked. "This is a very serious matter," he reminded her.

"Because, my love," she begun, "you are worth dying for. I swear to god."

"Really?" he asked with a sneaky smile. "And you know what?" He asked. "That very sad incident actually consolidated our relationship."

"Why?" she asked him. "Is it because I was insulted and almost beaten?"

They made little talk until Mboniwe dozed off, most probably under the influence of alcohol. Chishala took advantage of the silence to catch-up on some business literature he had taken from the office.

Mboniwe woke up and lunch was immediately served. They continued talking as they enjoyed the sumptuous four-course meal and dry red wine; courtesy of South African Airways.

They landed two hours later at Oliver Tambo International Airport in Johannesburg. After the immigration formalities, they waited for a while before boarding another SA flight to Cape Town.

In Cape Town, Chishala went to town in an attempt to impress his young mistress. Because he had been to Cape Town a couple of times before, he knew exactly where to stay and where to take her. They checked in at a four star Golden View Hotel, overlooking the picturesque and famous table Bay Mountain. In the evening, he took her to a cinema to see the premiere of Mandela – a Long Walk to Freedom. Mboniwe was extremely excited; she had never seen the opening of a new movie before.

On Saturday, they took a pre-paid bus trip with other tourists to visit a couple of wineries on the wine route near Stellenbosch. They went to three different wine farms, which had developed their wineries to international standards. Mboniwe had never engaged in wine sampling before. Chishala explained how it was going to be done; the ten wine glasses were for tasting nine different wines, with the extra glass for water, to cleanse the mouth in between the different types of wines. This was to ensure that only the bouquet of one wine is engulfed by the sampler at a time.

By the time they were done with wine sampling at the third and last farm, Mboniwe was tipsy; what with her swallowing the wine like water, and failing to spit it out as many amateurs do, which the real connoisseurs, however, would never do. In any case, Chishala never alerted her to this, but let her enjoy her first wine tasting experience without his influence.

In her alcohol-induced jovial state, Mboniwe could hardly remember the details of what really happened at the third winery; many boys call it postdrinking amnesia. However, she remembered one thing; wine tasting in Cape Town was great fun. Given another opportunity, she wouldn't mind going on the wine route of Cape Town once again.

Sunday was equally interesting. They took a tourist-bus southwards out of Cape Town. Mboniwe was amused as a group of baboons walked across the road with exaggerated ease as if deliberately blocking the road. Slowly and majestically, some moved along the road while others a few metres away from the road were picking whatever they found edible. It was very clear that these closest biological relations of man were not scared of humans or traffic. Cameras clicked on the bus as tourists captured the close cousins of the human species in the middle of the Cape Point National Park. The bus stopped at a few other notable exciting spots, along the way.

At Cape Point Farm along M65, Mboniwe was amazed by the size of the ostriches; they were gigantic, and totalling over 200. She and Chishala, like most of the passengers disembarked from the bus for a closer look at the huge birds. Besides the baboons and giant birds, Mboniwe enjoyed the scenic view as they gradually came to the south – most end of the African continent.

Mboniwe exclaimed with trepidation, "What is this?" she asked.

"Where are we?" she wondered.

"This is the famous Cape point," Chishala explained. "This is where the south most tip of Africa touches the two oceans at the same point," he added.

"Which oceans?" she asked inquisitively.

"The Atlantic and Indian oceans of course," he clarified.

"Oh! I see," she exclaimed, as some memories of her African geography came flashing back to her.

They went up to the light house in a funicular side, to have a clearer view of the place; where the two oceans really touched. There it was! Mboniwe saw a huge mass of water flowing in calmness and bringing a sense of serenity. She looked over the horizon above the waters; the sight of the calm blue waters on the eastern side against the sight of the blue sky. But the rough currents of the whitish Atlantic waters on the west kept constantly dashing into the calm blue waters; the very edge of the southern tip of the continent gave a spectacle she had never imagined before. Chishala took several pictures of the excited Mboniwe standing behind the signpost indicating that this was the most South-western point of the African continent. The other fascinated tourists queued for turns to pose at the now famous signpost.

A tour guide explained to the group that the cape of good Hope was situated at the junction of two of the world's most contrasting water masses, the cold Benguela current on the south west coast and the warm Águilas current of the southeast coast, popularly known as the meeting point of the Indian and Atlantic oceans.

"Oh my god!" she screamed. "I never dreamt I could see such a spectacle in my whole life time," she cried.

"You like it then?" Chishala asked, smiling broadly.

"Like it?" she retorted. "You are joking. What an understatement. I love it," she revealed. "I shall write to mum and my sisters tonight and describe this experience in great detail," she excitedly revealed. "I am glad we came here then," he suggested.

After listening to their tour-guide's detailed explanation of the history of Cape Point the excited tourists asked several searching questions and bought some souvenirs. Then Chishala and Mboniwe had lunch at a modest restaurant with other tourists.

They returned to Cape Town by late afternoon and rested at their hotel for a short while. Chishala then took Mboniwe to do her first shopping in Cape Town. He encouraged her to pick whatever she wanted irrespective of the cost; she picked what her heart desired, for herself and a couple of items for her parents and sisters.

They had early dinner at a posh seafood restaurant, at the waterfront.

On Monday, they visited robben island by a scheduled boat cruise and were happy to visit some of the cells of former political inmates, including the cell where Nelson Madiba Mandela had been incarcerated. This was a political highlight of the trip as far as Chishala was concerned. He would certainly refer to it in his brief report to the President, about his private trip to South Africa. As Minister, nothing was totally confidential to the head of state, especially aspects of a political or historic nature. Chishala would of course not mention Mboniwe anywhere in his report. He had to tread very carefully in the way he conducted himself as senior Minister.

The love birds also visited table mountain, and enjoyed the cable ride, from which they had a complete and clear view of Cape Town from above.

It was such an interesting and revealing trip. She now understood why many people claimed that Cape Town was one of the top ten holiday destinations in the world. For sure, Mboniwe would be happy to come back to Cape Town a few more times, funding permitting. As for Chishala, he knew even before they left Zambica that he had picked a great holiday destination, which had so many interesting options to visit within the well known South African tourist city and the countryside.

They flew into Johannesburg on Tuesday morning and checked in at the modest Court Yard Hotel in Sandton City. Its proximity to the Sandton Complex was a major attraction. They visited a number of interesting sites including the older part of Johannesburg. Many tourists had stopped staying in this part of the city due to increased robberies and muggings.

Chishala had nearly settled down and had learnt the basics of working in a government structure, using government systems and procedures. Subsequently, he even recognised and met his deputy minister more often than before. Eventually, he also got used to working and liaising with senior civil servants whose input he now valued and appreciated, as significant.

While minister Chishala was happy with the way he was consolidating his grip on the ministry and the unfailing support he was receiving from the President, the same could not be said about his domestic affairs, because relations with his wife were increasingly strained, leading to acute instability in their marriage.

Initially, Mwansa got rumours about her husband's infidelity. She first ignored the rumours, like most Lusiku house wives did, largely in the hope of keeping their relationships intact. One day, Mwansa received a tipoff with overwhelming evidence from a sympathiser who called her on condition of anonymity. She was seriously hurt by her husband's reported behaviour, which dashed her high expectations of a good life and a blossoming marriage now that Chishala was appointed senior minister in President Chaluma's cabinet. She remembered all the sacrifices the family had made in the past. Her high expectations were being frustrated by that immoral and skinny Mboniwe. She reckoned.

After crying and fuming silently, she resolved to gather more evidence, including her competitor's full names, place of work and residencial address. Armed with Mboniwe's vital data, Mwansa summoned her two trusted friends for lunch. After enjoying the sumptuous four-course meal downed with dry red Mediterranean wine at Marlin restaurant, she narrated her husband's heart-rending infidelity.

As expected, she received outpouring sympathy and support from her two confidants. Subsequently, they schemed the way forward, aimed at teaching the young mistress a lesson she would never forget.

Mwansa and her friends patiently waylaid Mboniwe on her way from work one evening.

"Good evening young lady," Mwansa greeted. "I am Honourable Chishala's sister and these are my close friends," she said in introduction.

"Good evening ladies," Mboniwe reciprocated. "What can I do for you?"

"My brother can't stop talking about you," Mwansa said. "I therefore wanted to be the first one in the family to set my eyes on you." She patronised her.

"What a beautiful young lady," Mwaka joined in. "No one can blame your brother for being mesmerized and obsessed by such a stunning young woman," she also praised. The other woman nodded in agreement. Mboniwe relaxed among the women she had never met before and felt highly appreciated.

"Just to get to know you a little bit, can you accompany me and my friends?" Mwansa asked. "We shall bring you back soon."

"Why not?" Mboniwe responded after reflecting for a short while. She joined the other woman at the back of the car. As Mwansa started the engine, the women engaged the young lady in what sounded like friendly social conversation.

Instead of driving to a coffee shop, Mwansa pulled up at an old cemetery in the old part of the capital city. With no one in sight at the time, the three women suddenly descended on the unsuspecting young lady, putting a gag of a thick cloth in her mouth and took turns at beating her up. Mboniwe was dead scared of the unexpected development and the cemetery environment and not in the least aware of her offence. She wailed emotionally as tears streamed freely from her large eyes.

"This is what prostitutes get for sleeping around with married men," intoned Mwaka. In no time, the older women started cutting Mboniwe's hair using blunt pairs of scissors, aimed at inducing excruciating pain on the defenceless young woman. Then, they applied white paste mixed with glue on her hairless scalp.

With her head completely but crudely shaven, Mboniwe looked terrible; her small now bald head had nothing to do with the fashion of the time. Feeling the pain and humiliation, she passed out, which suddenly instilled fear in her attackers, who thought that she had died. Not knowing what to do with the unexpected turn of events, the three scared women fled from the crime scene, leaving Mboniwe for dead, at the old cemetery.

The Minister of Defence was terribly upset, when Mboniwe's sister reported and described in crude detail the crime committed by his wife and her associates. Chishala fumed profusely and promised to teach his wife a lasting lesson. Thus, instead of going to the club as usual after working hours, he was driven home by his chauffeur. Initially, he blamed his wife of being a savage and a crook, for organising a lynch mob of her unmarried friends to attack an innocent woman, and before she could respond, he beat her up and called her all sorts of derogatory names. He also threatened to divorce her for embarrassing him and for carrying out criminal activities.

Instead of apologising as he had expected, Mwansa narrated a catalogue of events involving him and his mistress; stark details of rendezvous, restaurants and hotels they frequented. This angered the minister even more and instead of concluding the matter with his wife, Chishala drove to his girlfriend's flat he was renting for her. He consoled her and promised her his protection. Since he was minister of defence, protection was a simple matter. But Chishala was still curious; "how did his wife get all the details about his affair with Mboniwe? Did she employ a private detective to trail him?" He wondered.

With a swollen face, Mwansa confessed her misdeeds to her favourite uncle justifying what had happened. The older man who was of a sober character denounced her actions out rightly as childish and warned her to desist from following her unmarried friends, whom he called marriage-breakers. After a long admonition, he nevertheless promised to talk to her husband, who was on very good terms with him.

Even though the minister had a scheduled cabinet meeting in two hours' time, he agreed to see Mwamba, largely because of the seriousness of the issue and the mutual respect they had for each other. The visitor made clear to the minister that he didn't support his niece's criminal conduct influenced by her bad companions. But he also advised him to be cautious on how he conducted himself, especially in public.

On the other hand, while the minister regretted his misconduct with his girlfriend, he stressed that his wife and her accomplices had committed a crime of assault and attempted murder, for which they could be jailed.

"I know," Mwamba concurred, "but as minister of defence, you can surely do something about this misdemeanour," he suggested. The minister reflected further, but uttered no word.

"What brought me here really is to discuss the problem between you and your wife," said Mwamba calmly to break the obvious silence. Chishala nodded.

"The problem exists," he said. "But what is the way forward?" Mwamba asked.

"I know, I have my weaknesses," Chishala answered, "but my wife has gone completely out of line," he stressed. Silence pervaded the office again.

"What she and her friends did is obviously wrong," Mwamba admitted. "But marriage is a two-way traffic and a contract between two people." He advised. Chishala didn't get what he was driving at.

As if reading his in-law's mind, Mwamba added, "Minister, your wife seems to be reacting to something here, your infidelity," he put it bluntly to him. "Thus, what we have here is a cause and an effect," he reasoned.

"I see your point ba Mwamba," Chishala agreed. "However, my actions cannot justify such bad behaviour to desecrate the dead at their resting place, including the use of excessive force on a poor unarmed woman," he said. Mwamba nodded in agreement.

"In my position as minister," Chishala continued, "I shall be ruined both politically and financially should this story be leaked to the nosy members of the press," he told him. "I will lose my job and the negative impact will affect the whole family," he said. "The whole family," he emphasized.

"I shall talk to her sternly," Mwamba promised. "She will never repeat a silly stunt like this in future," he assured. The Minister nodded.

"She better never repeat an act like this," the minister said. "Otherwise, there will be no marriage to talk about." He threatened.

"I see," Mwamba replied curtly. "And as a man, I understand exactly how you feel."

"So, the question of self-defence on her part does not apply," the minister said. "What she has done is like a person setting her own house on fire in order to chase a little snake from the house." He reasoned.

"I will talk to her right away," Mwamba assured him again. They concluded their meeting on a lighter note by talking about tennis, a sport both of them immensely enjoyed. They arranged to play at Lusiku tennis club over the weekend.

Although Mwamba left knowing that his mission was partially successful, he had no illusions whatsoever; there was a lot of hard talking to be done with his niece. Chishala also knew that if there was anyone who could prevail on his wife, it was Uncle Mwamba. He therefore expected him to pump some sense into his wife's psyche.

However, what the minister didn't mention to his visitor was that an inquisitive reporter from a notorious private newspaper was already on his tail, asking him to pay a little fortune or else, the story involving his wife and his mistress would soon grace the front page of his newspaper. The corrupt and snooping reporter gave Chishala a 48 hours-ultimatum to pay up or else! The minister quickly, but quietly settled the issue fearing for his political career.

Thereafter, the minister shifted his attention to another important item; perusing through the agenda and documents for a cabinet meeting at state house, due in one hour's time.

CHAPTER 8

Fragile Economic Boom

Mwansa obtained more incriminating evidence and details of her husband's continued infidelity. She was hurt and felt rather embarrassed. She imagined that some people who knew her were already aware of her husband's perfidy; he had gone too far. She reasoned that she had already lost her marriage and had nothing else to protect.

With a pained heart, she went to Mboniwe's flat in the company of a friendly reporter and caused a nasty scene one evening. As arranged, her fight with her husband's mistress was subsequently reported on the front page of the Past Newspaper; to Chishala's annoyance. True to his character, Chishala insulted and intimidated his wife that night for humiliating him with her continued public misconduct. He warned her severely and threatened her with divorce again. For punishment, he chased her from a good government house they occupied in Morningdale. He further gave her one condition that she goes to her village to be counselled by banachimbusa(traditional marriage counsellors). She had to learn to be a decent wife to a cabinet minister, he commanded.

After further reflection and a meeting with Uncle Mwamba, she obliged, thinking that anything short of compliance would lead to divorce. She had to prevent divorce at any cost.

In the village, she went through her marital exile with mixed feelings but accepted her banishment as an inevitable bitter pill aimed at saving her failing marriage. However, she felt bad because she knew that she was the offended party which made her punishment more cruel and unfair. She also recalled that when she and Mboniwe fought, the good-for-nothing woman was very aggressive towards her, forgetting that she was the offender. Mboniwe went to the extent of biting her, leaving an ugly and indelible scar on her right cheek.

"Why are you bent on destroying my marriage?" She had asked her.

"Did I come looking for your husband?" Mboniwe asked. Mwansa hesitated to reply. "He came to propose to me," she continued.

"That doesn't give you an excuse to encourage him. You have no shame." Mwansa retorted.

"Where were you when he came chasing after me?" Mboniwe insisted. "It is not my fault." She defended herself.

"I warn you to leave my husband alone, or else." Mwansa intimidated.

"Or else what?" Mboniwe dared her. If I were you, I would firmly deal with my husband, instead of wasting time with an innocent person like me," she teased.

"I didn't know you are so rude." Mwansa said. "Where did my husband pick you from?" She asked. "From a cheap bar?" She further asked.

"It doesn't matter where we met," she answered. "Not a bar for your own information. We met at a five-star hotel." She bragged. "In any case, what's important is that he loves me. The biggest mistake you made was to try and kill me with your crazy friends at the old cemetery, because we have been very close since that incidence," she boasted again. "He can't love a skinny woman like you," Mwansa refuted. "I know him better than you do, he will soon dump you as he has done to many others."

"Those are others." Mboniwe responded. "I am totally different. I know how to treat a man, which you obviously don't seem to know." She bragged yet again.

"In any case, I know that what you are trying to do to me is in your family practice." Mwansa revealed. "Like your immoral sisters have done to other innocent women." She alleged.

"What do you mean?" Mboniwe asked with interest.

"Many people in the capital city know that your mother is a witch; she uses juju to ruin other women's marriages, and her daughters are the beneficiaries!" she insisted.

"That's a lie!" Mboniwe responded feebly. "You have no evidence." she said in a muted voice.

"Aren't your two elder sisters married to men whom they found already married?" She gave their names and some details. "I won't allow a witch like you to ruin my marriage," She warned. "Over my dead body!" The older woman ranted.

"That can be arranged with my mother!" Mboniwe said intimidatingly. Mwansa uttered no word. "Don't bother me. Leave me alone." Mboniwe shouted at the top of her voice, after realising that Mwansa had done her homework and was armed with negative information on her family. She also realised that Chishala's wife was dead scared of witchcraft. Mwansa drove quickly from the scene to avoid more embarrassment.

Instead of getting protection from her husband, Mwansa was banished to a remote village. It was like a double punishment. Obviously being a decent wife had not paid her any dividends; on the contrary, she was penalized for it. Nonetheless, Mwansa had hoped that her marriage counselling and training by traditional women in the village would save her marriage. Her grandmother kept encouraging her almost on a daily basis.

Upon her return from the village, Mwansa's hopes for things to get better were dashed. She was shocked to find that her husband had taken in her youthful arch-rival. She had moved into their matrimonial home as his new wife. She further learnt that during her brief absence,

Chishala had secretly married Mboniwe in a quiet civil procedure, to avoid any adverse publicity. To prevent their children being present at the time; he had sent them to Kasaba bay holiday resort, on the banks of Lake Tanganyika, on an all-expenses paid for vacation by their 'generous' father.

Mwansa was even more disappointed to learn that her husband had bought a nice and expensive car as a gift to Mboniwe. She thought her husband was extremely unfair. She remembered how they had sacrificed so much in the past when they were relatively poor, before the salaula business blossomed and started paying off. In fact, she had contributed to raising the initial capital to start sally's Boutique. What was so special about that skinny little woman anyway? She wondered, but rather belatedly. She concluded that her husband was mean and ungrateful.

A family meeting was held chaired by Uncle Mwamba. Mwansa described the pain and humiliation she had endured by being replaced by a naivelooking young woman, after all the sacrifices she had made in the marriage. While sympathising with her, most of the family members advised her to accept the situation and move on with her life. The meeting was inconclusive however, despite the majority advising her to file for bigamy so as to send Chishala to prison. This would teach the philandering Minister a lesson and would use him as an example, to deter other randy politicians from taking their marriage vows for granted. He would certainly be fined heavily for committing such a heinous offence.

Regardless, Mwamba and a few other senior family members advised her against litigation. They knew that the offence of bigamy was serious and non-bailable. It carried a very heavy fine and Chishala would definitely lose his job and be stigmatised in society forever. They were more worried about the future of the children, especially if their father went to prison. His imprisonment could also strain the relationship between her and the children, if she cut off their source of livelihood from their father.

The senior relatives therefore, advocated an out – of – court settlement which would also protect the future interests of the children. They coerced her not to take an antagonistic decision against the father of her children in her quest for revenge. Despite her earlier inclination to publicly humiliate her offending husband, Mwansa swallowed her pride and gave in and went for the out of court proposal advanced by her kith and kin.

Mwaka, one of Mwansa's accomplices at the cemetery incidence visited her as soon as she heard that her friend was experiencing more marital blues.

"Welcome my friend, how are you?" Mwansa greeted her warmly.

"I am just fine," Mwaka responded. "How have you been?"

"I could be better," Mwansa responded, "but am sure you heard that I have been divorced." She told her.

"No, I haven't," she answered. "What happened?"

"Nothing really. Except that my husband had changed." Mwansa lamented.

Mwaka nodded silently.

"Seems like political power had suddenly gone to his head!" She charged.

"Are you sure?" Mwaka asked. "Isn't he just like most Lusiku men? Changing women like shirts!" She postulated.

"Not at all." Mwansa replied. "He has had occasional affairs during our marriage," she sighed. "But this one was very different."

"What was different this time?" Mwaka asked.

"The difference was probably money and power," Mwansa explained. "In the past, he used to leave his girlfriends the moment he knew that I had wind of the affair. He used to dump them like hot potatoes."

"On this particular affair, did you tell him that you knew about it?" Mwaka probed.

"I did. We discussed it many times," Mwansa replied.

"And then?" Her friend asked further.

"Look at me. We even fought and that good-for-nothing skinny woman had the guts to bite me on my cheek!" She turned to the left and showed Mwaka the scar on her right cheek.

"No!" Mwaka exclaimed. I can't believe it." She stated.

"It is all over now." Mwansa conceded sorrowfully. "I can't fight her anymore," she pulled air in, and suddenly pulled it out. "I have lost everything." She cried. "Its now water under the bridge."

"I am so sorry," Mwaka sympathised. "Maybe we should have just disfigured her face with acid that day when we had the chance." She lamented. Mwansa smiled without saying a word. Her marriage was now like spilt milk; it was gone.

Chishala eventually realised that by punishing his first wife, he had been mean to her and to his children. The fact that he gave her a good out of court settlement and bought a house in a modest suburb for her and the children was not enough. What would happen to them if he suddenly died? He wondered, especially that he had not yet made a will; many Lusiku men didn't write wills, fearing that signing their last will and testament would probably trigger their own death. It was a primitive but common belief among some men.

There were also times when he gave her a lot of credit for having been a faithful and hardworking spouse. He resolved to support her no matter what, after realizing that he had wronged her by his actions, especially bringing Mboniwe to their matrimonial home. Mwansa didn't deserve that humiliation he reckoned.

In any case, he was very grateful to her for not going ahead with litigation for bigamy; if she had, he could have been ruined politically and financially. He would have also been languishing in jail. He now suspected that Mboniwe did not truly love him; she was probably lured by his status.

Chishala and some of his colleagues in the cabinet concluded that the previously declining economy had now opened-up to external capital injection and was progressively on the upswing. They praised their government's bold measures that had included the removal of exchange control regulations, tighter fiscal policies, and reduction in domestic borrowing by government and parastatals, bringing inflation down.

Under the new environment, many individuals, small and medium business organizations now freely embarked upon buying and selling ventures.

Armed with favourable information, Chishala thought of a way of empowering Mwansa to run her own business. However, as an economist, he suspected that the country's sudden economic growth was probably on a bubble, embedded rather on trade than production.

He was warmly received when he visited Mwansa one Saturday afternoon.

"Welcome home," Mwansa greeted, "this is a complete surprise. We were not expecting you."

"Good afternoon," he responded. "I know it has been a long while since we talked. The truth is I have missed you guys," he confessed.

They talked about a number of family issues, especially recent funerals, before he came to the main reason for his visit.

"Despite what happened in the past, it was not my intention to neglect you and the children," he said. "Please find some space in your heart to forgive me," he asked her. Mwansa nodded without saying a word. Her eyes, though less appealing probably due to worry, retained some of their youthful spackle.

"I have come to offer you financial support so that you go into business. I think it would be good for you to firmly stand on your own two feet." He sounded both serious and genuine.

"Thank you, father of my children," she replied. "This is very kind of you and I don't know how to thank you."

Chishala was distracted briefly by the sparkle in his former wife's eyes again. The eyes reminded him of her youth.

"You don't have to thank me yet," he advised, "after all, it's me, who should thank you for your civility. We would have been talking about something nasty if you had dragged me to the courts of law over our matrimonial differences," he countered diplomatically.

"As you know, I am not a serious business woman," she stated. "While I have sold a couple of paraphernalia imported from South Africa lately, I wouldn't know how to start a serious business concern as it were," Mwansa said, sounding honest.

"I know you. You already have a natural knack for business. With your usual commitment to assignments, all you need now is a little capital injection, moral support and some logistics for you to be up and about as a successful business person," he suggested. "I have no doubt you will be successful."

"You really mean your words?" She asked. "I hope it would be as simple as you put it," she said enthusiastically and smiled gently.

Those eyes, Chishala thought again. Those haunting eyes rather made his heart beat faster. Just like in the old days.

"I have no doubt in my mind," he assured her. "A number of serious women entrepreneurs today are making it already; what with our government's liberalization policy."

He gave her some details and examples on the subject; she felt greatly encouraged.

"Are you sure it can work as easily as that?" She asked with belated uncertainty inscribed all over her face.

"I mean it, mother of my children," he responded, to reassure her. "It will certainly work."

"That sounds really good," she smiled enthusiastically.

They discussed some details on the subject. He expanded on how many Zambican women were now involved in business. With dollars laden in their pockets, they would fly to South Africa or Dubai and other places and return with suitcases full of merchandise that they sold to individuals or shop owners; mostly Indians, Greeks or Lebanese that owned retail outlets. Sometimes, they obtained orders from institutions looking for imported merchandise or those planning events.

She asked a couple of searching questions but he assured her he would help her secure some initial orders with reputable shop owners.

He added, "if successful, which I can't doubt, you could extend the sourcing of merchandise further afield to countries such as China and Japan; the sky is the limit," he prophesied.

At the end of their meeting, he left her with some cash in the local currency, for local expenses and some of it in US Dollars. She couldn't believe it; it was indeed her lucky day; like winning a lottery in a dream-come-true experience. The rest was left with her to arrange travel plans after talking to some potential buyers and securing initial orders.

Mwansa was left wondering just how he had abruptly changed, and decided to support her that way without any request on her part. Who was she to reject a god sent gift anyway? That would be like looking a gift horse in the mouth, she resolved. She now thanked her stars and Uncle Mwamba in particular, for not dragging him to court, despite her strong feeling to teach him a lesson. She also remembered having called him all sorts of names. She reckoned that had he been languishing in prison; his new support could have not happened.

Chishala was delighted to learn that within a couple of months, Mwansa was looking forward to opening a new shop of her own; to concentrate on selling of wedding dresses and exclusive women's clothes and to have a permanent base to operate from. This would inevitably discard the image of a briefcase business person. She was extremely excited and the prospects were looking good. Chishala was particularly happy that the MMR government was succeeding where the ULP regime had lamentably failed. However, he also knew that the economic reforms largely aimed at empowering Zambican entrepreneurs, were at times being frustrated and hijacked by cartels and manoeuvres of some capitalist foreign investors with their own vested interests.

On the monetary side, the foreign exchange regime and interest rates had been liberalised leaving them to the open market of supply and demand, while excess liquidity was mopped up using open market operations. While this measure initially witnessed a violent rise in interest and exchange rates, they eventually stabilised after about 2 years, as the market became predictable, with confidence returning to the economy, as some foreign investments began trickling in.

The liberalization of trade imports and exports brought about a development in the economy, which most people had been waiting for. Riddled with chronic shortages of basic essential commodities, such as sugar, cooking oil, mealie meal, salt, etc, the situation suddenly changed. Big and small trading companies took advantage of the policy to import various goods and merchandise. Surprisingly, the shortages of essential commodities ended in just about 6 months of President Chaluma's administration. Thus, the endemic shortages prevalent during Jumbe's administration were quickly brought to an end. With more investment coming in, local production of many needed commodities started. This included bread, soap, cooking oil, drinks, toiletries, chemicals and a few others. Not surprisingly, Finance Minister Kasalu rubbed it in one day when he met the three notorious ULP MPs from the Eastern Province at Parliament. He said to them, "Just six months and the shortages are over! Compared with your 29 years of trial and error." They laughed but offered no defence.

It was now evident that the economic liberalization policies commenced by Chaluma's MMR truly transformed the country's economy as promised by the party during the 1993 elections campaign.

Now, inflation which was at 120 percent in 1993 and had practically destroyed the social fabric of the nation was brought down to 30 percent, even though this did not immediately fully reflect in prices or in the real value of wages and salaries. Chishala however, knew that the blossoming of the Zambican small and medium scale businesses was a clear achievement under President Chaluma. This was a vindication of their reasons for removing Jumbe's repressive and pro-socialist regime from power; not even the vocal and often biased opposition ULP party members would dispute.

Under the MMR, the economic reforms advanced considerably in the initial years, and significant changes in the economic policy regime were implemented, especially in the first three years. Within the first two years, the MMR government had completed the liberalisation of the external and domestic trade regime by eliminating tariffs and freeing the exchange rate and interest rates. Despite some exogenous shocks and sometimes, uneven implementation, the MMR government maintained an open trade regime. For instance, in october 2003, Zambica was one of the first countries in the region to implement the COMESA Free trade agreement.

Earlier, some formidable steps were also taken towards liberalising agricultural marketing and production. However, sporadic government involvement in the marketing of fertilizer, a critical production input for maize, the staple crop, contributed to market insecurity leading to an underperforming agricultural sector.

In any case, the agricultural sector suffered some setbacks under the MMR government. For instance, the ministry of finance and national planning gave farmers promissory notes, in lieu of actual payments. When the promissory notes were not honoured in good time, many farmers who had borrowed heavily from commercial banks, faced foreclosure threats at the time interest rates had ballooned. To mitigate huge losses or possible bankruptcy many commercial famers sold either farms, livestock or other assets. They were upset.

Nevertheless, the privatisation process was initially seen as successful, even on a world scale. For instance, the Zambican privatisation programme was hailed by the international press and the World Bank as one of the most successful, on a world scale.

Another business growth under President Chaluma was the transport sector, which under Jumbe had completely stagnated with bus owners having no capital to buy new motor vehicles or spares to service the routes in the capital city and the country. On the contrary, during Chaluma's first term, many Zambicans grabbed the opportunity of the waiver of customs duty on buses for a fixed period.

To begin with, most of them largely imported second hand motor vehicles, especially from Japan. Subsequently, minibuses replaced large expensive buses. In a short time, more minibuses arrived in the country and several routes were inundated with fleets of second-hand and new buses both large and small. This had the double impact of increased access to transport and reduced fares due to the high competition. Regardless, the travelling public was happy with the availability of cheap transport, which stimulated the expansion of small and medium businesses, coupled with the entrenchment of a rising Zambican middle class.

In no time, the Zambican transport system became a market driven competitive system founded by Zambicans and Zambican investors, with improving quality in terms of buses and services they offered. As President Chaluma had predicted before the reforms, instead of long queues of passengers at bus stops waiting for the buses, the opposite happened; the buses were now parked at the bus stops waiting for passengers!

Improvements in the transport sector were greeted with great relief by the travelling public. Under the previous regime, travelling under a crippled public transport sector using the United Bus Company of Zambica (UBZ) made provincial and rural area travel a nightmare – people had to wait for hours, in some cases days on long queues. To add insult to injury, the queues were controlled by the rough and rude ULP party cadres, commonly referred to as vigilantes, demanding payment or favours from passengers.

In a short time, the emergent middle class started to invest in property, such as real estate, to a level never seen in the country since the attainment of independence.

Even though Chaluma never provided direct financial support to the transport sector, the enabling environment created by his government was enough; it facilitated economic growth. In addition, Chaluma's government allowed the business sector to grow and thrive by allowing politicians to get involved in business ventures. This was a reversal of President Jumbe's rigid socialist rules and regulations, under the so-called leadership code.

Some challenges were however, experienced especially on unemployment. Even the MMR government at times, agreed that it failed to live up to expectations, although it sometimes blamed the failures on the ULP legacy, the global environment, lack of foreign aid and investment. The National Commission for Development Planning noted in its 1994 report that prospects for employment in 1995 were not very promising due to envisaged loss of jobs largely because of privatisation, retrenchment in the public sector, and continued credit squeeze while measures to control inflation were expected to cause a contraction in the economy and would also inhibit expansion in employment creation.

Its 1995 and 1996 reports were no different. It was evident, in most sectors that the results of the MMR's reform programmes were not very satisfactory. In fact, the Minister of Finance and National Planning then, made it clear to Parliament in his 1995 budget address, that in spite of the NERP and support from donors and lenders, some major challenges remained, especially inflation and unemployment, while low copper prices exacerbated the situation.

Strangely, forces of nature also seemed to gang-up against the new government, as a series of droughts devastated the 1993/1994 cropping season. If not well handled, the country was destined for starvation. However, the MMR government quickly worked out a strategy to avert serious hunger by sourcing yellow maize from Latin America. On a lighter note, witchcraft was suspected, as a possible cause, as rumours taking rounds in most Lusiku pubs were that Chaluma's electoral victory had certainly upset a combination of 'spirits' from Kwitonta and a neighbouring country.

While high expectations were justified, in relation to campaign promises made by the MMR, the environment was somewhat unfavourable. In May 1997, the country faced yet another severe drought. But unlike in the 1994 experience, the government was ready and made plans well beyond traditional reliance on foreign resources to assist affected communities. But rumours continued, especially in Lusiku and Kwitonta, that the combination of strong 'spirits' were still upset with what had happened in 1993! For a solution to the almost continuous droughts, it was suggested that witchdoctors be hired from Kwitonta and neighbouring Mawali, to exorcise and calm the upset 'spirits', to be followed by a traditional reconciliation between the adversaries, former President Jumbe and new President Chaluma.

As part of the privatisation programme, Zambica Airways was liquidated, rendering hundreds of workers unemployed, thus swelling the ranks of the 70,000 public employees already retrenched. Thus, instead of bringing Zambicans together, the privatisation programme seemed to alienate some people, creating pockets of opposition; those that had been laid off, inevitably blamed the government for their plight.

Some insiders were actually more sympathetic to the President, as his lack of experience in government seemed to have been exploited by some of his senior Ministers, especially those with vested interests. While the President was trying to clearly comprehend the challenges facing the Zambican airline, one interested Minister belonging to the notorious Abercon Mafia group had already leaked a cabinet resolution over the matter, to a representative of donors. Subsequently, the President was embarrassed at a closed-door meeting with some donors, when he was told bluntly that, "we are aware Mr President that while your cabinet is divided over the issue, the majority are in favour of the privatisation of the loss-making airline."

The President's jaw dropped, 'Who the hell was the mole leaking sensitive cabinet decisions to donors?' He wondered. This added more pressure on President Chaluma as he had already been accused of procrastination, despite his earlier commitment to the privatisation process, during the 1993 election campaign.

The economy also suffered some knocks; the IMF, World Bank and a few other co-operating partners wanted a speedy privatization of state enterprises. It was therefore, alleged that Chaluma embarked on privatisation of several companies in a hurry except those he felt were strategic, such as in mining, insurance, telecommunications, power generation, banking and textiles. In any case, President Chaluma had to deliver on privatization, one of his strong campaign promises, which made him the darling of western countries. In 1994, the Zambica Privatization Agency, sold almost 150 government companies to multinational corporations and private hands. It was rumoured that while Chaluma was under intense pressure to deliver on this front, some nationals wanted him to hold on to security-related companies.

Some economic analysts questioned lack of transparency and accountability, regarding privatisation proceeds – where was the money going and how accurate were the evaluations by liquidators? Lack of transparency seemed to be the case in the bid for one Kolala based antelope Mine, where a conclusive process to Last Quantum was halted against accepted world practice, especially that a new bidder, Lenani of India, that was allowed to join the negotiations at the last minute won the bid. This upset Last Quantum, alleging that their bid details had been leaked to Lenani, a company without any mining experience for that matter.

Old President Jumbe, trying hard to revive his old popularity never kept quiet either and joined the debate and often asked about where the privatisation proceeds were banked and also suspected some underhand methods in the process. As expected, Jumbe's involvement brought more excitement to the privatisation debate, while some well-read historians asked the old man to stop throwing stones while living in a glass house.

Jumbe was quickly reminded of his nationalisation programme whose details, including amounts raised remained a closely guarded secret between him and a few he had trusted and appointed for the exercise. It was also further argued that strangely some key players in the transactions became filthy rich in the process. The former President subsequently kept quiet, while Chaluma was happy with the outcome of the debate.

Under the MMR reforms, domestic resource mobilization for public investment was also changed. Tax collection from three government departments was transformed into an independent statutory body, the Zambica Revenue Authority (ZRA). This ended the civil service mentality, as workers were now hired on performance – based contracts. Subsequently, revenue collection improved tremendously, with ZRA often meeting targets or exceeding them, providing needed resources to support the health and education sectors, construction of roads and other public infrastructure and reducing government dependence on donor funding in national budgets.

The MMR government had also liberalised the telecommunications sector, making it competitive and communication improved. It was during this period that the first cell phones came into the country. On a lighter note, it is rumoured that the first service provider for cell phones had actually approached the ULP government, to supply the phones, whose concept was new in the region at the time. However, when Jumbe informed his cabinet, largely composed of old politicians, about the idea of a phone working without wires, most of them laughed and scoffed at the provider, suspecting him as a possible conman! Thus, the proposal was rejected, thereafter, until the new MMR government quickly implemented the project.

With the socialist policies of the ULP government, Zambicans were perpetually confined to poverty, as it was a crime under the socialist leadership code to own property or assets. Sometimes, Zambicans felt sorry for themselves. How come citizens in countries they helped liberate, such as Mibiana, Mozambique, Zimbabwe and South Africa were effective players in their countries' economies; they were making money, buying assets and some even invested well in manufacturing and other serious enterprises. They also felt very strongly about the question of owning land. Land was a birthright, and bequeathed to them at birth. How come this particular inheritance was not fulfilled by the previous government while in power for almost three decades? Was it a curse to be ruled by a socialist regime? Some asked.

President Chaluma often lamented about the high levels of poverty endured by Zambicans, largely thrust on them by their own government. Ownership of property or the lack of it often troubled the President. His government decided to empower some Zambicans to buy and own houses cheaply. All public enterprises that owned houses, rented council houses, government pool houses, and similar units were offloaded to sitting tenants at giveaway prices. Subsequently, some Zambicans owned houses legally and title deeds were quickly processed in their names. In doing so, former tenants were liberated from the 'slavery' of tenancy while the enterprising ones turned their new homes into rest houses, lodges, offices or motels. This created some business activities, local employment and transformed some individuals from being perpetual tenants to landlords!

House empowerment notwithstanding, the President was aware that empowering citizens with land was outstanding. As a member of the ULP youth League at Kabombe secondary school, he remembered how JJ and his colleagues used to campaign against poverty induced by the colonial government, and made several promises to change the situation once their party came into government. Some of their promises included three meals per day, one egg per person per day but one of the biggest promises was free land, as people's birthright. How come ULP leaders never followed up on their several promises once in power including the issue of land ownership? He reflected. His party must make the difference. He promised.

However, Chishala felt that objectively, the economy itself could have fared even better. He reasoned that the protraction of the implementation of the IMF imposed structural adjustment programme somewhat hurt the economy and apparent indicators were there to see. The base lending rates escalated in a short time and this particularly slowed down progress in the agricultural sector. Under the circumstances, some enterprising business people, especially observant foreigners, borrowed huge amounts from commercial banks and, instead of investing in agriculture or any meaningful productive business ventures to benefit the locals, instead bought government treasury bills, where high interest rates of around 50 percent at the time were assured, with the cash from the treasury.

Was the government sleeping? Some observers wondered. Since it was easier to externalise funds under MMR's liberalised regulations, it hurt the local economy, in the long run.

After playing Lawn tennis Chishala and Kaluba were having drinks with two women friends at the Lusiku tennis club one evening. One of the women, Towera, shouted "I love you Minister of Defence. With you on my side I feel totally safe and well protected." She beamed and leaned towards Chishala who in turn welcomed her with open hands.

"Thank you, honey." Chishala said, "but please don't shout. Keep your voice down." He advised. Though the bar was scantily populated, Chishala figured there could be some nosy journalists. He did not want to be a head liner during the celebration season. He also feared if his wife got wind of it, she would hit the highest roof top. Come to think of it, he should have been celebrating with her. He also feared they could be in the company of some ULP die-hards who were still hurt the deepest, by their very first loss in decades. He reminded himself that a wounded animal is the most dangerous.

"The most important thing is that the MMR has restored and stabilised the country's economy." Lungowe brought Chishala back to the bar. "I am very happy that shortages of essential commodities are now history."

"Wait a second. Do you really expect everything to get back to normal in just a short time? The former government really did a lot of damage. I don't think it will be that easy and fast." Chishala stated, in order to provoke the two women.

"No, no, no, comrade. Do not dampen spirits here. Lungowe and Towera, are you happy with our party and what it has achieved so far?" Kaluba asked, joining in ignoring his friend's cautious approach.

"Happy?" Lungowe quipped. "We are not happy. We are actually thrilled," she answered.

Towera raised her wine glass and clinked it with that of Chishala. When Kaluba tried to toss his too, Lungowe quickly extended hers. The two ministers exchanged knowing looks and smiled. These girls were keepers even though they knew the two ministers were married and possibly had numerous other side chicks. Towera, especially, made sure she used her time to the fullest with her big catch. This was her once in a week golden moment with Chishala. She winked at him, sipped a little and cleared her throat, then licked her red lips and said, "you see Lungowe, my sweetheart here is right." She then took Chishala's wine glass, sipped from it, deliberately painting it with her red lipstick and then planting a vicious kiss on his lips.

What a show, Kaluba thought. He felt a tightening in his throat. Was it jealousy? Chishala always got the beautiful, smart, intelligent, innovative and sexy ones, he thought deeply. Was he too slow? "Towera, what do you mean minister Chishala is right? You seem to be well vest in what is going on." Kaluba was trying the hardest to find ways to entertain this young lady who was seemingly oblivious of the fact that they were in a public place and they were ministers in Chaluma's cabinet. They needed to be careful or else they would be the talk of the town. That would be embarrassing. But he was also sizzling with jealousy, of course while Lungowe was busy gulping one glass of wine, after another. She was not as elaborate as Towera. "Minister Kaluba, we all believe that MMR is here to rebuild walls that had been broken down by the former regime. That won't be easy. But for women, due to the improved business environment so far, many now feel they are being empowered. They will now do very well in business," Towera, cut in. "Because of this development, many people, especially women are very happy with the ruling party and the bold economic measures of President Chaluma." She said. "President Jumbe was scared of implementing tough economic measures." she reasoned.

"This then confirms that the removal of old Jumbe and his ULP from power has paid dividends." Lungowe concurred.

"I'll drink to that," Chishala shouted, at the top of his voice, forgetting his earlier instruction to Towera, to keep her voice down. That did attract stares from the other patrons in the bar.

"Cheers," Kaluba shouted, raising his beer glass for a toast. The women friends joined them in the toast.

To divert the attention of the people who were now glued on the four, the two happy Ministers decided to buy drinks for all the patrons present at the club. With that out of the way, the four jolly lovers continued their celebrations mixed with political discussions. Towera had discovered that Chishala got tickled easily by politics. Any other topic sounded a bore. Slow Lungowe needed to learn that too.

"Have you seen how many people are now thronging soweto market?" Towera asked excitedly. "From nowhere, soweto is now packed with all sorts of vegetables and wares. If we continue like this, Zambica will in no time be the bread basket of Central and Southern Africa." She suggested.

"Mhm. That's true. It makes sense." That was all Kaluba could say.

"It does. Towera, you are deep in politics I can see." Chishala said proudly. "How can I not when I spend part of my life with an intelligent and popular politician? A senior minister for that matter? I am a good student, right?" Towera wriggled excitedly in Chishala's embrace.

"Lungowe, would you want to add anything, sweetheart?" Kaluba cut in. Unfortunately, his escort was already tipsy. But he patiently waited for her to respond. She struggled to raise her head and to open her mouth. All she could do was mumble one or two senseless disjointed phrases, unrelated to politics.

"Haa. Add more wine you mean? Yes I would love some more. These dunked wings are heavenly." Lungowe was gone to Kaluba's disappointment. He had hoped she would give intelligent political contributions like Towera. Instead, she was more interested in drinking and munching the chicken wings. What a waste! This meant Chishala once again had an upper hand; Mwansa, Mboniwe and now Towera. He will one day avenge his heavy defeats. He mentally made a promise.

"Leave her to enjoy herself. Knowing Lungowe, she will be snoring in no time." Towera rubbed it in. "Many people are hailing the new government, your government, for improving the transport system as well. We hear there will be buses and trains to all the 9 provinces. JFC is the man. He is a genius!"

"What about me? Am I not the man'?" Chishala teased.

"Ah ah! Look at your friend swimming in the deep lake of jealousy! No offence, but with my height can I ever entertain someone whose height is up to my hip? Heh minister Kaluba?" Towera knew just how to get the attention of these two men. She had them wound around her small finger. She was happy. Her seductive nature was already paying off. Minister Kaluba could not take off his eyes from her and this made Chishala very uncomfortable.

"What? Me, jealousy? No way. Try another description or tactic. Anyway, you mentioned transport system. What are people saying? What have you heard? What is the reaction of the people? I mean what is the response?" Chishala heaped his questions on Towera just to keep her busy.

"Phew!" Towera exhaled forcefully. "Do you want me to write a dossier?"

"I'm just curious my love. When we meet the boss tomorrow morning I will be able to lay it on the table." Chishala spoke slowly and lovingly.

"As I said, my darling minister Chishala, so far people are generally very happy. They are singing praises to god for sending a little Moses right on time. People cried and the Lord heard them." Towera said. "We believe JFC has it all. The good thing is that he also picked up his cabinet prayerfully and carefully. Is that because he declared our country a Christian Nation?" This Towera woman had her way with words. Kaluba reflected again and the winner is still Chishala, he concluded.

The two ministers and indeed the other male patrons succumbed to Towera's seductive tactics. When Chishala saw that all eyes, including those of his friend Kaluba, seemed to feast on his girl, he became very uncomfortable and insecure. Towera saw it too and quickly decided to visit the powder room. She knew her guy very well. Lungowe, on the other hand, was struggling to say something sensible. It was like getting water from a rock. She snuggled comfortably in Kaluba's embrace as if his potbelly and chest were her final haven of rest.

They continued drinking and chatting into the wee hours of the morning. Towera had been schooled well by her sisters: Never empty your very first wine glass when you are in the company of a 'sugar daddy'. As a result, she was not drunk when everyone else was seeing 20 fingers on her one hand. The two ministers were right where she wanted them; especially Chishala. The following day, the two Ministers informed the President about his increased popularity and that of the MMR. Kaluba went to the extent of advising the head of state to call a snap election, in order to catch the sleeping opposition unawares. While he was happy, the President laughed, he laughed; with some kind of scorn which brought tears from his small eyes.

Despite what some experts and a few disgruntled opposition MPs had said about the performance of the economy under Chaluma, many citizens were very happy about the economy, and their views were well represented by the two women Towera and Lungowe, in the company of the two Ministers at the club. For them Chaluma had liberated the country economically, in a short time; long and irritating queues for essential commodities were no more; shops and supermarkets were full of goods; the economy had been opened up to the extent that those who were enterprising and businessminded were doing their own thing – buying here and selling there.

Also, there were visible and practical important fundamental changes in the economy. While economists and other experts worried more about the stability of micro – and macro-indicators in the economy, these were dismissed by the majority as insignificant, because they never brought food on the table. In any case, while economic indicators were not visible to the common man, essential commodities were, and met people's everyday needs.

Kaluba and Chishala were certain that the majority of the voters in the country were still supportive of their economic liberator, aka red, Ka Moses, who had inherited a shattered economy from former President Jumbe and yet like a little magician, he did so much, to achieve a good measure of recovery, in a relatively short space of time. What some people say now made sense…that big things come from small parcels.

The economic achievements brought hope and built a firm foundation for further economic growth. Believe it or not, there was a boom in the country's economy, they concluded.

CHAPTER 9

A Missed Opportunity

The excitement that was there after the first elections won by the MMR was seemingly dying down. Almost every corner of Zambica was talking about the MMR propaganda. Even school children were finding politics an interesting topic. Break time, lunch time and short and long walks back home were punctuated with heated debates on how MMR had either achieved this or failed to achieve that. Women in the high density suburbs and in villages exchanged salt while talking about how politics was a dirty game. Village drunks too, competed in displaying their knowledge on where Chaluma had messed up or where he had excelled. Teachers and lawyers silently but craftily expressed their opinion to all who had ears to hear. Interesting scenario it was.

"My learned friend, any other party would have won the 1993 elections. People had been fed up of a one-party state scenario. You know when people get tired of nshima every day, the day they are given a choice between the same nshima and simply boiled sweet potatoes, three quarters will go for the sweet potatoes. Bottom line, people want change. Mr Ngomwalo, a well-known law lecturer submitted his analysis to his lawyer friend, Mr Sabe, as they were sipping slowly their wine.

"You are very right my learned friend. Remember the ancient and popular Lemba saying: 'to be remembered as a great leader, a shrewd leader picks a weak and ordinary person as a successor,'?" Mr Sabe asked his friend as a matter of fact.

"Yes. But where are you leading to?" Ngomwalo couldn't pick the direction his learned friend was on.

"Don't be impatient Ngomwalo! I am getting there. The same Lemba saying condemns such a shrewd ruler as selfish; thinking only of himself, or herself, and not his or her own country."

"I hear you counsel, I hear you now. You remind me of how former President Jerome Jumbe tried a young man from the Southern Province, mostly unknown, whom he had earlier made the Prime Minister, to take over from him as party President. However, President Jumbe must have totally forgotten that 'ancient and popular' Lemba saying when he later humiliated and unseated his own chosen successor in very suspicious circumstances." Mr Ngomwalo was now getting warmed up.

"Exactly. I wonder why you left the bar. You are good analytically my friend. You are good." He praised.

"Don't flatter me my learned friend. You know very well that those of us with big mouths could not have survived the JJ regime." Mr Ngomwalo burst out laughing. "Remember our learned lecturer saying flies cannot land on some people's mouths because the lips are ever moving." Once again the two friends' ribs cracked with laughter.

"And that was exactly what exposed the old man's ploy and confirmed what many people had suspected all along; President Jumbe wanted to rule forever, and would therefore not pick a successor." Mr Sabe concluded as he downed another long sip of his almost empty glass of wine.

"True indeed," Ngomwelo said. "But James Francis Chaluma was forced on President Jumbe by the people who wanted change. In this case, the flip side of that ancient and popular Lemba saying applied to his successor, President Chaluma. This was due to all the political and economic blunders old Jumbe committed in 29 years of his rule, and the outpouring support Chaluma received upon coming to power, from Zambicans and the international community." The conversation was truly that of lawyers and it was now getting legally deeper.

"But did the political engineer take advantage to distinguish himself as a good leader or even greater leader than his predecessor?" Ngomwalo asked a rhetorical question. "In the run up to the 1998 general elections, the first elections under its rule, the MMR seemed to face many challenges, some self-inflicted. Instead of consolidating on economic recovery, where some of the MMR stalwarts like Minister Chishala thought they had fared well, under the circumstances, they seemed to be pre-occupied with something else. The ruling party is no longer focusing on the main issues, which had brought them into power."

The two friends continued with their analysis of the underlying issues in the current politics. Of course they were not the only ones talking politics. It was the topic of each minute and breath.

Some opposition party members told Chishala off on several occasions concerning the economy. They told him that there was no real economic achievement for his party to write home about. In fact, some opposition members of parliament sometimes argued that the MMR government was mismanaging the economy. But Chishala dismissed their arguments, as sour grapes, from chaps who were still in denial and had refused to accept their humiliating defeat in 1993. In fact, denial of electoral defeat had now become siamese twins with the United Liberation Party!

However, as their name suggested, MMR was expected by many to enhance democracy in a multi-party dispensation. On the contrary, President Chaluma's party started to embark on what seemed to many like repressive electoral reforms, whose objective was not appreciated by some in the conservative circles and rather resented by the main opposition. Even some independents asked several questions which begged for answers. For instance, were electoral reforms a top priority at the time? Then, if the electoral system was biased in 1993, could the MMR have won handsomely against a well-entrenched and seasoned political party like the ULP? Thus, to many, the ruling party was merely on an electoral journey, designed by themselves, for themselves.

With growing disaffection, especially on the alleged internal repression, some leaders in the ruling party started getting pessimistic about their chances at the polls due in one year's time.

Chishala's friend, Kaluba, the Minister of Local government and Housing headed the President's think tank to assess the main political threat to the ruling party; the main challenges and needed measures to ensure that MMR continued its grip on power.

The Presidential and general elections were due in 1998 and most senior members of the party set their sights on retaining political power, in order to continue reaping associated monetary, material and other benefits. Even though Chishala was not a member of the think tank, he knew the main contents of the secret report sent to the President by the committee's chairperson. Kaluba had asked him to secretly proof-read the executive summary of the long report.

After attending a press conference addressed by the President, Chishala was left with no doubt; he knew what the head of state was insinuating in the electoral reforms. The President announced the creation of a permanent and autonomous election commission of five members; all the previous committees were on ad-hoc basis. The mandate of the elections body was to conduct elections, including local government elections, and to delimit constituencies. However, he felt that the body's composition needed approval by Parliament.

While Chishala expected many people to welcome the creation of an independent and permanent elections body, he doubted whether its autonomy would be recognised since its members, including its chairperson would be directly appointed by the President. He thought that for its credibility, such an important body ought to be appointed by the Chief Justice or Parliament. However, for obvious reasons, he kept his progressive, but dissenting views tightly locked and vaulted in his chest.

The other important item announced by President Chaluma was to do with the registration of voters; he stated that KUVUNI a private international company from Denmark was engaged by the government to carry out voter registration to capture eligible voters for the elections due in 1998.

Despite accepting the authority and mandate of government to engage such a service provider, Chishala was apprehensive about consensus to avoid problems after the elections; it was necessary to obtain consent from the major stakeholders, in order to put this issue to bed, once and for all. He recalled that voter registration was a fundamental issue for the credibility and fairness of any elections.

Chishala also knew that like him, some of his fellow Ministers in Chaluma's cabinet harboured the same views as he did, but dared not oppose a position endorsed by their leader to avoid risking losing their well-paying jobs. He still reckoned at the time, that there were very few jobs that carried so much influence and were reasonably well paying in the country, as that of a cabinet Minister. No wonder, many people were now jostling for becoming members of parliament, at a rate never seen in the country before.

Even more contentious than the electoral reforms were the constitutional reforms, which MMR suddenly embarked upon as if its political survival solely depended on them. Chishala did not see the need as well as the hurry for this second wave of reforms. In any case, the political reforms looked more discriminatory than the electoral reforms. The MMR was agitating for a new constitution, requiring that both the parents of a Presidential candidate should be Zambicans by birth or descent. Furthermore, a person who had been elected to the office of Republican President of Zambica on two previous occasions would not qualify to contest the elections.

In addition, chiefs were now required to give up chieftaincy in order to contest parliamentary elections. These proposed amendments to the republican constitution raised a lot of eyebrows in the country. The proposals were highly contested among opposition political parties. The proposed reforms were also opposed by some democrats within the ruling party as well as some non-nationals and naturalised Zambicans, especially those who had supported the country's liberation struggle and the reintroduction of multi-party politics.

Chishala and his close friend Kaluba had a heated discussion over the issues one Friday evening.

"You don't seem to understand the damage these reforms will cause to our party," Chishala said thoughtfully.

"What damage are you worried about?" Kaluba asked. "As a new party, there is no harm in implementing political reforms."

"But where exactly are these political reforms taking us?" Chishala asked. "Nowhere'" he answered his own question and continued, "especially that they are parallel to our own party constitution."

Kaluba cleared his throat, before answering. "Well, you will agree with me that Jumbe and his ULP overstayed in power, right?" Kaluba asked. Chishala nodded in agreement.

"In the process, his party, and government messed up everything." He continued. "MMR has the people's mandate to clean up the mess," Kaluba sounded confident.

"But Minister, you are now opening a door which is already ajar." Chishala contested. "We all know that Jumbe overstayed in power; one of the reasons for easily booting him out." Kaluba nodded.

"But some of Jumbe's mistakes ought to be corrected." Kaluba insisted while Chishala smiled. "Don't you think?" He asked.

"Minister, how can we correct a historic fact?" He asked him. "Jumbe ruled Zambica for a 29 year period. No one will ever change that." Chishala thought his friend's views were completely off the subject. Kaluba kept quiet.

"Then, you know as well as I do that the constitutional amendments we have proposed are not only contentious; they are also highly subjective." Chishala continued. "They are targeted at specific individuals."

"Which individuals are you talking about?" Kaluba asked, as if he didn't know them.

"The citizenship clause is targeted at Jumbe, one of our early freedom fighters who was also our first Republican President,"

Chishala replied, "while the chieftainship clause is aimed at his party Vice President, who happens to be a senior chief. What more evidence do you need Minister?" he challenged him.

"No!" Kaluba protested. "These reforms mean well for our country. Surely there's little wisdom in trying to recycle and give another chance to a 73 year old man who had ruled the country for 29 years, to return to ruin the country further." He said. "The same shall apply to all in his position." Chishala nodded.

Kaluba explained further, "the indigenous clause added to the new constitution is historic."

"What do you mean historic?" Chishala asked.

"The previous constitutional commissions during JJ's rule had recommended it," he explained.

"As for former President Jumbe, the man sacrificed so much to liberate this country," Chishala reminded him. "In addition, he ruled this country for almost 29 years and developed education and put up a lot of infrastructure. What will the international community think about the Movement for Multiparty Restoration? In any case, what shall we gain by stopping him now?" He asked.

"We shall gain something," Kaluba responded. "Jumbe abruptly changed his party's constitution many times to stop others from challenging him." Kaluba said. "This time, he's on the receiving end and reaping what he had sown!" Chishala remained silent.

"As for the chief, he superintends on subjects who belong to different political parties. If he runs on one-party's ticket, he will cease to be objective in handling subjects belonging to other political parties and consequently chiefs will lose the respect of their subjects. So these reforms are well intended." Kaluba insisted.

"Good point." Chishala nodded.

"Jumbe grossly abused the constitution of this country and that of his own party," Kaluba continued. "Someone has to correct the mistakes," he suggested.

"On the contrary it's our party making a grave mistake this time around." Chishala stressed, to break the obvious silence. "We should not take this route. It is a dangerous one," he warned.

"But Jumbe used to change constitutions in a very subjective manner and nobody cried foul." Kaluba alleged.

"Give a specific example," Chishala challenged him.

"How about 1980?" Kaluba asked.

"How about 1980?" Chishala asked back, trying to remember.

"He changed the ULP constitution just four days before the party conference," he paused. "It was an act targeted at Simon Mulenga Wampanga, John Mwendalubi and Robert Chalwe, to prevent them from challenging him for the party presidency." Chishala recalled and nodded. Kaluba smiled.

"It was bad, I recall," Chishala agreed. "But circumstances were quite different." He pointed out.

"What was the difference? The changes were still subjective." Kaluba insisted.

'The main difference is that it was during the one-party rule.' Chishala explained.

"One-party state my foot!" Kaluba retorted. "One-party state was introduced against people's wishes, and the worst part is that the proposed amendments were implemented before they were approved by delegates, by a show of hands at the conference." He emphasized. "That act was totally unconstitutional."

Chishala reflected silently for a short while before responding. "Regardless, two wrongs don't make a right," he argued. "Most importantly, we condemned all constitutional abuses in 1993 and won easily at the polls. Should we start making the same mistakes? If we do, observant Zambicans will kick us out." He sighed. "And they won't wait for us, as long as they did for Jumbe." He warned.

"Minister, you are also exaggerating the issue," Kaluba said. "Nobody, except a small number of Jumbe's sycophants will want to recycle an old tired politician." He answered. "And at the moment, Zambicans want to go forward, not backwards."

"I am sure everyone else will read it the way it looks." Chishala responded. "Especially in the region where Jumbe is still revered as the liberator of Southern Africa." He sighed.

"Why should they?" Kaluba mumbled. "You seem to be reading in between the lines."

"Because we are backdating the period he has already served." Chishala replied, "that's why." He emphasised. "It is very clear."

"I don't think so," Kaluba said. "Nobody will notice." He suggested. "Only philosophers like you will do that. Come to think of it, you should be teaching philosophy at a university, and not running a government ministry." He suggested.

"To be honest with you, many people including the international community will think that we are scared of JJ," Chishala insisted to break the obvious silence. "We beat the old man badly in the past when he was in charge; using the same old constitution. Why can't we beat him fairly for the second and last time and silence him and his supporters for good?" He asked. Silence pervaded the room. "Many people will think that due to the apparent resurgent popularity of the former President across the country, our party has sneaked in a constitutional clause, intended to bar him from standing as a Presidential candidate in the 1998 Presidential and general elections," Chishala insisted.

Kaluba listened thoughtfully. "As for the chief," Chishala continued, "he is of no consequence. Why should we give him the attention he doesn't deserve?"

"Well, that's beside the point," Kaluba responded. "The bottom line is that chiefs should concentrate on local government and traditional affairs," he said. "They should leave party politics to politicians, like us," he suggested, evading his friend's direct questions.

"But every person, including a chief, has a constitutional right to indulge in politics if he or she so chooses," Chishala pointed out. "I see nothing wrong with that. And the constitution is very clear about people's rights of association, whether they are chiefs, or not." Chishala said. "We should play a preventive role as political leaders." He suggested.

"You are wrong my friend." Kaluba responded. "We don't want chaos and confusion between chiefs and their subjects in this country." He stressed.

"Are you sure?" Chishala asked him.

"I am very sure," Kaluba responded. "Most of all, I am happy that God Almighty loves this country called Zambica. He anointed Chaluma to rule after Jumbe for a very good reason." He suggested.

"What do you mean? What good reason?" Chishala asked.

"History has come full circle my friend." He quoted Galatians 6:7, "Be not deceived; God is not mocked; for whatever a man sowed, that shall he also reap.' Chishala looked down, somewhat defeated.

They continued debating for a long while with no sign of some compromise on any single issue, as the polarity in their arguments seemed to increase with time. It was reminiscent of the growing divergence on these issues, even in Chaluma's cabinet. The only difference was that in cabinet, those with divergent views like Chishala were inhibited from expressing them openly. They quietly and safely kept their dissenting views to themselves, under the guise of collective responsibility.

While the debate for and against constitutional reforms continued in the country, ULP felt most aggrieved. Some of their members protested in different ways, but to no avail.

As if MMR had foreseen people and their parties going for litigation, they had sneaked in a preventive clause; that the nomination and election of a person as President could only be challenged in court by petition after the elections had been held. The question was, why after the elections? This meant that the appellant would be dealing directly with the accused, with the latter having the upper hand, through Presidential powers. Some political engineering for sure!

Despite Chaluma being the darling of the West during the 1993 elections, and early in his first term, the situation rapidly changed soon after he was seen to have excluded Jumbe from the 1998 elections, much as Minister Chishala had feared. As if the head of state got wind of some subtle but growing internal discontent about the proposed amendments to the constitution, he gave Chishala, Kaluba and two other Ministers a confidential assignment to assess the extent of the internal dissatisfaction; how it would affect election results, if the rift became open and to suggest the way forward.

In their concise confidential report to the head of state, the four Ministers confirmed that the discontent did exist within the party ranks, but that its threat was minimal. The report also projected that the most likely outcome was resignation of affected members from the ruling party to join any of the existing parties or to form their own parties. The two main recommendations were for the President to have private talks with the identified ringleaders; offer them a small political carrot and assure them of their continued value in the ruling party. The other one was on the extreme; to preempt the impact, and just fire the affected officials and probably expel them from the ruling party.

When Chishala and the others signed the rather subjective report to the President, Kaluba laughed mockingly. He felt he had the last laugh on his colleague; how come he had also signed, in view of the democratic tenets and principles he always loudly professed, especially when they debated the issues privately? He accepted that like himself, African politicians were deceptive, because most of them openly expounded what their leaders wanted to hear and not what they fervently professed or believed in. However, Chishala harboured opposite views. He felt that his friend was the real chameleon who put his own beliefs in the cooler, in order to propound his boss's views; typical of a chap with a banana backbone, he quipped!

As expected, the ULP's central committee analysed the constitutional reforms and concluded that the reforms were neither for the benefit of the country nor other parties. ULP leaders reasoned that the reforms were targeted at their party and their two leaders, in particular.

In their fury, ULP leaders stated that the Movement for Multiparty Restoration was damn scared of competing with them on an even playing field or else they would lose the elections. This somewhat boosted their morale and confidence. They now openly announced that MMR was a failed project, because the party did not deliver most of their campaign promises to the people. They further argued that the MMR had messed-up the democratization process because they wouldn't dare compete with the ULP in free and fair elections.

Subsequently, the ULP President held a press briefing stating, "the ULP strongly denounces the cowardly acts of the ruling party," said former President Jumbe to national and international journalists at Liberation House, his party headquarters in the capital city's central business district located on Egypt Road.

"The political repression by our brothers and sisters in the ruling party must be stopped immediately to allow for a level democratic playing field for all our people. We call upon the international community to join the ULP in condemning unwarranted verbal attacks by the MMR on ULP members. The ruling party has indiscriminately attacked our members in the morning; they have attacked us in the day and at night. Man is a sacred creature created in god's image, but our comrades in the MMR feel they are above fellow Zambicans who hold different political views." He sighed. "In their acts, they have turned Zambica into Animal Farm, and they believe they are more equal than all non-MMR citizens!" He said.

"I also wish to state clearly in the open that the ULP has no faith whatsoever in KUVUNI getting involved in voter registration; it is a recipe for rigging elections. I irrevocably state that the ruling party has singularly targeted the ULP, in order to exclude its membership from taking part in the 1998 elections. This is not the spirit of inclusiveness and selflessness upon which Zambica was founded," he said.

"I warn our inexperienced comrades in government that the country may be drifting towards a blood bath, if the MMR leadership does not stop its members from carrying out uncalled for cold-hearted, callous attacks on their brothers and sisters in the opposition. This is cowardly and undemocratic. Zambica was founded on the platform of One Zambica One country, so that all humans within our boundaries: black, white, yellow, – live in harmony. I wish to put it on record that the gallant ULP is the only credible opposition, in this country, without which the forthcoming elections will be a sham." He fumed.

The country's founding President, now in the opposition was apparently overcome with grief. Jumbe produced his famous green bandana and wiped out tears. "Comrades, I now wish to announce a major development in the history of our nation." Again, Jumbe paused and went through the theatrical motion of wiping out tears. Photojournalists jostled to strategic positions and readied their cameras to record the unfolding historic drama.

Jumbe went ahead, and announced that his party and five other allied parties had decided to boycott the so – called elections in which case MMR would only be running against small and new parties, to which his followers applauded. In view of their U-turn on democracy, he asked the ruling party to change their name from Movement for Multi-party Restoration (MMR) to Movement for Democracy Mutilation (MDM), to further applause from his audience.

It was later disclosed that while they resented the letter and spirit of President Chaluma's reforms, the majority of ULP central committee members wanted the party to contest the elections. They needed to avoid handing the MMR a blank cheque and not disappoint their local and international funders who had already contributed very generously to the cost of the envisaged elections. It is however, said that the ULP leader was furious and terribly upset for being excluded from the ballot and ordered his party to boycott the elections, which was a political blunder.

Despite being sympathetic to ULP under the circumstances, most citizens condemned the party's decision to boycott the elections, giving a carte blanch opportunity to the ruling party, since it was the main opposition party, while the other opposition parties were new and relatively small.

With increased polarity between the ruling party and the main opposition party, some people concluded that despite their stark differences in height and stature and being vehemently opposed to one another, President Chaluma and former President Jumbe had something in common; both of them being stubborn. Nevertheless, a good number of observers took delight in the idea of the former President being at the receiving end for a change. He was now being subjected to the same harsh treatment he had dished out to both his real and perceived political enemies in the past. What goes around, really does come round!

Nevertheless, some observers could not comprehend the basis on which the MMR leadership based its unexpected decisions. However, just when many people felt that without a credible opponent, the 1998 elections would be postponed, something unexpected happened. A handful of newly formed political parties announced their intention and readiness to participate in both the Presidential and general elections. In any case, two of the hastily formed parties were led by people who were dissatisfied with MMR over internal squabbles in the party and left to form their own parties. They included Donald Mwila who formed his own party and Mukelabai Lisilo and others who formed the Unity Party. Under the circumstances, the MMR leaders were bubbling with confidence of a win, even before a single ballot was cast. Instead of toning down to improve credibility of the forthcoming tripartite elections, Chaluma's government continued on their own political journey, by mounting unwarranted attacks on former President Jumbe.

Despite the international condemnation of the political manoeuvres, Chaluma's government went ahead with the legislation of the new law. Nevertheless, the rationalization of these tactics employed to exclude Jumbe on the basis of his purported Mawalian parentage was dismissed as morally repugnant by church and civil society in the country. This apparently politically-motivated move left a negative spat on Zambica's democratic ethos; it was definitely a missed opportunity to put things right politically and democratically after the one-party state had been abolished in the country.

A popular and internationally respected President of a Southern African country condemned the discriminatory piece of legislation during a regional meeting in neighbouring Mawali. But true to his form, President Chaluma was adamant and described the statement as interference in Zambica's internal affairs. However, after the bill was assented to by the President, former President Jumbe described the President as a 'frightened little man.' From his language and tone, it was apparent that the former head of state didn't accept Chaluma as the new leader of the country. Some people suggested that JJ's pain from his humiliating defeat in 1993 would go on for ever.

Elections day came and five candidates contested the Presidential elections with four from minor parties. Six hundred candidates participated in national assembly elections under twelve political party tickets, while ninety nine candidates participated as independents. As expected, MMR won both Presidential and parliamentary elections. They comfortably took 131 seats of the 150 electable seats in the National Assembly, while President Chaluma won 73 percent of the vote in the Presidential elections.

Four opposition party candidates, mostly former MMR officials jointly received almost 27 per cent of the Presidential vote while the success of independents in parliamentary elections was unprecedented. In 1993, no single independent candidate won; this time twelve independent candidates won. Seven of the participating opposition parties failed to win any seat, while voter turn-out was modest, at 59 percent. Nevertheless, many observers blamed former President Jumbe and his ULP for Chaluma obtaining a comfortable majority in parliament; their naivety of boycotting the elections gave Chaluma a big majority in parliament to do whatever he and his party wanted. The ULP has never recovered its political fortunes since.

As Chishala had feared, no international observers came to witness the polling, thereby sending a negative message to the rest of the world, while the three major independent election observer groups in the country declared that the elections were not free and fair. This was due to lack of a consensus on the adoption of the new constitution, public media bias being in favour of the ruling party, and suspected flaws in the voter registration process. However, the Christian Council of Zambia, together with a newly formed minor monitoring group, the Sympathetic Monitors and Observers (SMO), broke ranks with the umbrella organization and declared the elections free and fair.

In any case, upon further introspection, Chishala concluded that the MMR and his President had missed a golden opportunity. With the sympathy and outpouring support he had received in 1993, President Chaluma could have been the leader who liberated the country both economically and politically.

But Chishala was fully aware that President Chaluma had initially succeeded in sealing relationships with the international and donor communities who were pleased with the peaceful transition from one-party rule to multiparty democracy in 1993. They were also happy with the economic policies promoted by the new MMR government; almost making the country a model for Africa! The donors also seemed eager to promote an African 'success story' of dual reforms, as one of the few countries in sub-Saharan Africa to do so. This was evidenced by the country experiencing substantial growth in official development assistance, in 1993.

As widely expected, former President Jumbe's ULP challenged the legitimacy of the 1998 Presidential and general elections after they were held as the new constitution stipulated. They based their challenge on a defective registration of voters by KUVUNI, which managed to capture only 2.5 million voters, out of 4.7 million eligible ones. It was claimed further that some genuine voters were disenfranchised by having their names in the wrong registers and that amendments to the constitution lacked consensus. This justified old Jumbe's earlier assertions that the vendor from Denmark could not be trusted.

While the courts took almost for ever to listen to the petitioners, they finally reached a verdict; the election victory of the President and his members of parliament was upheld and the petition by the main opposition party was thrown out. Even though he was a beneficiary, Chishala was disappointed. He felt that the capitulation by the courts put paid to the Zambican people's aspirations for a strong democratic dispensation.

After the one – party state was abolished in 1993; it was not only the missed opportunity in the 1998 elections; it was a retrogressive move democratically. And objectively analysed, the political engineer, as his predecessor had done before him, failed to take advantage of the flipside of that old Lemba saying; about choosing or succeeding a leader. Under the circumstances, a new leader, performing even on average would shine, due to errors and blunders of the predecessor. Why didn't President Chaluma utilize that opportunity?

Chishala made his views known to his 'close friend', when they met for a quiet drink one evening. Seated in a secluded corner of the bar, to avoid the noise and intrusion, they ordered their usual drinks first.

Then he said, "What a golden opportunity to let go! it was sitting pretty, right there, on a silver platter."

"Why are you talking in riddles today?" Kaluba challenged, "What opportunity are you referring to?"

"I mean the President and our party have just let go of a golden opportunity to make history in Africa. We should have been the first ones on the continent to successfully implement political and economic reforms, what with all the overwhelming support we received from the people and the international community." He quickly let in air and then slowly let it out.

"But we have done very well under the circumstances," Kaluba responded, "and since we are still in power, this is an on-going process." He smiled, while Chishala stiffened and coughed uneasily.

"Sorry to disappoint you Minister," Chishala responded. "The rare opportunity is already gone, and we have probably lost it for good. Remember the old adage – a good opportunity knocks only once."

"No! you are being too harsh to the party and the President." Kaluba protested. "We are still firmly in charge of this country." He boasted.

"In politics my friend, once you miss a golden chance, it doesn't wait for you. It's gone." He concluded.

"But who can take over from us right now?" Kaluba challenged. "There is no one." He answered his own question.

"Any one will come on the scene and our mistakes will make it happen; remember the saying – 'the beautiful ones are not yet born'. Who knows?" Chishala asked.

"No! I don't agree with you." Kaluba protested.

Chishala pointed out to him. "Remember what they used to say about former President Jumbe; no one would ever remove him from power, he was too entrenched because of this, and that they would always say." Kaluba nodded in agreement.

"The rest is history; we all know what happened, don't we?" Chishala asked. "To his own detriment, even President Jumbe believed that nobody would ever succeed him. He used to call all MMR leaders 'ba Kalume' or small boys, until the 'little boys' shocked him with the most humiliating defeat ever inflicted on a sitting African President." "Yes," Kaluba affirmed. Chishala smiled.

"Problem with most African leaders is that after winning elections, power often goes to their heads! They don't sit down to analyse critically, why they won. They naively think they are extremely smart and popular." Chishala reasoned, "and yet the popularity is variable, it cannot be constant."

Kaluba nodded again. He suddenly remembered what President Chaluma had said to him when he sent him to support Chipulu's campaign in Lake constituency. "Don't worry about lack of resources. Through their own blunders, Jumbe and the ULP have done most of the work for us." And indeed, Chaluma and the MMR won with a landslide, against all odds, and against all the wrong projections from biased or paid journalists, and Jumbe's stooges, including general Silutongwe and his close friend general Ikolo.

"Yes, I fully agree with you on this one." Kaluba conceded.

Chishala nodded and smiled broadly, and then said "We make mistakes, and then we become cannon fodder for any opposition, weak or strong." He told him.

CHAPTER 10

A Silent Storm after the Elections

"We should have contested Jerome. I told you we still had pockets of loyals throughout the country. We disappointed them. Now look at what is happening outside." One of the ULP stalwarts, Comrade White Phiri, and Party Secretary General spoke to JJ with open annoyance.

"You mean those empty cymbals? Just leave them alone. Our withdrawal from the race has made a huge and very clear statement not only in Zambica; not only in the region or continent, but throughout the world!" JJ stood up and clapped his hands together in utter satisfaction. He then took his popular cloth and walked to the massive ULP office window.

"What are you trying to do Jerome? Don't dare….don't even try that! Let us not awaken a soundly sleeping bull dog. Please, I beg of you. My goodness! Your continued stubbornness will drag us all into the mud I tell you. You should know and accept that you are no longer JJ the father of the nation." White Phiri looked at the others who were still sitting down and nodding their mostly balded heads in agreement with him.

The moment JJ opened the big window and was about to wave his green cloth, his jovial spirit was dampened by what he heard from the crowd that was fast building up.

"JFC is number one! JFC is number one! Woyee number one!" The frenzied crowd, mostly youths, shouted, whistled and screamed even louder when they saw JJ's face.

"Need I say 'I told you so'? Sit down and lick your wounds of stubbornness. Ah! 29 years in power you can't read the winds of change! You are now being booed by your great great-grandchildren! What is all this?" White Phiri could no longer contain himself. He was the only one brave enough to speak his mind even when they had been in government; others were still scared of JJ.

"29 years!" The others chorused, clapped their hands together twice and signalled seven using seven fingers then shook their heads as if a very important person had just died mysteriously.

"The popular 'JJ is number one' is now 'JFC is number one'. Even when it is clear this was no election at all! People change like weather." JJ was deflated. Clearly, those youths had been paid and sent to poke him; to demean and embarrass him in broad day light. It is a tactic he used against political opponents, especially during the one-party era, he remembered. The statesman was gone in a flash just like that. "Comrades, I think I need to go home and rest. I can't take........." He could not finish the sentence before a group of journalists budged in; all competing in asking questions at once.

"JJ, what do you think of the recent elections?" One journalist asked without introducing himself.

"Yes, do you think your withdrawal has paid?" another one came in.

"What are your comments on what is happening outside?" Yet another journalist shouted at the top of her voice.

White Phiri could not take it any longer. Together with the other senior members of the ULP who were present, they tried to push the journalists out. JJ no longer had powerful security guards. He was now a nobody. That aura that used to engulf him wherever he went was all gone. His cronies started leaving the once upon a story time popular and revered ULP headquarters on Egypt Road one by one. Those who saw them leave knew that this was the end of the once powerful and feared political party.

Although happy to have retained the presidency and his party's good performance in the elections, Chaluma was conscious of the growing dissatisfaction over the electoral and constitutional reforms. When he met Chishala and Kaluba just before the elections, he had dismissed the rumours circulating in the country that due to the discontent, he may not even complete his second term of office before riots started.

Politically stubborn as usual, President Chaluma told his two Ministers not to worry; after all, the rumours were being concocted by a few disgruntled elements from inside and outside the party especially those who had resigned, to form their own little parties. In any case, he suspected that those making most noise included a few perpetual noise makers from urban areas. They had nothing to offer, unlike the contented majority of voters mostly based in the rural areas.

Immediately after the elections, Chaluma's first address to the nation was through an over – publicized press conference. He thanked the voters for giving him and his party a landslide victory at the polls. The President also explained that his reforms were objective contrary to speculations in some quarters that they were subjective. He further stated that as a true democrat, he would appoint a commission of enquiry to review the reforms, their impact, as well as the way forward and promised to be a good listener to experts' advice by addressing the commission's anticipated recommendations.

Then the President turned to the main agenda of his press conference; the unveiling of his new cabinet. He announced a few changes, but mostly cosmetic. The noticeable change was the elevation of Kaluba from the ministry of local government and housing to finance and national planning, while Chishala remained entrenched at the ministry of Defence. A few minor changes were also announced, especially those concerning deputy ministers and some permanent secretaries, mostly moved from one ministry to another horizontally.

Towards the end of the president's address, the first reporter to ask the President questions didn't mince his words. "My name is Speedwell Mwale, from The Times of Zambica," he introduced himself. "Congratulations Mr. President on the expected landslide victory over new and largely unknown political rivals," he paused for impact. This was followed by laughter from the audience, as anticipated.

"My question is: are you really convinced that the elections were free and fair, Mr. President? You had already knocked out a genuine opponent and his party well before a single ballot was cast through your reforms." He said bravely, as more laughter followed from the audience, while Chaluma nodded.

"Thank you, Mr. President." He said before quickly sitting down.

The President glanced at his scribbled note pad, with anticipated questions and their possible answers; he smiled, and then quipped, "thank you Mr. Mwale, or is it Mr. Speedwell, for your speed at asking tricky questions. Reporters from the east are always known for good questions," he paused, allowing in the laughter that ensued; but largely, to buy some time, while he reflected further on an appropriate response which was not on those anticipated by his advisors.

The President went through the motion of taking off his spectacles, polishing them with a silk handkerchief and perching them on the tip of his nose, to buy more time. James Francis Chaluma was definitely a politician of many qualities. Subtlety and sophistication in the use of words were notably among his strong points. Some observant citizens described him as a man who had the tongue and voice of an angel, capable of debating with the Devil himself.

"Firstly, I am very happy that as a Presidential candidate, I won with a landslide," he said. "Naturally, every winner should be happy with victory," he added. "Unless of course if the victory was fake, or if one only beat a frog or hyena!" More laughter followed. "The same goes for the victory of my party, over five other parties," he sighed. "They gave us tough competition; I can assure you." The audience remained mute, and he guessed they were not pleased with the last part of his response.

"Secondly," he continued, probably to break the obvious silence, "didn't I beat the same former President Jumbe handsomely in 1993 when he was totally in control of the country's affairs, including elections?" He asked, "Didn't I?" he stressed rhetorically. A group of party cadres clapped as laughter and more clapping followed.

"So, the question of being scared of former President Jumbe and his ULP does not arise at all," he continued. "However, our position is that even former President Jumbe and his party should abide by the law," he said. "The law is very clear and it is for everyone to follow. Even ba Jumbe should abide by the law as no one is above the law." He stated, as more silence dawned. He sensed the indifference by the audience again.

"Come-on guys!" He urged the audience on, glancing at the scribbled notes. Some people applauded while others laughed cynically.

"Otherwise, this country will be just like George Orwell's Animal Farm; some people will be more equal than others, even before the law," he continued, as more laughter erupted.

"At least Zambicans should give me credit men!" He paused. "I ran against real people, and not pictures of frogs or hyenas, which my predecessor used to do." More laughter erupted. He mentioned the names of some of his opponents in the Presidential race: Donald Mwila, and elder statesman Chewe Chakontoka. More laughter ensued largely because Chakontoka was perceived as a comedian by many people, and not Presidential material.

Another reporter Charles Mezo from The Past Newspapers stood up and introduced himself, before asking a related question. "So, you are happy Mr President with the outcome of the elections which you and your party won comfortably," he said, pausing. The President was not sure where he was going. "How about the credibility of these elections?" He said. "Are you not worried that no single international observer came to monitor the elections?" There was more laughter.

"In addition, all credible local monitors also stayed away. Are you not bothered by that Mr President? Just compare with the multitude of international observers, who came in 1993 and declared the elections which you won as free and fair?" He probed. "I thank you sir." The audience clapped enthusiastically.

The President looked at the note pad; the question was anticipated by the officials, and the answer was right there.

'Thank you Charles from the paper that digs deeper just like your questions," he said. "I agree with you that credibility of elections is important. However, you will recall that we did invite both local and international observers to come." The reporter nodded in agreement, while the audience kept quiet.

"Many decided not to come out of their own accord," the President said. "What were we supposed to do? Cancel our own scheduled and important elections? No," he answered his own question. Some people in the audience laughed.

"So, those who wanted to come came," he explained. "Just like the Bible story," he went on, "most people invited by the King to the wedding banquet didn't show up. The King didn't cancel the banquet; he sent his workers to invite people from the streets; to come to the wedding to eat and have fun." He smiled briefly. "As a Christian Nation," he paused; "that is exactly what we did. I don't see anything wrong with that. Do you Charles?" some people in the audience laughed, while others kept quiet.

"And in their wisdom, former President Jumbe and ULP decided to boycott the 1998 elections," he continued. "While that was a big blunder by the former President that was certainly their constitutional and democratic right." He ended. Laughter followed while the reporter acknowledged the President's reply with a condescending sneer.

"Mr President," another reporter stood up. "Since you are happy with the outcome and credibility of the elections, let me ask you a hypothetical question," he stated. The President nodded.

"You described yourself as a democrat in 1993, didn't you? Which, elections were freer and fair? The 1993 or 1998 elections? Please, answer me honestly Mr President. I beg you." He sat down. Applause and laughter followed.

"Well! Well! Well!" The President and political engineer said without glancing at the written script. "A hypothetical question certainly begs a hypothetical answer." He suspired, as laughter erupted from the audience. "Since we won very well in both elections," he said, "I liked both elections because they put a broad smile on my small face." He gasped.

How evasive! Thought the reporter. This President has a knack for avoiding tough questions, he concluded silently. However, his feelings were echoed by those of the silent majority in the audience, while others simply burst out laughing.

"But since you want me to choose," the President continued, "I will slightly prefer the last elections, because they are recent, and the joy of victory is still fresh in my mind." He ended. How clever, but evasive, some people felt.

"Mr President, I am Damiano Lungu from the Monitor Newspaper. You have insisted at this press briefing that the 1998 elections were free and fair, but the rest of the world thinks otherwise." He slowly, pulled in air, and then quickly let it out. The audience laughed.

"Many people in the country think that by your constitutional reforms, you had effectively restricted participation in the elections, especially by the main opposition party, the United Liberation Party. Are your measures not exactly the same as former President Jumbe's amendments to the party constitution just a few days before their party conference in 1980? Remember he knocked out Simon Mulenga Wampanga, Mwendalubi, and a business man, Mr Chalwe and won the race unopposed?" The President nodded. "Why do this Mr President, especially after exciting Zambicans about the need for a strong democratic space in the country?" The audience clapped.

"Thank you Mr. Damiano for an important and long question." the President answered. "I am also glad that you have asked it even though your comparison of 1980 to 1998 is highly misplaced. The two are like night and day. In 1980, President Jumbe was scared of two 'political giants' to compete against him at the party conference. True to his character, he changed the party constitution four days before the conference. That kept away Mwendalubi and Wampanga from competing, and yet they were paid-up members of the ULP. In addition, the two were chased from their own party conference; meaning that the amendments were unconstitutionally implemented before they were even approved by the delegates."

"JFC! JFC! JFC!" Some members chanted drowning Chaluma's own voice.

"On the contrary," Chaluma resumed, "our amendments came from people's submissions to a commission I appointed constitutionally," he confirmed as the audience kept quiet once again. "The records are there, including names of the petitioners to the commission. "No!" He protested. "1980 under ULP was unconstitutional while 1998 under the MMR was legal and constitutional," he elaborated to a thunderous applause by most in the audience.

A few more questions were asked and the President attempted to answer some and like an eel, evasively avoided some difficult ones.

Chishala knew well in advance that the questions at the press conference would be difficult. The President did answer some questions well but skilfully avoided a number of them.

On the other hand, Kaluba was very happy with his new ministry. In actual fact, his dream had always been a possible promotion to Finance or Foreign Affairs. How did the President guess just what his dream was? He was certain that as a good manager, he would perform well as controller of the country's assets and resources. There was no doubt he would perform well, he projected.

So, guessing games and subtle rivalry continued between the new Minister of Finance and National Planning and his erstwhile friend at Defence. All considered, Kaluba was certain that he was now better off at Finance than being at Defence, even if it was slightly senior. The silent rivalry between the two Ministers was certainly bound to be a hurdle in cabinet. Their discord started way back on campus, during their days at the University of Zambica.

Kaluba and Chishala entered the university in the same year. The freshmen were admitted in different schools. Chishala was in the school of Humanities and Social Sciences while Kaluba was in the school of Natural Sciences. Even though he had wanted to become a medical doctor, Kaluba did not perform very well in biology, and was therefore, redirected to another school at the end of his second year. Kaluba obtained a degree in environmental health and later graduating with a Master's in Public Health. Chishala on the other hand, graduated in Public Administration and later obtained a Master's Degree in economics from a University in Uganda.

Both Kaluba and Chishala joined the staff development programme at UNZA and were lecturers in their respective fields. Kaluba recalled that even at the University, comparisons were abound about who got promoted first from one grade to the other; who got a more beautiful girlfriend etc.

Then, the real acid test was that Kaluba dated Mwansa first and Chishala grabbed her from him in outrageous and unexplained circumstances. Although the two fought over Mwansa and later made a truce, Kaluba never really forgave his friend. In fact, Mwansa, then a secretarial student at a college in Lusiku initially had problems choosing between the two men, but later preferred Chishala.

Chishala and Mwansa later got married, and instead of boycotting the wedding, Kaluba did actually attend it, and he made a number of practical jokes at the wedding reception. One of them was to send a note to the high table, addressed to the bride whom he congratulated for looking so beautiful in her lovely wedding attire, but stated that she had made a grave mistake marrying Chishala, because he was a loser, and not the best guy for her. While the new bride smiled with indifference, she instructed her chief bride's maid to shred the mischievous note, and never reveal its contents to anybody, especially the groom.

⸺⸺⸺◦✹◦⸺⸺⸺

The two Ministers had another secret meeting at which they talked politics and analysed the previous press conference held by the President. While their analyses differed on many fundamentals as always, they however, agreed that all considered, the state of the nation although looking apparently calm, was rockier and more tentative. Chishala described the scenario in a few words, 'a silent storm after the elections.'

One evening, something unexpected happened. Chishala received unconfirmed reports that Mboniwe was having an affair when he was on one of his trips abroad. He was upset. To get more details, he engaged a private detective, whose report was inconclusive. Despite lack of conclusive evidence, but true to his character, he went home and shouted at Mboniwe and called her all sorts of names without giving her an opportunity to explain. She in turn reacted angrily and told him off.

Mboniwe felt confused. All along, She thought that rich people were not only generous but also kind. Her parents, her sisters, and her friends in Chandevu compound thought so too. Now after the almost physical confrontation and insults, she didn't think so any longer. She actually thought she had made a big mistake by agreeing to marry the old man.

"How could you shout at me based on mere rumours?" She asked, breaking the silence. "Don't do it again, or else,"

"Why should I bother to check?" He asked. "I knew from your behaviour and body language that you were guilty," he blurted out, "guilty as hell!" He shouted for emphasis. "Or else what?" He challenged her.

"You are neither judge nor jury," she reminded him. "After all, I have heard several negative reports about you myself." She moaned. "However, based on love and trust, I have dismissed the reports and given you the benefit of the doubt." She sounded rather mature for her age. He listened quietly and felt somewhat impressed with her mature reasoning.

"You are my wife," he reminded her. "I have the right to correct you whenever you step out of line." He stressed. She shook her head, in total disbelief. She had to spell it out to him.

"I warn you not to ever be violent with me again," she told him, "or else, I shall report you to the authorities for gender-based violence." She warned. Chishala laughed.

"I am the authority, the Minister of Defence." He told her. "Who else are you going to report me to?" He asked mockingly. "The President?" He teased her further.

"I shall report you to the Inspector General of the Police," she retorted.

"Oh! That guy is useless. He's always scared of me and my position in cabinet." She shook her head as tears rolled down her rounded cheeks. She now concluded that she was probably trapped in a violent relationship. "So, are you going to report me to myself?" He continued, as she looked down. "Don't give me that timid expression and those crocodile tears," he shouted. "I can beat you right now!" He threatened.

"What!" she screamed. "I didn't know that you were a child abuser. For your information, my father has never beaten me in my whole life," she told him. "And yet, here you are, threatening me with violence," she said, downcast. He listened attentively and said not a word. "And yet, you are definitely older than my father." She ended.

Chishala shook his head while dismissing her tantrums. He had known all along that he was slightly older than Mboniwe's father. "What has your father's age got to do with our relationship?" He snapped.

"It is relevant," she said between sobs, "because you are older than my father; you should not behave like this." She ridiculed him. Chishala was annoyed with that comparison and her unbecoming language and completely lost his cool. She watched him at close range shaking his head with rage. She was suddenly frightened.

"If I am older than your father," he said, with barely controlled rage, "how come you were the first one to approach me at the tennis club? How come you came fast to apologise when I left you at the hostels. Were you blind?" He bombarded her with a string of questions.

"Don't go into history and trivialities," she replied. "Let bygones be bygones", she advised him. He remained silent. "If I liked you then, tell me, was that a crime? Does that give you a licence to rough me up and treat me like an object of scorn, as you are doing now?" She ranted on.

"I just want to know if you had planned our relationship all along," he insisted. "Or is it that you have a special affinity for older and rich men?"

Mboniwe kept quiet. She felt insulted, and thought that her husband's arguments were rather childish.

"And when I left you after your rude boyfriend insulted me," he recalled, "didn't you know that I was older than your father? You came running back to me and apologised." He pressed.

Mboniwe was further upset. His language was just like that of her previous boyfriend at the college; crude, childish and annoying. Did she make a big mistake to leave one bad and vulgar boy for an equally crude and abusive old man? She wondered.

"I will not tolerate your insults anymore," she cried. "I am out of here," she announced without thinking. She went into the bedroom, hastily packed two cases, left the house, and drove off without telling him where she was going.

Over the weekend, Chishala and Mboniwe attended a family meeting at her parents' house. She had told her parents that her husband frequently physically and verbally abused her. He tried to defend himself but it was pointless as he was completely outnumbered by the family members of his wife. In spite of his age and senior government position, he was considered a son-in-law and treated as such in the marital dispute.

In the end, the couple was counselled on how to live amicably, and learn to settle their differences maturely. It was also resolved that Mboniwe could not stay with her parents, in her condition. She was four months pregnant.

She reflected further. Her husband repeatedly said that slum dwellers were the poorest of the poor people in Lusiku. For her, coming from Chandevu compound, one of the most densely populated in Lusiku with poor amenities, she reasoned that her family was in the same category of the really poor people, according to Chishala's classification. No wonder she didn't often want him to accompany her whenever she visited her parents, in their small house, in the crowded compound. She didn't want him to disrespect the lives of the people in Chandevu; they could never mock his own life or the lives of his close friends in Short Hecters or Morningdale.

She revealed her apprehension and told him how she felt one day, when he made the mistake of picking up another quarrel with her.

"Why do you dislike my parents?" she asked, looking him straight in the face. He kept quiet.

"Is it because they are poor?" She challenged.

"I actually like your parents. Who gave you that wrong notion?" He asked back after a short reflection.

"It is just the way you talk. You make me feel uncomfortable." She replied. "You actually give me a complex! As if you are superior to me and my family."

"To be honest, what I don't like is your arrogance." He put it bluntly.

"Don't forget that to every action, there is a reaction." She said. "You should learn to be gentle with me. I am a woman you know." Chishala thought that her argument was genuine. He sometimes reacted instantly, and never allowed any room for dialogue.

In the meantime, Mboniwe had confided in two of her close friends on how her marriage pendulum was now swinging from left to right, like a baseless yoyo. The youngsters called it pre-emptive damage control, just in case the worst happened.

Chishala on the other hand had only whispered his marital woes to one person he thought he trusted, Kaluba. However, gossip and speculation in the capital city were already rife about instability in the domestic affairs of the Minister of Defence. When the negative rumours got to him, he wondered just who was at the centre of spreading them. He consulted his old friend one evening. Kaluba suggested that it could be Mboniwe herself, while in essence he was the real culprit; so, the guessing games never ended.

Chishala and Mboniwe had expected an instant return to their marital bliss after their reconciliation in Chandevu compound, but that never happened. Consequently, they often engaged in unintended silence, carefully picking the right words to use; as if one was sizing up the other. It was as if they were courting all over again, with each one apprehensive of offending the other. The situation was exacerbated by Mboniwe having lost her pregnancy prematurely at the time.

Instead of taking the lead to make the reconciliation hold, Chishala rather took a backseat role and allowed their differences to continue and yet, he was the more mature spouse, with more experience in relationships and conflict resolution. In the process, he seemed to take advantage of the silence and less laughter at home and quickly returned to his old ways. He started dating Theresa, an older woman who had fancied him in the past.

"After the way you have treated me," Mboniwe said, "I miss my freedom to do what I want." She told him one evening during dinner, to test their reconciliation after they quarrelled once more.

"What freedom do you want? After all, I now travel often," he said. "You have too much freedom already, as it is," he challenged.

"But I don't like being beaten or molested on mere suspicion," she told him. "Without any discussion."

"I have told you before and I am telling you again. Marriage is a two-way process," Chishala replied. "It is always a give and take affair," he explained.

"What do you mean by that?" She asked innocently, still unconvinced. "To give what and take what?" She asked. Chishala smiled gently.

"You mean you don't know, my love?" He asked, sounding patient.

"I have no idea what you are talking about." She admitted.

"Please don't talk in riddles."

"It means you give up a bit of your freedom for instance," he advised. "And in return you have comfort, wealth, travel and a happy and a stable relationship."

She shook her head and thought that she had probably been bought by his money. How come she never thought about that before? She asked herself.

As if reading her thoughts, he coughed and cleared his throat first. "It is not too bad, is it?" He asked. "You know that I love you. But wives should always be obedient. We are Africans you know." She now realised that he actually meant well.

She reflected for a short while before responding. "Now, I understand my dearest husband. But why didn't you tell me this before?"

"It is only fair," he continued, ignoring her question, "that you give up a little of your freedom and arrogance for instance, so that you gain a lot more, in return," he stressed. "To be fair I should also give up something, like being hard and rigid with you, my beautiful wife." He sounded genuine and she liked what he was propounding. She nodded, and moved closer to him. He complimented her, holding her hand. "The business people say that there is no free lunch. Everyone partaking in the meal has to pay or contribute something." He stressed, "it could be one way or another." He said. "Everyone has to lose something, and also gain something in the process." He clarified patiently.

"Oh! You mean a symbiotic relationship?" She asked. "We learnt about it in biology," she remembered.

"Precisely," he echoed. "Not a parasitic relationship, which cannot last long because it is one-sided and exploitative." He expanded.

"Thank you, my loving husband," she said meekly. "You teach well. You can be a Professor in a university. We shall certainly work at it," she promised. Chishala recalled Kaluba's words, also suggesting that he could be a Professor at a university; some coincidence! "That's how married couples sustain their relationships," he said, pleased that their marriage might work out, after all.

He extended his hand, which she took gladly. She now knew they had made-up and he knew too that he had finally sunk the 'give-and-take,' theory in her little but pretty head.

They made love that night; she gave it all. She moaned each time they made love and pretended to achieve maximum pleasure. What difference did it make anyway, whether it was real or fake? She asked herself. What really mattered was to 'Give and take,' she remembered his theory.

Chishala smiled broadly. He was completely contented that his give and take theory had finally sunk in his wife's difficult medulla oblongata; it was now working both in theory and in practice.

Why didn't he preach it earlier in their relationship? He reasoned, rather belatedly. But nevertheless, he was very happy with the new development; it was in line with the old saying; 'better late, than never.'

"No! We have some catching-up to do, under the new theory." Mboniwe shouted at the top of her voice, while Chishala smiled radiantly.

CHAPTER 11

JFC and Political Enemies

President JFC probably surprised many political observers and commentators in the manner he firmly dealt with real and perceived political opponents. According to the grapevine, he targeted both members of the opposition parties and those in his own party, who differed with him or crossed his path. Nevertheless, first Republican President Jerome Jumbe was without a doubt JFC's chief political adversary, for a long time.

Chaluma vigorously opposed JJ when he worked as a trade union leader; and after the introduction of the one- party state JFC bitterly opposed and fought JJ. For this, he paid a heavy price including ridicule, insults, and imprisonment. In any case, JFC was never satisfied when he convincingly humiliated JJ at the polls in 1993. Then probably as pay back, he outmanoeuvred old JJ by successfully excluding him from participating in the 1998 elections, using Jerome Jumbe's own old tactics.

Inevitably, it was not long before the opportunity presented itself early in his first term; the President etched a plan to abduct JJ. Jerome Jumbe was arrested at Easter. The former head of state was accused of masterminding a coup code named the maximum option. Suddenly, the state machinery swung into action at 02.00 hours. Heavily armed police officers surrounded Jumbe's residence.

JJ heard some footsteps outside and he wanted to go and check. In any case, JJ was feeling uneasy. In fact, he had premonitions throughout the week. The previous night he could not sleep. Something kept gnawing at his conscience as if to remind him that something bad was about to happen.

JJ stood up heavily and slowly, went to the window and drew the curtain just a little. He was stunned! He saw them; a multitude of them. His heart stopped briefly. Has Chaluma turned into a beast with multiple heads?

The police were outside and were heavily armed. The house was surrounded. I am finished, JJ breathed. This gun is no match to the guns I have seen outside.

He forcefully opened the door and three or four policemen fell into the house. JJ chuckled and forgot he was now face to face with the enemy. The other policemen rushed in and held him as if he was a dangerous prisoner.

"Handcuff him! Quick! Quick! We have no time to waste. Take that toy gun from his hand." The so called commander did not give Jumbe any chance to say anything. JJ was also too shocked to even scream.

"Boss, I'm afraid I can't! This is our father. He may be our political prisoner right now but he is our father, the founder of this nation. I beg you; let us just walk him to his prison cell without humiliating him." He must have been a second in command. He felt terrible treating the once upon a time father of the nation like that. He also knew that Jumbe still had many supporters in the country.

"To be effective, you should only recognise the current and not history." He preached, showing no mercy to the former President. He should have been drilled well. However, his junior froze, making no movement and taking no action.

"You! Do as you are told. My friend, we have no time for history. Orders from above are neither discussed nor opposed. Move it!" The commander had no mercy for JJ at all. "You and you and you, give this house a thorough search. Old habits die hard you know."

The former first lady heard the commotion and swiftly followed the direction of the noise. What she saw shocked her to the core, and she briefly froze. The police did not bother to explain the situation to the brave but shocked former first lady. But they all knew that she was still widely respected in the country, as a kind and compassionate lady. She and her family sacrificed a lot during the freedom struggle and yet she was known to be generous and shared the little her family had with other needy party members.

"Where are you taking my husband?" she raved, "you ought to be protecting us, but you come here armed to the teeth; you exert undue force against harmless senior citizens at the crack of dawn! You should be ashamed of yourselves." She charged.

However, the squadron of law enforcement agents comprising plain- clothed officers and uniformed officers in battle fatigue and armed with assault rifles had been well briefed and took no notice of the feral by the former first lady. She cried hysterically. A brood of grandchildren that had come to spend Easter with their grandparents was awakened by the hubbub. The little ones, though still half asleep cried their lungs out when they saw their respected grandmother crying; they had never seen her so distressed.

The police took away the ageing Jumbe and hurriedly bundled him in a truck. They drove him to the Remand Prison, charged him with treason, and threw him into a small cell, already crammed with more than twelve people.

A week later, they flew him by helicopter to a Maximum Security Prison in Chibwe and bundled him in a bare cell, save for a single bed and scanty beddings. Sharp lights from a naked bulb flooded the cell.

The former President was virtually in solitary confinement.

Paradoxically, Jumbe had first visited the facility at independence in 1966 in his capacity as the first President of Zambica. The former President observed that the prison had limited capacity as congestion posed a great challenge in managing the correctional and rehabilitative roles expected of a prison. It was one of the 53 prisons left by the British colonial masters to house 5,500 inmates countrywide and yet, the prison population at the time of JJ's detention stood at 15,000.

As JJ found out, the conditions at the prison were deplorable. For instance, 152 inmates shared a cell for 40 prisoners. The so-called lavatories were nothing but plastic buckets. The cells mirrored years of neglect; the floor and walls were chirped and covered with indescribable stains; cockroaches roamed even in the day while bed bugs and lice relentlessly feasted on the blood of the inmates. Food was the inevitable half-cooked nshima with kapenta or beans, swimming in over- salted water for soup. Drinking water was cloudy while at night, fat mosquitoes preyed upon the unprotected inmates.

The pace of the criminal justice system in the country moved at the pace of the chameleon for commoners. It was reported that some prisoners in the country waited for four years or more to have their appeals heard. The court system had unnecessary adjournments linked to overwhelming schedules by judges and sheer incompetence. Another rumour was that sometimes, prisoners on death row at the maximum prison had their files missing in the court system. The prisoners cried foul because without case files, they could not exercise their constitutional right to petition the President for pardon.

There were a number of deaths of inmates and prisoners from suspected AIDS- related illnesses and sodomy was linked to the spread of HIV at the facility. Thus, life came to a complete halt when one was incarcerated at that prison. The wheels of life simply stopped, as living ended for the individual. In the trappings of the cold, dark and intimidating cell larked self-pity, the cause of more deaths among inmates than any disease. Weak inmates stopped to dream successes or promises for the future. They withdrew into themselves; lack of hope deflated their spirits; some inmates suffered from extreme loneliness amidst prison crowds. Thus, life at the maximum prison was so hard to the weak-minded inmates that they saw nothing to widen their life's horizon; life there was a living hell on earth.

The former President reflected on the prison calamity and was deeply worried. Why didn't he know this when he was in office?

A warder assigned to guard the block in which JJ was locked-up was deeply worried on day two. He had to address the former president.

"Sir," the warder said, "you have not had food or drink for…"

"Young man, I am fine, very fine," JJ said, interrupting him.

"But sir, you must eat and drink," the warder suggested.

This time JJ did not answer. Instead, he took his guitar and hummed his favourite song- Rock of All Ages.

On day three, word reached the prison Commandant that the former President had not taken food or drink. When the Commandant failed to persuade JJ to eat and drink, he whispered to the Minister of Home Affairs about the fear of the old man's health. The Minister of Home Affairs arranged for JJ's grandchildren to take food and water to their grandfather. He reasoned that JJ would definitely break his fast if grandchildren took the food to him cooked by the former First Lady. To the dismay of the Minister, JJ remained taciturn. The first Republican President declared that he was on hunger strike; JJ said that he would not rescind his decision until he went home.

The news about JJ's hunger strike worried President JFC. On the local scene, JJ was the founding father of the nation, the people could rise against the MMR, and JFC leadership should JJ's health decline. The international community was closely following the political development in the country. Since JFC had built an image of a rising African democrat; he needed to act quickly to forestall the detention of JJ from backfiring and tarnishing that image. If JJ's health was compromised and he died in prison, everything JFC had worked for would crumble as a castle built on sand. He needed to act swiftly but cautiously so that his enemies did not capitalise on the embarrassing situation.

President Chaluma therefore, summoned his closest confidants, the Minister of Finance and National Planning and his colleague at Defence and the Minister of Home Affairs. They brain stormed into the small hours of the following morning.

The three ministers together with the Minister of Foreign Affairs engaged the High Commissioner of a neighbouring country in secret talks. JJ followed the developments to which in public he played mum while JFC the political engineer meticulously reversed what could have backfired and possibly cost him the Presidency.

The rest is history; one of JJ's contemporaries and probably closest living friend, the former president of a neighbouring country intervened. He flew in with his wife, met JJ in prison, and persuaded his friend to end the hunger strike. Subsequently, JFC gave in and asked his Minister of Home Affairs to move the former leader from the Maximum Security Prison to his residence. President JFC sighed with relief. The storm passed and his Presidency survived from a possible major dent. To the unsuspecting public, however, JFC remained adamant and declared JJ's home a private jail.

Subsequently, Jerome Jumbe was released on a 'nolle prosequi' order by the DPP, after the President of a powerful Southern African country intervened by sending his Minister of Defence to procure a deal. No details are known about the deal. According to many critics, Chaluma was probably saved the embarrassment of Jumbe being found innocent; exactly what Jumbe's lead lawyer had wanted, by insisting on a trial, while others argued that Jumbe was saved from likely imprisonment; the debate continued.

JFC's regime also arrested some members of JJ's ULP. They were charged with planning to overthrow the democratically elected government with support from foreign countries, a project famously called the highest-option-plan. To back-up his allegations, he acted as JJ used to do and declared a state of emergency under the provisions of a specific article, of the constitution. Those arrested included two of JJ's nephews and Brown Ruwe, popularly called BR. It was speculated that some of the detainees were tortured.

In a closed door meeting with the ministers of Foreign Affairs and Home Affairs, the visiting former head of state humorously stated, "the problem with Jerome is that he doesn't think there is a good life after leaving the presidency." He however, implored the two Zambican ministers to look after, and protect his close friend, and Zambica's first Republican President.

The Zambican Home Affairs Minister responded, "Unlike you sir, many of your former colleague Presidents in East and Central Africa seem to believe that once in power, they must die in the chair, as Presidents."

The former head of state smiled gently and said, "true indeed."

However, though the Zambicans were first divided over JJ's imprisonment and later house arrest, some registered their dissatisfaction in different fora such as church, weddings etc. Many Zambicans remembered the several sacrifices Jumbe and his colleagues made while fighting for the country's independence. Hardly a sermon or a speech would end without referring to the on-going mistreatment of the founder of the Zambican nation. As days went by, half of the nation was crying foul. Some people could not stomach what they thought was the ill treatment of the founding legend. Many people asked why the President could not forgive the old man. That was the African practice. The Christian and human in Chaluma listened though he publicly acted tough. Those closest to him whispered that Chaluma was fast softening towards the former President.

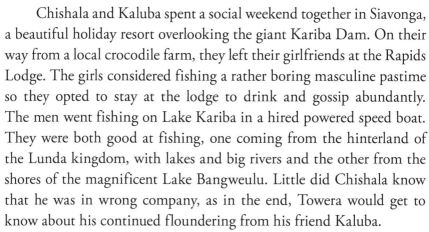

Chishala and Kaluba spent a social weekend together in Siavonga, a beautiful holiday resort overlooking the giant Kariba Dam. On their way from a local crocodile farm, they left their girlfriends at the Rapids Lodge. The girls considered fishing a rather boring masculine pastime so they opted to stay at the lodge to drink and gossip abundantly. The men went fishing on Lake Kariba in a hired powered speed boat. They were both good at fishing, one coming from the hinterland of the Lunda kingdom, with lakes and big rivers and the other from the shores of the magnificent Lake Bangweulu. Little did Chishala know that he was in wrong company, as in the end, Towera would get to know about his continued floundering from his friend Kaluba.

The two ministers, as usual engaged in deep conversation. They first discussed relatively lighter issues. Then they delved into politics, the topic of their deep passion. The party faithful would have considered their subject sacrosanct but the two ministers and close 'friends' had no cause for caution. After all, they were alone in a boat, far out on the rough waters of the biggest man-made lake in Southern Africa. They felt safe from any prying eyes and attentive ears; their talk was therefore open and completely unguarded.

"Why is the President pre-occupied with issues surrounding the former Republican President?" Chishala asked. "He should simply let go of JJ and leave him to the annals of history," he suggested.

"Why should he do that?" Kaluba countered. "I have said before, and I can repeat it without fear of contradiction, that no one is above the law," he said. "That includes old JJ of course."

"Minister, I told you before that banning JJ from the 1998 elections was a big mistake; it was misconstrued by some people that JFC was scared of contesting those elections against JJ. That single act suddenly turned JJ into a new hero, as if he was being victimised by the President."

"I have also told you in the past that JFC could not be scared of JJ. He beat the guy fairly and decisively in the 1993 elections," he sighed. "After that, JJ became history politically as far as I am concerned."

"That's beside the point." Chishala replied. "You know as well as I do that during the one-party dictatorship, JJ had successfully silenced almost all political enemies, except JFC who remained like a lone political thorn and voice in the wilderness," he explained.

"Yes," Kaluba agreed. "That I accept without any argument."

"I knew all along that we have some common ground, on some issues," said Chishala, "this being one of them."

"That's right. But you still haven't proved your point," Kaluba challenged him.

"I was coming to that," he said. 'The point is that when JFC was like the lone person, courageous enough to oppose JJ during the one- party state, JJ misfired by continuously disparaging him; calling him names... that he was only four feet, blur, blur, blur. It was silly of the old man to try and discredit JFC's leadership of the Trade Union

Movement, because he was the workers' representative." Chishala argued.

"Yes. To a certain extent, JJ did build and market him politically by his anti-JFC messages." Kaluba sighed, and then continued. "They inadvertently built him up."

"Thank you," Chishala said.

"Thank you, for what?" Kaluba interrupted.

"Today, we might be very far away from a civil blood bath than ever before." Chishala observed; ignoring his friend's direct question.

"There is no need to worry," Kaluba said.

"The situation on the ground is contrary to your wild assertions," Chishala replied.

Kaluba remained silent.

"The anti-JJ campaign; all those acts against him are building the old man to the extent that he may defeat JFC in a free and fair contest," Chishala suggested. "History my friend has a funny way of repeating itself."

Kaluba shook his head, before asking, "which are those acts, making JJ popular once again?"

"Minister, are you asking me about things that are in public domain?" Chisala asked. "Some of the issues we have discussed in cabinet and were later implemented," he reminded him.

"Yes minister," Kaluba responded. "I want to know which acts are so serious to influence the people to turn to JJ again," he said. "We dealt the final blow against the old man in 1993, and the rest is heresy and conjecture."

"Let me refresh your memory, if I may," Chishala offered, 'detaining the father of the nation and later releasing him on a nolle was a big blunder, denying JJ his legitimate terminal benefits on the excuse that he had not retired from active politics was a serious mistake. Then attempting to deport the old man to Mawali after he had liberated and ruled this country for twenty – nine years is yet another. Accusing the former president of stealing state property only to find his personal books that he had kept on the bookshelves of the study at the state house is rather sad. The list of falsehoods by our government against JJ is endless."

"I know that some of our actions against him have actually made the old man popular, largely based on empathy," Kaluba agreed. "But I can assure you, the President didn't mean any harm. He was simply safeguarding the security of the nation," he explained. "The President had to take certain measures, such as arresting JJ and investigating him thoroughly, since he was allegedly implicated in serious crimes."

"How about his immunity?" Chishala asked. "He had total immunity in accordance with the Republican Constitution as a former Head of State," he said. "The best the President could have done under the circumstances was to go to parliament; table the charges and try him, only after parliament had revoked his immunity."

"But on security matters, he couldn't wait. The country was being threatened. Have you forgotten that JJ himself locked up so many people largely based on trumped-up charges?" Kaluba paused and then continued, "and yet, no one raised any dust." He smiled, thinking he had made a good point.

"I do agree that many innocent people were detained or jailed under JJ, on flimsy charges and later released," Chishala concurred. "But honestly, two wrongs don't make a right."

Kaluba shook his head in disagreement.

"But much more importantly," Chishala continued, "none of those detained or jailed by JJ were former Heads of State; they had no immunity we can talk about," he stressed. Kaluba listened in silence; his friend had made a very good point.

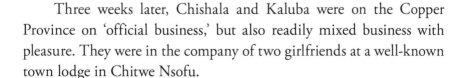

Three weeks later, Chishala and Kaluba were on the Copper Province on 'official business,' but also readily mixed business with pleasure. They were in the company of two girlfriends at a well-known town lodge in Chitwe Nsofu.

From their conversation with the women the ministers concluded that once a stronghold of the ruling party, the President's popularity in the area was declining. This was largely attributed to what many perceived as increasing intolerance to divergent views in the ruling party. While this was more evident to Chishala's ears, Kaluba disputed what he heard and dismissed it as mere gossip. As they often did, the two ministers found a moment to be on their own. They continued their covert analysis of events in their party and the country, with Chishala's allegations of their leader's apparent high-handedness in dealing with either real or perceived political foes, which Kaluba obviously strongly disputed.

"The President had developed the habit of intolerance to divergent views in the ruling party," Chishala charged. "It doesn't augur well with our pre-election promises on democracy," he said and surprisingly Kaluba gently nodded in agreement.

"These acts are diluting the impact of our party on key issues and at the same time strengthening the opposition, which is actually growing." He said. "This is what our girls from this province have almost confirmed." Kaluba reflected before responding.

"I know that we promised a stronger economy and a solid democratic dispensation," Kaluba echoed. "But the girls may be exaggerating. Anyway, what politics do they know?" He challenged. "They are just fly-by-night business women."

"I am happy you haven't forgotten the pillars of our genesis as a party." Chishala appreciated. "As for the girls, they are ordinary I accept. But they don't need to be politicians to know what people are saying about our party and our leader."

"But that said, some of our colleagues are rubble rousers," Kaluba alleged. "They need to be dealt with firmly. The President knows exactly how to deal with them."

"Look at young Donald Mwila. What problems did he cause the party?" Chishala asked, "to be arrested, detained and, humiliated like a common criminal?"

"I recall that before the 1993 general elections, Donald was perceived as a blue-eyed boy of the party president. He was literally the chief economic advisor to JFC at the time," Chishala added.

"I also clearly remember that," Kaluba echoed. "For instance, when it was evident that MMR was poised to win the elections, JFC undertook a quick trip overseas to market the party and to fundraise. He took only two party officials and one of those was Donald; he was very close to the party president, more so after we formed government," he recalled.

"What went wrong then?" Chishala asked.

"He made a great political blunder," Kaluba said emphatically.

"What blunder did he make?" Asked Chishala. "Tell me." He sat at the edge of his seat, highly engrossed in his colleague's analysis.

"He suggested that the economy was too porous to external capitalist abuse and that we needed to slow down a bit on the economic liberalisation process," Kaluba explained. "JFC would have taken it lightly if the blue-eyed-boy had uttered the damaging words behind closed doors. But he spoke on a private radio station, on an enemy platform for the whole world to hear! He further rubbed it in by repeating the same words at several public debates. That was tantamount to undermining the Presidency."

"But in a democracy, those suggestions should have been taken as constructive criticism," Chishala countered. "After all, the young economist was trained in America. I am sure he still believed in the open American democracy; in freedom of expression and in the greater American dream."

"This is Zambica, in Africa," Kaluba reminded him, "and not America. We have no Zambican dream, but that of the appointing authority. Only the President's bigger dream matters here. The rest are smaller and silent dreams. It was a big mistake...political suicide I must say."

"That's the real problem," Chishala intoned, "a minor difference in approach towards the same democratic goal with the boss's ideas was enough to force Donald to resign. Later, he was detained and it was rumoured that he was tortured by a government for which he passionately worked. It was total dictatorship," he concluded.

"Sometimes people have been tortured in the name of the President, but without the President's consent or knowledge." Kaluba explained.

"I know that, but in his case, the President could have intervened at some stage." Chishala suggested.

"We all tread a very thin line. It makes a big difference between drowning and survival," Chishala continued, "whether he made a mistake or not, Donald was broken after that detention." He argued.

"I'm sorry, I missed that." Kaluba mumbled.

"I have no doubt Donald should have been compensated handsomely by the courts for the torture," he continued. "It's a great pity, for such things to be happening in a multiparty system and what terrible abuse of state resources!" Chishala countered.

"The punishment was too personal and rather hard," Kaluba agreed. "But African politicians should always tread carefully," he suggested.

"It is us the senior party officials who make African leaders into ruthless dictators," Chishala argued. "Young Donald's punishment was totally disproportionate with the perceived offences," he said.

"My friend, Africa will always remain Africa for a long time." Kaluba said. "It can't be changed into America or Europe overnight. The law of the jungle is still here."

"Just look at what eventually happened to Donald" Chishala said. "He ended up contracting Tuberculosis in prison," he said sympathetically. "And he went to prison at the instigation of his own former personal friend and party leader… a party leader for whom he sacrificed so much!"

They discussed on and on. As always, they reached a deadlock in their political discourse. Kaluba continued supporting the party and their leader, accepting only a few of the arguments advanced by his colleague while Chishala advanced contrary views. Chishala also observed that several victims of President JFC's vendetta were later released through politically engineered nolle prosequi, due to lack of evidence by the state. But in any case, the accused persons were often humiliated. Kaluba countered that similar things happened during old JJ's reign.

"How about the exclusion of Chilala Munkombwe from the party?" Chishala asked. "Can it be justified in a democratic era?"

"To some extent it can," Kaluba replied meekly. "Depends on the circumstances."

"Admittedly, the man was highly educated. He was economically independent too," Kaluba said.

"Is it a crime to be rich?" Chishala asked him.

"You know what? " Kaluba responded. "The case of Chilala or CM as he was commonly called has been misunderstood by many people. The bottom-line is that he was overly calculating and ambitious. He single-handedly wanted to hijack the party and the Republican Presidency by using shortcuts."

"No. I would dispute that." Chishala protested. "CM was told by JFC to start from the bottom of the party hierarchy and he did comply."

"Did he?" Kaluba asked. "How did he do that?"

"Well, he went to the lowest-placed party unit, the ward in his community. There, in the shanty compound, Chilala rose rapidly to the position of deputy branch Chairman and, before we knew it, his motor vehicle was parked at state house," Chishala narrated. "It was very undemocratic for JFC to get involved in a case that was really beneath him."

"Well! Well!" Kaluba exclaimed. "I give credit to the President on this one," he said.

"Credit for what?" Chishala chuckled. "For being oppressive?" He asked him.

"For being observant in the first place, and for quickly nipping the whole naughty scheme in the bud," Kaluba explained.

"I don't understand," Chishala said. "What scheme are you talking about?"

"You know it," Kaluba answered. "The guy came late to the party and he wanted to use his wealth to quickly get to the top," he explained. "The President did the right thing for our party and the Republic. I can assure you. Never reap where you did not scatter seed, that's the moral teaching."

"I strongly disagree with that," Chishala protested. "First, Chilala committed no offence I can tell you this. In any case, who doesn't use available resources to get what they want, including getting to the top?"

"You and I, for starters," Kaluba responded.

"You and I, my foot!" Chishala exclaimed. "We have both used the resources at our disposal very effectively; our expertise and little monies, to get to where we are in the party and government," he explained. "How do we differ from Chilala?" He asked him bluntly.

"The difference is that Chilala had lots of resources, and was well connected to multi-national companies," Kaluba answered and then smiled.

Chishala explained what really happened, ignoring his friend's rather academic opinion. Chilala Munkombwe was democratically elected as deputy branch chairman in the area in which his massive mansion is located. But before he started celebrating his sweet victory, he was suddenly summoned to state house.

"To do what at state house?" Kaluba asked. "Anything to do with his position as Managing Director of an international mining conglomerate?"

"Not at all." Chishala replied. "Much to do with his little new position in the ruling MMR."

"You can't be serious!" Kaluba exclaimed, "such a junior position!"

"Now listen to this," Chishala interrupted. "At state house, Chilala, found the President seated with his party Secretary General, Chief Cobra. They told Chilala that they were aware of his little scheme to use the MMR as a ladder for his future political ambitions."

"What did Chilala say?" Kaluba asked.

"Chilala laughed, first thinking it was a joke." Chishala said. "When he realised they were serious, he told them both that he had committed no offence, under the Zambican laws."

"And then what?" Kaluba asked impatiently.

"You have to resign now," insisted the party chief, Chief Cobra, "and there are no negotiations."

"But Chilala was not intimidated." Chishala said. "He knew his rights, probably better than you and I, and declined to resign."

He then explained that the meeting at state house was so unfriendly that Chilala abandoned his car and hired a tax to take him home while the branch elections were immediately nullified by the party chief, who ordered fresh elections in which surprisingly, Chilala won the same position again, but in absentia this time, since he was out of the country. This time however, the entire branch executive committee was instantly dissolved, for insubordination; a disturbing and worrying development! He added that word had it that the President had a confidential report on Chilala's meeting in Brussels with his close friends whose main agenda was to prepare him to become the next Republican President.

Surprisingly, the two ministers failed to make sense of Chilala's case. Was it tribally or politically motivated or both? They wondered.

After being chased from a political party of his choice, it was not surprising that Chilala Munkombwe formed a new political party, called United Democratic Party (UDP), on whose ticket he ran as presidential candidate in the 2003 general and Presidential elections. He came very close to winning, after leading the count for some time, but ended up a close second, obtaining 29 percent of the vote compared to the winning candidate, who had 30 percent of the vote.

"Irrespective, it was wrong of the President and Chief Cobra to behave in that manner," Chishala insisted.

"Maybe there was something more than meets the eye, in Chilala's case," Kaluba suggested.

The MMR amended its constitution to regulate the ascendancy in the party hierarchy. Accordingly, everyone without exception had to start from the branch going up. You could not aspire to a higher party office except after serving a minimum of 3 years. Chief Cobra, then MMR national secretary, was the real architect of the constitutional amendments. The grapevine had it that Chief Cobra perceived Chilala Munkombwe as a major hindrance to his own ambition of taking over the helm of the party and to subsequently lead the country.

Thus, Chief Cobra thwarted Chilala's Presidential ambitions. He convinced JFC that Chilala was after his position. "How can you explain a man of high standing accepting to serve at branch level, let alone as deputy chairman?" He asked an equally baffled President.

Surprisingly, in this case JFC seemed to have been dribbled by Chief Cobra. The President fell for Cobra's lie hook, line and sinker. Inevitably, Chilala was hounded out of the party of his choice, thus, paving the way for Chief Cobra to pursue his own personal political ambitions.

Kaluba smiled again, but offered no defence.

"Chaluma also got rid of some of his critics within the MMR," Chishala remembered.

"Which ones are those?" Kaluba asked.

"How about his first Minister of Finance; some people believe he was the chief architect of the party's economic liberalisation policy."

"But in all governments, people are hired and fired, depending on their performance," Kaluba replied. "This is not only peculiar to this regime." He defended. " In any case, one's contributions should not be used as a ticket to misbehave."

"But your response is rather too general minister." Chishala pressed. "You should be more specific." He demanded.

"For your information only," Kaluba whispered. "The President actually liked that guy; to the extent he wanted him to be his successor." He revealed.

"What went wrong then?" Chishala asked. "Why was he fired instead?" He pressed.

"I am sure that with his wide and privileged sources, the President discovered a blot he could not tolerate. I hear there was pressure from a strong constituency to have him removed. Besides, he belittled the President, and told some donors, that he would do a better job, because he was more educated," Kaluba disclosed.

"I see." Chishala conceded. Kaluba smiled.

"Nevertheless, the former minister of finance was also politically excessively ambitious." Kaluba said.

"What do you mean?" Chishala asked curiously.

"Kasalu and two other former ministers who resigned from MMR formed a political party, the National Union, and went on to challenge their former party in Presidential and general elections, but their performance was dismal," Kaluba told him.

"Why did they perform so badly?" Chishala asked. "I hear they were well educated, and had the necessary resources."

"Education and wealth are beside the point." Kaluba argued. "If they were the most important, the United States of America and Europe would always be ruled by professors and billionaires," he reasoned. "In addition," he continued, "the new party's senior leaders developed serious disagreements about the outcome of their first party elections."

"I agree with you on that one. But minister, is it a crime to form a political party after being fired from cabinet?" Chishala asked him.

"No, it is not." Kaluba answered in the affirmative. "However, in this case, his actions went on to prove all the rumours circulating in the media that the minister of finance had formed a political party." Kaluba revealed, as Chishala nodded. "Yet, he was still a cabinet minister at the time.

"No President anywhere in the world can tolerate such indiscipline and insubordination from a senior minister," Kaluba continued.

"The President did the right thing to fire him." Chishala admitted.

Kaluba further explained that any head of state had a lot of information, including sensitive information from the state machinery that is often used to make important decisions. He gave examples of two top business executives who were relieved of their duties but later re-instated when relevant state organs found them innocent. He also revealed that one of these business executives later became a close friend of JFC, proving that the President was not vindictive.

Besides dealing firmly with political enemies, JFC was accused of using unorthodox ways of dealing with business executives who had fallen out of favour with him. For instance, he summoned a very experienced agricultural economist to state house and dangled a juicy carrot before his eyes. The President instructed the expert to support the government in its fight against corruption. He told him, that due to his reported prudent business management, he was sending him to a big commercial institution to put things right there and stamp-out the reported corruption at the organisation. The President promised to compensate the expert for his time and expertise.

When the new MD arrived at the company's Head Office on Egypt Road, he was in the company of a top police officer, and they forced their way into the MD's inner office without waiting for clearance from the secretary. The old MD was told to vacate the office immediately and leave things with the new boss; he was denied to take any of his personal belongings.

After a few weeks of probing, the new MD and his team failed to find evidence of the alleged corruption at the organisation and he made a report through the Minister of Finance to that effect. He however, tried to curb political interference, and dismissed a top management official, who was close to a powerful minister for financial fraud. Instead of getting the promotion he had been promised by the head of state, he was demoted and sent into Foreign Service without any explanation. The expert tried to seek audience with the appointing authority, but it was not forthcoming.

As usual, the two ministers continued their discussion and Kaluba insisted on the president's innocence.

"I will tell you that the President is a peaceful and a committed Christian." Kaluba said.

"Why do you think so?" Chishala asked.

"Why do you think he declared Zambica a Christian Nation?" Kaluba asked back.

Chishala smiled but uttered no word.

"He offered the country to the Lord," Kaluba continued, "that was a big decision my friend."

"It was a big decision I agree," Chishala conceded. "But actions speak louder than words," he countered.

"'I have heard that general argument before," Kaluba responded. "As far as I am concerned, the president did his part. I think many Christians in the nation didn't follow his footsteps in prayer." He reasoned. "Nevertheless, for matters of spirituality, it's better to follow the leader's advice, rather than his personal actions." Kaluba pontificated.

"You mean do as I say, and not as I do?" Chishala asked him.

"Absolutely," Kaluba concurred. "You must understand that leaders are human and also make mistakes along the way," he explained. "Look at Biblical figures like King David and Solomon; they also made mistakes, and yet God used them to bless and lead their people."

"I see," Chishala conceded.

"And I think there were other forces at play at the time" he clarified. "I could easily suspect that the Devil himself never had a wink of sleep after the President's bold declaration." He concluded.

Chishala nodded. "You think so?" He asked him.

"I don't think so." Kaluba retorted. "I know so."

"I see," Chishala said.

Kaluba smiled broadly, satisfied that he had finally put his message across to his friend's difficult and hard skull.

CHAPTER 12

A Costly Third Term Bid

Chishala's entrenchment at Defence was finally broken when he was moved to Foreign Affairs in the same capacity. The President's mini cabinet reshuffle took the former Minister of Defence by complete surprise. Until then, he had broken the record of being the only cabinet Minister in Chaluma's cabinet who had stayed the longest in one ministry. To some extent, he didn't mind the move to a ministry which he knew would give him maximum exposure to the rest of the world.

The Vice-President and the Minister of Foreign Affairs compared notes after returning from their respective foreign trips. Chishala cheerfully talked about his captivating trip to the United States while the Veep happily but cautiously informed the minister about the political situation brewing in neighbouring Mibiana, particularly that country's incumbent President's declared interest to go for a third-term in office. However, the Veep did not mention their own President's apparent personal interest in the subject; that would always remain strictly confidential, as directed by the head of state.

According to the country's constitution, a sitting President had a total tenure of two five-year terms, giving a maximum of ten years. By all initial indications, James Francis Chaluma was not at all interested in another term of office, and seemed ready to comply with the appropriate clause of the constitution when his maximum tenure came to a close. To this effect, the President had intimated to his Veep: "off the record, just find out what my brother in Mibiana is up to, concerning the third – term debate in that country."

"Yes Mr. President," the Veep had responded obediently. "I understand sir," he said politely.

"And your report should be confidential," the President emphasized. "Strictly for my eyes only. Do you hear Veep?" he stressed. The two had a very good rapport; many political observers thought that the Veep was destined to succeed JFC and Veep himself held similar views.

Upon his return from the weeklong trip to Mibiana, the Vice President made an official, but confidential report to the President, which was delivered using the usual official channels. But he personally typed another but shorter report, for the President's Eyes only,' which, not even his secretary had access to. The Veep drove to state house in his private vehicle without the noisy motorcade and used a private side gate, away from the prying eyes of nosy reporters, security officers and political vultures, and sought audience with the head of state.

He was ushered inside the inner office and was welcomed by the President, who was apparently in his characteristic jovial mood. There were no aides or witnesses to the meeting of the two most powerful men in the land. The President was uncharacteristically dressed informally in a pair of Jeans, golf shirt complete with matching shoes. After some awkward silence, the VP cleared his throat and then reported:

"Mr. President, your brother in Mibiana is very serious about going for the third term." He said.

"Is he really?" The President asked eagerly.

"Yes sir," the Veep responded. "They will be amending the constitution soon, to prepare the way for it." He replied.

"What!" The President chuckled. "Are they serious really?" He asked.

"Absolutely Mr President," the Veep reiterated. He gave some specific details, on the matter and the President seemed to relish it.

"You are laughing, Mr. President..." The Veep asked.

"I know that this is a very serious issue indeed. But why should the President distort his own legacy?" He asked him. The Vice President nodded in agreement and then smiled, probably in anticipation of his own future after Chaluma's presidency.

"After what my brother has done for that country," he complained, "and the heavy sacrifices he made, especially during the long and bitter liberation struggle,' he continued. "Why does he want the third – term really?" He wondered.

"I know, Mr. President," the Veep replied, sighing. "From what I observed, your brother in Mibiana seems to have enough support on the issue from his party, backed by a partisan Parliament." He stated. The President nodded.

"That could be his main motivation." The Veep suggested.

"Support is not the issue here," the President pointed out.

"This is much more of a moral issue," he said cunningly. The Vice President nodded, but remained mute. "It's like shredding the country's supreme law, for personal gain." The Veep nodded again.

"I know Mr. President," the Veep echoed, waiting for him to continue.

"What will the rest of the world think of us African leaders if they succeed?" President Chaluma lamented, trepidation inscribed all over his face. "In any case, what is it that one can achieve in another five years which he can't do in the first ten years?" He reasoned.

The Veep 'chewed and swallowed' the confidential discussion. At the time he was leaving the President's office, he had no reason to doubt that the head of state was totally against the amendment of any African constitution to enable a sitting President serve more than the prescribed duration. He felt greatly encouraged, and looked to his own political ascendency, at the end of the President's tenure of office.

A few days later, the Vice-President whispered his assessment of what was brewing in Mibiana to Chishala when they travelled together on an official trip to Southern Province, away from the noisy capital city. However, besides that story, Chishala observed that the Veep was elated over something else.

"Why? Mr. Vice-President," he asked him bluntly.

"Why? What? Minister," he asked him back.

"You seem to be elated by something sir!"

"It is nothing," the Veep said.

What he could not reveal to the minister was that, as Veep and with only ten months left before the next elections, he stood a good chance to be adopted as his party's presidential candidate; all he had to do was work extremely hard, and remain totally loyal to the head of state as he had done in the past. However, little did he know that the political engineer of a President had other ideas.

One month later, the President held a press conference. The Veep, most Cabinet Ministers, and Members of Parliament were not in attendance since the President's less-publicized press conference clashed with an important scheduled parliamentary session. The VP was obliged to present and defend the government position on a number of important bills and answer various questions from honourable members of parliament, as leader of the House, as was always the practice.

Meanwhile, the debate in the House went on and on as usual, until the Honourable Mr. Speaker brought that day's sitting to a scheduled close. Immediately, most members shuffled out of the chamber. As he exited from the National Assembly building, the Veep noticed some unusual movements against the established protocol; ministers and some ordinary members of parliament streamed out before him, and yet in the past, they would wait for him to leave first, as Leader of the House.

Outside, he also observed that his motorcade was not in his official parking lot. 'Did his team go to refuel?' No! He reflected. He waited impatiently as seconds ticked away. Fifteen or so minutes later something unusual happened again; the Minister of Foreign Affairs came to offer him a lift to Government House, the VP's official residence. The Veep hesitated for a while, and then agreed instinctively saying, 'why not?' In any case, the minister seemed to know something, but could not tell him; he didn't want to probe either.

At Government House, the usual Vice President's security deployment was missing. This was most unusual! A cold sweat ran down the Veep's back. Normally, his tall and beautiful wife waited for him in the spacious living room down stairs, but the room was quiet and empty. Then, he thought he heard someone crying upstairs. He tossed the briefcase on a couch and hurried to the master bedroom located on the first floor. The sobs were louder as he neared the bedroom. A retired General, he thought about the safety of his wife first. He quickly went for his gun in the right-side pocket of his trousers. After turning the safety gadget off the Revolver, he very slowly turned the door handle and then entered the bedroom. There she was; he swiftly secured the safety gadget to his gun and put the weapon back in his pocket. She did not see him because her back was turned towards the door. She turned when he cleared his throat.

He ran up to her, puzzled. Grace's face was in a mess; the makeup suffused her teary but beautiful face.

"Grace, sweetheart," his voice was charged with emotion, "why arc you crying?"

Large drops rolled down her pretty face, as if in response. She hunched her shoulders and wailed aloud like a child.

"Why has he done this to us?" She asked mournfully, "why?" She sobbed.

He held her tight and felt her body shudder with each sob.

"Who has hurt you Grace?" He insisted. He feared that someone may have crept up the house, entered the bedroom and ...His thoughts cringed. He prayed that no one had molested his wife. Anything was possible, what with the sentries to the immense Government House not at their designation.

He hurriedly poured and brought a glass of water from the side fridge by the bedside. She sipped some of the water and became somewhat composed.

"The midget, cockerel, son of a..." She didn't finish.

"What is going on Grace?" He interrupted; he could hardly contain the suspense.

"Oh! You mean you don't know?" She asked.

He watched her without saying a word.

She slowly walked to the mantelpiece, groped above the fireplace, and got the television remote control. She switched on the video, rewound the tape and played back the President's whole press conference. Only then, did he know that he had been demoted from the position of Vice President to that of Minister of Local Government and Housing. His jaw dropped. He was baffled; why did the President do this to him? All along, he had given him the impression that he was very happy with his performance. He recollected the events of the day; the unusual conduct of some ministers and members of parliament; they should have known by then that he had been demoted. He wondered why the President took away the bodyguards and sentries to Government House just like that. Why didn't he just tell him in advance? He could have willingly stayed at home, instead of making a complete fool of himself in Parliament, handling the business of the day when he was no longer Veep and leader of the House. He felt terribly belittled by the little man he had trusted so much.

For the former Vice President, the thought of resigning from government immediately crossed his mind; but he understood African politics too well; his reaction could easily be misconstrued as insulting the President. It could attract unnecessary animosity from the ruling party, a party he had truly worked hard for as General Secretary, before they formed government. Besides, he also knew too well that financially, he was far from being ready to do without government pay and privileges. His measly government pension from the army was nothing. In addition, his beautiful young wife and their children had already tasted good living. It would be unthinkable to emotionally flush all that into a garbage bin. No doubt, the President expected him to resign but he would surprise him. He would keep the little man guessing at his own game; he would therefore stick around. This was not the last time Chaluma and the country had heard about him.

After all, some members of parliament had told him in confidence that he would make a very good president. The greatest attribute the army experience had taught him was never to give in to rush thinking. One day he would ascend to the most powerful office in the land, whether Chaluma liked it or not. Zambicans would one day give him the mandate to rule and, he knew that Grace would make a perfect First Lady.

However, as the President wished, the former Veep was quickly replaced by a New Vice President.

Like other political parties in the country, the MMR was holding its provincial party conferences to prepare the ground for their national general conference. However, the MMR's provincial conferences gave conflicting indications concerning the future leadership of the party. At the end of the well-attended Kaole party conference, the President whispered in Lemba to the provincial party chairperson, in Chishala's presence; 'Ndemishila ichaume ichakosa, balya abatula amatwi' (I am leaving a real strong man to run the country; they have a primitive practice of piercing their ears). His description was clearly fitting the new Vice-President. It was crystal clear, without further explanation. From that day, Chishala, now a pragmatic politician started treating the new VP as the president in waiting. "What more evidence did people need about the incumbent President's desire to respect the constitution?" None, what-so-ever, Chishala answered his own question.

However, the following and final provincial conference of the MMR in Chitwe Nsofu in Copper Province, gave contrary indications. The President, despite his well-known rhetorics was not a known singer. This time round, however, he started his important address with an old Lemba romantic melody, at Chitwe Nsofu's Independence Park. Before taking to the podium, the President was seen pointing to his watch, an apparent reminder to the last speaker, Minister Bismarck Mwiinga that the President was itching to take the podium.

In response, the seasoned political honest broker swiftly wound up and announced the final and most important act of the well-attended political conference; a final address by the head of state himself. As he moved to the podium, President Chaluma opened his little mouth and belted out, the 'Bushimbe nabumpesha mano…mayo bushimbe tune; the song of bachelors lamenting on their plight, while seeking for a bride. But the head of state was already married; so, what was the melody all about? What followed thereafter was real confirmation that the President was actually searching for a bride or had probably found one as his marriage with the First Lady was reportedly in turmoil.

From nowhere, and almost out of the blue, a hint of President James Francis Chaluma's third-term bid surfaced and quickly gained some momentum. Initially, the move was suspected to have been masterminded by party cadres on the Copper Province and amplified by other cadres in a few other provinces who chorused as if by arrangement that the President had done the impossible by bringing back multi-party politics and fixing the shattered economy and, also did this and that... and therefore, deserved a third – term of office.

Even though this was untenable under the existing Party and Republican constitutions, some gullible cabinet ministers, who should have known better joined in, while others were not so sure but soon jumped on the band wagon, calling for a third term for their leader. Surprisingly, Kaluba was at the forefront of the political demagogues. Nevertheless, with the information he had in the past from the former Vice-President, Chishala was initially indifferent to the whole idea. However, quietly, the CEO of the party, Chief Cobra, was also urging the President on saying. "Sir, you are so popular, you will easily get the third-term."

In a short time, the calls for Chaluma's third term were getting louder while the gossip and rumours were also gaining momentum. This was confusing because Chaluma made public statements on a number of occasions indicating that he would step down at the end of his second term. When he had a quiet moment alone with the President, Chishala decided to be professional and put it bluntly to the head of state, "Mr President, there are strong calls for your third

– term," he said, hesitantly. "What is your stand, sir, so that we know how to handle this?" He asked his boss.

"Minister," he hesitated, "I shall let you know later," the President replied curtly.

Chishala was baffled further; the President's body language and his lukewarm response were almost 90 percent in the affirmative, and yet the President never officially announced his intentions to go for a third-term of office. He was curious because he believed all along that Chaluma would not go for a third –term of office. Besides the discreet information from the former Veep he was also certain that almost all legal minds and non-partisan thinkers in the country agreed that the constitution did not allow President Chaluma to stand for a third term. Although disappointed, he had to be politically correct and prudent and follow the wind. In any case, it did not take long before it became common knowledge that the President, the political engineer himself was actually behind the calls for his third – term.

Public speculation about Chaluma's intentions on the third-term increased when the President, early in 2002, refused to name a successor, but warned his cabinet members about stating presidential ambitions, allegedly to prevent open conflict within the ruling MMR. In any case, after a series of MMR by-election victories in 2002, the third-term campaign intensified.

Government actions also fuelled more speculations. For instance, the budget presented to Parliament in January 2003 set aside US$ 400 million for establishing 72 positions of District Administrators (DAs), allegedly to improve service delivery in rural areas. However, while DAs were considered civil servants, they were provided with motor vehicles and offices outside the formal local government structures. Tasked to help coordinate various government activities at the District level, the DA's privileges sharply contrasted with the working conditions of local government officials. In addition, the DA's were personally appointed by the President and were structured to report to the President, through the Provincial Administration.

Many people including some from the ruling MMR were surprised and disappointed with the turn of events. They included Chishala and many senior party members. One of the former Vice Presidents was even more puzzled; what had happened to the President? The President had made a complete U-turn. In the process, the party was divided right down the middle, between those for and those against President Chaluma's latest political scheme.

The state of affairs led to indifference, among a few principled ministers from the cabinet as they did not like the idea of mutilating the party's constitution, which they had heavily campaigned against in 1993. Instead, some of them resolved not to resign and decided to fight the President's machinations within the party. His two immediate former Vice-Presidents were also disappointed and openly rebelled, with no less than nineteen Members of Parliament strongly rejecting the ploy. They were joined by the church, civil society, some institutions of higher learning, and the donor community.

As the 2003 elections drew near the Movement for Multiparty Restoration was, therefore hit by a political crisis caused by President James Francis Chaluma's desire to go for a third-term, against his earlier assurances that he would not seek a third – term of office.

A consortium of the church society dabbled 'The Desert Committee' was born and somehow finally put spanners in Chaluma's wishes. People were told that the JFC's scheme would take the country back to one-party state. Strong campaigns were mounted against Chaluma's third-term bid with support from church mother bodies and more NGOs to emphasise the message against Chaluma's latest manoeuvres. Concerned citizens wore green ribbons and honked their car horns every Monday afternoon. Ultimately, the growing resistance scared the President's third-term campaign.

The President was insulted, called all sorts of names, and one newspaper in particular started calling him a thief, while a few of his former ministers were among those shouting the loudest! Even regional governments and some donors were also disappointed with the unexpected developments. For instance, the South African and Botswana governments pressed the President not to amend the constitution, while some foreign aid donors also expressed their displeasure.

Some vengeful private tabloids especially those funded by members of the cartel, also seized the opportunity to get at Chaluma to settle old political scores under the guise of practising journalism and sided with the protestors in criticising and disparaging the President. Other than divide the nation, the President gradually realized that it was a battle he could not win, though it had worked easily in neighbouring Mibiana.

A political schemer, Chaluma publicly called himself a political engineer; and that was not for nothing. He therefore planned his revenge against his new 'enemies', whom he described as 'rebels.' The President suddenly issued instructions that no MMR party official was allowed to start campaigning for the presidency until he said so. Nevertheless, a campaign was started through various groups pleading for him to stand, in national interest.

As expected, the MMR party convention expelled the 21 'rebel' members of Parliament by a resolution of the Convention. An injunction by the 'rebels' to prevent the conference from taking place flopped and the party constitution was amended to remove the two term limitation. James Francis Chaluma won the party presidency unopposed, but his party still had no presidential candidate for the 2003 general elections, since his third-term bid had been shot down.

However, instead of the conference electing Chaluma as the party's presidential candidate, as was the previous practice, the conference mandated the party's National Executive Committee (NEC) to head-hunt for a suitable candidate. By then, the MMR was now in a fix as the main opposition parties had already announced their presidential candidates who were in fact quietly campaigning. This encouraged the expelled former leaders of MMR, who saw a window of opportunity and quickly formed their own parties, while Chilala Munkombwe and his new party were consolidating their campaign and became optimistic about their chances.

It is rumoured that unknown to most of the party hierarchy, JFC had already printed on A3 gloss paper (in colour) third-term campaign posters. These posters were first delivered to the Copper Province via the offices of the District Administrators (DAs). The DAs in the province were secretly instructed to set apart those vuvuzelas or praise singers from those who were critical and analytical on issues of democracy. Those who insisted on a two-term tenure for the presidency were ostracised.

President Chaluma used the African leaders' old trick and tried in vain to convince the nation that he had no intentions of going for a third-term, but if the people demanded it, he would be obliged to bow to their wishes. But reading the uncompromising general mood of the people against his third – term bid, the President finally relented and announced that the constitution would not be amended, meaning no third-term for him. That effectively ended the third-term bid debate, to the great relief of the nation.

His opponents including old Jerome Jumbe celebrated a victory they thought they had won. However, it was reported that the President was terribly upset: How could the chaps who were nobodies; whom he had propelled to political prominence treat him like that? With the Chief Cobra playing a loyalist trick on him, by urging him to go for it, he therefore was unhappy with a group of his senior party colleagues who he believed had betrayed him. He was convinced that they were largely responsible for the failure of his bid for an extra term of office. However, if he thought his former ministers had betrayed him, the worst was still to come.

With rumours circulating about the likely presidential candidate for MMR, some ministers were apprehensive about Luka Mwambwa being a suitable candidate. Two of them Peter Mabo and Gold Mandi plucked up courage and spoke to the President in confidence, over the issue.

Mandi said, "Mr President, are you sure this man will work well with us and look after you?"

"Yes, he will," the President assured, without hesitation. "What are your concerns?"

"Mr President, please avoid getting a man you will be leaving in your chair, who will start looking for faults of what you did." Mabo joined in.

"No! That wouldn't arise," the President said, "But even if it did, what would be there to find?" He asked them.

"Thank you for the assurance Mr President." The two ministers said almost in unison. "We just wanted to be assured that all will be well." Mabo continued.

While several citizens were scared of approaching President Chaluma over his preferred candidate, one person wasn't. As soon as he heard unconfirmed reports that Luka Mwambwa was the front runner for adoption as a candidate for the Movement for Multi-party Restoration, Lewis Chanda, sometimes called LC, summoned his courage and decided to do something about it. A fearless freedom fighter, LC had directed the implementation of ULP's five point master plan, during the liberation struggle, and was passionate about democracy and the interests of Zambicans.

After trying to seek an appointment to see the head of state for two weeks, he was finally granted one. He was told to report at state house at exactly 08:00hours on Monday morning. With vast experience in the tactics of persuasion, Chanda asked an old colleague, Chapwa Chileya, who was an old schoolmate of the President to accompany him. The two senior citizens arrived at state house at exactly 07:45 hours, thinking they had fifteen minutes to spare. Oh boy! They were terribly mistaken.

They were well received and given comfortable chairs. But there were also other people in a crowded waiting room. From time to time, some names were called; some people came out, while others went into the President's inner office. The two senior citizens glanced at each other, and smiled simultaneously, but said nothing. After waiting for about two hours, the President's Special Assistant came to them and apologised.

They continued waiting patiently for another one hour, before an apologetic presidential aide called their names. They were at last ushered into the President's inner office. He greeted them cheerfully and cracked some old jokes about Kabombe secondary school. He also gave them a long sermon about the structural adjustment programme; how he loved it, and how it was still working in Zambica. He then personally saved them tea with cakes before asking old Chanda to unfold.

"Thank you so much Mr President for allowing my colleague and I to see you, despite your very busy schedule." Chanda said.

"The pleasure is mine gentlemen." The President answered. "And you are always welcome here at state house." The two visitors nodded.

"Mr President, the main purpose of our visit is to quietly inform you that the person you are considering as party presidential candidate is not suitable!" He stated bluntly.

"What do you mean not suitable?" He asked Chanda. "Can you elaborate?" He was short of asking him for his source of information since the name was still confidential, but he decided to spare the respected old man.

"Let me take you back into political history, if I may Mr President," Chanda reasoned. The President nodded. The senior citizen went ahead and provided the head of state with detailed information against the preferred candidate.

"I shall have that investigated." The President promised curtly. His eyes were mostly fixed at one point of the ceiling, while tapping his right foot. Chileya knew that gesture of the President; he had already made-up his mind on the subject.

"Is there another issue?" the President asked impatiently.

"Yes Mr President. The second issue is that Luka Mwambwa left your administration a very bitter man, something he never hid from his close friends. He has continued to harbour hatred against you," he revealed. "He may humiliate you while in office, if you gave him this chance." He told him.

"Is that so?" The President asked, while Chanda nodded.

"Are you sure about that?" The President continued. "My friends from the intelligence service have scrutinised him," he sighed. "Their report indicates that he is as clean as sterilised water." He told them. Chanda was baffled and it showed on his face.

"Mr President, please. I beg you, don't make the same mistake Wampanga and I made in the past, and you may live to regret it for the rest of your life." He warned him.

Chaluma smiled. "When I leave office soon, I shall, become former President," he said. "But there will be no need for me to look over my shoulders," he preached. "Because, I have done nothing wrong. Nothing whatsoever, Mr Chanda," he emphasised.

"Mr President!" LC pleaded again. "Vindictive people like him don't need a crime!" He sighed. "They can always manufacture one." The President and Chileya nodded.

"The third and final reason Mr President is that, unconfirmed but reliable information indicates that the candidate and President Jumbe, your arch enemy are already in tandem; they are working together." He said. "Their partnership would work terribly against you Mr President. I know how he works Mr President. I worked closely with him for a long time." He ended.

"No! It's not feasible," the head of state protested visibly. "But those two are enemies and Jumbe is totally against Luka Mwambwa's adoption." He raved, shaking his head.

"Mr President please," Chanda pleaded yet again. "As former Minister of Home Affairs, I worked with many intelligence officers at the highest level," he said almost boasting. "In my humble opinion," he continued, "Jumbe is simply creating a smoke screen, in order to divert people's attention." He advised, sounding, as if he had more intelligence information than the head of state.

"I see," the President intoned. "That's a possibility then."

"And on the intelligence reports Mr President," Chanda said, "they have failed you sir."

"In which way have they done that?" the President asked him firmly.

"From my humble experience, weak or subjective officers, report on what they know the boss wants to hear," he alleged.

"But they don't even know Luka Mwambwa personally," the President argued. "What's going on?"

"A lot is going on Mr President," Chanda said, sighing. "For instance, do you know Mr President that today, one senior member of the Luka Mwambwa family has been meeting a very senior officer from the intelligence at a private place?" he asked.

"What were they doing?" he asked. "What were they discussing, Mr Chanda? Are you sure?" Chaluma probed further with belated interest.

"Mr President, I have never asked to see you since you became President." He said. "I know how busy this office can be. I came now because of the gravity of the situation and I can assure you that my sources are impeccable!" Chaluma's eyes were fixed at a part of the ceiling again, while tapping his right foot – mission impossible! Chileya concluded.

"I wish to thank you both for your useful information senior citizens," the President said looking at his watch, attempting to quickly conclude the meeting. Chileya nodded.

"Mr President, please reflect on the information I have just given you before it is too late," Chanda reminded him. "Its for the good of the nation." He pleaded.

"Intelligence officers shall investigate further, and appropriate action will be taken," he promised, without conviction.

However, with the President's defensive stance and body language, Chanda concluded that their mission was a flop. What a waste of valuable time? He breathed. They left the President and state house soon after that.

Against all expectations, President Chaluma convinced his party's National Executive Committee (NEC) to elect his first VicePresident,

Luka Mwambwa, who had resigned from government, citing corruption and other vices as the reasons. However, the elections were suspected to have been flawed. Besides, it is said that the President had a secret one-on-one meeting with each voter just before the election; what was that meeting all about? Some political engineering, obviously.

As widely expected the President's handpicked candidate won the secret ballot. Thus, with only a few months before the elections, the MMR now had a presidential candidate. Without a contingency plan and in a hurry, President Chaluma banked on Luka Mwambwa to win the presidency for him and the party. But even some staunch party supporters insisted that he was a 'wrong choice'. Ostensibly, the choice of Luka Mwambwa was meant to teach a big political lesson to his former colleagues who had been expelled from the party.

The divisions in MMR were accentuated by the choice of Luka Mwambwa as presidential candidate, leading to speculations that Chaluma had hand-picked a successor whom he thought he could manipulate. The choice of Luka Mwambwa resulted in the exit of MMR's influential but tricky national secretary, Chief Cobra, who had been in the forefront of Chaluma's third-term campaign. After his resignation, Chief Cobra ironically claimed that he had never supported Chaluma's third-term campaign bid, but was merely defending the government and party positions and that he was only doing his job as the party's Chief Executive Officer. Shortly afterwards, Chief Cobra announced that he was going to run for the presidency under his newly formed political party.

Despite being preferred by the President, the adopted presidential candidate was unpopular among most members of the NEC who opted to keep quiet in order to keep peace with the political engineer of a president. However, Chishala and a few other brave members whispered to the President that the party's presidential candidate was rigid and too legalistic; he could betray him as soon as he assumed the instruments of power. But the President scoffed at the insinuations with a characteristic laugh, saying his decision was final. Political analysts though believed that Chaluma's decision was largely motivated by his desire to teach the 'rebels' a lasting lesson. Little did he know that he wouldn't have the last laugh, and that his own bitter lesson was still to come.

Suddenly, the razzmatazz about the President quietly divorcing his wife of many years with whom he had several children took centre stage. No reasons were advanced other than the standard jargon that the marriage had irretrievably broken down. He was marrying another woman. The cat was therefore, finally out of the bag and provided possible answers to two intriguing questions that had boggled the minds of many people in the nation, who wondered why James Francis Chaluma a non-singer, had publicly poured out amorous lamentations by singing that old but sweet romantic Lemba melody at the party conference in Chitwe Nsofu.

It all suggested that he was seeking a new bride and also a good reason for his change of heart to go for a third-term, against his earlier strongly held views. With the new evidence, it was now further speculated that he was dictated to by his beautiful new lady's desire for two things; a state wedding and the status of First Lady, after listening to Chief Cobra's husky whispers. But the two tied the knot in a private service as her new husband failed lamentably to deliver on any of her two wishes after the third-term debacle.

The President established campaign committees, and appointed some ministers to them. Some of his special assistants were tasked to write speeches for the candidate, in order to bring his speeches to presidential level. To make him look different from other opposition presidential candidates, officers from the police, army, and intelligence were instructed to salute the MMR candidate. The President was damn serious and did everything possible to market his chosen presidential candidate.

For his own safety, the candidate seconded his trusted people to the committees set-up by the president to monitor and spy on what was being said and done, and in particular to report anyone with anti-Luka Mwambwa sentiments. The MMR and President Chaluma campaigned very hard to have the candidate elected Republican President and the candidate himself knew it. In fact, he often boasted to his close friends that he had directed President Chaluma to work like a servant for his campaign!

Nevertheless, President Chaluma campaigned very hard for his chosen candidate; it was as if his own life depended on the candidate's victory. It is reported that due to prolonged campaign hours and the overall stress of the frequent election campaign trips, the President developed high blood pressure. His doctors advised him to take a break from the campaign and to seek medical attention abroad, but the President declined, fearing that his absence would lead to his candidate losing the vital elections.

⸻ ⟨•✴•⟩ ⸻

The atmosphere at Chishala's home had changed drastically. For a few weeks, he usually came home late and tired, often giving one excuse after another, and showing little interest in the beautiful young woman he previously adored so much. That caused suspicion and more silence in their bedroom. Mboniwe realised that there was a bigger problem than she had previously imagined. Instead of bottling it up or confiding in an elderly woman as she had been taught by her grandmother, she decided to give vent to some of the pressure differently. She decided to talk to a man!

That prompted her to call on Kaluba; of all people.

"I am worried about your friend," she said. "He might be seeing someone else," she suggested.

"You can't be serious," he replied. "Do you have any evidence?" he asked.

"Not exactly," she replied. "But I can tell from his long unexplained absence from home, endless excuses and body language. You know what I mean," she put it to him.

"Sounds like mere suspicion to me," he said. "If you need me to assist in any way, you need to be more specific" he suggested. "I'll need details and facts and you should trust me with any information. You know your husband very well. He could be quite defensive."

"You also think so?" She asked.

"No. I don't think so," he responded. "I know so."

"That's interesting. I have equally found him to be quite defensive." She concurred.

"In cabinet, they used to call him the perfect Defence Minister when he held that portfolio. Even now, he talks and behaves defensively all the time." Mboniwe nodded.

"I am not as young as I look," she told him, changing the topic. "I have had relationships with men in the past," she revealed.

"You!" he exclaimed, "Relationships?" he teased. "That sounds like a joke of the decade," he ridiculed her. "Let me tell you that those in the past were probably mere picnics. This is the real thing called marriage!" He explained. Unknown to Towera, his real motive was totally different. To dig more and get to the core of Chishala's marital problems, after all it could finally pay him dividends one day.

"Besides my time in primary education, I spent five years in secondary school and then two years in college," she explained. "And during that time," she continued, "I have had three serious relationships," she stated, while he listened with utmost attention. "Your friend is behaving like one who has lost interest in me or is having an affair." She moved closer to him. He swallowed saliva hard, but held her hand and prevented their bodies from touching; just to tease her further.

"You are a very beautiful young woman," he complimented her. "You are more beautiful than Cleopatra." He praised her further. "Sometimes, I feel that my friend is very lucky to have you, at his age."

"Thank you, for your compliments," she replied and smiled invitingly. "What is your fear then?" she challenged. "And besides, age is just a number." She put it to him.

"You are so smart and attractive; it will be a real pleasure to hold you in my arms one day," he complimented her again.

"What is preventing you then?" she teased him yet again. "You have inhibitions Minister?" she asked, looking him squarely in the eyes.

Kaluba could not believe his luck. Mboniwe was hot, no doubt about it. There and then, he felt like crushing her against his body, but he managed to look detached. He would tread slowly and carefully. Better that way. There was no need to hurry. Age and experience were on his side. He would take the role of the cat; play with his prey for some time, before closing in for the final kill. But this was like the mouse bringing itself uninvited, to the hungry cat!

"First, you want me to help you and Chishala in your marriage, right?" he asked instantly.

"Yes, I do," she agreed. "That's why I came to see you." She said. Her real motive was initially to find a way to make Chishala jealous.

"If I am going to help you both," he said, "I rather help to solve the problem first, and then you and I can have the pleasure," he suggested. She smiled at him. Her eyes dilated. She could not tell whether it was fear, excitement or both that made her eyes feel weighty.

"Two," he paused, looking her firmly in her pretty face. "Your husband has been a close friend of mine for a long time. If you and I become intimate, you should not betray me," he cautioned her bluntly. She nodded, and slowly drifted backwards, before replying.

"What do you mean by that?" She asked him.

"You should not kiss and tell," he stressed. She smiled at him gently.

"Are you scared of Chishala?" She challenged him.

"No. I am not." He replied. "I like him actually; we have been buddies for years."

"Then tell me," she challenged him again. "Between your number one and number two reasons, which one is more important to you?" She bluntly asked him.

"I give both the same rating," he replied without hesitation.

Mboniwe again gave him a grin, like a Cheshire cat, without saying a word. He smiled back at her. But she suspected that he too fancied her, probably more than she did. He was only being diplomatic and playing hard to get. Apparently, she was familiar with that tactic, even though it was more common among women.

As Mboniwe had suspected, Kaluba was not being honest to himself. He had a craving for her for some time. However, he now wanted more details about their marital problems; stuff he could probably use against Chishala. This was aimed at settling old scores, totally unknown to the young lady.

In any event, it wasn't long before Kaluba started whispering Chishala's marital can of worms to the President's special assistant for press and information. He hoped that it could eventually reach the President's sensitive ears, but the professional gentleman at state house declined to get involved in what he considered as a purely domestic affair.

Thus, the silent rivalry between the two, 'close' Ministers, continued tenaciously; little did the Minister of Foreign Affairs suspect that he had a big mole in his relationship with his oldest friend. On the other hand, little did Mboniwe realise that she could end up being used as both a pawn and catalyst, in the long simmering, but undeclared war between the two 'good' friends.

CHAPTER 13

Former President Sold Down the River

"Mr President, how much do you trust our candidate?" asked Dr James Ndalya, one of the two image builders President Chaluma had secretly assigned to work with the candidate in order to improve his image; polish him up and make him look presidential.

"Very well," the President replied. "Why do you ask?"

"He seems to harbour feelings of hatred against you, Mr President," he disclosed. "I am afraid he may hurt you later."

"Why do you think so?" The President pressed.

"He makes subtle and careless hints." Dr Ndalya said. "It's like he was mistreated in the past by you and a few senior members of the party." He disclosed.

"You really think so, Doctor?" the President queried.

"Yes, Mr President. He seems to have left the party and government a very bitter man."

The President promised Dr Ndalya that he would investigate, a promise he had made to others, but never kept. Nevertheless, the President kept on receiving worrying intelligence reports about the unexpected attitude of his party's official candidate during the climax to the elections campaign. A few people, including some trusted ministers, also informed him that they suspected the candidate to be a trojan horse, but he did not believe them due to the stubborn element in him.

The President and his team worked extremely hard to sell a difficult candidate. He had to raise a lot of money from various sources to support the man's campaign. He also sacrificed a number of his colleagues from the MMR, and yet most of them had served him well.

However, Chaluma's candidate won the presidential elections against the opposition which was badly divided. In fact, it was rumoured that the president did everything legal and illegal to secure his candidate's victory. The candidate of the MMR managed to secure the narrowest of victories, in the country's history, managing only 30 percent against the candidate with the second highest votes, Chilala Munkombwe, who got 28 percent, while a new party, Democratic Forum for Development(DFD) came third, in terms of parliamentary seats scooped. Thus, Luka Mwambwa won by a simple majority, in accordance with the existing first past the-post constitutional provisions. But put together, opposition parties garnered a hefty 70 percent of the votes cast. President Chaluma's candidate was therefore, a minority President. In popularity, he was as good as rejected by the electorate.

It was obvious, therefore, that if the major opposition parties had formed an electoral alliance, President Chaluma and his MMR could have been sent packing, and probably gone into political oblivion, as had happened to the former ruling party, ULP. But as it were, the self-styled political engineer survived possible embarrassment and his preferred candidate was hurriedly sworn in as the country's Republican President, amid protests and accusations of vote rigging.

Nevertheless, the President was over the moon. He had achieved his major objective; having his handpicked candidate elected as Republican President. Despite the unconfirmed negative reports about the President-elect, his promoter was probably sure the new development was an opportunity for him to continue ruling by proxy. What better way was there than having a 'surrogate' as the new leader?

By hindsight, the President regretted having wasted his valuable time and resources on the now dead third-term bid.

The High court premises in Lusiku were a hive of activities. Preparations were advanced for the inauguration ceremony to swear-in the third Republican President, Mr Luka Mwambwa. It is said that former President Chaluma had prepared a moderate reconciliatory speech for the President-elect to tone down tempers in view of the bitterness and name calling that had characterised the campaign, and also due to the very narrow margin of his victory, but it was ignored. Instead, the new President's speech was full of hyperbole and warnings. In a hot breath, President Luka Mwambwa showed anger and annoyance at his critics, stating that now that he was Republican President, he would deal firmly with those insinuating that the elections had been rigged. Many people in the audience were dumbfounded; those were words of a bitter man and not a new minority President who had just taken his oath of office to protect and defend all the citizens.

When Chaluma arrived at state house, his body guards asked him to pack his belongings quickly; an instruction apparently given by the new President. The director general of intelligence was instructed to supervise the shifting of the former President. Everything was being done in such a hurry and without a definite plan. No wonder some of the former President's belongings ended up at a private warehouse. Thus, like a miracle, the former President had moved to his new house. As he himself had done for Jumbe, he had expected the new President to give him time before moving to another house. That was definitely bitter lesson number one for Chaluma. At 19.00 hours Chaluma's cell phone brought him back to the new reality.

"Hello. Good evening eh Mr eh ....sorry ...I mean Mr President sir." Chaluma responded to the phone that had been whirring for more than three minutes. Until then, he had been used to the luxury of someone answering all his calls.

"Where are you Mr Chaluma?" the President asked nonchalantly. "I would have thought you would have waited for my arrival so that you usher me into the state mansion as well as orient me and my family."

"I am sorry sir …. but…" the former President was baffled.

"Your excellency you mean" the President cut in with an authoritative demeanour.

"Your Excellency, my apologies. I am at my new home." The former President responded.

"Hah! your new home. Where is it? I see. Why didn't you wait for me?"

"Your Excellency, I was given instructions to the contrary. My sincere and honest apologies." Chaluma said.

"I hear you. In future, you should only act upon instructions from the head of state." The new President instructed. "Is that clear your exc….oh sorry, I mean Mr. Chaluma." The new President rumbled his forced laughter and dropped the phone unceremoniously.

Chaluma could not believe how his world had turned upside down within one day. What next? He wondered.

As expected, opposition parties petitioned the election results, but the High court ruled that while it was true that there were some irregularities in the election process, these would not have altered the outcome of the election results. Nevertheless, this sounded like a textbook judgement, by a partisan jury in view of the thin margin obtained by the winner.

Admittedly, the 2003 general and presidential elections were fiercely contested, especially there being no incumbent in the race.

There were no less than eleven presidential aspirants, a record at that time. The outcome of the elections was also regarded as highly controversial due to the fact that the new Presiddent won only by a few percentage points. Consequently, three opposition party leaders, including one former Vice-President under the MMR went to court and challenged the outcome through a petition.

However, after a deliberately protracted hearing, the court ruled in favour of Chaluma's candidate, who was already president in any case.

Meanwhile, a development was brewing which shook Chaluma to his core. It was only a short time after Luka Mwambwa's inauguration when former President Chaluma started seeing the 'true animal' character in his chosen candidate. Initial indicators were rumours to the effect that Luka Mwambwa was telling his close aides that he was now in the perfect position to avenge his mistreatment and that of his close allies at the hands of the former President, when he was in government.

Then, Chaluma received confirmed reports that Luka Mwambwa and Jerome Jumbe had met and formed a secret alliance whose objective was not known but worrying. The scenario did not make political sense. How could Luka Mwambwa do such a thing when Jumbe had publically opposed his adoption as the MMR candidate and openly called him a cabbage? The former President also remembered that at that time, some women shoppers at most urban markets seemed to agree with Jumbe's vegetable description of the then MMR presidential candidate. The women would mockingly ask for a 'Luka Mwambwa' when buying cabbage, often sending suppliers and observers into wild laughter. But the well-informed suppliers knew better, and would not ask for clarification, they would actually provide their customers the real cabbage, and not Luka Mwambwa!

On a serious note, Chaluma now regretted having dismissed the warning from Lewis Chanda about the dangers of adopting Luka Mwambwa as MMR candidate. The old and respected former freedom fighter seemed to have done his homework, but he had dismissed his report instantly. At least Chanda's warning came at the right time, just before Luka Mwambwa was officially adopted.

Then Chaluma asked for his first favour from the Republican President. He sent in a confidential list of seven names to be included in the new cabinet and one to be appointed as Veep. The President laughed at the request, but surprisingly retained Chaluma's last Vice President in the post, even though he was not on the former President's list. Then for the position of ministers, he picked two from Chaluma's wish list. One of the two was none other than Kaluba, a former minister in Chaluma's cabinet, and Chishala's 'close' friend. While the former President's request was not directly responded to, he got the message when the President announced his first cabinet. What ingratitude! Chaluma thought.

To everyone's surprise, Kaluba became the most ardent supporter of the new President against his former boss and mentor. It also became a talking point that while Kaluba was appointed Minister, Chishala was left out like many others from Chaluma's former cabinet.

Without a doubt Kaluba had clearly been favoured above many ministers by the former President. In fact, some senior ministers at the time thought that he was the most likely minister to succeed the President, after serving his two terms. However, instead of being grateful to the former President as expected, Kaluba's behaviour was rather indifferent and almost similar to that of the new President.

Once he got the minister's new mobile number, the former President put in a call to him one morning and they talked for a short while.

"Congratulations minister for the deserved appointment," the former President said, "even though I thought you deserved a higher portfolio."

"Thank you Mr President," Kaluba responded. "It is very kind of you to call."

"You are most welcome minister," Chaluma said.

"I am reliably informed that I owe the position to you sir," he said.

"My recommendation to the head of state was purely on merit," the former President responded.

"Thank you, all the same, sir," he said. "They say that there would be no outcome without an input," Kaluba reasoned. "My appointment is the outcome," he continued. "But your recommendation is the input here, sir." He emphasised sounding polite on the line. "You are welcome, minister." Chaluma responded.

They talked briefly about the results of the elections. Kaluba pointed out that the new President's victory was clearly due to the former President's strategy; funding and overwhelming support. Otherwise, the situation could have been different.

"You think so really?" Chaluma asked.

"Without a doubt, Mr President." He replied. "Even the President knows that." He added. "He has often talked to us about it."

"That is good to hear." Chaluma intoned. "There is one important issue I would like us to discuss privately as soon as possible," he intimated. "When can you find time?" he asked the minister.

"We have a cabinet meeting tomorrow. I shall call you after that, sir," he promised.

It was now four days and the minister had not yet called. Because the issue was urgent, the former President dialled Kaluba's number which rang for a short while and then was cut. He rang the number once again and this time got the 'network busy' tone. In the evening, he tried the minister's number yet again but drew another blank. What was happening? Was it poor network? He wondered.

The following morning, Chishala paid the former President a visit and they discussed a number of issues. Then finally the former President complained about his problems in accessing Hon. Kaluba's number. He was totally flabbergasted by Chishala's laughter.

"What is it?" Chaluma asked him.

"Mr President, you mean you don't know?" He asked.

"Know what?" He sounded totally ignorant.

"Kaluba has always been like that – opportunistic," he revealed.

"What do you mean?" Chaluma asked. "Do you think that he is deliberately avoiding talking to me?"

"Most likely, sir," Chishala confirmed with a smile. "Many of my former colleagues in your cabinet are fully aware of his unbecoming behaviour."

"I can't believe it," the former President said, shaking his head. "There must be some other explanation. Not after all the many favours I extended to him," he recalled.

When Chishala gave him some details on Kaluba's motivation and pattern of behaviour, the former President nodded in understanding. To prove his theory, however, Chishala put in a call to Kaluba's number, using a phone whose number was not known by him; it went through. He passed the phone to the former President who greeted the man on the other side and they talked briefly before the minister gave an excuse, and promised to call later that evening, as he was chairing a meeting at the ministry.

"I can't believe this," the former President said.

"No exaggeration sir," Chishala explained. "Fits into Kaluba's behaviour perfectly," he said. "I have known him for many years," he quickly pulled air in, and then gently let it out.

"Really?" He asked him.

"He has always been very quick, blowing with the wind, as they say." Chishala mockingly stated.

"How come I never knew about his bad behaviour all those years?" The former President asked. "I feel like a fool," he confessed.

"Sir, don't even feel bad about it," he suggested. "You couldn't read the minds of many people who served in your administration," he explained. "Some were genuine while others were opportunists." He said. "Just like my friend Kaluba," he intoned.

"My! My!" said Chaluma. "I was certainly duped by some people I truly confided in," he regretted.

Chishala smiled. "They don't call him gold-digger for nothing."

"Gold-digger!" Exclaimed the former President. "How appropriate." He concurred. "He is exactly like Judas Iscariot I should say. If he behaves like that."

"Exactly, sir. Correct description, fits him like a glove, he always blows with the wind." The former President nodded, without saying a word.

On his own, after Chishala had left, the former President was annoyed. Kaluba was the minister he had trusted a lot. At some point, he had thought he was suitable to be President after him but he didn't pick him, in order to give a chance to someone from another province. While he had made him a very senior minister in his cabinet, he recalled that he also protected the chap from investigations by the anti-corruption commission, when he received corruption charges against the minister.

Chishala reflected on the predicament the former President had found himself in. While Kaluba's likely betrayal might be the worst from Chaluma's former ministers, he anticipated others to follow suit. What with the rumours Chishala had heard about the new President; wanting information and evidence to enable him nail his sponsor, and predecessor, to the hard cross. How ungrateful! While Chishala had secretly criticized some of Chaluma's actions while in office, he still had great respect for the man's courage. Without his courage and sacrifice, Jerome Jumbe would probably have still been in power, as almost all potential political leaders were scared of him.

As per practice the party had just launched its annual national card renewal at a posh conference centre in the capital city. This was followed by the party's executive committee meeting, chaired by the party president, the former Republican President, with the Republican President in attendance. This arrangement was unusual and was happening for the first time. In the past, Chaluma was both Republican and party president just as JJ used to be during the ULP reign.

After formal introductions, the atmosphere in the hall suddenly became tense, with the majority of members present looking agitated and exhibiting hostility to the new President, for what he had done, or what they perceived he had failed to do. This was strange and consensus was channelled through the former minister of science and technology, Vested Kunda, sometimes called VK, an old and seasoned politician and ardent fan of Chaluma. VK had also served as a Member of Parliament in a constituency in Luapita Province during JJ's rule and differed bitterly with the then head of state over his dictatorial tendencies. VK had paid a heavy political price for standing up to JJ. A good orator, many people listened attentively when he stood-up to speak. VK first recognised the party president, who was in the chair and then went on to congratulate the President for the victory at the polls.

"I am sure, Mr. President, that you know too well that many of us in here worked extremely hard to make your victory possible under very difficult conditions," he puffed, without elaborating as Luka Mwambwa nodded silently.

"However, what the ancient Romans did after a deserved victory in battle was to sit down and objectively plan how to share and enjoy the spoils of war," he sighed. This was followed by a deafening applause from the audience, probably reading his direction.

"Can you come to the point," Luka Mwambwa interrupted. "Mr chairman, we have a long agenda." He appealed.

"I know Your Excellency, er......er.....state counsel," VK replied. "Please allow me to express myself. I think we are still in a democracy, which we fought very hard for, from old Jerome Jumbe," he paused. "And I am also certain I am speaking on behalf of most party faithful's in this room and in the country." He said. Luka Mwambwa fumed, as shown by his facial expression while Chaluma smiled gently.

"For the Romans, the spoils were shared equitably and in proportion to rank and contribution." He continued. "After the emperor it was the generals, after the generals, it was the Brigadiers, then the colonels, the Majors, the captains and there after came the lower ranks. They did not apportion part of the spoils to those who never took part in battle at the expense of the soldiers who fought and brought victory." he explained. The big hall was silent; one could hear a pin drop.

"At the end, everyone was happy with what they got since it was in proportion to their own inputs," he stated. "This assured unity of purpose." The audience applauded instantly.

"Mr chairman, what has the Roman history got to do with our agenda and the Zambican situation today?" Kaluba interrupted.

"Mr Kunda, please come to the point." the chairperson appealed.

"In a moment, chair, in a moment." VK responded. "I can assure you, it is pertinent." Others clapped, with some shouting, "VK! VK!" "Please go on," the chair encouraged.

"However, in what we all thought was our victory, but now looks like your victory alone Mr President, the sharing seems to be rather unfair," he continued.

"Yes!" came the thunderous chorus from the audience.

"In your victory sir, we have seen free-loaders, who never really participated in the campaign and who had been insulting us and our party, now being preferred over those who worked very hard. What is the meaning of this Your Excellency?" He asked, and then sat down. The audience erupted again in response, giving him a standing ovation, which was embarrassing to the head of state.

"I understand how you feel, and how closely you worked with our former Republican President, and how you personally supported my campaign." Luka Mwambwa stated bluntly. "However, under the Zambican constitution, and not the old Roman empire one," he teased VK, "the President has sole powers to appoint members to the cabinet," he stated. Silence pervaded the hall. The chairperson nodded, but uneasily.

"In any case, as for you VK," he continued as if to break the obvious silence, "I considered the possibility of having you in my cabinet due to your qualifications and vast experience as a parliamentarian. Unfortunately, I couldn't because there is still a court case against you," he said, rather undiplomatically.

"Hmm! Hmm!" Came the murmurs from one corner of the hall.

"Mr President, your excellency,' VK responded, 'with due respect, please don't expect us, party faithfuls to jump with joy when your first major act seems like destroying our party unity; the unity we worked so hard to build."

"How about some of us without any cases in court Mr. President?" Asked a woman, a strong party supporter.

"And honestly Mr. President. Is it fair to treat your own members like this?" Asked Chalwe in a deep voice. "You are a lawyer, just like I am a lawyer too." He continued. "Before the law, everyone is presumed innocent until found guilty by the courts of law."

"Yes!" came resounding and excited loud cheers.

"Therefore, how can you, our own President, who only a few days ago swore before the Bible to protect us all, start persecuting us before we are found guilty?" He asked subtly as more applause erupted, almost causing pandemonium in the big hall. Chalwe then sat down with ultimate satisfaction.

"Order!" the chairperson shouted. "Order!" Pounding the gavel on the table.

Was it an organized revolt? Luka Mwambwa wondered. He felt he needed protection from the little man in the chair. But true to his character, the President was upset to the core and his trembling voice betrayed him.

"Let the President speak," the chairperson said. "Excellency, the floor is all yours."

"Thank you Mr chairman," Luka Mwambwa appreciated.

"Chalwe, you for instance, you may be a lawyer," he paused, as many people wondered where he was driving to. "I can't appoint you to my cabinet," he hesitated. "Because, if I did, the whole country will be laughing at me," he said bluntly. "I don't want to be a laughing stock," he stammered with rage.

As the noise engulfed the hall, the President put a false smile on his broad face and then said, "there are two other people from the old cabinet I have appointed, who are taking too long to reply." He sighed.

"Through the chair, who are those?" VK asked him.

"This is confidential," the President replied. "But Mr Chishala here is one of those. I have appointed him as Deputy Minister, Foreign Affairs, a Ministry he knows very well, where he cannot get lost, even at night." He said teasingly with a sarcastic smile on his face, inducing laughter from the audience.

"What?" Was the strong response that came from the audience, "a demotion?" They echoed almost in unison.

"Well, when I appoint people to important positions," he said, "they have only two options. To accept or decline." He clarified. "The choice is theirs, but the time limit is mine; determined by me alone." He emphasized impatiently, sounding like a strict primary school head teacher.

While he now realised that the majority in the audience were not with him, the President also appreciated the fact that he had absolute power. He therefore went on unchallenged, discounting one name after another and discrediting them against appointment to his cabinet. These included other former senior members in Chaluma's cabinet; it was like demeaning the former President's capacity to pick a credible cabinet.

Chalwe raised a point of order through the chair, "Mr chairman, critical minds have analysed the composition of the new President's cabinet. It looks like it is a cabinet of an opposition party to MMR." He paused as clapping ensued. Luka Mwambwa's face tightened. "Is it in order Mr chairman, for our own party sponsored President to appoint a cabinet, whose majority are known or perceived to be critics of the party President? Is it in order Mr chairman?" He repeated, before sitting down.

"Yeah! Yeah!" came a chorus from many people in the hall. James Francis Chaluma smiled gently, feeling somewhat protected.

"Thank you Mr Chalwe for your observations. However, because of the sensitive nature of the issue you have just raised, the matter will be discussed by a select committee of the National Executive Committee, at its scheduled meeting next week." The chairman ruled tactfully. "Then recommendations of the select committee shall be referred to this body." He advised.

While Chalwe's analysis was accurate, he was diplomatic and didn't want the gathering to turn into a kangaroo trial of the President. He was optimistic though that the NEC could put the head of state in check. Despite the chairman's diplomatic handling of hot issues, the majority of members present were happy that some complaints were made directly to the head of state, in a neutral setting.

The former President felt publicly insulted for the first time after handing over the instruments of power to Luka Mwambwa. How can this blatant humiliation come from a chap who had no chance in hell, but whom he picked and ordained as his successor against his better judgment? Little did he know that Luka Mwambwa's act at the meeting was just a prelude to worse things to come.

After finally dispensing with other pressing matters, they tabled the issue of the party presidency which, until then, Chaluma had thought would secure his retirement. However, with the way things were turning out, Chaluma decided to step down as party president and handover the office to the Republican President now, and at that very meeting.

Chaluma's statement was met with unhappy faces and quiet disapproval by an overwhelming majority of those present. However, Kaluba bravely stood up and stated that he supported the idea of the party President stepping down, to promote unity in the party. There were murmurs of incredulity from members in the hall, at Kaluba's unexpected statement. Most of them wondered how party unity could be assured by giving the party leadership to a man who seemed intent on destroying the party and humiliating its founding president. Many could see that Kaluba was such a cheap sell out!

When the President replied that he didn't care much about the party post and did not mind the former President continuing in it for some time, it became a serious discussion and boiling point at the meeting.

Most vocal among the contributors on the issue was none other than Kaluba, who headed a very senior ministry in Chaluma's cabinet. He put it bluntly:

"To unify the obviously divided party, it is necessary for the former President to relinquish the party presidency," he shouted at the top of his voice against loud hostile murmurs from most of those present. "Silence," ordered the chairperson. "Let him speak."

The President nodded, with a broad smile; as the former President remained silent.

"Those of us who read newspapers daily have seen how the former President is being attacked and brutalised constantly," Kaluba continued. "They may be mere accusations," he suggested, "but these are serious charges. I therefore propose that the former President leaves the limelight for now in order to enjoy his retirement," he paused. "And of course to prepare his defence carefully against these serious cases." He ended. The President nodded smiling smugly.

Several members shook their heads in total disbelief and wondered amongst themselves. How could a chap who seemed to be the chief supporter of the former President now turn full circle against him?

Chalwe stood up, "Mr chairman, if this august gathering of the party wants my advice, let us leave things as they are. We have two democratically elected presidents!" he paused, "Let them remain in their respective positions and work together." He advised as most in the audience clapped. "Otherwise, we have to amend the constitution to make new changes and then hold fresh elections." He suggested. "If we do it now, it will be unconstitutional." He warned.

"Yeah! yeah!" shouted most in the audience.

"That's the democratic way." He said as he sat down, while most in the audience clapped enthusiastically.

"I concur with the respected lawyer's advice," Vested Kunda stated. "Otherwise our party will be regarded by the country as undemocratic like the ULP."

"Sense!" some of the people shouted.

One apparently neutral member warned the two factions, "Let's work hard to ensure that our two democratically elected presidents work in tandem, otherwise it is our party to suffer the consequences!" He warned.

It was a few days after the NEC meeting that Kaluba met Mboniwe secretly at a Lodge on the outskirts of the capital city.

"Congratulations Bwana Minister," Mboniwe greeted him as he entered the room.

"Thank you, love." He replied. "I am happy that you are proud of my continued success."

"Who wouldn't?" she responded. "It gives a good feeling when your man is appreciated by the new President."

"Didn't I tell you, that I am a smarter politician than your husband? Didn't I?" He asked her, smiling broadly. She smiled back uttering no word. "That's why President Luka Mwambwa, a distinguished lawyer, and clever politician has left him and many others like him out of his cabinet." He boasted. "They never saw it coming!"

"But he's not left out completely." she said. "I am reliably informed that he has been offered something at the ministry of Foreign Affairs." "Oh! What's that?" He asked mockingly.

"He has been offered the post of Deputy Minister at Foreign Affairs."

"What an insult!" Kaluba exclaimed. "That's something I cannot accept in any ministry." He said. "But the worst would be in a ministry where I was the boss."

"Why do you think so?" She asked him innocently.

"Honey, I understand politics like the back of my hand." He bragged. "The President is merely humiliating him further." He said. "That appointment is in bad faith, I can assure you." He concluded.

"What do you mean bad faith?" Mboniwe asked. "Is the President cheating him or what?"

"Not really. The bottom-line though is that the President knows too well that he is very close to the former President." He sighed. "Normally when elephants fight, it is always the grass that suffers." He explained. "In this case, Chishala is the grass."

"I see." Mboniwe replied. "I never thought it could come to that. How about you? I know you were very close to Chaluma when he was President. In fact, it was rumoured that you were his chief defender, all the time." She challenged him.

He smiled, "I told Chishala during the campaign; to show special respect for the party's candidate. But he couldn't listen." He revealed. "As for your other questions, it is like riding a bus. You must know when precisely to jump out; seems like your husband had no clue." He charged.

"I see." Mboniwe said. "What exactly did you tell him?" She probed. "To offer special services to the candidate for instance, to support his campaign? Are you sure he didn't do that?"

"I know that he didn't do much." He said. "In fact he is one of the senior people in the party who disparaged the candidate!"

"But how did the candidate come to know who was supporting him and who was against him since Luka Mwambwa was the sole party candidate?" She probed further.

"Good question," he responded. "But I also knew that our candidate was smart. He had spies in all our committees. They often used to give him confidential reports." He revealed.

"Oh my god!" Mboniwe exclaimed. "Are you sure about that?"

"Absolutely," he answered. "The candidate then knew that Chishala was one of our ministers who had opposed his candidature."

"How unfortunate," she said, now suspecting that Kaluba could have betrayed his friend and others to the candidate; he was now being paid back.

"I know for sure that he is one of our people who used to describe him as a cabbage," he paused, "because of his principles, he didn't do much to support the campaign."

"How about you, did you support him during the campaign?" she asked changing the direction of the conversation.

"I did everything possible," he replied. "And I made sure that either the candidate or his spokesperson knew about my contributions."

"Now I know why he lost out! Too bad for him." Mboniwe said. "He doesn't listen to any advice." She added. "I also advised him to be prudent and be nice to the party's candidate after he was nominated. But he couldn't; he believes too much in his self-ego."

"I agree with you, honey, because I know him too well." Kaluba responded. "But I also know that his time of reckoning has just started." He projected. "We shall see if his so-called integrity will bring bread on his table." He ended.

"As for me, I shall not accept my standards to be lowered by anybody." Mboniwe hinted. "Life is short. I know exactly what to do."

"Just leave him to eat his principles." Kaluba encouraged. "You and I should make a permanent item." He suggested. "You make me so happy, you know."

They talked more about Chishala whom they both pitied under the circumstances. They also discussed how Mboniwe could desert him in order to embarrass him.

Then, they engaged in the real romantic reason for coming to the secret rendezvous at the lodge.

On another day, Kaluba was with his friend's wife at another lodge. After having a good time, he was in the bathroom having a cold shower. He was feeling on top of the world; he had finally avenged his several losses to Chishala; now, he felt that they were eventually even.

Mboniwe heard a faint knock on the door. "Who is it?" she asked.

"Room service," came a female voice. Half-naked, Mboniwe slowly moved forward and opened the door.

"Take that." Pumulo shouted, as she hit Mboniwe with a strong punch to her nose. Blood started oozing out.

"My god!" Mboniwe yelled. "What have I done?" she asked.

"You think I don't know?" Pumulo asked back. "You have been sleeping around with my husband, you twit." She shouted.

"You have no evidence." Mboniwe responded. "I am innocent," she claimed feebly.

"I will teach you a lesson." Pumulo threatened in a firm voice. 'It will stop you from prostitution!"

"You can't prove anything." Mboniwe insisted, ignoring her other allegation.

"We know your little schemes of grabbing other people's husbands." She shouted at the top of her voice which attracted several people at the lodge. "Just like your silly elder sisters have done."

"I don't know what you are talking about." Mboniwe insisted on her innocence.

"Didn't you steal Chishala from Mwansa? Is it not true that you now want to steal my husband from me? Is it because Chishala is no longer in employment?" Pumulo asked a string of searching questions. Mboniwe reflected for a short while.

"Liar." Mboniwe murmured in a low voice. Without answering back, Pumulo advanced quickly to mete-out more punishment. She slapped her hard on the left cheek.

"If you slap me again, – – -," Mboniwe did not complete her sentence, Pumulo advanced swiftly and slapped her harder on both her cheeks and she fell to the ground.

With only a towel around his waist, Kaluba suddenly emerged from the bathroom. "Stop it!" He yelled, advancing to hold his wife, who was older and much bigger than Mboniwe, who had stood up to try and defend herself. Kaluba managed to separate the two combatants; a crowd had already formed with people showing interest in the fight.

"So it's you?" Chishala shouted coming forward, dressed in a tennis attire.

"What are you doing here?" Mboniwe asked her husband. "It's not what you think." She said.

"What a crude little bitch!" Pumulo shouted. "She lies even when she is caught red-handed with her pants down." She said, as many people in the audience burst out laughing.

"I was just trying to help save my friend's marriage." Kaluba said. Many people in the audience laughed again. Some onlookers knew them well, as both had served in Chaluma's government for a long time.

"Liar." Pumulo told her husband. "Just say that you were helping yourself to a little loose bitch that has no scruples and sleeps around with rich men," she said. "And yet you call yourself my best friend!" Chishala chipped in and challenged Kaluba. "I rather trust an enemy than trust you." He swore at the top of his voice.

"Leave him alone." Mboniwe interjected, defending her lover. "It takes two to tangle!" She volunteered her willing participation in the secret affair.

"Now I know why you declined to play tennis with me today." He recalled, ignoring his wife's ranting and confession. "You had a date with my cheating wife, and yet you lied that you had an appointment with the President. You shameless liar and Judas Iscariot!"

"Do you wish to know why?" Kaluba asked him, "we are now even." He said.

"Even over what?" Chishala asked him.

"You took Mwansa from me when we were on campus." He told him.

"Such a long time ago?" Chishala asked reflecting back, "I thought we discussed and settled the matter permanently."

"No we didn't," he replied. "In Lemba they say 'umulandu taubola, elo taupwa kano uwamulandu alipila (a case is never forgotten until it is settled)'. Now it's settled for good."

"Have you forgotten?" Chishala asked, "and in any case, Mwansa preferred me over you." He revealed.

"That's that then," Kaluba concluded. "What goes around always comes around!" He said.

"What do you mean by that?" Chishala asked challengingly.

"Now Mboniwe has shown her preference for me over you!" He retorted smugly. "You jobless loser." He shouted. "Don't bother me anymore!"

'Oh my god!" Mboniwe screamed louder. "I am finished. I am the real loser here," she reasoned.

"You deserve it. But what do you mean, you fool?" Pumulo ridiculed.

"Can't you see? These two foolish old men have just used me as a pawn in settling their old university scores!" She shouted at the top of her voice, collapsing to the ground. A few people moved forward to help her.

"I suspected she was having an affair." Chishala explained. "That's why I hired a private detective to trail her." He revealed, as more laughter ensued from the crowd. "Little did I suspect it could be you." He confessed. "You are worse than the devil, you Judas Iscariot!" He swiftly moved forward. "Take that." Chishala moved with speed and rocked his friend with a hard uppercut to the chin. Kaluba staggered. Other people moved in to separate the two old friends from hurting each other, as Kaluba timidly tried to cover his face with his bare hands, with the towel falling down.

⟶•✳•⟵

In just 3 weeks, bitter truth and reality soon dawned on Chaluma as the President quickly pushed him out of the presidency of the party which naively, he had believed he would use to curb excessive powers of the Republican President.

Then, within 6 months real and worse calamity struck. The President went to address a special session of Parliament against all odds and presented 170 detailed but unsubstantiated charges of theft and abuse of office by the former President while in office, which he termed prima facie charges. He demanded the removal of Chaluma's immunity.

On his first day to court, Chaluma kept on feeling hollowness in the pit of his stomach. He could tell that something unpleasant was awaiting him. A number of his cronies had already disassociated from him for fear of victimisation by the Luka Mwambwa government. He could not believe the turn of events.

"Kawalala (thief)! Kawalala! Go and rot in prison." The once upon a time women who would sing praises as he was passing along Kamwala, shouted and some threw potatoes and rotten tomatoes at his passing car.

"Now who has the last laugh, JJ or JFC? Uuuuuuuuu? Liar!" Another marketer shouted at the top of her voice and others responded. "Eeeee!"

"Where is your prowess JFC? Where is your arrogance? We are now the same. Come let's sell kapenta together. Hehehehehehehe! All that has wings lands. Iyeeee." Others shouted all together all at once. Obviously they took advantage of the congestion caused by the traffic jam. This was a big case so it would seem all heads and cars were heading to the courts.

Chaluma wished against wish that they could find a quick way out. Though he had started working on the road network when he was President, there were still a number of roads that were narrow. As a result, it seemed as if traffic was at a standstill.

"Boss, do not raise your head." Chishala advised. He felt a lump lodge itself in his throat. No matter how much he tried to dislodge it, it remained there and was seemingly growing. He knew the only way out was to shed tears, bitter tears mixed with anger and annoyance. He felt for his friend. At that moment, when he cast an eye in the direction of Chaluma, he made a firm decision and commitment again to stand by him no matter what. "Chishala, are these not the same people who voted me into power twice? People are unpredictable. I am wondering where all this is going." JFC slid backwards and covered his tired face with both his hands. He had been betrayed by the same person he thought was going to pamper him. Life was fast laying sharp thorns wherever he tried to step. He could not see the way out.

As they continued the bumper to bumper drive, they invited the silence of the tomb; their brains switched on to fast mode as they thought of what lay ahead. Kingship is dew for sure. They knew in no time they would be at the courts.

As allowed under the constitution, the President had demanded for the removal of Chaluma's immunity, in order to pave the way for his prosecution. Surprisingly, the motion had gone through easily and a long and protracted prosecution of the former President commenced. This was unprecedented in the country's history and in the region.

It looked irregular for Parliament, and subsequently the Supreme Court to accept the removal of immunity from the second Republican President Chaluma without hearing him first. The nation was stunned because the principle of natural justice or audi alteram partem means that the other party should be heard and demand that no one should be condemned unheard. Surprisingly, in this case, the Republican President, Luka Mwambwa, a trained and experienced lawyer ignored these important requirements and pressed for the removal of immunity from his predecessor without offering him the all-important opportunity to be heard.

CHAPTER 14

Heartaches, Regrets and Vindication

Luka Mwambwa's hatred for Chaluma was probably deep rooted. However, it was publicly unleashed when he took charges of abuse of office to Parliament. That speech poured out the venom and demanded for his predecessor's immunity to be removed. In addition, President Luka Mwambwa set up a Task Force to prosecute Chaluma, sidelining existing prosecution institutions, the DPP, the Police and ACC thus, the rule of law was not followed in Chaluma's case. Instead, Luka Mwambwa used Law fare to prosecute, persecute, and break the former President, and his Kingmaker.

Subsequently, poor Chaluma ended up with more enemies than he could have ever imagined. Stripped of his Presidential immunity unconstitutionally by a man he favoured and trusted most, and made President, but was now working in cohort with others who disliked him and were seeking revenge for whatever offences he had committed. They were quickly joined by those who saw an appropriate opportunity to make the former President pay for what he did, or what he didn't do for them while in office; Chaluma was finally as vulnerable as a boxing punch bag.

The 'hatred club' was obviously facilitated by the President's appointment of Chaluma's known enemies to the Task Force and sending some of them to Parliament, to testify against him. Some who ganged – up in the crusade to humiliate Chaluma were unprincipled like Kaluba, who had benefited a lot from the former President and used to support him unconditionally but now deserted him, turned full circle, working with the new President. Thus, the man with a tongue of an orator was now silenced and could only defend himself in court through lawyers, against a multitude of reducing and changing criminal charges.

Nevertheless, a few people saw the grave injustice against the former President and some sympathized with the man they saw as the loneliest former President on the African continent; Chishala was among the few, and yet, he had quietly disagreed with some of Chaluma's excesses when he was in power, largely expressed during his several heated political arguements with Kaluba.

Now, some people remembered a particularly harsh example, a Zambican Past Newspaper writer, Ray Charles, who ran a recurring column which lampooned President Chaluma during his time in office as "vain, crossdressing, high-heel wearing, adulterous, dwarf, thief, etc". Thanks to Luka Mwambwa's removal of Chaluma's immunity, others, not as brave as Ray Charles, jumped on the band wagon and threw lots of mud on the lonely and defenseless former President. Some even borrowed Ray Charle's satirical charges and traits in their attacks on the small and lonely man.

Chief Cobra was one of them and was furious. How could little Chaluma skip him and go for Luka Mwambwa, his known political enemy to succeed him? He also played Ray Charle's now popular stereotype of Chaluma, charging that the former President's thinking was as tall as his height! "We are not going to steal money, we are not going to plunder, and we are not going to buy shoes. We are not going to buy suits; we are not going to give girls houses. We shall simply empower the people to stand on their own."

But Chief Cobra himself was a very complex character and a dribbler too. After playing a major role in the expulsion of the 21 mostly senior officials from MMR, he was very sure he was the last one standing and could easily succeed the then President. Strategically,

Chief Cobra had advised Chaluma to go for the third term, and yet knew it would flop in the end and he would pick up the pieces there after. To make sure the President fell for his political trick, he often whispered to the President's new wife, "you should insist on a state wedding and then you can become first lady because you deserve it." He had closely worked with her in the party, when she was in-charge of the party's women's affairs and he was the party chief. Ironically, Chief Cobra had pretended to be the most loyal to the then head of state. But his true colours and contempt for the President were revealed after he too, was dribbled, when Chaluma skipped him and picked Luka Mwambwa as presidential candidate; it was the story of two dribblers dribbling each other. Chief Cobra felt hurt and did not hide his anger. He immediately resigned from the government, and formed his own political party called National Front.

In no time, others, mostly opportunistic enemies of the former President joined in to have a go at the former President. A strong force among them was led by members of the cartel, who had a big bone to chew against the small and now vulnerable man. They were insulated by one powerful private newspaper called the Past. They dug up dirt and innuendos against him, published and circulated them, whether true or false! New political adversaries could not be left out either, they included two former ministers of finance in Chaluma's government; all subsequently orchestrated a 'Chaluma is a thief' chorus. Taking this group to court for defamation of character never helped Chaluma's cause either, it simply exacerbated his position, as insults and accusations were amplified and circulated, for more people to read.

To add insult to injury, a petition went round the country accusing Chaluma of theft and some of those who signed had been in Chaluma's inner cabinet, lending credence to the accusations and insults. Chaluma was terribly upset. He concluded that, all this largely came about because of his naive third-term attempt which led to his wrong choice of Luka Mwambwa to succeed him. By hindsight, it now sunk into his head, but belatedly that he himself started the crap, leading to his unthinkable persecution and humiliation. As he sobbed,

Chaluma realised that his intransigence had cost him a lot; including distorting his own legacy.

Around 01:30hrs in the morning, many thoughts flooded Chaluma's brain. It was as if he was watching a movie of his own life story. He recalled his childhood in Mwasanga village; his primary school days; his work with southern african road services; his work on a sisal plantation in tanzania which led to his speaking fluent swahili, and his work with atlantic company (Z) Limited eventually rising to the leadership of the Zambica Congress of Trade Unions. He also remembered many friends and relatives up to the time he left the presidency.

Above all, Chaluma remembered his children from his two marriages and those from out of wedlock. Thoughts became his breakfast, lunch and supper. Thoughts deep thoughts engulfed his being and he could not recognize himself. Thoughts, unfortunately are always related to regrets here and there. The saying 'god's waiting room' flashed across his already tired mind. This waiting room was no waiting room for reminiscing. Though there were many enjoyable past events to think about, in this stuffy, congested and smelly 'waiting room' only regrets, fears and the like became his unwelcomed companions. He really needed god, His son and the Holy Spirit as well as the angels to rescue him.

Chaluma shook his head slowly, shrugged his shoulders, and threw his short hands in the air. He then looked at his current wife as she slept soundly next to him. It was clear, judging from his countenance, that he resented the fact that he had made many positive and negative choices in his life. As he didn't want to disturb her, he crept out of bed slowly and went to the next room which contained his library. As was his habit, he knelt before god and prayed a long prayer outlining his sins to the god of Abraham, Isaac and Jacob. He even prayed for his enemies, some of whom just a few months back and years ago had been his best friends, often seeking favours from him.

He recalled that the magistrate had originally read a myriad of charges against him in court and he had not pleaded guilty to any of them. In the final analysis, the court had now reduced them to just 6 charges but none were those that led to the removal of his immunity by parliament as directed by President Luka Mwambwa. He asked god to give him wisdom and to forgive his sins and if it was god's will, to restore his legacy. By this time, Chaluma was covered in sweat and his heart was pounding in his small chest. He sat in his chair and wiped his face with a towel and began going down memory lane, sifting through memories of old and recent events.

He reflected on his divorce from the wife who had given him many lovely children. The reasons for the divorce were very personal and painful to him. He felt that his marriage to his current wife was not satisfactory. In any case, he condemned himself for marrying so soon after the divorce, making some people suspect that he had divorced his former wife because of her; far from it. He even wondered how her views often coincided with those of Chief Cobra, the MMR secretary general, especially on persuading him to go for the third term.

He recalled how Bismark Mwiinga brought Michael Chuma to be his advisor on the third term issue. In retrospection, he couldn't believe Michael would be the chief prosecutor and chairman of the Task Force on corruption. He remembered the attempted coup de tat by Captain Bele and how the Director of intelligence had failed to foil the coup attempt. He reflected on how he was fooled by Luka Mwambwa's praises and show of loyalty during the third-term debate, the money he spent buying him a good house, paying his huge debt, buying him vehicles and giving him campaign funds and campaigning for him to win the presidency. While he thought he was a good reader of character, he had been completely blinded by the show of loyalty by the same people he had worked with.

He now realized that the respect he had been accorded was not for him but the office he had occupied. He felt lonely, sad, and afraid for his life and that of his children and legacy. He recalled how Jerome Jumbe had treated the man who had made him President and the tactics being used on him as reminiscent of the ULP era. He remembered what the old and wise politician, Lewis Chanda had told him; that Luka

Mwambwa had been planning revenge against him. "Why didn't I see him for the trojan horse he has turned out to be? Why didn't I listen?" Chaluma asked himself rather belatedly. He blamed his intransigence again for this.

Chaluma recollected that at no time did he constitute a Task Force to prosecute corrupt citizens. He left the anti-corruption commission (ACC), Drug enforcement commission (DEC), Police and Director of Public Prosecutions (DPP) to do their work professionally, without his interference. He also recalled that he never, in his ten-year administration; castigate the judiciary for passing judgement against the state. During his term there was separation of powers among the executive, the Legislature and Judiciary.

He also recalled that no chief justice was summoned and told how the judiciary should handle cases. In his case, however, the DPP was made to resign for trying to do his work professionally. Contrary to the President's wishes, he had proposed that the charges be investigated first and brought to the DPP for scrutiny before prosecution as was always the case. However, President Mwambwa hastily formed a Task Force to speed-up prosecution to convict him. It looked as if prosecutions in Luka Mwambwa's era were being directed from state house. Special magistrates were appointed to convict people Luka Mwambwa called 'plunderers'. The press was also allowed to comment on cases before courts while the President willingly interfered in the three wings of government as the situation became intimidating and uncertain.

Democracy became compromised to such an extent that the Inspector General of the Police was being asked to arrest a person for no offence. The Inspector-general resigned when given the order to arrest Chief Cobra, a president of an opposition party and enemy of the Republican President. There was also a MOU signed between the government and five foreign governments aimed at prosecuting and convicting Chaluma; equivalent to surrendering of Zambica's sovereignty. As his security detail had been withdrawn, Chaluma hired his own security guards. As Chaluma agonized over these issues, he felt that he had made a fool of himself by insisting on installing Luka

Mwambwa as President. It was, however, too late to amend his terrible mistake and he instead braced himself to face the 'monster' he had personally created.

———⟶·✹·⟵———

Former President Chaluma was reported to be quite sick and his doctors had recommended that he be taken to South Africa for intensive medical evaluations and possible treatment. However, Luka Mwambwa's government was reluctant to facilitate his evacuation; suspecting it could be a ploy for him to run away from the highly publicized trial.

The Minister of Defence was alerted by some concerned citizens about the developing and worrying situation of the former President's deteriorating health. After visiting Chaluma at his home, he plucked up courage and went to state house to alert the President.

"Your Excellency, I am afraid we have a serious situation concerning the former President's health!" The Minister reported. "I suggest that you do something quickly sir."

"Wait a minute," the President responded. "Are you sure he is in a bad condition?" He asked." Is he not merely seeking attention?" He continued.

"He is a pretender and a coward, you know."

"I have seen the man, Your Excellency, he is in a very bad condition. They also showed me his doctor's report. He has a serious heart ailment and the Doctor has recommended immediate evacuation." He said. The President nodded.

"We have to act promptly; otherwise if the worst were to happen, everything you have worked for sir will be shredded to pieces." He advised.

"You think so minister," the President asked, with belated worry ringing in his voice. "What makes you say so? Is it because you are from the same district?"

"Your Excellency please, I beg of you. Do something, as quickly as you can possibly do," the minister urged him. "Otherwise history may judge you very harshly." He advised.

"The minister might be right." Reflected the President. And yet some of his ministers had advised, "Let the little man die, he is a thorn in your flesh and can remove you from office if he had a chance."

That same day, the President and the First Lady visited Chaluma at his home. Despite his earlier reluctance, the President approved a quick evacuation for the former President for medical attention in South Africa.

Chaluma was given a chartered plane to fly him and his wife to South Africa.

Chaluma arrived in South Africa and was harassed at the airport by the Zambican ambassador to that country, who told him to surrender his passport but he refused to give in. He hired an ambulance to the hospital where it was discovered that his heart was functioning at its lowest capacity. The cardiovascular specialist was surprised that the man was still alive. Those who knew Chaluma's resilience called him 'shikalume kalyonso', meaning a man who survives irrespective of harsh conditions. Afterall, he did survive during the harsh treatment in the one-party state era. In other words, he was a brave and persevering character. The next day after his arrival, Mwambwa's government announced that they had been generous in sending him for medical treatment.

After some weeks, Chaluma, the 'Shikalume Kalyonso', came back home and although he had not fully recovered, Luka Mwambwa's government insisted on continuing with the trial.

Chaluma's trial was resumed immediately after his return from South Africa. He recalled vividly the last question he was asked by the counsel.

Counsel: "What would you like to say about all this?"

Witness: "From the day my immunity was unconstitutionally lifted, I was harassed and humiliated for seven long years, called a cheap thief by people whom after close scrutiny can be found very wanting and very lacking indeed." He said.

"I am only worried about what has happened to many lives in this process, in the attempt to bury my legacy. The security system has been reduced to nothing, destroyed. The regions are no longer interested in dealing with this system knowing that one day they may be exposed and suffer shame and embarrassment. When political turmoil starts, no one will ever be spared; they will be swept in the whirlwind which will be of man's creation. That is how it started in Rwanda and we have heard of genocide." He sighed.

"I want to say how grateful I am that no matter how humiliated I am, we know that the courts will grant us justice.

Thank you very much."

RMS: "Thank you, Your Honour. That is all from this witness."

———•✳•———

Two weeks later, Chaluma called Chapwa Chileya to arrange a meeting with Lewis Chanda, at any place. While Chanda tried to avoid meeting the now humiliated former President, Chileya persuaded him to do so. A meeting between the two was therefore arranged at Chileya's residence in Lusiku West. The place turned out to be the same one often used by late Simon Mulenga Wampanga to rest, reflect, and run away from swarms of reporters and Jumbe's prying spies.

The former President was the first to arrive at the farmhouse and was made comfortable. As soon as Chileya stood-up to welcome old Chanda, the former President went on his knees and said, "I am terribly sorry sir, for not listening to your timely warning about Luka Mwambwa. Now your predictions have happened, as you know. Banjeleleko mukwai." (Please, forgive me sir). He begged. The old politician instantly asked him to stand up and forgave him, using Lemba wisdom: kanofye ishilu elingome ichitumbi (only a mad man can flog a corpse). They shook hands and smiled at each other warmly and gently.

While a divided nation debated the harsh treatment of the former President at the hands of his handpicked successor, some simply said it served him right; he probably had something to hide. But many questioned the President's motive for such unprecedented and harsh actions against a man who favoured him so much above all his former colleagues and made him President against all odds.

Subsequently, rumours were rife about Luka Mwambwa acting under the covert hand of the cartel which was composed of guys who wanted the former President to be persecuted to settle old scores, only known to themselves. Earlier, members of the cartel had informed the President that they had overwhelming evidence to easily convict Chaluma, for financial crimes committed while in office.

The excited Luka Mwambwa thought he would make a good name for himself as the defender of the nation's assets and persecutor of the high and mighty, his predecessor and his former client. In any case, if Chaluma was very corrupt, a lot of corruption should have taken place during his own adoption as MMR presidential candidate and the expensive campaign, of which he was the major beneficiary. Thus, under the circumstances just how clean was Luka Mwambwa himself? To many, it just looked like the same old story of 'kiss and tell!'

The evening was relatively cold. The former President had been to court, for the never-ending trial and persecution. As they had often done on trial days, his political enemies had organised party cadres to insult him and pronounce obscenities against him; accusing him of being a thief, and predicting that at the end he would be rotting, or even die in prison.

While he forgave the paid cadres sent to torment and insult him, he was upset with their paymasters, most of whom were nobodies and he had supported and propelled them to political prominence. Nevertheless, all of them were cowards, totally silenced by Jerome Jumbe, only he summoned his courage and stood up to the old dictator, risking his own life and the livelihood of his family in the process.

Suddenly he felt the heavy load on top of his small and fragile shoulders. Being a born-again christian, he knelt and prayed to his creator:

"My god! My god! I know I am a sinner; I have made many mistakes in my life and committed several sins, for which I repent and ask for your forgiveness. My Lord, I also know that it was not within my will and power to dedicate my life to fighting political injustice and to liberate this country from dictatorship and later to dedicate and offer this beautiful land to your glory, as a Christian nation," he said.

"I am nothing, but you used me as a tool and gave me the courage and protected me against so many dangers along the way. It was your will, Lord, and power working through me, that made my contributions possible. I thank you most sincerely for your amazing grace and favours, which I hardly deserved. There were probably many others more deserving than me to perform this arduous task, but you picked me Lord, for which I thank you."

He continued praying, still on his bended knees, and then suddenly, like in a dream, all his political and militant life came quickly flashing back to him.

Oh my Father! What a mess I am in! Hear my cry I beg of you Lord. I believe all things went haywire the moment I succumbed to the pressure of the third-term attempt and my poor judgement on picking a successor. I was aware of the old Lemba saying about choosing a successor; it says something about picking a weak or an ordinary leader to enhance one's legacy, but I was wrong; it says nothing about picking a cabbage!

Hear my cries Lord… Hear me Father…I am your child….

I surrender my life to you….Take me as I am Lord……….

Chaluma cried his lungs out until slowly, he reminisced from his slumber. Fully conscious again, he confessed his sins once more and prayed for a fair and just conclusion to his trials and tribulations.

After years of trials, the eagerly awaited judgement was delivered to a packed and anxious courtroom by Principal Resident Magistrate Charles Pingula.

The experienced Magistrate outlined the duration of the trial; defence and prosecution arguments; key witnesses and evidence and exhibits from both the defence and prosecution. He stated the delays in proceedings and their causes, including the sickness of the accused, and constant interference to the proceedings from commentaries in the press. In some cases, press interference irked defence counsels who made requests to the court to institute contempt proceedings.

The Magistrate was mindful that justice delayed is always regarded as justice denied, but also stated that justice hurried can amount to justice denied.

After going through arguments on the 6 charges in detail, giving examples of similar cases, to provide insights and the judgements passed, the Magistrate concluded, "I would also like to comment before I end that the undoing of the prosecution in this case was their failure to secure the testimony of the intelligence chief, a very key player, without a doubt, in most, if not all of the transactions that constituted the charges in this case. But then, this is my view. Having considered the evidence in the manner that I have done, I am satisfied beyond reasonable doubt that the prosecution failed to prove that the accused stole funds."

The Magistrate noted that even the supreme court of Zambica had concluded and ruled that there were President Chaluma's personal funds in the Lamdrop Account.

Chaluma was therefore acquitted of all the charges.

Thus, for former President Chaluma, the pronouncement of the not guilty verdict by the Principal Resident Magistrate set him free after almost 7 years of accusations, ridicule, insults, and torment. This verdict also brought shame to the perpetrators of Chaluma's prosecution and persecution, including the public and some private media, which had tried the former President many times over and had subjectively found him guilty, as many times through their biased stories and editorials. However, the non-guilty verdict clearly showed how malicious and malevolent the press had been in their writings against former President Chaluma.

Thus, despite the humiliation, Chaluma was vindicated. It seemed he had endured all this persecution for nothing. But he knew he was in god's waiting room. For him to see the light and know who was who in his former cabinet, he needed to be in the stuffy, smelly, and unbearable waiting room. He had probably grown wiser after the event and was now a better judge of people. Inevitably, Chaluma again remembered with sadness the wise words uttered by Lewis Chanda at their first meeting at the state house. The wise old man had warned him that his preferred candidate had plans to drag him to the courts of law. Chaluma had however, dismissed the idea out rightly and stated 'there was and would never be evidence'. The old man said then that a hateful and vindictive person would manufacture evidence against him. How prophetic and correct that statement had been. Yet in the final analysis, the Lord god almighty had fought for him and he was acquitted of all charges. He prayed and thanked the Lord.

Asked about how he felt after the verdict in his favour, Chaluma smiled gently and said, "Glory be to god, the almighty, for ensuring that justice is finally delivered after years of injustice and falsehoods. He knew all along that I was innocent of all trumped up charges. I can't question Him. He is god; He was with me all the way, all the time." He ended.

Some critics questioned Chaluma's acquittal but it was evident, however, that even public sympathy had been growing in Chaluma's favour during the seven-year trial period, as government blundered and kept changing charges and applying unconstitutional manoeuvres in the case. But it is also clear that the political will to prosecute Chaluma had evaporated.

Some of Chaluma's former ministers had deserted him, mostly scared of Luka Mwambwa's wrath as those closest to the lonesome former president were being targeted. However, word was circulating that some real cowards among them were prepared to trade even false information on Chaluma's financial dealings while in office to remain in good books with Luka Mwambwa's administration. A few brave ones, however, stuck with him, some even getting closer to the lonely JFC than before. One of them was Chishala who used to meet him more regularly.

"You sent for me, Mr President," Chishala said as he took a chair and sat close to the former President.

"Mwaiseni mune, mmm that habit of yours of calling me President will land you in trouble very soon." He welcomed him in Lemba as well as cautioned him. However, he loved hearing that title. "How is home?"

"Home is fine sir," he responded, not wishing to burden him with his own domestic challenges especially knowing that the man though acquitted was still burdened by the public humiliation of the removal of his immunity and having been paraded before the courts of law for several years, like a common criminal. "You will remain my President. No one can stop me. Once a President always a President." They then looked at each other knowingly and laughed before hugging each other endearingly.

"I called you for a frank chat today because I trust you," Chaluma intoned. "I have come to trust you even more than when we were in office." Chishala nodded silently.

"This is because your support and friendship seem to be genuine and not induced by material expectations."

"Thank you so much Mr President," Chishala appreciated. "I continue to admire you sir, largely because of your rare courage, without which we could probably still be in a one- party state." He praised.

"You think so?" Chaluma asked nodding gently.

"Mr. President, your patience and endurance have also been tested to the maximum limit by the prolonged and unfair prosecution, ending with your vindication for which we should all thank the almighty god," he breathed. "Others could have easily crumbled." He stressed.

"Amen! Thank you for the compliment minister," Chaluma responded. "I called you here however, because despite my acquittal and my innocence being proven, something bigger than me is still bothering me."

"Bigger!" Chishala exclaimed. "You are now supposed to be at peace sir, celebrating your victory in the courts of law," he told him. "What is consuming you Mr President?" He asked with worry after seeing sadness inscribed all over Chaluma's face.

"Zambica!" Chaluma replied. "Zambica is much bigger than all of us," he clarified. "As you know our country is endowed with lots of arable land, abundant mineral and other natural resources. But it has not progressed," he lamented. Chishala nodded, though not knowing his trend of thought.

"In fact, in terms of natural resournces and valuable minerals, our country is among the top five on the African continent. Therefore, we should be among the richest on the continent." He concluded. "But we are among the poorest." He lamented. Chishala nodded again.

"The question is why?" He asked.

"Probably because the first three Presidents, including myself had missed key points." He answered his own question.

"What do you mean sir, missing key points?" Chishala asked. "Don't be hard on yourself sir, you have made tremendous contributions already. Future leaders can also make their own contributions."

"No!" He declared. "I called you here because I want to be honest and frank with you and through you, the Zambican people." He slowly pulled in air and quickly breathed out. Chishala nodded timidly.

"It should not be about me and not about the first or third Republican Presidents, either." He said. "It must be about Zambica and the Zambican people."

"I see Mr President," Chishala said nodding while appreciating Chaluma's reasoning. Chishala moved to the edge of the chair, engulfed in Chaluma's frank exposition.

"You said the three first Presidents missed key points," he commented.

"What are these points, sir?"

Chaluma's eyes dilated and he certainly saw more light. "Not keeping and fulfilling our promises, we betrayed our people for selfish reasons. We the leaders have no right to bequeath misery and poverty to the next generation. Who will now hold the Zambican flag high in a country's history marred with distorted legacy?" He quipped, mourned and regretted it all, as Chishala nodded.

"Despite making immense contributions to the liberation struggle, first President, President Jumbe, was unfortunately easily intimidated by political competition," he said. "That was the main difference between the late Simon Mulenga Wampanga and Jerome Jumbe. Subsequently, he started fixing and sorting out real and perceived political opponents," Chishala nodded again.

"Many suffered in the process," he continued. "Including Wampanga, his childhood friend and his kingmaker, Ngenda Mwanawina, the fearless politician and Mubanga Nkole for articulating the need for true democracy in the party and the government. In addition, while JJ and his team were dedicated freedom fighters, they were very poor economic managers; consequently the country's economy was crushed under their watch."

"But why did the ULP central committee fail to intervene?" Chishala asked impatiently. "All the MCC's were there."

"Good question," Chaluma responded. "For ULP, dictatorship and one-man rule commenced at their Nagoye party conference in 1964, when divergent views were crushed and too much power vested in the party President then, Jerome Jumbe, by the central committee itself." Chishala nodded.

"Now, during my own tenure as second Republican President it was an achievement to unseat an entrenched one-party system and we seemed to start on a good note implementing challenging economic and political reforms," he stated, as Chishala nodded again.

"Initially, I was even regarded as a rising African democrat," he continued. "However, I too was later accused of developing intolerance against those with divergent views, evidenced by early resignations from my cabinet and the expulsion of senior party officials for exercising their democratic rights."

Chishala cleared his throat and reflected before asking. "Do you think you also made subjective electoral and constitutional changes?" He asked him bluntly.

"Yes, I was coming to that," Chaluma responded. "We did as you know carry out constitutional reforms which excluded some political competitors from the elections. In the process the former President could not stand after constitutional amendments." He admitted. "In any case, while the origins of our reforms had a historic basis, they were misunderstood by some people." He conceded.

"Why do you think they were misunderstood?" Chishala asked.

"Well, some people felt that we were targeting the former President and his party."

"Why was that course of action necessary when we had campaigned against subjective reforms during the 1993 elections?" Chishala asked with renewed courage.

"First, the submissions to the commission of enquiry we setup were overwhelming on the parentage clause, and we also found out that petitioners in the previous commission had also demanded for that particular amendment to the constitution," He answered. "That was the main motivation." He clarified.

"How come that particular recommendation had not been implemented by the previous regime?" Chishala probed further.

"To be honest with you, I can't answer for the previous government and our meeting today is not about blame games, it's about being open and totally honest," Chaluma replied. "However, it appeared that Jumbe and his colleagues opposed the parentage clause for obvious reasons. But it was clear also that the remaining freedom fighters were afraid of JJ since they were more or less appointed by him." He said with regret.

"Mr President, in retrospect, what are your views now about excluding JJ from the 1998 ballot?" He asked him.

"Thank you, my brother," Chaluma replied. "Despite submissions on the parentage clause to the commission I appointed, I should have been man enough and said for democracy's sake, bring him on, and let me take him on like I did in the 1993 elections."

How Chishala wished that sell-out Kaluba was there to hear for himself from the former President. He remembered the heated arguments with Kaluba over the issue. He wished that Judas Iscariot and gold digger of a man could have heard it from the horse's mouth, he sighed heavily.

"Nevertheless, I also regret that as party leader I should have prevented the expulsion of almost 21 senior party members for opposing my third–term bid." He said with regret.

Chishala couldn't believe what he was hearing! How he wished he captured Chaluma's regrets on tape, he breathed in heavily. "Why did you go for the third-term Mr President, against the MMR constitution and your earlier statements that you could retire at the end of your maximum two terms of office?" Chishala asked candidly and breathed out gently.

"I know I was totally against third-term bids in Africa in the past," Chaluma replied. "In any case, it all happened so fast, from cadres and some stakeholders demanding that we needed another term to complete what we had started and so on."

Chishala nodded.

"In the end it was my fault entirely," he continued. "I wasn't strong enough to stop the process, through which unfortunately many innocent people were victimised."

"By innocent people, do you include senior members of the MMR who were expelled from the party?" Chishala asked.

"Yes, I do," Chaluma said. "Much more than anyone else, it was my fault for not stopping the unconstitutional development and they were within their rights to reject what they believed was wrong. There were also others in some provinces that were called traitors and plunderers, just because they differed with the group agitating for my third-term of office," he revealed.

"Mr President, a related incidence to the third-term bid was your choice of a presidential candidate, your successor as Presidential candidate for the MMR." Chishala stated. "Do you also regret that action Mr. President, especially in view of what happened there after, leading to your persecution?"

"Very much so, my brother," he agreed. "I had no right whatsoever to impose a Presidential candidate on my party, whatever my motivation was," he responded in the affirmative, as Chishala nodded again.

"As you already know, instead of teaching my colleagues a lesson by picking Luka Mwambwa, it is me who was taught a bitter lesson through this humiliation," he said with regret sounding in his voice. "Therefore, I too seemed to have forgotten the main reasons for making sacrifices and fighting President Jumbe for the reintroduction of a multi-party system in our country."

"Are you sure of your regret over this issue Mr President?" Chishala pressed.

"Absolutely," Chaluma responded. "I regret my decision and actions in this regard and wish to ask for forgiveness from the Zambican people," Chaluma answered taking a deep breath and gently breathing out. "I could do things differently if I had another chance," he moaned.

"How about late President Luka Mwambwa, how would you assess him?" Chishala asked.

"It was unprecedented. A man I chose, financed, and campaigned for, my own preferred successor wasted no time to implement nasty acts against me, my close allies and all those he thought supported me," he lamented. "As you know, I got the worst treatment, ending up with my immunity being revoked based on unsubstantiated false criminal charges."

"Mr President, do you think your successor was acting alone to harass and humiliate you like that?" asked Chishala.

"It's not possible! The information we had is that he had a pact with other powerful people, and members of the cartel were at the centre of fabricating criminal charges, which as you know failed to hold in the courts of law." He explained.

"And the persecution process had marks of what used to happen during the one-party state era. It couldn't have been coincidence surely." He reasoned.

"For indications of what used to happen during the one-party state, like what?" Chishala probed further.

"Well to disregard the separation of the three arms of government and instruct Judges what to do is one of them. To deny a person charged with criminal offences an opportunity to defend himself; to orchestrate a lynch mob to interfere with the due process of law, and call that a public outcry, was yet another; then the attempt to incriminate a charged person by planting banned drugs in his home under his carpet and rug is certainly another. These gestapo tactics were vintage of the one-party era. What more evidence would we need?"

"Mr President why do you think your own sponsored President did all these terrible things to you?" Chishala asked. "Do you know the real reasons?"

"There are no comprehensible reasons for the actions Luka Mwambwa took against me." Chaluma replied. "However, his actions seemed more vengeful, and certainly not in national interest." He continued. "He also suffered personal inferiority complex. I know for instance that some powerful people, warned him against me and he unfortunately believed them that I was a threat, even without power."

"Mr President, how do you then summarise what has happened under the three first Republican Presidents, including yourself sir?" Chishala asked curiously. "In relation to your earlier comment, that all the first three Republican Presidents missed key points?" He asked him.

Chaluma smiled gently with his face lightening up, "yes that's the bottom line," he agreed. "All the three of us, seem to have something in common irrespective of how we started. For instance, during elections we all promised so much to voters and yet delivered much less. It's like telling your crying child that if necessary, I shall bring down the sun for you. And yet in reality when necessary, you fail even to touch the moon for the child; turning the child's hope into despair!"

"That's a very important conclusion Mr President," Chishala observed. "It can help us for the way forward." He suggested.

"Certainly, and I am coming to that," Chaluma declared. "Firstly, I sympathise with our people. We excite them; we promise so much during the campaigns; we literally promise them heaven on earth, raising very high expectations among them in the process. The question is do we deliver on our promises, and are we held accountable by the people?" He asked. The excited Chishala moved to the very edge of his chair again paying full attention, like a final year university student, listening attentively to his Professor, a few weeks before the final examinations, as silence pervaded the room. Chaluma realised too, that he was receiving undivided attention.

"My earnest prayer is that people, the people, failed by all their leaders, me included, should develop the courage to engage and demand more from their elected leaders," he suggested.

"Mr President, I like what you are saying," Chishala retorted. "What type of engagement? What type do you mean, and what kind of demands can the people make under the prevailing circumstances?" He probed.

"Very good questions again minister Chishala," he complimented. "I am coming to that. It is the essence of our meeting." He explained.

"Thank you, sir," Chishala appreciated.

"First, the people should always engage their members of parliament and other local representatives on their needs. Then during commissions of enquiry and other fora their voices should be very categorical on what they want." Chaluma suggested.

"They should be alert too and prevent leaders from stealing such opportunities to sneak in their own changes, unrelated to the wishes of the people," he continued to break the obvious silence.

"Then, the constitutional making process should be transparent, and Presidential powers need to be trimmed; while Parliament should have more say. In addition, intra-party democracy should be enhanced, while members of party central committees should be elected and not appointed by party presidents."

"Very good, sir," Chishala intoned. "Any particular changes that need to be considered now?"

"Certainly," Chaluma said. "One important change which we need in this country is an adequate transitional period to effectively deal or dispose of emerging electoral disputes. Such a period should provide an adequate interface between the incoming and outgoing administrations. This should also provide sufficient information on the state of the nation to facilitate a smooth handover of power," he suggested.

"Thank you, Sir. Very important and currently missing in our political system," Chishala agreed with him.

"You're welcome," Chaluma responded. "In addition, I pray for a new breed of patriotic and committed leaders to emerge in this country who will learn from all our mistakes during the three republics and beyond, whose own prayers to their creator should be for wisdom to rule for the good of the country, to tolerate divergent political views and the capacity to treat all citizens equally, irrespective of their political, religious affiliation, tribe and race," he stated as Chishala nodded in total agreement.

"In addition, all new leaders should be ready and willing to move on from the presidency after serving their prescribed maximum terms of office and to exercise tolerance for perceived political offenders and desist from the current habit of crushing and getting rid of real or perceived political enemies," he concluded.

"And finally, Mr President," Chishala hesitated slightly, "I want this to come straight from your heart."

Chaluma nodded.

"After all that had happened to you, name-calling, imprisonment, humiliation especially in the Second Republic. Then more humiliation, fabrication of criminal charges, a long and torturous trial and finally vindication and acquittal; as a Christian, have you forgiven your brothers the first and third Republican Presidents?" He candidly put it to him.

Chaluma smiled broadly, "Without a doubt! Who am I but God's creation?" He replied candidly. "It is there in the Lord's Prayer for each one of us to forgive the brother or sister from the heart and unconditionally." He sighed and continued. "As a sinner myself, I always ask for forgiveness from my God, and in the same vein I ask Him to give me the capacity to forgive others because it is not easy on my own. It is clear that when we forgive, we behave like God who forgives our sins even before we repent." He paused. He quoted Ephesians 4:32: 'Be kind to one another, tender-hearted, forgiving one another as God in Christ forgives you'. To answer your question directly, yes, I've forgiven my two brothers absolutely and I hope they will also forgive me for my transgressions against them," he ended.

"Finally, Mr President, is there an African President who has publicly forgiven those who humiliated or offended him or her before coming into office or even when in office?" Chishala asked further.

"Oh, yes!" Chaluma responded without hesitation. "Late President of South Africa, Nelson Madiba Mandela, is the greatest example. He forgave unconditionally those who tortured and humiliated him for so many years. Mandela had said: The mentality of retaliation destroys states while the mentality of tolerance builds nations."

Chishala nodded but uttered no word.

Chaluma continued, "Mandela also said: The WEAK can never forgive....... FORGIVNESS is the attribute of the strong."

"Thank you very much Mr. President, "Chishala said. "It is a rare honour and privilege to have had this open and frank conversation with you, sir." Little did Chishala know that that was his last meeting with former President Chaluma, as he passed on at his home 24 hours later.

Made in the USA
Columbia, SC
13 October 2024

44273393R00176